MW01169243

An Ocean Away

Mike Aldridge

1st WORLD
PUBLISHING

An Ocean Away

Mike Aldridge

© Mike Aldridge 2009

Published by 1st World Publishing
P.O. Box 2211 Fairfield, Iowa 52556
tel: 641-209-5000 • fax: 866-440 5234
web: www.1stworldpublishing.com

First Edition

LCCN: 2009928152
SoftCover ISBN: 978-1-4218-9097-5
HardCover ISBN: 978-1-4218-9096-8
eBook ISBN: 978-1-4218-9098-2

To my Mom and late Dad,

And to Evan, the backbone of my life.

"I've done a bit of smuggling, I've run my share of grass, I've made enough money to buy Miami but I pissed it away so fast, Never meant to last, never meant to last."

—Jimmy Buffett
A Pirate looks at 40

I can finally see the ivory-colored lighthouse as my boat makes it through the dense fog and the unusually rough waters for the Sea of Cortez. Fog is rare this time of year. I was expecting a calm evening. The ocean is different. It's unpredictable. Mysterious. Dangerous. One second she's your friend. And next? You're pleading for your safety. Or even more, your life.

As I approach the coast, I kill the engine, hoping the crashing waves will camouflage my presence. I'm looking for "Check Point Charlie," a phrase that I picked up watching old American war movies as a kid in Tampico and the nickname for my dropping point. It's where I will make the last delivery of my illustrious career as a drug dealer.

I spot something in the distance. Small beams of light are flashing in my direction. My heart is racing and I can feel my blood pressure rise by the second. After 20 years of doing the Devil's work, I am now convinced that I must step to the other side. If it wasn't for Lucy and God, I may have never decided to retire my illicit ways.

I'm getting closer, but something is going terribly wrong. I'm drifting south and the rough waves aren't helping any. I start the engine. It turns over on the first try. I begin to regain control of the boat. But the engine sounds much louder than normal. I forward the throttle as my boat thrusts north, but I can no longer see the beams of light. I signal for direction with my own spotlight, but no response. I am beginning to feel more and more abandoned by the second.

The noise is getting louder as I go faster. I'm having a hard time deciphering between my engine, the crashing waves, and what appears to be general chaos around me. This can't be happening! It's my last time. Have they left me? I've got 250 kilos of dope on board that I need to unload for the last time. I plan on running the orphanage full time.

It's now unbearable, the noise. But now I can see the lights again. Bright lights. Too bright for a flashlight. My breathing is becoming erratic. I can't be this nervous. I've done this many times over the years. My heart feels like it's about to pound through my chest. The noise continues to escalate. My breathing is out of control. I'm panicking. I feel a burning sensation in my back, neck, and chest. I look down at my feet in front of the helm and realize that I'm standing in a pool of blood. I'm in shock! This can't be happening! But it is. I hear voices and a screeching sound up above, but I'm losing it. I see a very bright light that drowns out the rest of my surroundings. But I'm not dead. Not yet. I've collapsed to the deck of the boat. I lose consciousness. Silence.

I regain consciousness at the violent impact with the shoreline. I roll over and look up. I'm staring at the barrel of an AK-47. My life as a child begins to flash through my mind and suddenly, nothing.

CHAPTER 1

They say at one point in their lives, my parents prospered. But by 1970, hurricanes had destroyed the beautiful gulf coastline of Tampico, Mexico. It was in the early seventies when I was about 2 that I was given away like a cheap, hand-me-down shirt by my folks. I remember my mom's face as it was swollen from tears and sorrow, and my dad just rushing her out before things got any worse emotionally. That morning, I went from being a son to an orphan.

It was at the time that this beautiful colonial city had lost its appeal to the international travelers and the native citizens from the inland. In essence, Tampico was dead. And so was my soul.

You see, nothing is more painful than seeing young couples walk through this orphanage and hand pick a child like a finicky housewife in a produce market. I guess I was the bad apple because they never picked me.

I quit making friends because by the time I got close to another orphan, he was gone with their new family. Friendship to me only bred envy and jealousy. It went on like that for years. I was an introvert and very anti-social. When a new orphan showed up, I held nothing but contempt for that person. I knew that he would go before me.

In 1980, everything changed. If there was a God, I thought that maybe, just maybe, he was looking out for me. The Ramirez couple, in their early forties, decided to adopt me after several trips back and forth to the orphanage. At the time, I just didn't understand why. But I went along with it and even the kids who I was mean to, seemed to be genuinely glad that I was leaving to start a new life with a new family.

"Jose, the Lord has found you a home," Sister Maria's gleaming face stared into my eyes. "Hand picked by one of his own ambassadors. I want you to meet your new parents." I was awkwardly thrown into the mix with my new parents.

Sister Maria's smile radiated throughout the orphanage that day as I gathered my things together, preparing for the departure to my new home. In retrospect, it was obvious that she couldn't believe someone would actually adopt a 9-year-old child. Although I was told that this is what I had wanted ever since I was dropped off at the orphanage, I had become accustomed to the daily routine of orphan life. With that routine came a hard shell that I had developed around my emotions and feelings. In reality, the homely Sister was the closest thing that I had ever had to a mother, except the ocean, of course. I'll save that for later. But in a way, it was a sad day as I stared at Sister Maria's waving hand from the back seat of the Buick Electra 225 as a cloud of dust slowly erased her into a tiny spec as I departed for good. I never saw or heard from Sister Maria again.

I was taken to the Reverend Tomas Ramirez's home that evening. My new parents had a quaint little flat on the outskirts of Tampico in a small rural development. Their home was right next to the Protestant church that my new dad preached from every day. I had my own room and felt it odd that my new parents were so much older but never had any kids. The two had been what appeared to be happily married for over 20 years. Why would they be adopting now? If they couldn't have kids because of biological reasons, why wouldn't they have adopted years ago? Valid questions for a 9-year-old kid going on 21. I guess it would just take some time to find the answers to these questions.

From the start, the relationship with my new parents was awkward. I never really felt any love or affection in the household. Not that I had ever experienced love or affection before in my life except from my real mom, from what I could remember. I had only assumed what a family should act like, and more importantly, feel. So it was strange at first, and only got worse.

It had been almost 30 days since my new childhood began. I was enrolled in the private school at the church, where both my mother and father taught class to about 15 of us. Every subject had biblical overtones, including the science that we learned. Life was boring and I was beginning to miss the orphanage. People were disappointing, and the family life was severely overestimated in my young, humble opinion.

I had turned 10 even though no one knew my exact birth date. They just made one up and I had a birthday cake made out of chocolate. It was held at the church and all of my classmates were there. Most of them were either very little or in their late teens. No one really cared except when it came down to having cake and ice cream. I received one present from my parents, a sombrero that I never wore. It made me look silly and was entirely too big on my skull.

My intuition proved to be right when it came to my father. Something was wrong with this man. He gave me odd looks, usually when no one was around and asked me strange questions about certain feelings and attractions. I had a level head and considered myself smart for a 10-year-old. But I didn't always understand where he was coming from.

It was in the early hours of the night when I was suddenly awoken with his hands stroking my genitals.

"What are you doing?" I screamed at the pervert.

"Quiet, Jose" as he yelled under his breath, "you'll wake your mother!" He tried to continue the assault. My natural instincts followed as I whacked him as hard as I could in his face, causing an adverse reaction.

"You will pay for this, young man," as Mrs. Ramirez began calling out his name, asking if everything was all right. The reverend scurried out of the room as I could hear him saying something about how he was only checking up on their son.

I got up from my bed and went for the closet, where I found the small aluminum baseball bat in the corner. I would be prepared next time. His questions now made sense. My father was a child molester, obviously using his position for personal gain. I understood it now and vowed for it never to happen again.

That morning, while my father went into town, I tried to tell my mom about the incident. She became so enraged that she began to beat me with a heavy wooden spoon that she used to mix up large batches of pinto beans for community meals at the church. When my father returned, he was told of the snitching, where he immediately carried on the beating. My face was so badly swollen that they had to lock me in my room for almost a month while my wounds healed.

When I was finally allowed to come out, I had my escape and journey planned. It was like being in solitary confinement. You had nothing to do but think. And one thing I learned at an early age was to think. I began to play the part and my ignorant parents became convinced of my compliance with their mission in life.

I began to go to church and volunteer to clean the vestibule every day. It was there that I would steal a few pesos out of the collection plate. Within weeks, I was a trusted member of the Lord's team, getting bolder and bolder each week. Within two months, I had over a hundred pesos stashed away in my room at home. The couple representing God's team wasn't exactly shrewd when it came to business. If I didn't fear so much from a second attack by the reverend, I could have stayed on longer and made it a very lucrative side job. But that wasn't going to happen. I knew it was just a matter of time.

At night, I never really got any sleep. I traded the baseball bat for a hammer, as it was smaller and just as effective. I would wait and wait until I would finally fall asleep. It was awful and rather scary, not knowing if you were going to be violated or not.

It was the night of November 23, 1980, when the Reverend Tomas Ramirez molested his last child. I kept beating him long after he was dead, I presumed. I had never seen such rage come out of this 10-year-old body. A victim in self-defense.

That night, this child became an adult and snuck away with several hundred pesos and blood on his hands. I had snagged the money out of his wallet, which added to my small fortune that I had accumulated. My so-called mother slept through the entire incident. I would have never hurt her if she had woken up. She either didn't know that her husband was a pedophile, or she was too dense to realize what was going on.

I didn't want to think of how many kids he had molested over the years. I guess at this point, it really didn't matter. Justice had been served. He was dead and would never have the opportunity to molest again.

I followed my escape plan that I had put together over the past several months. I followed the only route I knew. East, towards the docks. I would wind up where Sister Maria always took me when I asked. The Ocean.

It's hard for people to imagine that a 10-year-old kid could make it on his own. But the fact is, Mexico is so poor that a child wandering aimlessly around the streets with no parent in tow is no big shock. I was scared for the first several weeks that maybe the police would come looking for me. But they never came. At least I wasn't aware of it. I really don't think they cared. Perhaps if they knew about Reverend Ramirez's other side, perhaps they would pin a medal on me for instant justice. I couldn't figure it out. And for the longest time, I walked around with a bit of paranoia hanging over my shoulder.

The docks of Tampico were where I belonged. I met several fishermen who taught me how to filet the day's catch and fed me in return. Within a year, I was sleeping in my own cardboard shack outside of Pancho's casita. They called him Pancho because his last name was Villa. His real name was Ricardo, but if you called him that, he would kick your ass. And me being just a boy, that wasn't hard to do.

I didn't spend a dime of my money unless it was an emergency. I had it made. A free place to stay, goodies from the sea, and small tips from the few foreigners who came to Tampico to fish and enjoy the nightlife. I dug up my bank in the sand every night and made a deposit. But things got better. They always do.

CHAPTER 2

I really didn't have anything to compare it to. They say times were tough in Tampico during the seventies and eighties because of the hurricanes and then the oil spills. For some reason, I never felt the pinch. I was recession proof. For me, getting by was never a problem—I was resourceful. One of the few lessons that I ever learned from the Ramirez family was that there will always be poor people in this world. Actually, now that I think of it, I read that in the Bible while staying with the Ramirez family. The point is that I decided early on that I didn't want to be one of those poor people, although statistics indicated otherwise.

Even though there are poor people in the world, I also knew that it wasn't my responsibility to take care of them. If there is a God, let him deal with it. Which really brings me to my next point. Religion is nonexistent in my eyes. If God's ambassadors were of Reverend Ramirez's caliber, then I needed a dose of God like the north pole needed a blizzard. Why did my people in Mexico weigh so heavily on the God factor? Most of my countrymen were suffering in one way or another. If there were a God and he was truly almighty, why did he allow so much pain and suffering in my country and around the world? No one I had ever met could answer the question. So, basically, religion simply didn't play a role in my life as a kid unless you consider the financial boost it gave me when skimming the collection plate.

I needed to be by the sea. The sea was my only family. Mother Ocean. I made a pact with her from the moment that I laid eyes on her in the back of Sister Maria's station wagon en route to Miramar Beach several years ago when I was about 6 years old. She was overwhelming with her strength and beauty. I saw her on her angry days when she washed the *mulicán* clean with her turquoise waters. Yet, it was never long before she allowed me to wade in her shallow waters when the tide was out. She was human to me, with emotions like a roller coaster. One day pleasant, the next day a bitch! But in the end, pure respect. So I was actually raised by a single mom up until this point. Mother Ocean.

Throughout history, men tried to conquer her through valiant efforts at sea. But to this day, and to the last, my mind tells me, she will always win. Mother Ocean only answers to Mother Nature herself. And a smart man knows that, in the end, the woman always wins.

CHAPTER 3

The year 1983 turned out to be a great year for me. I was 13 years old and I met my best friend, Miguel Agosto, and my mentor, Mr. Eduardo Robles. It was this boy and man who had the biggest impact on my life.

Miguel and I shared a common bond together. We were both orphans. Miguel's story was a bit different than mine, even though you could trace the same pattern back to the beginning. Miguel did not have patience like me. Whereas I hung around the orphanage until I was almost 10, Miguel had escaped and lived with different families on and off as a child. He always told me when the subject was brought up that an orphan was no different than a dog at a kennel. The oldest and ugliest ones stayed the longest. So why would anyone wait?

Unlike me, Miguel simply ran away. It was early one morning when he was about 7 years old. He had earned the respect and trust of the other children and their caretakers. He was highly intelligent and street-wise. Unlike me, he had too much pride to steal money. Instead, he hoarded food and water for a couple of weeks until his path determined his destiny. But like me, he wound up on the beaches of Tampico. Specifically, he found himself on the fishing docks, looking for food and work.

When I first saw him at a distance, I was filleting fish for an older couple from the United Kingdom. They had come from a small coal mining town called Barnsley and had never been anywhere else except Paris and Spain. The Grahams were amazed by how inexpensive and beautiful Mexico was and even offered to adopt me. I laughed it off until a young boy had caught my eye, staring directly at me from across the pier. I realized right then that we would become friends.

He was wearing a Los Angeles Dodger's cap that towered over his big brown eyes. Once we made eye contact, I noticed his contagious smile, inviting friendship. Was there something called friendship at first sight? I motioned him to come over while I kept the British couple at bay with my mediocre English and silly fishing jokes. As he got closer, I realized that his face was not serious. Although a stranger may have guessed that his plight thus far in life was desolate, his features hinted otherwise.

I had a good sense about people but Miguel wasn't always an easy read. He was a very competent person but varied in his confidence levels depending on what he was doing. As similar as our backgrounds were, and as close as we had become, I felt like I could never fully break that barrier that he held so close to himself.

Mr. Robles was an early influence in my life, although neither one of us was aware of it at the time. It was like working for the government and claiming the president was your boss. Technically, this was true. Mr. Robles owned the entire fleet of boats and I was on the bottom of the totem pole, simply a deckhand who baited hooks and filleted fish. I swore to myself that one day, I would be just like him: successful, respected, and most importantly, rich.

CHAPTER 4

By 1985, this 15-year-old felt like an adult. I had more money than most middle-class families in Mexico because of my job benefits. I had gotten to know Mr. Robles a bit better and he was kind enough to give Miguel and I a plot of land a few blocks from the docks. It would turn out to be one of the many good investments that I made over my lifetime.

Mexican labor is cheap and I had guys twice my age working for me. When it comes to money, age has no barriers. I wanted to design the home to reflect the colonial architecture of the historical city. I tried to bring Miguel in on every aspect of the plan, but he would look at me like I was crazy. He wasn't one to pay attention to detail. I think he was just happy how fortunate he was to have a roof over his head that he could call his own.

Going into this project, we had a simple partnership. We both ponied up some cash to get the foundation and basic structure going. We then decided to pay as we went. Miguel would work the boats to bring in his wage and tips. I supervised and helped out on the construction of the home.

Mr. Robles provided the labor, but I worked out the details with the men myself. It was easy: bricks and mortar for a few pesos a day. I negotiated with each laborer on a daily basis. How much I paid depended on the skill or trade involved. A few of the men got a bit testy with this teenager, but they shut up quickly once Robles found out about it. In the end, the guys were happy because they could depend on a cash payout at the end of each day.

This project fared well for both of us because we had a home now and were able to get to know the "Old Man," as we affectionately referred to him behind his back. Periodically he would stop by and check on the construction, apparently curious as to how we were getting by. He seemed sincere and interested in our plight. He was friendly, but in an odd way. I always sensed his generosity beyond the material things in life, yet he was very intimidating, constantly making innuendos about loyalty and productivity. Little did I know that he was weaving a web that if you weren't careful, could literally strangle you.

The plot of land from Robles had been a surprise, especially for such lowly deckhands as ourselves. But more surprising to him was how quickly we acted on developing the property. One day he dropped by after all of the workers had left.

"So, Jose, it looks as if things are really coming along," he said smugly.

"Sir, Miguel and I would have never been able to do this without your help. We simply cannot thank you enough for your generosity," I said, stumbling for words. "I can only ask myself, why? What did we do to deserve this?" I asked intently.

"My son, it's not about generosity, but loyalty."

As his eyes met mine, I could feel the powerful projection of subordination radiate throughout me. It was as if his eyes were doing all of the talking and his words only played a supporting role.

He knew just by looking at me that I was intimidated by his presence. I was another loyal servant to the king—King Robles, that is.

"Well sir, you know where my loyalty stands," I said as I kicked the dirt in front of the half-finished structure, then looked up. "You have given Miguel and me one thing those orphanages could never give." I looked back down at my dirty sandals half buried in the dirt.

"And what may that be?" the old man asked with an amused look.

I looked up at him and paused. "Opportunity, sir. Opportunity."

Robles did not respond immediately, but digested my words. He then placed his hand on my shoulder. "Jose, you are my rising star," he said with a big grin. I looked at him as he began his sermon.

"Most kids in orphanages are only praying for someone to come rescue their pathetic selves." Robles could be insensitive and downright cruel I had heard. But he was also unusually honest.

"But you and Miguel are different. You didn't get chosen because you both knew deep down that getting chosen would not have produced the lives that you wanted to live. These do-gooders who think they can patrol an orphanage to get one more kid off the street reminds me of shallow-minded fools who think they're going to save the world by adopting a dog at the pound."

Was Robles comparing orphanages to pounds, and orphans to animals? I thought to myself.

"Don't get me wrong, Jose. You guys are not animals. But the other ones might as well have been, all sitting around trying to look pretty so that they could get picked and thrown into a whole different world. You two bastards got it right!" he smirked and gave me his famous left-eyed wink. "You really didn't want to go in the first place, and when you did, you did it on your own terms."

This was partially true. Deep down, although I was eventually adopted, I knew that I was a loner. As tough as it was to swallow Robles's words, I knew that he was right.

"Jose, the only thing you've ever wanted was opportunity. But that's only part of it. The rest of it is taking advantage of that opportunity and turning it to your benefit. That's what you have done. And that's why I have given you and Miguel this land."

I was still confused but I went along with it. It at least sounded good to this teenager.

"Look at what you've done since I have given you this land," the old man said as he spread out his arms as if he was embracing the new structure. He then continued, his breathing getting harder, his voice louder and more intense. "You've already begun to build your home. You have no training in construction or management. You don't need it because you're a natural, Jose. You are a leader! You make things happen!" He was yelling at this point. "Miguel is a good kid. You, Jose, could be the best!"

I didn't know how to respond, so I didn't. The old man gave me another wink, spun around on the heel of his leather cowboy boot, and walked to the car. As he opened the front door of his Lincoln Continental, he turned and his eyes had become cold as stone. "And just remember, son," he said, his words hanging in the air just long enough for me to feel uneasy, "don't ever let me down."

CHAPTER 5

Everything in my life since I left the orphanage happened very fast. As I waited during those long days and nights at the orphanage hoping my situation would change, it never did until I literally had given up hope. It was when I lost that ray of light in my soul that the Ramirez couple came swooping in to save the day. If I would have been older and wiser, I would have realized immediately that these degenerates, who used the cloth for their personal gain, were up to no good. Although I never regretted killing the son of a bitch, I did regret not knowing any better.

The house was finished and times were good. I had just turned 16 and would still get guilty feelings on occasion over the land that the old man had deeded us. There obviously was a reason, but I just didn't know. And his words, as comforting as they were at the time, really didn't add up. People just don't give things away for nothing, unless you're Mother Theresa.

So it was at the age of 16 that Miguel and I were dispatched to Mr. Robles's headquarters somewhere in the hills outside of Tampico on the Panuco River. My comrades always said that if you were invited to the compound, it was either to be rewarded heavily or punished severely. I couldn't think of anything that I might have done wrong. But either way, Miguel and I were nervous. It was our first time going to the Robles's residence.

We were picked up in one of the company Suburbans. The drive from our house was about 20 minutes. We pulled off of a main road, where we were stopped by a security gate and three armed guards. The doors of the Suburban were opened and all the occupants were patted down. It was obvious that Robles had layers of security in place. Odd for the owner of a fishing fleet.

We were cleared through the gate and made our way up a rather steep hill. Green foliage brushed the dark tinted windows as we ascended to the top. The flowing waters of the Panucha River came in and out of view as Miguel and I stared out of our respective windows. My mind kept turning over how Mr. Robles was able to buy and build such a fortress. I assumed he had other interests at hand, such as investments and what not. I considered myself smarter than the average Joe and knew there was more than the eye could see.

We reached the top only to encounter another security gate. This time, we were not inspected. As we drove through the gate, two armed security guards awaited our arrival. The compound looked as if it were built in the middle of the rain forest. Unlike many of the structures in Mexico, Mr. Robles's house had dark mahogany siding, almost like a cabin that you would find in the mountains up in the States. It also had giant windows that you could not see into. I presumed you could see out. It was unlike anything that I had ever seen or read about.

We exited the vehicle and were quickly escorted into the foyer of the home. Shoes were to be removed in the foyer along with any other burdening items such as coats, purses, and such. As Miguel and I were removing our shoes, a beautiful young girl no older than 20 greeted us and asked if we would like a cocktail or soda. We both nervously declined.

We were then escorted into the main area where we were met with open arms from the Old Man himself. I was already beginning to realize that we were there because of good things, and not because Miguel and I had screwed up. It was a relief.

"Well, hello, my son." He greeted me with a bear hug.

"Hello, sir," I awkwardly replied.

"Miguel, it's great to see you, too." He extended his hand, indicating obvious favoritism towards me.

"What will you boys be drinking this evening?" he asked as he snapped his fingers towards one of the servants.

"I'll have a Coke, if that's all right," I said.

"And what would you like in your Coke, my son?" he said with a smile.

"Is it OK?" I asked stupidly.

"I'll tell you what, boys, I'll order for you." He snapped off an order for three Bacardi and Cokes.

The drinks arrived within minutes and we were invited to take a tour of the house and the grounds. We started outside, where we climbed a set of thick wooden stairs that took us to the observatory deck. The view was tantalizing as you could see a huge portion of the State of Tamaulipas, including the cities of Madero and Altamira. What was most impressive was how his home was hidden on a tropical mountaintop, yet never lost the unbelievable view of the Gulf of Mexico. The top of his roof was barely exposed for this view alone. The three of us sat there for what seemed like hours, staring off into the huge body of water and admiring her strength and beauty.

"Shall we see the rest, boys?"

"Ah, yes sir—yes," I said as I walked back towards the stairs with my head turned, staring at her waters.

"It's incredible, sir."

"Well, think about it, Jose. She is my lifeline. She is what helps me succeed in what we do. As much as I like to be away from the city below, I never wanted to lose sight of her," he said, winking his left eye. *Neither do I,* I thought to myself.

As we went down the stairs, the Old Man began showing us his collection of plants from around the world. While I wandered around the massive backyard, I noticed that in front of each plant, Mr. Robles had placed small placards indicating its biological name and native habitat. *Collecting trees and plants?*

We were led back into the home after viewing the grounds, where we were politely asked to wash up for dinner. When we sat down, I was reminded of a scene from *The Untouchables,* where all of Capone's henchmen were seated around the table while the mob boss gives a speech on loyalty—because that was exactly what Mr. Robles did. As he walked around the table slowly introducing the reason for being there, I sensed everyone's nervousness. Dozens of employees and guards waited around the table while a waiter was pouring shots of Don Julio 1942. Everyone got one, including Miguel and me.

Miguel looked as if he were in a daze. I tapped his left foot with my right and signaled him to pay attention with my body language. Robles got to the point in his speech where we all had to raise our glasses and toast our loyalty to the Cartel. *Cartel?*

The same waiter came back around and poured shot number two. I never really liked the taste of tequila, but this was smooth and had been slightly chilled. A younger gentleman then came around and laid a thin cigarette next to our silverware with a gold Zippo lighter bearing the Robles Fishing Charter Cooperative logo.

"And before appetizers are served, I would like to introduce to you two young men who have showed their loyalty to the organization for several years now. Please raise your glasses and let's toast Jose and Miguel for being here this evening for the first time."

We drank a second shot and my head started to get light. Cheers and applause erupted from our colleagues around the table. I wasn't sure where this was going and I didn't necessarily like the attention. I looked over at Miguel and his face was bright red, a combo from the embarrassment and the tequila I'm sure.

"And now, let's have a smoke so we can disinhibit our appetite for the wonderful dinner that we are about to enjoy."

Miguel and I followed suit as we opened up the Zippo lighters and lit the thin cigarettes. We barely puffed on them when we immediately began to choke. Laughter spread throughout the room as everyone else dragged heavily and seemed to hold the smoke within their lungs for several seconds.

"You must inhale the smoke," Robles said, "and hold it in for a little."

I did as I was told along with Miguel. This time I told myself that I wouldn't cough and I didn't. It was actually smooth and enjoyable. I always liked the smell of tobacco, but this was different. It certainly didn't taste like it smelled.

"Miguel, Jose," the Old Man said, singling us out, "it's marijuana." Robles laughed and the rest of the table followed suit. I didn't know what to say. I had never smoked anything before, no less marijuana. But within minutes, I began to enjoy the smoking over the cactus juice. It relaxed me and made me think of things that I had never thought of before.

The expansion of the mind that evening made me realize that other dimensions of this world exist, even if it was only in a cognizant manner. And the food that was served tasted better than any food that I have ever eaten. Lobster, scallops, shrimp—goodies that I dined on daily because of my profession—never tasted so good.

I looked over at Miguel and started to laugh as I unshyly bit into a large prawn. His large brown eyes were surrounded by a squinty redness—I thought he was going to die of the smoke inhalation and the powerful substance. It appeared as if he didn't enjoy it. I, however, thought it magical and pure. God's herb, as I overheard someone at the table describe it.

I didn't know it at the time, but the unique herb would control the rest of my life personally, professionally, and financially. And just when I couldn't get any higher, and finally thought that I had made it into Mr. Eduardo Robles's inner circle for a great evening of indulgence of life's best offerings, I was smacked face on with a sobering blow.

CHAPTER 6

The intoxicants had kicked in. Although the food neutralized the buzz from the tequila, I was still as high as an astronaut from the smoke. I wasn't quite aware of it, but everyone had left the table except me, Miguel, and Old Man Robles himself. A waiter came by with some flan and fresh coffee, which none of us declined.

"So guys, how long has it been since you joined the Robles organization?" It was obvious that the Old Man knew the answer, but it was a good introduction to what was going to be a serious conversation.

"Six years come August, sir!" I said with certainty.

"And you Miguel?"

"The same as Jose, sir. Six years. In fact, sir, with all due respect to the conversation, that's a lot of fuckin' fish filleted!" He burst out laughing.

"Yes, Miguel, it is a lot of fish." The Old Man had to laugh at Miguel's immaturity and the fact that he had gotten him stoned. "But let's get serious for a moment." His demeanor changed instantly. "We need to talk a little business during this festive gathering."

A flash of sobriety hit us simultaneously.

"Do either of you know why you are here this evening?"

"Actually, sir, no. I can't speak for Miguel, but I wasn't quite sure. We aren't in any sort of trouble, are we?"

"No, no, Jose. Don't be ridiculous."

Miguel piped up foolishly, "Uh, sir, I ah, I thought that it just may be a company get-together."

"Ah yes, Miguel, a company get-together," the Old Man smiled in his response. "Actually, you're right. This is a company get-together of sorts," the Old Man choosing his words carefully.

"I have watched the two of you from day one. Jose was here first and you showed up within a couple months afterwards," he said, turning to direct his words at Miguel. While the Old Man was speaking, I noticed a police officer walking through the side of the dining room into the kitchen. *That's odd. A police officer present with marijuana in the air,* I thought.

"Jose, do you remember coming here like a lost puppy searching for leftover scraps at Mr. Villa's home?"

"Yes, sir. I never knew you noticed," I said in complete surprise.

"My friend, I notice everything. What I don't see, my people do and report it to me immediately."

I swallowed hard, not knowing what to say.

"When you first arrived on the beaches of Tampico, Jose, you had nothing, correct?"

"Well, actually sir, I had a few pesos to my name."

"Oh yes, the pesos that you stole from that queer priest you later killed," he smiled.

My face went as white as snow. How did he know? *Only Miguel knew and he swore on his life never to reveal it to anyone!*

"Don't worry, my boy, I would have done the same thing. In fact, Chief De La Hoya over there in the kitchen came sniffing around the docks looking for you." The words seemed to roll off the old man's hardened face. "But I intervened. Yes, I did that not because you were of any value to me at the time, but because your determination to filet that fish gave me a knowing feeling that you had it together. Something told me that even a poor bastard like you had purpose."

I suddenly felt the need to use the restroom. I wasn't sure which end it was going to go out—I just knew it was coming.

"Mr. Robles, with all due respect, I must use the bathroom please!"

Out of nowhere came one of Robles' henchmen, who snapped his fingers at me, rattling off something about respect. Robles quickly intervened, overriding his command. "No problem, my son. It's straight ahead, off of the main hallway."

My vomit barely made the toilet. A wicked combination of seafood, tequila, and bile stripped my throat unlike any sickness that I had ever encountered. But that wasn't what made me sick—it was the knowledge of what Robles knew for the past six years that was now surfacing. What once was a kept secret between two people was now known amongst the most powerful men in the State of Tamaulipas. I quickly cleaned my mouth with the complimentary mouthwash in the medicine cabinet, trying to regain my composure.

Once I returned to the dining area, I noticed Miguel's face was whiter than before, as if fear was tattooed on his cheeks. Mr. Robles had left and Miguel did not say a word. I knew our lives would never be the same.

CHAPTER 7

That evening changed not only our lives, but our job descriptions and responsibilities as well. It had taken six years, but we were now officially members of the Eduardo Robles Drug Cartel. We stayed in one of several guest rooms that he had and were treated like royalty the rest of the weekend.

Mr. Robles and his subordinates put us through a crash course on what they did and how the organization was structured. There were several layers of "management" designed to protect Mr. Robles.

I had many questions. One that was answered was why the police chief was at the house the previous evening. He was there to protect all of Robles' employees and his organization. In return, he and many officers were on the payroll looking the other way while Mr. Robles supplied North America with all of the drugs that he could deliver.

Trust and loyalty were the only things that Robles was looking for. There was really nothing else that one had to know to keep out of trouble. Drug dealing did not require a degree and there were certain standards and methods that had been established that produced a reasonable degree of success. Oh, it also required a lot of balls. Fortunately, Miguel and I possessed those in no short supply.

The property now made sense. Over the weekend, the deal on the plot of land had been finalized. We both knew it. Robles knew that we would never turn the offer down. And we didn't. What we didn't know is that we were now partners for life. There was no escape. We made our beds and we would either lie in them—or die in them.

Robles utilized the fishing operation to launder the money and take cover for the transportation of the illicit substances. It was just a mirage for a much bigger enterprise, one that dealt with everything bad in the world.

It was Sunday evening and we were told that we would be driven back to our home in Tampico within a couple of hours. We had one last meal with Mr. Robles that consisted of a traditional Mexican meal. The only mention of business came with two envelopes with 2000 dollars in each one. They were American greenbacks, which we all preferred because the peso was so unstable. It was a huge amount of cash for two teenagers living in Mexico in the eighties.

Although both of us had a considerable amount of money saved up, it was from a few bucks here and there. Never a G note at a time. So not only did we have a new profession that evening, the two of us considered ourselves rich. And we were. Especially with opportunity.

CHAPTER 8

"I can't believe that we're so lucky," Miguel whispered as two candles illuminated his dark skin and probing eyes. "We have been blessed by the good Lord," he said peacefully.

Unlike Miguel, I did not believe in a higher power. No reasonable God could possibly produce such mayhem in the human race.

"Miguel, this isn't the Lord's work, as you would put it. This is our reward for being loyal and honest. Can't you see that destiny is only created by our actions of the past? Anything else is simply luck!" I exclaimed as my body continued to fuel up on the new substance that I was introduced to that weekend.

"Good men see the virtue in other good men based upon their actions. There is no intervention by some invisible man in the sky!" I said, my point emphasized with a new aura of false confidence. I could see and feel the rage building in Miguel's features as I expressed my minority opinion of this silly belief in God and the phony men who disseminated the myth.

"Jose, you will go to hell speaking like that. Regardless of how you feel, you aren't old enough to know better! How else can two teenage boys like us wind up in such fortunate circumstances?" He slapped the end table next to the chair he was sitting in.

I had heard never to argue religion or politics, so I found myself deep in the thick of things. *Going against the grain.* Even though I briefly shut up and pondered the mystery of the universe while staring into the candlelight, I knew this would not be the end of the conversation between us about God. I didn't have the answers to these mysteries, but after having read the Bible, I quickly dismissed its merit from a spiritual point of view. Sure, it had historical roots and I believed in Jesus Christ as a good person. But him being the son of God was a stretch to say the least. One day, when Miguel grew up, he would be mature enough to meet the truth. In the meantime, I might as well have told him that the moon was made of cheese.

Many of my friends and co-workers had questions about man's fate, but there simply was no evidence except those men's opinions as depicted in the Bible. Plus, there were many different versions of the Bible. So whose to say what opinion was true and which one was false?

I had quickly realized that organized religion was led by salesmen who profited from their congregations the same way salesmen profit from the consumers who buy their products. Miguel, like billions of others in the world, had been brainwashed because they were simply scared to die. And when it was their time, they wanted some false sense of security to tell them that they would live in heaven forever.

It was a game—life, that is. For me, it was a game in which only the best made it to the finals. The others simply followed in our wakes and eventually faded away. Religion too was a game. A game in which I did not participate.

Minutes of silence passed. We were drunk and stoned and silently agreed to disagree, if that means anything. "Maybe we'll pick this up tomorrow after a good's night's rest," I said, knowing that it wasn't worth arguing over.

Miguel stood up, nodded his head, and proceeded to exit the room for his bed.

"One more thing Miguel…while you're up."

"Yes Jose."

"Could you bring me that leftover box from the Old Man's house before you go to sleep?" I smiled.

"Will do, stoner."

CHAPTER 9

I had never met him before, but his eyes were as cold as the north pole. You knew that he was a killer by just looking at him. He examined me like an interrogator would his prisoner. However, the Geneva Convention would not be followed. He would do whatever it took to extract information. There was no other side to "Shark," as he was called. All business and no friendship. He was here to train us and not make new friends.

Shark had been a key member of the Robles Organization and carried more influence than anyone except the Old Man himself. He was recruited from Columbia from the Escobar organization. Rumor had it that Pablo himself did not want to lose him, but owed the Old Man. Apparently a massive shipment of cocaine had been intercepted on the way up from Columbia to Tampico. Robles had paid in advance. Shark was part of the remuneration.

Shark had a barrel-like chest with massive biceps. His fingers were short and thick. He had a single tattoo of Che Guerva, the Argentine revolutionary, on his right forearm, accenting the massive muscle tissue beneath his skin. It was rumored that he had never cracked a smile or laughed in his lifetime. It was hard to believe until you came into contact with him. It was probably true.

His specialty was logistics. In Colombia, he trained people how to get cocaine to the United States from the jungles outside of Bogata. His job was to make sure the product got to its destination without detection. He was the best in the business. And he meant nothing but business.

Another rumor about Shark was that he killed those within the network who did not follow his specific directions and who put any facet of the operation at risk. Like the Mafia, the only way out of this organization was in a body bag. We were never specifically told that— it was just an understood fact in this business.

The blow to Miguel's face was proof that Shark's reputation was genuine and that he didn't screw around. While Shark was speaking, Miguel's mind was wandering. Eye contact was lost and, consequently, so was his consciousness briefly.

"When I'm fucking talking, you best listen and look me in the eye." His words echoed as his fist pummeled Miguel's mouth. The blood of Miguel's face splattered like a ripe tomato hitting a brick wall.

"And what about you?" he screamed in my direction. "Consider my fist a bullet and now you're fucking dead!" He smacked his fist hard into his palm.

"Let me make this perfectly fucking clear!" he yelled. "You're fighting a war on the front lines. We don't do this just for money, do we? We do this for many reasons, including that we can get away with it. You cannot become complacent or you'll die. You got that assholes?" His face turned bright red. He then turned and focused his attention strictly on me.

"The old man says you're a rising star?" I could smell his morning's breakfast on his breath. "I don't fucking believe it!" he spitted into my face. I didn't flinch. I just let the saliva drip down my cheek, eventually dropping onto my boot. "Talk is cheap, sailor. I'll be the judge of you," he raged, his eyes piercing me like a fine syringe.

He was testing me and he knew it. He knew I knew it, too. I think it was more show for Miguel than anything. I never once took my eyes off Shark, regardless of the nasty saliva that I could smell with every breath I took.

Shark had clearly defined a distinction between Miguel and I. And at that particular moment, I had little concern for loyalty to Miguel. My safety and livelihood was on the line and I was looking out for number one. I had witnessed Miguel wander off twice now when things were really important—first with the Old Man, and now with Shark. That was dangerous. For the first time in my life, I was beginning to see a side of Miguel that could prove detrimental to our safety. Drug dealing was serious business, and as the Shark had demonstrated, nothing could be taken for granted.

In my peripheral vision, I could see Miguel lying on the ground with a bloodied face. My instincts were to go over and help him, but I didn't move. My loyalty was to the Cartel at that very moment. And whether I liked it or not, it would be until the last day of my life. Or so I thought.

CHAPTER 10

Miguel's jaw was fractured. He was taken to a local hospital in downtown Tampico. Mr. Robles was not happy with what Shark had done to a 16-year-old kid, but did not question his actions. Shark had his own way of dealing with subordinates within the Cartel. My own senses told me that even the Old Man was afraid of him.

Miguel was released that day and was driven home to recover. I continued my training one-on-one with Shark. My first hands-on lesson was the use of a Ponga boat and its role in the drug trade. I knew Pongas firsthand from my experience as a deckhand and fishing boat captain. These Pongas looked similar—however, they were quite different. First, they were much faster, more powerful, and had very technical instruments on them. Second, they were designed to move drugs for hundreds of miles—not to leisurely fish around a bay. In short, they were beyond impressive, compared to what we were used to in the fishing trade.

Shark was given credit for developing new technologies within the drug trade as well as his expertise on logistics and defensive tactics. It was rumored that he had developed a rather large container that latched to the bottom of the Ponga, capable of stowing and towing large amounts of cargo—in this case, cocaine and marijuana. It had an electric contraption that allowed the density of the container to fluctuate, allowing the cargo bin to sink or rise behind the boat and beneath the ocean's surface. This type of technology was crucial as a countermeasure to the latest technology that the United States was using in its feeble attempts in the war on drugs.

It was further rumored that a former governor of California, a real cowboy type, was going to become president and pump billions of dollars into the fight. Not only was technology crucial, the wisdom to stay a step ahead of law enforcement was a must. Shark was that man.

With Tampico's strategic geography as a distribution point for the United States and the Caribbean, and the massive demand for cocaine and marijuana in the late seventies, I had job security as long as I didn't get caught, which was tough to do given the system that Shark had implemented for the Robles Cartel. If any member of the Cartel was interdicted by authorities, we could release the cargo underneath and behind the boat by pressing a disengagement latch. Once the cargo was released, the seal on the container was shifted to where it would take on water and sink the load to the bottom of the ocean. Granted, we lost the load, but we retained our freedom and protected the secrecy of the Cartel.

As time went on with my training, I knew 99% that Shark was in my corner. I would often ask him over to the house for a cocktail or dinner, but he would just stare at me as if I were crazy. I didn't know if it was because Miguel and I were roommates or some other reason, but he always gave the same, robotic response: "I don't associate with any of my colleagues on a personal level." I respected him for that. He was disciplined, although I felt his yearning for something outside of his job. In the end, I never witnessed him fraternizing with any of the members, including Mr. Robles himself.

I was determined to be the most successful operator in the Cartel. I had already become the best fisherman of the bunch because I focused on my job at all times and on how I could differentiate myself from the rest of the brothers. It was in this new job that I really began to work circles around Miguel.

Ironically enough, it was Shark who reinforced my dedication to the trade with his relentless pursuit of perfection. I was beginning to respect him more and more on a daily basis, despite his gruesome beating of Miguel. It was evident that Shark had no respect for Miguel and I quickly came to the conclusion that Miguel simply didn't take to the drug trade as he had fishing. In fact, I had lost trust in his ability to succeed in this business. And in him for that matter.

CHAPTER 11

Eventually Miguel decided to move out of the house that we built together. Apparently, he had found a girlfriend. Although the girlfriend's parents were staunchly opposed to their shacking up, because of their strict Catholic faith, neither was dissuaded. I'm sure the pressures of Miguel's job had something to do with it.

I was worried about his safety and how he was doing within the Cartel. Personnel issues such as these simply were not discussed among the gang of brothers. It was considered disloyal and unproductive. It would have gone against the code of the organization. But I held Miguel above the weight of the Cartel itself. I considered him my only brother, and yes, he was a fellow orphan.

I had never received any accolades from members of the Cartel with the exception of the Old Man himself, but I knew that I was respected and, more importantly, trusted. I never felt that I had to look over my shoulder with this group of criminals. And yes, I was a criminal. A rather wealthy one.

After some time I was able to confirm the girlfriend. She was 18 and the relationship was serious. I don't think that Miguel had ever been laid until meeting her. He conformed to that strict Catholic rule of not having sex before marriage. I myself had been lucky enough to lose my virginity to a Canadian woman in her late twenties after I took her and her girlfriends out fishing one afternoon. She had recently caught her husband with the babysitter and decided to splurge for a weeklong trip on his credit card in retaliation. They weren't shy about telling me that

I was going back to their hotel room to romp on this semi-overweight woman. It was over within a minute, but I was glad for that one minute. This one experience paved the way for many nights of surly behavior and downright hedonism.

Once he was set up at his new pad in a very nice, upper-class neighborhood in Tampico, I went for a visit. Many of the guys who worked on the oil rigs and tankers lived in this area. It certainly didn't look like the Mexico that I knew. Miguel had money and as far as anyone knew, he was just a boat captain, fitting in with the rest of the seamen in the neighborhood.

Miguel had rented a small flat with two bedrooms and one main bath. It was just under 1000 square feet but very nice and modern. Although rumors were scant within the Cartel about any personal issues that Miguel may have had, it was obvious that he was hiding something. I supposed that maybe his girlfriend was pregnant or that there was some other embarrassing situation. I knew, however, that whatever it was, it would not be tolerated much longer by the Cartel. Miguel had made the fundamental mistake of not getting permission from Robles himself to move anywhere, especially in with a woman. The secrecy of the Cartel could never be compromised and I finally felt the obligation to set down some rules with the only man I truly had ever befriended. But he wouldn't budge. For the first time that I ever noticed, he was actually cocky regarding this situation. I asked to speak to him out on the veranda and he respected my demand. But it was a no-go. He said his loyalty was strictly to the Cartel but I knew better. A stiff prick had no conscience.

I left and allowed the pains in my stomach to dictate my mood. Something didn't feel right. But I still felt safe. I decided right then and there that the only man I could look after at this point was me. I couldn't control Miguel nor should I. If he was to trip up, I couldn't compromise my own safety, nor the Cartel's.

I returned home and decided to go over my financial situation. My goal was to retire within the next 10 years. I analyzed my co-workers. Although many were good, most of them dabbled in coke. None of them had the money that I had amassed. They were too busy snorting it up their heads. My wealth had been accelerated because I didn't mess with the powder. I couldn't understand how people could trade away their lives like a pummeling stock knowing that it would never pay a dividend. There were no winners with coke addicts.

Marijuana, on the other hand, was different. I operated on the skim—skimmed product, that is. I always pinched the load for not only personal use, but for the extra cash as well. And I didn't need that medicinal bullshit that was *super* natural. I just needed that high that I had been adjusting to so much recently.

In this business, we paid our own bonuses. We, the distributors. Cartels didn't give a shit about you. They only looked at the big picture. Cartels were dealing with millions of dollars every day. It was up to us to make sure we got taken care of. It had nothing to do with honesty or loyalty. That was a given. We wouldn't be risking our lives if we didn't possess these characteristics. It was self-preservation. Like I said, we all skimmed—only I saved my extra cash while everyone else was blowing a line up their face. I was stoned and counting my money.

I was a functioning stoner. I was stoned all day, every day. But cocaine was different—weed was to aspirin as coke was to cyanide. If I were going to die in the drug trade, it would not be from some idiotic self-inducement of "blow." It would be at the hands of the authorities who would shoot first and then ask questions. Most of my colleagues were hooked on the powder, and consequently, screwed. Their days were numbered.

Shark once mentioned how people in the Escobar organization would disappear. It was scary to hear. But I knew what was up and it was Shark's way of saying, "I killed the fucker." The cokeheads got in over their heads. They got way too deep into the shit. They no longer had control of their lives or their actions. They were simply liabilities. And because of the sensitive nature of their duties within the Cartel and the knowledge that they possessed, they were eliminated. We heard about summary executions all the time—I'm sure Shark and Robles were no strangers to the practice.

I had read that many drug lords made their victims dig their own graves before they were murdered. That had to be intense because it gave them time to think about how they screwed up and how they wish they could change the past. And then—Bang. You're dead.

CHAPTER 12

For my 19th birthday I had celebrated over shots of Sauza Tequila and loose women at the Robles ranch somewhere in Vera Cruz, south of Tampico. We were never told of the exact location—it wasn't smart to identify a home of a drug dealer. What I do know is that I was flown in on a small Cessna single-prop plane and landed on a dirt airstrip a few hundred yards from the beach house.

The house was once used as a delivery point on the drug route to the States. A major delivery hit some really rough waters right off the coast and the boat capsized. For the next three days, cellophane packages washed up on the beach and literally flooded the town with coke and weed for weeks.

It immediately caught the attention of the local Army headquarters, which confiscated hundreds of pounds of dope. The local police tried to get in on the action but the federal government, in this case the Army, had jurisdiction in the matter. Unlike the police in Mexico, the Army was generally honest and had a bonfire burning for days. It was rumored that all of the washed-up druggies hung around and were stoned the whole time from the fumes.

So Campo de Vera Cruz was now off limits to any drug activity within the organization. The house was used for parties and retreats only. And speaking of retreats, it was standard practice in the organization that if your load of dope was ever intercepted, you were immediately sent on a retreat whether you wanted one or not.

It shouldn't have happened to me. For years I had always taken the utmost precautions on every facet of my route and never got compla-cent. Nearing my 30th birthday, however, I was nicked by the U.S. Coast Guard, which was working in conjunction with the Drug Enforcement Administration (DEA). I had to drop and sink a load worth about a half a million dollars to the Cartel. I had no idea where they had come from but they came in hot and heavy—it wasn't just a routine patrol. It was odd. Perhaps it was just chance. It had happened to every one at some point in the Cartel but I had believed that I would be the exception. I was not. I viewed it as failure, although I was told not to worry about it. So I tried not to. I was to stay for two weeks to re-evaluate my experience. And I did. Before the partying began each day, I mapped out just what I did and how the experience went down. I couldn't have done anything much different, I concluded, than I did. It had to have been chance?

I spent the mornings catching *corvina* from the shore and making fish and clam omelets every morning for the guests, whom I didn't really know. My pilot, Carlos, was also a bodyguard for the Robles organization. He was here to party, but also to take care of things. He certainly took care of things, especially himself. I had never seen such a large appetite for cocaine, booze, and women. Robles had a local who made sure the house was cleaned and stocked with food, beer, and of course women. At present, there were three local hookers from a strip joint in town that he had arranged for prior to our landing. Carlos and I didn't have to spend a cent—anyway, we were ordered not to leave the premises, unless we were going off-roading on the beach with one of the many toys Robles had stowed in the garage off of the back.

It was nice, but I did things every day to remind myself that this was not a vacation. I worked out every morning by doing push-ups and sit-ups on the beach and then going for long jogs in the sand. I also tried my hand at some new recipes after I cooked everything I knew from heart for my guests. The best one that I had come up with was a light-ly breaded *huachinango,* or red snapper, fried in olive oil served Vera Cruz style. It was delicious if I said so myself and concocted it on my own just by talking to a local fisherman.

All in all, the retreat was a good way to clear my head. But I need-ed to get back to work.

Carlos left us on a Friday and returned Saturday with Robles in a bigger plane, the Cessna 210. Robles brought a couple of his goons and we had a meeting that afternoon before we tore it up one last night. Robles seemed satisfied that there was nothing unusual about the situation. I just happened to be in the wrong place at the wrong time. Unfortunately, this wouldn't be my last retreat.

CHAPTER 13

About 2 years later, I was cruising on the midnight run headed for the Gulf Coast where I was to make contact with my American counterpart. The sky was starless and moonless; the boat was taking directions from my own dead reckoning. I was lost in my own world as I indulged myself with half a joint and cold glass of Coca Cola. My deckhand Felipe was busy preparing cold tilapia sandwiches made with fresh Mexican rolls and a regional garnish heavy on the onion and cilantro. We had been on the seas for almost four hours when I spotted a vessel on the radar. It was coming towards us at lightning speed. I called Felipe over to verify what I was witnessing on my instruments.

I quickly instructed Felipe to prepare for the worst. There was no way that this bleep on the radar was our counterpart, or they would have radioed us in advance to the change of our original plans. In this trade, there were enemies and then there were the authorities. Rarely did we find ourselves in conflict with the Mexican task forces because Robles had that handled at a higher level. It was the competing Cartels that could pirate your ship, or the American military or the DEA targeting you for a bust. Our American counterparts often utilized yachts or cargo ships to mask the illicit goods with luxury or legitimate cargo. Robles didn't care as long as we got the goods so he could get paid or make good.

Within minutes, we realized that it was the U.S. Coast Guard and I found myself getting sick to my stomach as I tossed my bag of personal stash into the water. With that small bag followed my livelihood and probably my life. I motioned over to Felipe and swiped my hand over my throat, instructing him to sink the goods.

Felipe dropped the load as we saw a large amount of white, sudsy bubbles surface to the top of the ocean. The air in the cargo hold was being replaced with water, rapidly sinking the evidence. *What is Robles going to do with me now?* I thought. With every second that passed, the precious cargo sunk a few more fathoms.

Within seconds, a screeching foghorn penetrated my ears as the vessel approached our boat. The boat was staffed with several armed soldiers, all aiming their weapons at us. We were warned in Spanish to raise our hands above our heads and we did. It was no longer coincidence. I had lost my first shipment of dope upon my return to the lucrative drug trade. The first time may have been chance, but not the second. There was no warning, no surveillance on their part, or suspicious activity on ours. They had just come straight for me. It was a backdoor deal. A setup.

Two lost loads back-to-back generally sent you into retirement very quickly. And in this profession, the retirement party normally consisted of a funeral out in the middle of nowhere. It was a turning point in my career for sure. I wasn't just nervous. I was scared.

As the Spanish-speaking officer boarded the vessel, we were detained in wrist bracelets and taken to the American cruiser. I could care less what they had to say. I had bigger worries and they had no evidence. I never saw Felipe while I was in custody because they had separated us immediately. Shark had trained all of us in the tactics used by law enforcement officials. These guys were easy. We were fingerprinted, photographed, and interviewed by the DEA. With that interview came a profile and I placed in their database of suspected drug dealers. Again, all I could think about was Robles and the Cartel.

After being slapped around a little bit, I was free to go. Felipe was on the boat waiting for me. His brown skin looked a lighter shade and sweat had formed around his brows, despite the cool temperatures. He was nervous and lost for words. He was just a poor fisherman who always remained loyal to Robles and the Cartel. And Robles was slowly destroying his life and his family by moving him into the trade. Felipe should have been out on the ocean fishing, not running drugs. A simple man. I felt sorry for him as the gloss of sorrow washed over his iris and pupils. He deserved a better life and for the first time in ages, I felt that maybe, just maybe, I had a heart.

It took everything I had to radio the Cartel and inform my bosses that I had been intercepted. Everything we did over the communications network was in code, and the last code I ever wanted to give was *Sunset Red.*

When the Cartel answered my call, there was silence on my end before I could gather enough muster to say the deadly words.

CHAPTER 14

I had spoken the words *Sunset Red* and listened to silence on the other end. Felipe had not said a word the entire trip back. I was paralyzed in thought and had no recollection of the trip home as I disembarked from my Ponga boat at the dock. Like old hat, Felipe cleaned up the boat as I stared at the faces of Robles' henchmen, serious and somber.

I regained some composure as I walked tall towards the black Suburban. The back door was opened for me and slammed behind me as I fastened my safety belt over my lap. I had noticed a second vehicle parked behind us and wondered why it was necessary. Did they think I was going to flee? That would have been admitting guilt. I was not a flight risk. In fact, I was as loyal to the Cartel as any. But what did it matter? I was making the arguments to myself and no one else because I didn't know what to expect.

I could see the lights of Tampico in the driver's rearview mirror as we made our way to the outskirts of the city. I didn't know if this would be the last time that I saw my home. We entered the guarded gate of the compound and began the steep climb up the hill. My nerves began to take a turn for the worse. I was sweating profusely and was further panicked because now I even looked guilty, with my moist, shaky skin. The second gate was opened and I immediately noticed Shark talking with Robles on the sidewalk running parallel to the steep gate on the perimeter of the property. This obviously wasn't a surprise party.

I exited the vehicle and made a firm approach towards Mr. Robles and Shark. I noticed more armed guards than normal, but quickly dismissed it as paranoia. I didn't do anything wrong and I was going to let Robles know it.

The Old Man's look was indifferent as he began to approach me. I stopped short of the sidewalk as he greeted me with a hug and left his hand around my shoulder.

"Come with me, Jose, where it's a bit cooler inside," he said, leading me towards the front door of his home. The foyer of his house was unusually cool and I could see the reflection of Shark behind us in the stained glass archway. Nothing was said as we continued to walk through the hallway into the living room. Robles handed me off onto the couch; he sat down across from me. Shark made his way in, where he sat perpendicular to us like a referee at a boxing match.

"Jose, I'm sure you can guess why we're here," Robles said in a calming voice.

"I have a hunch, sir, but I promise you, I never...."

Shark cut me off with a simple finger over his mouth. This was an improvement over the verbal abuse he gave me on the first day of training.

"Jose, I'm not questioning your loyalty to the Cartel. You are aware, however, that we have suffered tremendous losses at the hands of your boat. And though we have monitored you for the last two months, we have found nothing out of the ordinary."

"You've what?" I asked with a look of surprise on my face.

"Shut up!" Shark yelled. *I knew he still had it in him.* Robles turned to Shark and looked at the thug in disgust and then turned back towards me with a sarcastic grin.

"Well, Jose, we had to. But we haven't figured anything out. There's obviously a problem and we just don't know who's compromising the Cartel." His words echoed in my brain.

"But it's OK, Jose. Time always reveals the truth." He rose and walked towards the hallway, then stopped, paused, and slowly turned around.

"You're free to go, Jose. The boys will see that you get home safely."

"But sir—is that it?" I asked in bewilderment.

"Yes, Jose, that's it. Shark will wake you in the morning," he said with a smile. "You'll be staying in Tampico until things cool down. We've got plenty of other work to do here on land. Good night." He gestured with his hand and walked through the hall.

I turned and looked at Shark, who had indifference written on his face.

"So that's it?" I asked again in disbelief.

"Jose, we both know that you aren't responsible. Your demeanor this evening was proof enough. Now get out of here because I wake up early," he said, rising from the lounge and stretching his muscular arms above his shoulders.

I slowly got up feeling relieved but not entirely trustworthy of the situation. I still felt like a prisoner getting word that his new cellmate was in for rape. I walked towards the entryway, where I was met by armed security who escorted me to the Suburban. The next thing I remembered was being nudged by the driver, telling me that I was home.

I went straight for the kitchen and grabbed some weed out of the freezer along with a cold Modelo from the fridge below. I was still nervous in the head but the numbness put my body at ease as I lay down on the futon flipping on the fuzzy black and white TV.

If someone was compromising the Cartel, I should have a clue because it was me who was getting caught. But who? I thought. It was then and there that I decided that I would be a survivor no matter what. I would never perish at the hands of ignorance. Even if it meant I slept with my eyes open from now on.

CHAPTER 15

Shark wasn't joking when he banged on my door just shy of 5:30 in the morning. "Get some coffee going, Jose," he said, storming into the house. I was sure I wasn't dreaming because Shark had the tendency of sobering up anyone in his path.

I lit the gas stove as I poured the strong blend into the percolator. Minutes of silence passed until the coffee began perking. Shark did not hesitate to touch the scalding liquid to his lips as if he invited it with challenge.

"So, do you have any idea who it could be?" he asked me as if he was asking a friend for a smoke.

"I don't have a clue. I really need to search my memory before I go down that road of thought."

"I can imagine, Jose. I would hate to be in your shoes...you know, not knowing who's looking over your shoulder...calling every move..." his words trailed off.

Shark did have his way with words, I thought, pouring some milk and stirring some sugar in my coffee.

"I used to drink my coffee the same way, Jose, until I started the midnight runs as a kid."

I looked up as the aroma enriched my senses.

"What do you mean?"

"Well, nothing tastes better than a hot cup of coffee when the wind chill of the ocean is freezing your pecker into the smallest specimen known to man," he said with almost a smile. "But who has time for milk and sugar? Coffee is an acquired taste like a good scotch. Why fuck with it?"

I wasn't sure what his point was, but I took it in as if I agreed and let the sipping sounds consume the moment. I was lost for words and I think Shark was too.

"You're going to sit tight for a while here in Tampico. Like Mr. Robles said, time will cure a lot of things and eventually reveal the truth." He looked up at me and stared into my eyes.

"Yes it will," I said with a determined look. "Yes it will."

"You will have your choice of working with me or the Old Man himself. It will be up to you, Jose." He sniffled and then wiped his nose. "Frankly, I don't have much use for you except on the boat. You're one of the best I've seen and would like to keep you there. But right now it's not possible. Perhaps you should just take some time off and tend to some personal needs until we get this shit figured out."

Shark knew that I was a workaholic and that I liked money. Not that I needed anymore, I just enjoyed making it. Shark left abruptly and I lay down on the couch and tried to close my eyes. It wasn't working. As tired as I was, I couldn't sleep. I had too much on my mind.

The chill of the air rustled through my home and a taint of loneliness filled the room. Miguel was gone and I missed his company. He had fallen in love with a woman with two kids. She was widowed and needed him more than he needed her. He was crazy to take that on. Gold digger, freeloader, whatever she was, she was no good for him. He was too young to screw up his life by playing Daddy to another man's kids. Granted, he was dead, but they still weren't his.

I climbed off the sofa and stripped my clothes off. The hot water felt good in the shower, but it wouldn't last long. The water heater was only 20 gallons. I stepped out of the shower into some warm clothes and set out to find Miguel. I hadn't seen him for over a week and thought I would take him to lunch.

I found him at home cooking a pot of beans alone. He invited me in and I embraced his small and skinny frame. He had lost a lot of weight and didn't look well. She was off in Chihuahua visiting her family. He was obviously lonesome and longing to tell me something. But the words never came. His facial expressions said it all. I just absorbed what I could and made no comment one way or the other.

He was a changed man. A family man. It was obvious that the pressures of drug dealing were getting to him. We smoked pot openly and freely at the small wooden dining area. She had no clue except that he was a fisherman. She didn't know about the money either. It wouldn't look good.

She was mounting intense pressure for a formal union. Miguel would have to go to confirmation in the church. Take classes. Become a good little soldier for God. It was ridiculous, but he had agreed. She could no longer live in sin, especially with her kids beginning to wake up to the fact that their mother was living like a whore.

As little as I wanted to admit it, Miguel was meant to be a family man, not a freewheeling bachelor like myself. He knew it and I knew it. But Robles did not nor would he tolerate such evolution among one of his own. Miguel was a lifetime member whether he knew it or not.

CHAPTER 16

Life was boring except that I was able to see a lot more of Miguel. His wife did not approve of our association because I never hid the fact that marijuana was part of my daily regimen. It went without saying that a day without pot was a day without life.

Almost nine months had gone by since my last attempted delivery. Then the call came in. I was psyched. A load was to be delivered to Key West, Florida, and I was to go about my business the same way that I had done in the past. But this time, I was not going to be moving any shipments of coke or weed. It was a test to determine who was ratting me out. The only people in the organization that knew otherwise were Robles and Shark.

I wouldn't be making any money, but the fact that I was making my way across the ocean once again gave me chills. I arrived at Miguel's home to give him the good news. He had been resting on the couch. He looked pale and nervous. He was obviously ill. For a moment, I was inclined to tell him that this was only a practice run and that I wasn't actually going to be carrying any goods. But something told me to remain loyal, regardless of the company of your best friend. I played it safe though it bothered me that I couldn't even tell Miguel.

He was so quiet, shy, and timid that I almost didn't recognize him. He looked like an AIDS patient. Something was wrong and I didn't know if it was physical, mental, or both. The departure was awkward. We said our farewells and I realized that we both had grown older. The old adage rang true in my mind that nothing remains the same. I left Miguel's home that day, never to see him again.

CHAPTER 17

The winds were blowing about 15 knots behind us. We were plowing waves like a cigar boat on Biscayne Bay. Our vessel was small, but always made the trip with relative ease. According to our coordinates, we were about 200 knots from Key West. I slowed the boat down and had my deckhand take over. I was tired and stepped into the cabin for a power nap. What a difference between the old Pongas and the leisure yacht that Robles upgraded me to.

I fell into subconsciousness. It was a dream—a bad dream. Miguel flashed through my mind. He was in danger. His body was naked, bones sticking through his flesh. His eyes were screaming out for help. He was being tortured. I couldn't help him no matter how close I got to him. I tried to touch him, but my hands went effortlessly through his body as if he was a ghost. He couldn't see or hear me, and therefore didn't acknowledge me. But I was there, irrelevant and ineffective. Shark was also there—with Robles—taunting me with scornful words of hate and betrayal. Robles was laughing at me. It was then that Miguel finally took notice of me. He acknowledged that I was trying to help him and his emotions became a wreck. He sobbed and lashed out as his tormentors continued their horrendous acts. A pistol to the head. The screams piercing my ears. The burning of flesh. The penetration of skin. The dismemberment of body parts. And a sudden loud pop and flash of light.

I jumped up in a heavy sweat from the hard bench seat and sweatshirt that I rested my head on. My body was tense and shaking as

I was jolted from my dream. I could hear a loudspeaker in English and a spotlight on our boat. It was the authorities. Again.

My deckhand was panicking because he knew I was the only one who could give the go ahead to release the shipment. But there was no shipment and he didn't know. I tried to calm him but he wouldn't listen. I grabbed him as he set into full panic.

"I have a family, Jose. Please, please," he begged me.

"Kino, calm down," I screamed. "We have no drugs. Nothing will happen to you!"

"You are a traitor, aren't you, Jose?" he wailed as I tried to constrain him.

The boat was a U.S. naval vessel with armed personnel aiming their rifles at us. I heard the loudspeaker in Spanish, but was concentrating on Kino. He thought I was a mole. He had no confidence in his captain and I finally released my grip around his torso. He ran to the stern of the boat where he found an AK-47. As he picked up the weapon, I was praying to a God that I knew didn't exist. It was over for him. Within a second, machine gun bullets ricketed the back of the boat, leaving Kino bait for the sea. He just didn't know and I was not at liberty to tell him. There were no drugs this time. And now, there was no Kino. Whoever gave the authorities the heads up, was directly responsible for the life of Kino Gomez. Friend, father, husband, brother, son, and loyal deckhand.

I stepped into the cabin of the boat to avoid the gunfire. I tore the white tee shirt off of my chest and wrapped it around the tip of a fishing rod hanging from hooks up above. I slowly raised the pole up out of the doorway in a sign of surrender. I was hoping that they wouldn't shoot first but recognize that I was not there for a deadly confrontation. A loudspeaker asked me in Spanish to slowly exit the cabin with my hands up. I was confused because my left hand was holding the fishing rod. But I did as I was told and kept the rod gripped. They instructed me to drop the fishing pole and slowly make a 360 degree turn, making sure I wasn't sporting any weapons on my backside.

Two agents boarded the vessel with M-16 automatic rifles and quickly tackled me to the ground, then they handcuffed me. Two more agents boarded to search the boat for explosives and drugs. And the last thing I saw before I disembarked was the dive team, obviously getting ready to search for Kino. As I looked back at my boat, I could see the extensive damage done to it by the short bursts of machine gunfire. I was lucky it hadn't sunk.

Within minutes, I was being interrogated as to where the drugs were. But I said nothing. A few slaps in the face later, I finally communicated with them by lifting my middle finger. This solicited a firm fist to the side of my temple which certainly did not put me in the mood to talk. The agent then instructed the captain to take me to the Key West Naval Air Station for additional questioning. *Ah, Cayo Hueso,* as we would say in Spanish. That was the one spot in Key West that I didn't want to be.

As we sped towards the air station, my mind meandered back to the nostalgic days of the town of Key West. It wasn't that long ago when one could roam freely throughout the lively beach town without sanction. Immigration was a nonentity and I had spent some of my best nights there partying on Duval Street with unruly characters from Canada to Cuba.

Key West was and had been home to many famous and colorful characters. Hemingway found solace in Key West along with Harry Truman and Tennessee Williams. Jimmy Buffett had made it famous again in my lifetime and had to finally leave because it had become to trendy for his tastes, due to him putting it back on the map. But I, on the other hand, did not want to be Key West's new celebrity out of notoriety. I would have much preferred to slip under the radar.

I was transferred from the boat into a holding cell before being processed as an international criminal, apparently. I had nothing to say except to myself. *I think I have seen the last of my drug-dealing days.*

CHAPTER 18

"You're lying, you brown piece of shit!" said the fat, balding civilian who opted to attend the pow-wow.

"I never knew shit to be anything but brown, with few exceptions, sir," as I stared up at the man's pudgy face. "In fact, I've never seen white shit until I first took a look at you!" I said defensively, in a rare moment of cockiness.

For the most part, I knew that it was not the habit of the United States to abuse their detainees with the media and all of the international watchdog groups these days. I could tell the guy wanted to hurt me, but everything was being recorded on video. He conveniently left the audio off when he called me a piece of shit.

The fact was, they didn't have anything on me except assumed information from some narc. I knew this would be the last time I ever stepped on Key West again. I wasn't afraid of these guys. At least not like I feared Robles and Shark. This was just an exercise in futility as far as I was concerned. I almost tuned them out entirely until I heard the fat guy pipe up to his buddy, "John, go and get the photos from our contact in Tampico." His words penetrated my eardrums as my demeanor turned serious.

"Did you say Tampico?" My tone was now sober.

"That's right, am-ee-goo," he drawled, emphasizing his redneck slang. "I think you'll find these pictures rather interesting." He flashed me his arrogant smile.

The room was unusually cool, but sweat continued to drip off of me as the low-ranking seaman stepped back into the room with a large paper bag in his right hand. I was no longer in control of this situation even though they had nothing on me. They knew more than I suspected—where I hailed from, where I was living. I should have known.

"Do you recognize this picture, asshole!" he said as he slammed an 8 by 10 photo of Miguel down in front of me. It was his mug shot and the computerized date on the bottom right-hand side of the picture was from almost a year ago. Panic and fear peppered his face like freckles on a redhead, but his face was tanned and normal looking, not milky and bony like it had been when I saw him just a few days ago.

"No, doesn't look familiar," I lied through my teeth.

"Try again, taco boy," he said as he exposed his yellow, crooked teeth with pleasure.

"Can't help you, gringo," I replied, trying to hide my fear and nervousness.

The civilian continued to smile as his eyes focused on mine. He swung his hand to the right and asked his assisting seaman for the second set of prints.

"Well, perhaps you'll recognized this photo." He placed the next print on the table before me. It was a gruesome photo of Miguel, barely recognizable. It was an autopsy photo clearly showing the bullet hole through the middle of his forehead. There were other photos too, showing the various stages of torture.

They didn't need an acknowledgment from me at this stage as the tears began rolling down my cheeks. *How could this be?* I asked myself, overcome with emotion. *My only friend in the world.*

Nothing was said for several minutes. A new team of negotiators were called in and I had nothing to say. They were playing nice guy and wanted me to cooperate in bringing the Robles Cartel down. They were out of their minds. I denied all of their requests until they stamped me as being uncooperative. I slept that night in a bare jail cell with not even a roll of toilet paper. It was their way of having control. If I wanted anything, I would have to give up some information. I never said a word until they finally gave me the free pass to go. They couldn't just hold me on their soil without any charges. They couldn't keep the boat because there was no evidence of anything illegal. It had been badly damaged but apparently rendered seaworthy because they told me to leave the country immediately. I was surprised to see my short-band radio still intact, although I knew it was bugged. My wallet wasn't missing any money and I was surprised to see some K-rations and a case of bottled water neatly stowed on board, courtesy of the U.S. Navy.

I was not going to trust this boat all the way back to Tampico and decided to head for Havana, 90 miles south. I didn't have a passport, but rumor had it that as long as you had a little cash, you fit in like family. I was starving and my mind wandered off to that little Cuban restaurant that I frequented, snacking on the *medianoche* sandwich. It was thinly sliced, slow-roasted pork with Swiss cheese on fresh, crunchy Cuban bread. It was so delicious that I never had the nerve to order anything else. The old man whose name escapes me would tell stories of Old Havana before the Revolution in the late fifties that brought me back to those nostalgic days. This would be a perfect time to relive some of those stories and gather my thoughts and senses.

As I approached the communist island outside of Havana Harbor, a gunboat stopped me. The officer demanded my identification and questioned what I was doing. I told him the truth and gave him 50 bucks. With that, I thought that I had met my long, lost family. Within an hour, my boat was being repaired and I was given several options on where I could eat, clean up, and get a nice lady for an evening at a first-class hotel. It all sounded great and I went along with everything. The gal was beautiful and the hotel cost me practically nothing. But for some reason, knowing I had to make that phone call to Robles, I was scared. Even more worrisome was that for the first time in my life, I felt lonely.

CHAPTER 19

I just didn't have the balls to call the Old Man upon my arrival, which had never happened before. As much fun as Havana had shown me that initial evening, I couldn't pick up the phone. I needed some time and the time wasn't right. I had been down this road before—the road of turning up empty handed, with only excuses. I merely assumed who murdered Miguel, as I hadn't spoke to anyone from the Cartel. The boat would be finished in the morning and I would have one last crack at the Havana nightlife before I headed west to Tampico to face the music.

The night came and went. I found myself sleepless, knowing that I owed my boss the courtesy of notifying him that I was still alive, even if he wanted to kill me. So I mustered the courage and called the Old Man at seven in the morning from a dingy pay phone outside an old market. If I hadn't have seen the pictures of Miguel, the call wouldn't have been so intimidating. The Old Man answered and seemed indifferent. I was simply told to get home. There were no questions on my whereabouts and I assumed they thought someone was recording the conversation. There was a mole in the organization—no chances were being taken.

It was a long journey and I took my time. I scored an ounce of weed from some crackhead in Havana. It was schwag, but it got me through the trip without any incidents. Upon my arrival in Tampico, I was escorted in by two Pongas from the old charter fleet. Apparently, they thought I might flee, even though Robles knew I wouldn't. Shark, however, never took anything for granted or become complacent. Procedures were in place and were never to be deviated from. He was an asshole and I accepted it, always reinforcing his lack of trust in me.

We docked the broken vessel and I was driven to the compound. There was no half-smiles or glad-handing as in the past. Robles was deadly serious, unlike I had ever seen him. He greeted me like a teenager who had just come home after running away. He still loved me but was pissed off.

The tequila offered to me seemed to mellow the moment. The waiting game was predictable. Several armed men swarmed around the perimeter as Shark came in and out of the room. I sipped the tequila and thanked myself for being so calm. Normally I would have been high but thought it unwise to get jacked up on dope. So I sat as Robles planted his men around the room to elevate his confidence in the situation.

My mind was at it again as I studied this mogul of everything dirty and corrupt. Robles was really just a small piece of the puzzle. I thought of how guys like Shark basically did as they pleased and expected the boss to turn a blind eye. He always had to have 20 guys around him as if they were some type of foundation for his existence. I was beginning to lose respect for the Old Man the longer I lived and the wider my eyes became.

I stood up as the Old Man entered the room like the Pontiff at Saint Peter's.

"Sit down, Jose," he said, seeming to talk through me. I sat back down on the couch and prepared for the worst.

"I think you know why we're here," the Old Man continued, as a small grimace outlined his face.

"I believe I do, sir."

Silence reigned and I noticed all of his henchmen staring at the Old Man and not me. These guys were puppets with no balls or leadership—only big guns.

"First off, I want to thank you for your dedication to the organization," he said sincerely. "You've been my best apprentice even under unusual circumstances."

"Thank you, sir. My loyalty has been with you from day one."

"Yes Jose, I know" as he moved his head slightly up and down. "Second, I know that we have all been baffled by the recent events of the past."

"Yes, sir."

"And I'm here to tell you that in no way do I, or the Cartel, hold you responsible in any way. None whatsoever."

I drew a sigh of relief because I knew his words were sincere.

"We have conducted an investigation as you well know and we we're able to conclude several things…"

I already knew but didn't want to admit it. Robles was talking to me as if he was reading a speech at a Rotary luncheon. My days with the Cartel were over. I didn't care what he had to say because I didn't know if I loved him or hated him. He was giving me the "at a boy" speech and I no longer cared. My livelihood had ended in a really bad chapter and I was longing for something new.

Robles finished his spiel. We stood up together. I was already looking past the Old Man and his group of cowards who got paid to lick his ass and couldn't think on their own.

"You will be debriefed, my friend, and we will talk soon."

"Thank you, sir."

"You're welcome, Jose. You're welcome."

Without a handshake, he did a 1-80 and left the room. I wondered if I would ever see him again.

CHAPTER 20

Shark's debriefing was more of a gruesome show-and-tell than any-thing. The Cartel knew before they sent me off to Key West but had to prove it definitively to themselves. As much as I hated what Miguel had done to the Cartel, I was too naïve to believe that it could happen to me. My best friend was a traitor and it almost cost me my life.

In hindsight, I began to get complacent about Mr. Robles and his ability to effectively run the organization. But Shark's debriefing changed my opinion. They had photographed every stage of Miguel's torture, which reinforced the fact that I was dealing with some very dangerous people. The final picture showing Old Man himself holding the gun after he pierced Miguel's head with a 9-mm bullet was the final straw. I had to step outside to puke in the gravel, hating both men whom I once loved.

I overestimated Miguel throughout the years because I was always drawing comparisons with my own pathetic life. We were both orphans, so I immediately placed him on a pedestal. In reality, he was weak and he should have never advanced into the drug operation. He compro-mised everything and lost, folding like a rookie poker player in Vegas who bet the rent money. And now he was dead, leaving a fiancé and her children to the wolves.

Shark had broken into his home and ransacked the joint. Anything that pointed Miguel to the Robles organization was destroyed when he burnt the place down. They had found over a 100,000 dollars in cash, which Shark loyally gave back to Robles.

I also reflected on why he had actually moved out of our house. Yes, Miguel had all of the characteristics of a family man. But to pick up the baggage of a widow with two children seemed odd. The real reason was obvious. He could no longer face me as he committed these treasonous acts against not only the Cartel, but his best friend as well. If I had known, maybe I would have done the dirty work myself but in a much cleaner way. He was my only family, and he could have had me jailed for life, or worse yet, killed by the Cartel.

The cycle was vicious. Robles was able to get bank records that showed the large amounts of cash that Miguel had deposited into his offshore accounts. The same money that the DEA confiscated was being redistributed to guys like Miguel in exchange for crossing over to the other side. And the sad thing was, the DEA knew it would only be a matter of time until guys like Miguel got caught. And then? Problem solved by the Cartels themselves. It was the collateral damage in the war on drugs. He was raw meat for the piranhas.

I was sick to my stomach and really pissed off. I had been scarred. I was now known by the boys up north and on a forever-wanted list. Robles knew this, and he knew that I would never step back and take some type of supporting position within the Cartel. The ocean was my life and the risk was my fuel. It would be a cold day in hell when I would work as a gopher for the Cartel, or any other tyrant living life on the edge. It was time to move on and become my own boss. And if there was ever a time to escape this prison without sanction, it was now. So I did.

CHAPTER 21

It was 2001 and I was done with Tampico. As beautiful as the city was, from my chaotic childhood to my drug trafficking failure, my life there had started badly and ended badly. The farewell party thrown was attended by most of my colleagues in the Cartel as an unofficial endorsement that I was not leaving them because I was disloyal. It was unspoken that my luck had run out.

As the party wound down, the primary principles of the Cartel stayed to ponder the future and reminisce about the past. They did their best to forget the true reason for the departure. I was ready to go but out of respect stayed to absorb the conversation. It would be my final celebration.

I was driven home as I had been so many times from Robles's mansion on the hill. I had made arrangements for another up-and-coming trafficker to purchase my home with a small amount down; I would carry the mortgage payments. This all happened, of course, at the hands of Robles and with his blessing.

It was a good business deal for me, like most. I received the property at no charge. I took down from the new owner about as much as I had invested in the entire home. Miguel was dead, so I doubled my equity. I would have a few bucks coming in for the next five years. Not bad for a guy who never invested in real estate. In addition, I got 500 bucks in gringo cash for all the personal belongings and furniture that I didn't want to take with me.

My life was about to begin on a new journey. How I got to Tampico no longer mattered. The future was the only thing to look forward to. As I left my house, I did an about face like the soldiers did in all those old American war movies. I raised the tip of my right hand and touched it to my temple and said goodbye to the docks of Tampico, along with my childhood, my education, and an old way of life.

CHAPTER 22

I boarded the old diesel bus early the next morning. The bus ride lasted close to a day, but I needed the break to think. I came with everything that I owned, fit in two suitcases. The biggest baggage I had was the emotional scars of failure. As much as I dreaded sitting on a crappy bus for 24 hours, the experience was humbling and allowed me to see how many other people lived.

I chose Mazatlan because it was on the ocean and I had read a great deal about its fishing. Many of my friends in the trade argued that next to Cabo San Lucas, Mazatlan came in a close second for game fish. This made sense. Directly west of Mazatlan was the tip of the Baja peninsula, where Cabo was located.

Like most Mexican cities, the outskirts were dingy and poor. The bus station fit right in, epitomizing the worst of Mexican poverty. Bums lined the terminal, using the filthy bathroom as a mainstay and the floor as beds. I felt sorry for them in a sense, but felt no need to dole out the few pesos they were begging for. I always believed that most bums were there by choice and didn't buy into the theory that they had other issues that weren't solvable on their own.

I immediately flagged down a cab, escaping the grotesque scene. I would be staying at one of Mazatlan's finest, the El Cid hotel, on Seven Mile Beach. Because I was so cheap, I had never stayed in a five-star resort before even though I could certainly afford it. I also wanted to take a stab at golf, having always been fascinated by the game. The El Cid offered a nice course from what I read.

On my way to the hotel I pissed off the cab driver because I offended him. I only asked him where I could score some good dope. Maybe he should have joined the priesthood if something so trivial sent him into a rage. In amends, I offered him a rather large tip—the tip of my middle finger as he screeched away from the hotel without a single peso more than the fare.

The bellhop caught me by surprise; I almost kicked his ass when he tried to take my bags. My ignorance was shining. I didn't know what a bellhop was, so my natural instinct was that I was getting jacked by some pretty boy in a faggoty hat. I was reassured that my belongings would be fine by the concierge and was given a strange look when I pre-paid for my room in cash. I had a credit card from a bank in the Cayman's but didn't need to be leaving any trails for law enforcement agencies, domestic or foreign.

My room was on the top floor overlooking the Pacific Ocean. My first priority was to call my banker, who at this point was really my only confidant. Because of the amount of money I had invested with him, I agreed to let him know my whereabouts now that Tampico was no longer my home. I promised that I would keep him updated and let him know when I found a permanent address. He made arrangements to supply me with money from a contact in Culiacan, about 100 miles north of Mazatlan. I had to make the short drive to pick it up, but I didn't have better things to do. I didn't care what I had to do to get it, as long as it was kept confidential and it was available to me when I needed it.

My new passport and fake identification would take a week or so. I would then be able to set up a bank account where I could access money throughout the country. In the meantime, I had to let my mind do the working and my body the relaxing.

My fuel of life was missing and I needed some of nature's best. It wouldn't be hard to find in a town like this.

CHAPTER 23

Valentino's sat on top of a rock formation overlooking the ocean. It was a trendy tourist trap for foreigners and natives alike. I was told that if you ever go to Mazatlan, Valentino's was a must. Although drinking wasn't high on my list, I probably could score some good smoke in a place like this. And I wasn't into the "club" scene or the music, but it was spring break for many American universities and the hard body sporting the Arizona State beater made it very tolerable.

Likewise, even though my English was good, chatting up teenage gringos wasn't my style. It wasn't that I lacked confidence in myself when it came to women—quite frankly, I simply didn't like their company. In fact, the best woman I ever had was in a massage parlor in Key West back in the early days. It cost me 200 bucks and was worth every penny. I never saw her again yet still maintain great memories of her. It really is the best way to have a relationship with a woman in my opinion.

Soon the glamour and the excitement over the teenage bimbos had worn off and it was time to take care of business. I am a calculating person and didn't want to take unnecessary risks. I knew no one in town and didn't feel like getting set up over a bag of dope. I have an odd mentality. I'll risk kilos but not grams. So I continued to wander around the busy club feeling awkward and out of place. I approached the bar and ordered the cheapest shot of tequila they had for no other reason than courage. And within minutes, the courage came and the discretion was tucked away in some other mental compartment.

The doorman seemed like a wise place to start and I immediately struck up some conversation with him. As we were talking, I placed a twenty spot in his shirt pocket and asked him if he could lead me in the right direction. He nodded in a positive manner and briefly excused himself. Within minutes, I was staring at this overweight guy who was introduced to me as Raul.

"How are you, Raul?" I said in a casual tone. His eyes lit up with the prospect of moving some product my way.

"Good, thank you," he smiled sincerely. "What's your name?"

"Jose. My name is Jose, Raul," I said, giving him my fakest smile.

We went through the customary bullshit of breaking the ice and all the other phony formalities before I cut to the chase and told him that I was looking for a connection in town. He pointed to his car and we began to follow his finger's direction. He told me to get in and I obliged.

"Jose, would you like an appetizer?" He pulled a perfectly rolled joint from his shirt pocket and rolled it under my nose like a fine cigar.

"Hydroponic shit, my friend," he said as he winked his left eye at me.

I could tell the weed was top notch and grown under "extraordinary" circumstances. I pulled a Zippo from my pocket and lit the magic in Raul's car.

"I hope you don't mind if I smoke now," I said, inhaling the wicked substance. "It's been a couple of days and I'm having withdrawals."

Raul kept the smile on his face as I closed my eyes and let my lungs absorb the smoke.

"I'm going to my apartment and you can choose from a variety of shit, my friend."

I looked in the passenger side view mirror and could see the lights of Valentino's getting smaller in the mirror. I had no idea where Raul lived nor did I care. I was reaching a high that I had never experienced before. I had some good dope in my day, but I was used to smoking the schwag. There was no comparison. This was one hit shit and I loved every second of it.

We arrived in a middle-class neighborhood within minutes and pulled up in front of Raul's apartment. It was nothing fancy and rather evident that Raul did not enjoy the same success as myself. He was a typical wannabe with nothing to show except bullshit. It was OK with me because I really had nothing but time to find a local connection and trace it to the source. Furthermore, I needed the contact for my own personal gain.

For the first time since I started smoking dope, I declined a second hit. My mind was on the moon and I needed nothing more at the time. I was almost tempted to try the hash that Raul pulled out for a little dessert but followed my better senses. The combination of the long bus ride and lack of sleep, not to mention the killer bud, put the brakes on any further indulgence. I was done for the night. But Raul wasn't. He had to pull out the last trick from his bag and offered me some pure Colombian cocaine. I just shook my head as I was quickly figuring this guy out. He snorted a line and then another and my stomach began to turn as he polluted his body like a glutton out of control. *This will be an interesting time with this Raul character,* I told myself.

CHAPTER 24

It was a rough night for my newfound friend but I was up at my customary time at five in the morning. I found orange juice in Raul's refrigerator and sucked it gone. It was fresh, which is always nice. We never got around to doing a business deal because Raul proved to be very careless. He was wasted by the first hour of arriving at his house and never yielded to the two coke whores who showed up from his neighborhood.

They were fairly decent but I had opted to decline not knowing where they'd been and not having any protection handy. Although I needed some smoke to make me content, I was here on business and Raul had already dropped the ball. After he had passed out, I decided to take it upon myself to explore the household, where I found a large amount of cash hidden on his person, along with several ounces of weed. He was quickly proving to be a jerk off and I decided to let him learn the hard way.

As I hailed a cab a block from the neighborhood off the main throughway, I began to feel sorry for the girls. I was sure that he would blame the missing cash and dope on the girls when he woke up empty. I justified the theft to myself rather quickly and knew that it would be brought up again the next time that I saw Raul. I would eventually throw the whores under the bus and deny any accusations that came my way, if they did. But I was in the drug trade. There was nothing noble or honest about my profession and I certainly didn't need to further justify my scandalous exploits.

I made it back to the El Cid, finding solace and comfort in a huge breakfast of *machaca* and eggs, along with black coffee, rice, beans, and fresh tortillas. It was an early breakfast by Mexican standards, but no one was keeping time.

I went to the pool where I bellied up to a submerged bar stool. *What a great idea,* I thought. *A pool bar.* I did my best at a tequila sunrise, but wasn't impressed with its lack of THC. I needed some smoke and followed my nose to my hotel room. Raul's variety was rather impressive and I opted to try some of the hash that I declined the night before. I was all about destroying the evidence.

As wasted as I was, all I could think about was wasted opportunities and what I missing out on. I was a workaholic and having difficulty in relaxing. I had never been on a vacation and really didn't know how to enjoy one. The hash was kicking in a bit quickly and I decided that it would be best to lie down for a while and stare at my eye lids. I stretched out on the king size bed, where I was quickly in an advanced stage of rapid eye movement. I was awakened by a sudden urge to piss, so I talked myself out of the rack. The alarm clock was the only thing lit up. I realized that I had slept past sundown. I was sweating from wearing my clothes and the warm air in the room. I stripped down to my underwear and opened the sliding glass door leading to the balcony. If there were a God, I thought, the ocean breeze was his air conditioner. With another joint in tow, I slowly smoked my dinner in my briefs on the balcony overlooking the Pacific. *Many of men have tried to conquer that water,* I thought to myself. *But for what reason?* I pondered the thought. Why would I want to conquer my Mother? She was the only family in my life. As I stared her in the face and watched her wandering moods, measured by the differences in the tides, I knew that no matter what happened, no matter how far she drifted away, she would always come back, always be there for me. She was my only relative. Mother Ocean.

CHAPTER 25

I rang the doorbell for more than five minutes. I knew the idiot was home because his Ford Taurus hadn't moved since I left the house yesterday morning.

"Wake up, Raul!" I screamed and pounded the door. I was anxious to see what kind of state he was in and if he had even noticed that his cash and stash was missing.

I had just about lost all patience and was ready to give up when I heard the latch of the door unlock.

"Who is it?" asked a sickened Raul in a groggy voice. I said nothing.

"*Who is it?*" Raul's toned increased in volume while I simultaneously kicked in his door.

"It's Ricky fuckin' Martin," I replied as the door clipped his head and he fell back into a ball of cowardice.

Raul was taken by surprise. I was aggressive and wasn't shy about it. This guy was so lackadaisical in his attitude that he would trade dope to a stranger and then allow him to stay the night in his apartment. And I wasn't a female and he wasn't gay? I had robbed him of his cash and crop and a day later he was still clueless, trying to rid himself of the deadly downer. It wasn't hard for me to come to the quick conclusion that not only was Raul a loser, he was a danger to himself and those of us in the business.

So I did what I did best besides transporting drugs. I took advantage of the weak. And ultimately, Raul would be my next victim. Not just financially by stealing his last bit of cash and the tools of his trade, but socially, mentally, and if he really pissed me off, his life. If idiots like Raul could just be eliminated based on their actions in this world, the rest of us would be much better off.

He got up off the floor slowly and tried to picture me with his rusty mind in motion. But I didn't give him the chance to ask the first question.

"Where's my dope, Raul?" I said as I grabbed him by the collar and tightened it around his neck.

"Uh, what dope? I never…"

"You never what!" I screamed in his face. "I paid you 200 dollars and you're telling me that you don't remember!" I yelled and shoved his overweight frame across the room. Raul hit a sofa and stumbled back to the ground. He quickly got up and backed into the other room. I followed with my threatening demeanor.

"Hey, mister, please, please, just don't hurt me. I will get whatever you want," he said while he continued to back himself into the adjoining room.

Inside the room the two bimbos slept through the entire episode. It was obvious that Raul had had his way with both of them—or maybe they had their way with each other. Who knew? It was sad what women would do with a loser like Raul just for some coke. I'm sure Raul could read my disappointment on my face as I stared at the whores in silence.

"Mister, I forgot your name. I'm sorry," he spoke his words nervously.

"Forget my name, Raul. Where's my dope?"

"OK. I will get it right away. Right away," he said as he became further panicked at the thought of getting hurt. I heard some rumbling around and some cursing, but surprisingly enough, he entered the room with a large bag of green buds. He approached me and held it out.

"Mister, please, help yourself." I grabbed the Ziploc freezer bag from his hand. I opened it up and sucked in the potent aroma.

"Mister, I'm sorry. I remember you now from Valentino's but I forgot your name."

"It's Jose," I said as my mood suddenly changed with the newly found bud. "This isn't the same shit you had two days ago, Raul. Is it?" I asked like a detective talking to a suspect.

"Well, no Jose. Honestly, this is the best of the best. It goes for 200 bucks an ounce on the street here in Mazatlan. That bag will last almost forever," he said, giving his best attempt at some humor.

"Well Raul, thanks a lot." I placed the bag under my jacket and began to exit the apartment.

"But Jose. You can't just, just…"

"Just what, Raul?" as I gave him a sarcastic grin.

"You haven't paid. That's almost 2500 American dollars worth!" his mood changing from timid to pissed.

"Raul, I'll inspect the goods tonight and come talk with you tomorrow. Maybe you can make up your loss on the next large load that I purchase. Unfortunately for you, this one's mine because you tried to fuck me on my very first buy" as my face tightened up with anger. "Or did you forget because you were too fucked up on coke?" I added hammering my point home.

Raul said nothing. He still hadn't realized that I had ripped him off of everything else. I missed the good stuff but it didn't matter, I had it on me. Raul was stupid and careless. He would not last in this trade. His kind never do.

CHAPTER 26

Since the move west to Mazatlan, I tried to adjust to the free flow of alcohol that seems to be served at all hours of the day in this resort town. For a man who labeled himself as a nondrinker, I drank more here than in my entire life. And because I wasn't working, I truly became chronic with the weed. No matter how hard I tried, I simply would never acquire the taste of alcohol. The smoke won the contest hands down.

I had done nothing for days. I was burning another bowl and letting my mind wander back and forth like the little Hobie sailboats coming and going as they chased the ocean's breeze. I would go crazy if all I did was sit back on a resort balcony and get drunk, eat, and sleep. But as much as I wanted to work today, it would've been premature. Patience is truly a virtue in the drug trade. A man without patience is a man without a pulse.

My hunger kicked in and the shrimp quesadillas at the swim up bar were calling me. I put on my board shorts, packed a few greenbacks in the side pocket zipper, and headed towards the elevator that would take me directly to the pool. I thought of those old movies that I watched as a kid when elevators had attendants and my mind tells me that I would have loved to live during those times.

As I descended in the elevator, I heard the sounds of water splashing and kids playing, sounds I never remembered hearing as a kid. I didn't have swimming pools and vacations, no less at least one parent that all these kids inevitably had here. It was all very foreign to me.

The doors opened to the large pool, as busy and overcrowded with youth as it had sounded. The seat at the pool bar was submerged in water, which was perfect in temperature. The bar had a great view of the ocean and Mazatlan's turquoise waters were calling me. Sailing might be in the picture today. Then again, maybe I would just stay in the pool all day, eating and sipping fufu drinks with little umbrellas shading the concoction.

The drink was good because I couldn't taste the alcohol and the anticipation of food was growing. I felt uncomfortable as additional thoughts crossed my mind. Certain people may think I was dead—others may have thought I was still alive. I was a man of circumstance, and so was whatever evidence someone might have had against me. They knew what I was and what I had done, but they couldn't prove it—at least according to me they couldn't. Had I embarrassed anyone, aside from anyone at the Robles Cartel? Maybe that would motivate someone to go outside of the bounds...maybe break the rules? You know, maybe they were out to eliminate me. But I couldn't worry about that.

OK. I needed to snap out of it, to get focused and keep away from the past. I thought that I should go and see Raul tomorrow—play this one out and find out who's supplying the fool. Middlemen were annoying and had the tendency to dampen profits. I was safe. If people were looking for me, their efforts were concentrated in the Gulf and the Atlantic. If their trail ever led them here, it would take some time and I'd be long gone.

In the meantime, the Betty at the bar was flirting with me. The waiter brought me my food, but my eyes didn't leave her face. She couldn't have been more than 25. Yeah, it had been a while and quite frankly, she was hot. Smoking hot.

"One more strawberry margarita," I asked her in English. She knew I was Mexican, but I taunted her with my antics. She smiled at me as she envisioned a large tip, I was sure, as I racked up my food and bar tab. I was beginning to get a bit drunk, but that was always good in the long run. One more hangover to deal with in the morning would motivate me to do what I do best: turning the stash into cash.

She was still smiling at me as my mind refocused on her beautiful face. I smiled back as I chewed the fresh shrimp melted in hot cheese. I went for it and asked her out later. She told me she was off at five and committed with a wink and a smile. She was hot, but like every other girl I'd been with, she'd be a one-night stand. I'd chew her up and spit her out by dawn. I always traveled light.

CHAPTER 27

"I know we started out of the wrong foot, Jose, but I can get you in touch with anyone when it comes to the goods. Everyone knows me in Mazatlan," Raul said with awkward confidence.

"So I hear," I said as we stared at one another across from his kitchen table.

I had showed up at Raul's early that morning to see if he had gained any composure since the day before. I found out he was on the ball because he was broke and out of dope. He didn't even have enough money for a cheap bottle of booze. *A real winner,* I thought.

"Have you had breakfast, my friend? I can make up some eggs while you burn that fatty that you have behind your ear," he smiled suspiciously.

Raul was not only broke, he was scared and we both knew it. This was probably the first time in a long time that he was sober and not hung over. *This will be his true awakening before his final rest,* I thought to myself.

"Yeah, Raul, breakfast sounds good," I said, pulling the joint from my ear and lighting the end with a cheap disposable lighter I had lifted from the convenience store at the hotel. I inhaled the substance hard and my lungs argued with my brain to slow down.

I was going to use Raul like toilet paper. When I was done with this low-life scrote, I was going to flush him like a good bowel movement. He could only get me in trouble.

As Raul cooked up breakfast, I shared the rest of my joint with him in hopes that he would loosen up and give me some more information.

"Raul, I know that you don't know me that well, but I think I know you. I think I know you because you sold me drugs without knowing me whatsoever. So I think I know you well enough to know that you don't work for the government."

Raul laughed at the statement. "Hell no! I don't work for no government, Jose!" he continued to giggle.

I was hesitant to carry on my next sentence because I didn't want to reveal too much of my past, but I also knew that it wouldn't be long before I destroyed the evidence. "I'm from Tampico, Raul. I used to work for a very large Cartel..."

"Which one?" he interrupted.

"You'll find out later. My point is, I know what the hell I'm doing. I know this business better than most. Everything I've done since I was a child has revolved around this business and some of the most important people who control it."

I stared into Raul's eyes to let him absorb some of my words. He couldn't hold a stare for more than a couple of seconds. The little time I had staring into his eyes were very enlightening. Yeah, he was a coward. But more serious was that he was a broken man. The wrinkles in his face and the dark clouds beneath his eyes showed a lifetime of bad decisions and hardship in general.

"Raul, I need a few things from you."

"Like what?" he said a bit defiantly.

"Well, I'm new to town. I need to meet people, the right people, you know, to do some big things."

"What do you consider big things?"

"Well, I want to get back into the action and, you know, you'll always be taken care of," my lie sounding credible.

"That's what they all say!" Raul yelled. He slammed at the table and teared up like a newborn.

I continued to play the part. "Why the tears, my friend? I don't understand why you're upset."

"Because..." he said, his tears turning to sobs.

He got up and walked to the kitchen. I could see the tears drip from his cheeks as he went for a paper towel to dry his face. As he wiped his eyes, he turned and I gave him my best look of concern without blowing my insincerity. This was beginning to get really weak and I was thinking that maybe he was gay. It was like he was inviting me to hold him in my arms and stroke his hair. But I continued to play into the bullshit.

"Take a breath, my friend. Not everyone in this business is cutthroat." My words echoed through the air.

Whatever Raul was upset about, he was confused. He negotiated my rhetoric like an amateur pilot on his first landing. His eyes were red and flooded with tears. He was the typical loser, thinking that his consistent bad habits would render him different results.

Although nothing else was said between the two of us that day, I had already made a deal with Raul. Little did he know that he was dealing with the devil. If his words didn't commit, his expressions in response to my acting certainly did. For a guy who just went into business with me, I don't think he was too happy.

CHAPTER 28

Guaymus was an old fishing and naval port a few hundred miles north of Mazatlan on the mainland. This was where Raul got his dope. I began to map out the logistics of bringing dope down from the mainland. Most of the drugs that went into Guaymus probably passed closer to Mazatlan and were most likely destined for the States. But Guaymus looked strategically sound because of its proximity to the Mexican Baja. I had mapped over 20 different routes on the bus coming over from Tampico and based on my knowledge of the business, heading west into the Baja made sense.

Baja, California, as it was known, was the wild, wild west of Mexico. It was virgin territory and virtually untouched in terms of trafficking drugs. It was known for its desert climate and warm summers. It was a proving ground for anything off-road, and was often invaded by the gringos up north a few times of the year for the Baja's 250, 500, and 1000 races. Not only did it intrigue me for my profession, its desolation made it a desirable habitat, accommodating my reclusive lifestyle—not that I was a rock star, but I wanted to be in a place where no one knew my name. And this would have a further advantage if I wound up on a wanted list. The Baja would be the last place the authorities would be looking.

I convinced Raul to take me to the port city up north to meet his contacts. At this point, I strictly tried to control his movements. It was imperative that his dealers knew that we had been lifelong friends and that I had a lot of experience in the business. It was also imperative, based on the trusting relationship that Raul and I would perceive to have, that his contacts knew we had the capability of moving much bigger loads—and of course, with quantity comes price reduction.

I would have preferred to do all of the talking, but it didn't work that way in this trade. I was the new guy, the odd ball, the one who had to prove himself or die. Somehow I was not afraid. The Robles organization was the best, trained by the likes of Shark. These guys had nothing on me except their established territory. Then again, my mind was just racing. I really didn't know what to expect until I got there and observed these guys.

We left early in the morning, around 4, so we could get there at a reasonable hour. An airplane would have been preferred because I had the money, but Raul's old pile of shit would have to do. I broke the silence as we began to enter the outskirts of the city.

"Are you awake or just sleeping with your eyes open?" I asked sarcastically.

"I'm awake, Jose. But this is going to be a long trip. I'm used to smoking a bowl for breakfast, but it will tire me out to quickly."

"I see," I said indifferently, under a seize of stonage.

The trip seemed to go on forever with idle chatter here and there. The Ford Taurus sounded like an overweight amateur trying to climb Mount Everest. At any second I expected us to be walking. After several hours and closing in on our destination, I once again had to break the silence.

"So, when are we going to meet your contacts?" I asked softly, carefully choosing my words.

"I will call them now and let them know we are here," he said nervously.

Raul dialed the number on his cell phone and waited several seconds for an answer. I listened to the one-ended conversation with curious intensity. From what I could gather, we were to meet at some marina dock at nine o'clock tonight. I could tell that the other party was doing most of the talking because of the long breaks on Raul's end. When he did speak, he was stuttering his words and his face seemed to lose pigment.

"I want you to meet an old friend of mine too...." He barely got the words off. I could hear the increased tone on the other end of the line, but could not decipher what was being said.

"Carlos, relax. Everything's fine," he said delicately. "He's my new partner and it will be a good thing for all of us."

Raul suddenly looked down at his phone. "I think I was disconnected," he said as he placed the phone back against his ear. "He's gone." He looked over at me with a fake smile.

"I hope that I have not caused any problems, Raul?"

"It'll be fine, Jose. Just fine."

Another 30 minutes went by without a word spoken. We drove all the way through Guaymus towards the resort town of San Carlos. Raul pulled into the Paradiso Resort where he had two rooms booked for the night It was still early but the hotel had several vacancies and the desk clerk allowed us to check in early. We unloaded the car with our belongings and, surprisingly enough, Raul had money for the rooms. I'm sure it was borrowed funds and he was thinking he was going to make a lot of money with me.

Little did he know...little did he know.

CHAPTER 29

The 9-mm in the center of my back was of little comfort. The henchman, Carlos, didn't screw around. I was stripped down to my boxers and literally frisked to my balls.

"Easy there, cowgirl," I said as one of his assistants shoved me in a corner.

"Don't fuck with me," he snapped back. "I'm checking for wires."

"I know, I know. You can never be too careful in this business, can you?" I said, staring the thug down.

"He's clear," he yelled to Carlos. "You can put your clothes back on."

I quickly put my clothes back on, as the chill of the air spread goose bumps throughout my body. I was interrogated for a good 15 minutes about my past, including my ties with the Robles organization. But I wasn't impressed with their techniques or their questions. Like Raul, I was dealing with amateurs and was patiently waiting to show these guys who they were dealing with.

"You're a very lucky man, Jose," Carlos said as he coolly drew on his cigarette.

"And why is that?" I asked with intrigue.

"Because my boss is good friends with your boss. In fact, they have done business together in the past."

"That's interesting, Carlos, because I don't have a boss. I'm my own boss," I rattled back.

"Let's not split hairs, my friend. You work for Mr. Robles…"

I rudely interrupted him. "I used to work for Mr. Robles, Carlos. I still consider the old man a friend and mentor. But let me make it very clear to you. He is no longer my boss." I raised my voice to emphasize my point.

"I see, my friend. The little cub is going out into the wilderness without his mommy."

I sat and digested his insults, not knowing if I was going to punch him out and hand him his head or play along with his little game. I chose the latter.

"So Carlos…big guy" I said sarcastically. "Are we going to sit around and play patty cake or are we gonna to talk business?"

"You sure are a cocky one, aren't you my friend?"

I really didn't like where this conversation was going. He was beginning to piss me off, but I held my composure.

"Carlos, I really don't need anymore of your bullshit. I'm here for business and business only. If you want to try and prove in front of these punks of yours that you're a bad ass, let's just take it outside. After I kick your ass, I'll help you off the ground and we can start over. Is that what you want?" I said as I stared him in the face.

"Jose, don't!" Raul intervened.

"Shut up, Raul!" I continued my stare.

Carlos was frozen and said nothing. I ran with my instincts and leapt forward, grabbing his neck as his hands braced my arm. The rest of his team drew their guns, but I quickly snagged his 9-mm in my other hand and pointed to his head.

"Tell your thugs to drop their guns or your dead," I said as my hand gripped harder around his neck while his choking got louder. "Tell them!"

"Drop your weapons," he barely whispered from his red cranium. I heard the guns hit the concrete and I did a visual to make sure my ass was covered. I relaxed my hand and Carlos began to cough uncontrollably. I kept the pistol at his face and laid down the law.

"Are we done, Carlos?" I asked, squeezing his neck for emphasis.

"Yes, Jose, we're done. I am sorry," he said sincerely.

"Carlos, you know if anything ever happened to me, you would open up a whole new turf war and you would surely be dead, right?"

"I understand," he replied, his face still showing fear.

"I am the best and Mr. Robles is depending on me to open up new routes for him, I'm sure," I said, relaxing my arm from his neck, then gently shoving him away from me. "Why do you think it was necessary to manhandle me the way you did?"

"Because I don't know you."

"But you deal with Raul. Don't you trust him?" I asked.

"Actually, not really," Carlos admitted as his words hit me like a cinder block.

"Really?"

"Really. Raul is careless so I didn't trust him when he told me you guys were related or best friends or whatever the fuck he was lying to me about. So I apologize. I have great respect for your boss. I'm sorry." He gulped as his coughing began to subside.

I handed the gun back to him and told him that we should take a walk, man to man in private. We walked out of a side door of the warehouse onto a dock and I placed my right arm behind his neck in a comforting manner. I knew none of his thugs had the balls to follow.

"Carlos," I initiated the conversation, "as you know, we're both dealers." He shook his head in agreement. "You and I are the smart ones out of this bunch," I said as I began to slowly build trust between us. "If we weren't, we'd be taking all of the risk and only making a pittance of the load. So, unfortunately, we have to depend on dipshits like Raul and the like," I said as we walked past a boarded-up fish stand.

"How long have you actually known Raul?" Carlos asked.

"Honestly, less than a week," I stated as I heard a sigh of stress from my newfound acquaintance.

"You've known him less than a week and he brings you up here and misrepresents the situation?" he said in disgust.

"I had to do what I had to do to make a reputable connection." The end of the dock was near.

"Well, like I said, Raul's not known for his brilliance," he said as I tried to conceal the smile on my face. We both stopped at the edge of the dock, where we stared at the boats under the starry sky.

"So where does this leave us, Jose? What do you need from me?"

"To start with, I need a reliable contact. You appear to be that man," I said with little conviction. My intentions were to cut this fool out of the equation until, eventually, I was dealing with the source.

"Where will you be shipping the goods?" he asked squarely.

"All I can tell you is that I plan on running my operation out of Guaymus with a final destination to the Baja."

Carlos continued to fish and I kept stealing his bait. I gathered that he didn't much care where I was shipping to as long as I wasn't stomping on his territory and interrupting his pocketbook.

"The Baja is a long stretch, my friend."

"That it is, but it's still the wild, wild west of Mexico. Interdiction efforts aren't nearly as prevalent or sophisticated. And I've got some close contacts in some of the areas."

Carlos seemed surprised. "I didn't know you knew anyone on the Pacific side except Raul."

"Well, my contacts in the Baja are simply the family of a friend who was killed in the business a few years back. I knew him from Tampico. He used to vacation there once a year and we became rather close. We used to trade stories and the Baja always intrigued me. We both lived for the excitement of trafficking in general. We were like brothers."

"How was he killed?" Carlos asked with a slightly stunned tone.

"Not sure. Don't know if I want to know. I'm sure I'll find out eventually. I do know that it was drug related."

"Did you ever..."

"Carlos!" I rudely interrupted him. "I really don't want to talk about it. Let's just get back to business."

Silence ensued as I thought about my next approach. I was going to go for the big fish and cut Raul out of the deal if I could.

"What can I get 500 kilos for? Me, and me only. No Raul or any other middle man?"

Carlos was silent but it was because he was thinking how much money he could make off me and he wasn't prepared for a heavy hitter.

"Let's talk price, timing, location, you name it. I don't want to stall this project off any longer."

Carlos continued his silence because he was still trying to arrange in his mind the best deal for himself. But he wasn't that smart and I knew it from that point on. I needed to get Carlos out of the picture soon enough, but I would deal with him for now.

"You know, Jose, the Humberto Cartel will require a large cash deposit up front."

"No deal, hombre. I don't play those games. Your boss, if he truly knows Robles, will testify to the fact that I'm not short on cash. I will pay you in full upon delivery. Nothing more, nothing less."

"Jose, that's not going to work," Carlos said as he stared at the dock below him. "We always require a deposit up front."

"I understand Carlos, but if that's the case, I'm gonna have to take my business elsewhere."

Carlos didn't say a word, but the redness on his face said a lot as he thought about all of the money that he was going to lose. He wasn't very slick. In fact, Carlos was just another clown in the drug trade. He could take my deposit and never deliver the goods. I had never dealt with him and wasn't going to fall for an elementary game like this. Shipments could be intercepted, stolen, lost, anything, and I would be out the cash. It wasn't going to go down that way and I was much too smart for these simpletons.

"I'll tell you what, Carlos. Because you forgot your fucking calculator and your ball sack back at your house, you can reach me at my hotel. I'll let that little prick Raul give you the name and address of the place. I'll give you until midnight to make a decision. I'm not fucking around any longer!" I turned and walked away. The drama and theater was startling even to me as I had never acted before.

"What's in it for me?" he yelled at my back in desperation.

I stopped and turned around. "Only you can answer that question, Carlos. I'll see you at my hotel room tonight," I said as I made the decision for him.

It didn't take much to figure out that he would be on the phone immediately doing his research on me. I politely pointed my middle finger at his two henchmen as I walked past them towards the car. I could hear my chauffeur follow behind me. Little did my new business partner realize that I had just bought him out with virtually no money invested.

CHAPTER 30

In hindsight, I must admit that I was a bit startled as I heard the knock on the door. I'm not one for paranoia, but I didn't know who it could be. I slowly opened the door with the chain still fastened and was surprised to see Carlos so soon.

"Well, come in, my friend," I said, shaking my head in surprise. *Surely he hadn't done his research and made a decision this quickly?*

"Thank you, Jose" he said, walking through the door. Behind him were his cohorts who had drawn down on me earlier.

"You two can wait outside," I said, slamming the door in their faces.

"It appears that you do not like my colleagues," he said with a serious face.

"Well, personally, you may be right. But more importantly, I like to do business on a one-on-one basis, not a one-on-group basis. Perhaps it's just my style," I explained as I made an indifferent gesture.

"Well, they're like brothers you know…they're…"

I motioned my left hand back and forth, close to my chest, and ordered, "Stop, Carlos!" I invaded his space. "Shut up," I continued firmly. "You're missing the picture, my friend. We're here to do business and nothing more. In fact…"

"Yeah?"

"Don't say another fucking word until I give you the green light, comprehende?"

"Yes sir," he said obediently.

I think Carlos knew that I had lost respect for him based on my exit at the docks. But this surely had to reinforce his thoughts. I had now made the decision to cut this dimwit out of the picture as well once I made a connection with his superiors. Carlos had come across like a gangster from L.A. and I had him disarmed within 15 minutes. He was too weak for my blood and it was no surprise why he dealt with Raul.

"You're aggression is uncalled for."

"Yeah," I said, as I dragged on a joint in anticipation of his next words.

"I'm here trying to help you out and you're treating me like a dog!" his voice gaining confidence.

"Carlos, you obviously came here for a reason and if it's only to try and change my manners, you're free to leave. Otherwise, I need to know if we have a deal or not."

"Well…"

"Yes or no!" I shouted.

"Yes!" he shouted back. "My boss is willing to accept your terms."

"What else did your boss say?"

"He said your commitment to buy the load was good enough for him because if you didn't come through, you're a dead man," he responded, backing away from his final words.

"That's good enough for me," I said as I smiled and smashed my joint into the ashtray. "That's good enough for me."

Silence permeated the room for what seemed like minutes before there was another knock at the door. It was Raul, looped out of his mind. He had a cheap bottle of Montezuma tequila and held it out for offering. By the looks of the bottle, he had been celebrating for some time. He was getting more pathetic by the second.

"Raul," I said as politely as I could. "Come back in 15 minutes."

"OK, boss," he giggled and pulled the door towards the jam.

I stepped towards the door to shut it tight. In the little bit of time that I knew him, Raul had learned not to question me when I made a demand. He immediately left and I could hear him offering the guys outside a swig off the bottle. *Nothing worse than dealing with a bunch of sloppy, incompetent drunks.*

"OK. I'm going to need 500 kilos within the next two weeks..." and I explained the terms and details to Carlos.

The deal was set in motion and I would use Raul as my buffer if the deal went south. It was my first experience with the Humberto Cartel and the details would be finalized over the time period when my boat was built. Raul was expendable and his time with me would be short.

I didn't need the money but a deal for me was long overdue. I had to regain my confidence and shed my mind of failure. In regard to Miguel—well, that was truly my fault because I allowed him to gain my trust. And trust from this point on would be gained by no one. Not a single soul. Trust, like Heaven, was only a made-up concept to help insecure people fee warm and cuddly. I would trust no one with anything unless I had the power to verify it and not get burned. No handshakes or verbal bullshit like "my word is my bond." You either produced the goods when you said you would or you were full of shit. No excuses. No apologies. And my new associates who crossed me would find out the hard way.

CHAPTER 31

The deal had been struck. Raul had tried knocking on the door after Carlos had left but I ignored him and called security. Within minutes, I heard him arguing with one of the hired personnel who threatened to have him removed from the premises if he didn't go to his room. I felt good that the initial deal had gone so smoothly. I skipped dinner and fell asleep on the couch, leaving the TV on all night. I was awakened by the morning news and the bright sunlight smiling through the blinds. I slipped off my shorts and took a cold shower to clear my head. I had work to do and was anxious to get going.

I opened the front door of the motel room and found a complimentary newspaper. I breathed in some fresh air and continued on with my morning routine. I made some instant coffee, giving me the needed caffeine boost, despite the taste. I tried calling Raul but he wouldn't answer. I suspected that he was passed out.

I loaded up the car with my personal belongings and bribed a maid to open up Raul's room. I found the keys to the ignition on the dresser next to his wallet. I opened up his wallet and pulled out roughly 200 bucks. It was all the money he had, I presumed. I noticed an empty bottle of tequila on the nightstand next to a small bag of what looked to be cocaine. I flushed the white substance down the toilet and ransacked the room. Raul didn't bother raising an eyelid.

I started up the car and got on the toll road headed back to Mazatlan. Raul would have to make way on his own. The guy was never going to learn, especially at my expense. The drive was long but allowed me to mentally map out the next steps of my future. I made it all the way to Culiacan, where I finally pulled over to smoke a snack and grab a soda. I couldn't help but wonder what Raul was doing. For some reason, in my own demented way, all I could do was laugh when I thought how I nicked him twice now for his cash. Wow.

I still had a hundred miles to Mazatlan and had to be up early to meet with my boatman. Old man Gomez is what they called him and he apparently was the best. He said he could have the boat done within two weeks, fitted to my exact specifications. Unfortunately, we Mexicans weren't known for our timeliness and efficiency. A couple weeks often depended on who was keeping time. Either way, the old man seemed credible and it would be out of my hands once I gave him the deposit.

My timing couldn't be better as I pulled into the El Cid with smoke seeping from the hood. It was obvious when I got out that the radiator was leaking as the green fluid covered the asphalt. I jumped back into the car and drove it over to the El Patio restaurant where I would enjoy a hand-cut steak and a glass of red wine from the northern Baja. As I pulled into the parking lot, I heard something combust under the hood. I had blown the engine just as I had hoped and left it for abandoned. *What a great ending to a trip with Raul. Maybe he'll think that he was actually ransacked if he ever finds his car.*

Dinner was great as expected and I took a cab back to the resort for some well-deserved rest. The red light on my phone was lit up and I called down to the front desk to retrieve the message. There were actually three messages, all from Raul. I was staying under an alias but I had made the mistake of giving him my room number. I would switch rooms in the morning.

The messages were nothing surprising. As she read them to me, I just laughed to myself, knowing that Raul was screwed and abandoned in Guaymus. He was broke and didn't have more than some change to make a couple of calls. It would probably buy me a day or two without his company, allowing me to get some things done without unnecessary distractions.

I thanked the clerk at the desk and asked her not to put any more messages through to me. I hung up the phone and couldn't wait until morning. I closed my eyes and thought again about Raul. I smiled to myself as I fell asleep. What a loser he was.

CHAPTER 32

I spent the next couple of days sailing, fishing, smoking dope, and relaxing. I was thrilled to know that Old Man Gomez was making faster progress than promised. He apparently was a man of his word. He told me that he would be done by the first of the week and I was anxious to pursue my goals. The weekend went by very slowly, although I spent every morning in the massage parlor getting rubdowns and hand jobs.

Monday afternoon came along with the phone call from the old man. The boat was ready for inspection; he would meet me at his shop within an hour. I hailed a cab to the southern docks where my boat stood out like an albino in Ethiopia. It was new and pristine and gorgeous. The looks of it alone had exceeded my expectations and I couldn't wait to get it out on the open sea.

I gave the cab driver a ten-spot and told him to keep the change. I raced towards the barbed wire fence and found the gate to be unsecured. Gomez hadn't arrived yet, but he had two hands in the back welding something or other on a transom. They didn't share in my excitement as I walked around my new vessel. My dream was coming true and my second chance at drug dealing had just begun. *Look out, George Jung, because I'm gonna make you look like a grain of sand on Seven Mile Beach,* I laughed to myself in excitement.

Gomez pulled up in a rickety old F-150 pickup truck with a bottle of cheap tequila in one hand and a Tecate in the other. I could tell he was proud of his work and opted to start celebrating before he arrived for the final inspection. He met me halfway in the yard and handed me the bottle. I politely declined the cheap cactus juice but told him that we could share a drink after a test drive on the ocean. He agreed, smiling, then laughed.

Gomez hooked the boat up to his pickup truck and slowly pulled out of the fenced yard. We turned right onto a dirt road that ran parallel to the coastal highway. Without a blinker or other notice, he cut another hard right and headed straight for the ocean. Within minutes, the old man had the new vessel floating in the sea, ready for its first test. Although it wasn't actually its first voyage, the old man handed me the bottle of tequila to break on the stern and I did.

He handed me the keys and I fired the dual Evinrude 200s on the first crank. It was music to my ears and by the look of the old man, his also. I put the boat through every test I knew and it negotiated every wave like a seasoned diplomat. The speed and power were unmatched by anything that I had ever captained. In fact, I was tempted to get on the horn to Robles and hook him up with the Gomez Boat Company, but I had more important matters to contend with.

I spent more time then I wanted with Gomez, but he covered the whole gamut with thorough care. He was a perfectionist and he wanted to prove it to me. So I gave the old man the courtesy and played out the afternoon with patience and compliments. He had 40 years of hard work on his brow and he deserved that bit of respect.

As we headed the boat in, my cell phone rang. The caller ID indicated that it was a private call. Not many people knew my number, so I presumed it would be the wrong number.

"Hello?" I answered cautiously.

"Jose! Jose! Are you there?" a frantic voice pleaded.

"Who is this?" I said in a lowered tone, not recognizing the caller's voice.

"It's me, Jose! It's me!"

"Who is 'me'?"

"Raul, Jose! It's Raul!" he screamed into the phone.

"Oh Raul, of course." I had to pull the phone away from my mouth as I tried to cover up my laughter. "I was wondering what happened to you. Why did you leave me?" I asked with a serious voice.

"What do you mean, 'leave you'? I got up and my money was gone and so was my car and so were you!" he said in a spastic tone.

I had to hesitate as I regained my composure, trying not to laugh. "I don't understand, Raul. I got up the next morning and your car was gone and no one answered your door. I only assumed that *you* left *me*."

"No, no, Jose, no. I'm sorry for whatever happened. I had never gone. Did you get back to Mazatlan?" he said in confusion.

"Well, yeah, I did…eventually. It cost me a pretty fortune as well, Raul. You see, I had an appointment with Mr. Gomez, my boatman and I don't break my appointments. So I had to hire a taxi to the airport and fly down just so I wouldn't be late. It cost me 500 dollars and a lot of heartache. In fact, I'm really pissed off at you for leaving me!" I did all I could to not start laughing.

I heard the pathetic apologies and I threw in the "I always do what I say" jargon to old Raul and let him rattle on. "Yeah Raul, I understand…." as I continued to play along with his game. The conversation went on and on as the old man and me put the boat away. And then the question came that I was expecting.

"Jose, my friend."

"Yes, Raul?"

"Is there anyway you can send me some money so I can get back to Mazatlan?"

And that was it. I hung up the phone. My days with Raul were finished as far as I was concerned. If he ever found the means to make it back, I would deal with him then. The phone continued to ring after I hung up, but I didn't answer.

Old man Gomez gave me a lift back to the El Cid where we would settle up with the money. I had made prior arrangements to have the boat docked and secured upon completion. I was looking forward to taking it out again tomorrow and working out any bugs. I didn't have to say much to the old man on our way back to the hotel because my demeanor said it all. It was evident, however, that the old man was a bit tanked, as he crossed the centerline frequently while we approached our destination.

We valet parked the old beater at my insistence and I handed the attendant a ten- spot. We made it over to one of the many restaurants where Gomez was ordering a shot of Don Julio Anejo before we were seated. The lobster tacos sobered him up a bit, but I insisted his son join us before we settled the debt. It was rumored that the old man made great money but had a weakness for the whores and booze. And unfortunately, paydays like today could bring out a man's vulnerabilities.

Junior Gomez showed and declined any food or beverage. As cordial as he was, he wanted this transaction done. He knew his old man all too well. We made it up to my room, where I peeled off over 10,000 dollars in cash. The son immediately intervened by tucking the money into a fanny pack on his waist. The old man started bickering but quickly backed off. As he was still suffering the effects of tequila, I turned my focus to his son.

"The only other thing I request is that your father paint the name of my boat on the stern," I said politely.

The son smirked and replied, "That should be no problem, sir. What would you like to name the new boat?"

"Carpe Diem," I answered.

"Carpe Diem? Latin?" he answered with an educated guess.

"That's correct," I said.

"May I ask what it means?"

"Of course," I said. "It's Latin for 'seize the day.'" I smiled.

Gomez's son smiled with admiration. The name epitomized my life and what I lived for.

CHAPTER 33

The knock on the door came too early for even my standards. As I rose from my peaceful sleep, I slipped into my sandals and placed the elaborate bathrobe over my body. I had a suspicion as to who it was but didn't quite believe that this fool could have actually made it back to Mazatlan so soon. I was mistaken. Raul had found me and I wasn't happy.

I didn't have much to say as I witnessed a man in desperation. He lived here in Mazatlan so I didn't understand why he was at my door in a five-star resort built for tourists. But then again, it kind of made sense based on the recent history between the two of us. He was broke and needed a helping hand. And he was broke because of me. But he didn't know that, nor would he ever. And perhaps I was less than noble, taking advantage of a fellow Mexican for reasons none other than I could. It really wasn't greed. And unfortunately, I felt no remorse.

I gave in to Raul's presence a bit because my sleep canceled out my intoxication. I was weak because my high was now low. I was just the opposite of most people: I operated at my peak when I was stoned—not sober. Or at least I thought. In fact, the more I thought about it, I had been stoned at least 50% of my adult waking life. Like a diabetic on insulin, I simply self-medicated on a daily basis to ensure sustainability.

"Raul," I said, looking down at the floor to shield my eyes from the light from the hall, "do you know what time it is?"

"No, Jose, I don't. But I need help! I have no money, no car, no..."

"Slow down, amigo. Stop! Take a deep breath," I said as I squinted my eyelids, allowing a bit of the light to absorb into my sockets. "What do you mean you need help?" I said. "Successful drug dealers aren't broke, Raul. You mean to tell me that…"

"Yes Jose," he said, cutting me off. "I do want to be successful but I'm not yet. In fact, the house that I live in I only rent. In fact, I'm going to get kicked out because I'm a couple of months behind on the rent. That's why I hitched a ride in the back of an empty cattle trailer so I could get here and start working with my new partner…"

There was no way in hell that I would be partners with this clown. However, I remained discreet, even though this guy was really pressing my nerves at this point. I decided to change the subject.

"Raul, I've got good news. My boat is done and I would like to take it out this afternoon. Would you like to join me?" I asked with little sincerity.

"Oh Jose, I knew it. It would be an honor. We could then maybe catch up on our new venture together."

"Yes…" I hesitated, "our venture. "I'll see you here at the hotel at six o'clock tonight. Don't be late!"

"Jose, I wouldn't think of it."

"We'll take the boat out and discuss our venture," I said sarcastically.

"Great, Jose," he said with joy.

"One other thing, Raul."

"Yes?"

"I'm not giving you any money, so don't even ask. If you're that broke, maybe you can get a hold of those two coke whores from the other night." My harsh words clashing with his drooping face.

I could see the disappointment in Raul's eyes. I simply had no feelings towards this man except that I wanted him out of my life. He was disposable like a throw-away camera after it was developed. I had already used him for everything I could. But then again, I still had one thing that needed to be done that he could probably accomplish for me.

"And by the way, Raul, if you want to be partners, you best bring some loot or dope with you. I'm tired of sporting the whole way. A partnership is equal contributions from both members. Remember that."

I finally shut the door of my hotel room and wondered if he would actually show up, especially with any cash or dope. Something told me that he would. I walked into the bathroom and slipped my underwear off in front of the mirror. I was getting older and my body was beginning to show slight hints of my age. My hair was still intact, but I was growing hair in areas that only older men do. My eyebrows were beginning to close in on one another and my ears and neck often competed with my beard. My eyes were still cold as ice and I think they had been since the day I murdered the pastor who tried to molest me. I knew that I was not a good man. In fact, I epitomized the worst in man. But then again, so did people like Raul.

I knew what drug dealers had to do at times to clean up their trade. I finally had the opportunity to make my contribution in a few hours.

CHAPTER 34

To my surprise, Raul showed up early at my hotel room with almost a hundred bucks and a rather large quantity of smoke. I stashed the smoke in my briefcase and told him that he was buying lunch. We made it down to the pool area where we dined on *ceviche* and tomato juice at the swim-up bar. I decided that I would draw out the afternoon a bit because I wanted to take the boat out just before sunset. It was important for me to get a feel for the boat in the dark as I would be making my runs at night. Raul agreed, as if I needed his assurance.

I finished up my lunch and was ready for a nap. I left Raul at the bar and went upstairs for a couple of hours. When I awoke and got back to the bar, Raul had lost all discipline and was jacked up on tequila and beer. *What a surprise,* I thought. I ordered a soda and just listened to his rambling about being rich soon, blah blah blah. I finished my coke and approached the front desk and requested a cab. There was one already out front. I went back and got Raul and off we were to the docks.

Within minutes, we were at the dock where my boat lay perfectly intact. I loaded in a cooler and a beach bag with some miscellaneous items. Raul immediately became nosy and started fishing through my items.

"What's the tarp for, Jose?"

"You'll see," I said, smiling at him.

As Raul attempted to climb into the boat, he slipped off the dock and landed face first on the fiberglass floor. It didn't look or sound very pleasant. I left Raul to see to himself and pretended I didn't notice his mishap. I untied the rope from the cleats of the dock and started the dual outboards to my stern. The noise was magic to my ears as it fired again on the first crank. I powered up all of the instruments and gadgets, including the ones that I didn't need, while Raul fumbled to gain his composure. Upon doing so, he smiled and dug to the bottom of the ice to find another beer. *I hope he enjoys it,* I thought.

We slowly trolled through the marina obeying the no wake rule. I was anxious to open up the throttle but settled for the beautiful sunset sinking to the west. We passed the final buoy and I opened it up slowly. The power and speed were amazing—no less the velocity. It was a rather choppy surface as usual, but the boat held its own as it plowed through the waves with little resistance. Raul was wasted and was smiling back at the ever-building lights of the seaport. The tarp began to catch air pockets and I slowed the boat down almost to an idle. We were quite a way out from the marina. I moved the ice chest onto the tarp to secure it and asked for a beer.

"No problema," he said. As he stood up, I floored the throttle and watched Raul crash down over the cooler and tarp. His head had hit the bench seat and his face gave a slight smile before I severed his carotid artery with my eight-inch blade. He tried to scream, but it just wouldn't come. As his body painted itself with blood, I shoved the cooler aside and wrapped him up with the canvass. I then tied rope around the tarp and secured an anchor to the end. I dumped the lifeless waste into the ocean and hoped the sharks would smell the blood. *All in the life of a drug dealer,* I thought.

I dumped the remaining beer from the cooler and used it as a bucket, trying to get all of the blood off the sides of the boat. It took a few minutes but I was able to conceal the scene of the murder. I continued to head north up the coast of Mazatlan, past Seven Mile Beach. The North Harbor was where I was to meet old man Gomez. I had him rent me a van and a trailer; we were going to pull the boat out of the water. I would then head up to Guaymus, where I would begin my first run.

I allowed myself plenty of time to get to the harbor and had an opportunity see the city from the ocean looking in. It was a beautiful city with a magnificent coastline littered with high-rise hotels and nightclubs. I even recognized Valentino's with its laser beams of light isolated out on the rock. For a minute I began to feel guilty about old Raul and his careless life. But I had to justify the murder to myself and it was for my own safety. If they ever found him, who would care anyway? He was just another scumbag drug dealer—and a bad one for that matter. Something told me that he would not be missed. I almost felt sorry for him.

CHAPTER 35

The Humberto Cartel had most of the Mexican naval personnel on its payroll. They were told to look the other way when it came to their boats in and out of Guaymus Bay. It only took one floater, a dead body with a Navy uniform, to get the message out. Plus, the extra money came in handy.

As in most third-world countries, the dope traffickers had more power than the government. What options did they have? Risk your life doing the right thing and risk getting you and your family killed, or shut up and make some extra cash. Option two had more appeal.

The drive to Guaymus from the North Harbor was long and boring. Carlos met me at my hotel room and briefed me on the Navy and what times were best to leave the port. We agreed to meet the next night, a mile offshore just to be safe. My boat was new and the Navy could be flaky. We agreed to use an obscure channel on our two-way radio system for all communications.

As we poured through the details, I could feel my heart racing out of excitement. I was back in the game but this time, running solo. I would keep all profits and take full responsibility for everything good and bad. I would be chancing my life for me and only me. I wanted a fortune and I was willing to risk it all to fulfill my dream, whatever it was.

The plan was set and Carlos left the hotel. I went downstairs to find a bite to eat. I forced down a shot of tequila to mark the eve of my first drug deal solo. It was smooth, but my body still told my brain where to go. My dinner arrived, calamari steak with steamed vegetables, rice, and beans. The steak was a bit tough but wonderfully seasoned. As I ate my meal, I mentally reviewed the conversation that Carlos and I had and the coordinates and contact information for in the morning. One thing that Robles taught me at a young age was to have as much information memorized that you could. Things could always go awry and the more you had written down, could always be used as evidence in a court room. Let's face it, drug trafficking had its detours at times and I always wanted to be prepared.

I paid the bill and headed back upstairs to my room. I turned on an old John Wayne movie playing on the tube as I lit up a joint. *The Man Who Shot Liberty Valance* was a favorite of mine, especially that Andy Devine character. I probably knew more about old American movies than most gringos because that's how I learned to speak English. There were always subtitles in Spanish and, eventually, I could recite an entire movie in English by memory. And once I began to understand what the words meant, not only did I appreciate the movies, I learned to love them. Who would have thought that John Wayne was my hero and that I always rooted for the good guys?

I tried to catch some sleep but I was overcome with anxiety and excitement. Although I never try to show weakness, I knew deep down that I was a bit scared. For weeks I'd been having reoccurring thoughts of being intercepted by the Americans and tried for my past crimes. But I continued to remind myself that this was going to be different. I was only moving drugs from the mainland to the Baja. I wouldn't be stepping on American soil and I was quite sure the gringos didn't patrol the Sea of Cortez with their Navy or Coast Guard. I only had the Mexicans to deal with and they were light- years away with their interdiction efforts compared to the Americans. I was now working smarter as opposed to harder. It was a catalyst that may or may not lead to bigger things. It didn't matter. I was in control of my destiny.

As the weed sank in, I began to have an internal debate with myself about politics and the drug war itself. All of the users were pissed off that both governments criminalized drugs, which were expensive and made the user a criminal. But us guys in the trade were happy about it because that's how we made our outrageous sums of money. If drugs were legal, the big tobacco companies would be reaping all the profits. Who would be able to compete with Phillip Morris and R. J. Reynolds? They had tens of billions and I knew that most Cartels didn't have that kind of money.

The authorities had spent close to half a trillion fighting us, but we were still supplying all of North America with relative ease. In Mexico, the Cartels had most of the Mexicans paid off from the southern border all the way up to the United States. We always laughed when the new Mexican president every six years stood up and talked about fighting the drug war. Few knew that the president and his cabinet often accept the largest bribes from the Cartels. The dynamics of the drug war, in fact, was just like Prohibition in the first half of the 1900s in the States. It was simple economics of supply and demand.

But I didn't want to go that deeply into the politics. Leave it be— that was my philosophy. I enjoyed the risk and the rewards that it brought me. My new mission was simply to bring large quantities into desolate areas like the Baja and that was it. What my contacts did with it from there did not concern me. It was like working an assembly line.

Overall, I felt very good coming into my opening game, but like a professional athlete, a bit nervous and like I said earlier, scared. And rightfully so.

CHAPTER 36

I can't remember sleeping a wink. I was wide awake and decided to get up earlier than the alarm was set. I would regret it later I assumed, but there was no use lying in bed doing nothing. I got up and made some of that crappy instant coffee in the hotel room. As bad as it was, I filled up my thermos, knowing that the restaurant was closed and would be for some time. The caffeine and the heat would see me through the grand opening of my new business.

The air was cold and blowing as I walked out of the lobby of the hotel. I took a cab to a block from the marina and never gave the driver any idea as to where I was heading. You could never be too careful in this business. I did a double take and walked past the sleeping guard at the security gate. I had every right to be there, but one less witness was a stronger defense for me. I tried to conceal my footsteps as they clicked on the dock; halfway there I gave up. The dipshit security guard could care less. If he had any ambition in life, he wouldn't be working where he was.

I found my boat and everything appeared to be unscathed and in order. I could actually hear the faint sounds of snoring from the security shack and it quickly brought a smile to my face. I know water carries sound but how embarrassing as I physically shook my head and climbed into the vessel. A joint would have been appropriate to some degree but my discretionary side kicked in. Complacency and carelessness had no room on my virgin voyage.

I stowed my cooler and thermos under the front passenger seat where I could easily get to it and checked the locked compartment to my side. I had a Glock, a 9-mm gun, with several hand clips of ammunition if I needed it. With that small exception, I was gun free.

I untied the boat, boarded, and did a visual around me one last time before I set off. It looked clear. The boat fired on the first start and nothing moved out of the guard shack. I backed out of the slip and slowly headed the boat out of the marina. I could see a few cabin lights on, yet something told me that all was quiet in Guaymus Bay.

I got out into the open sea where the water was still relatively calm and headed north towards Kino Bay. As I opened up the throttle, the wind began to scar my face with coldness. I set the boat on autopilot and opened up a compartment, retrieving some gloves and a scarf. I abandoned the helm and allowed the boat to do the thinking and steering while I made some coffee to warm up. It would be a good 30 minutes until I reached my destination and would allow me to warm up with some coffee.

I set my radio to Channel 5 and waited for a call. Within minutes, Carlos was asking about my position. Everything was right on course. Carlos was where he said he would be and was quickly proving to be a man of his word. I could see a handful of shrimp boats from my location, which helped me blend into the mix. There was nothing unusual as far as I could see. Within minutes, I was tying my vessel onto Carlos's boat.

The transaction happened quickly and there was little small talk. Carlos was a poor negotiator but he handled his business like a pro. Perhaps I had underestimated him. Sometimes hard work and loyalty get you promoted into a position that doesn't bring out your strong points. Sometimes it's better to give a man a raise and keep him in the same position in which he appears to excel at. This seemed to be the case with Carlos.

I didn't know it then, but I shook Carlos' hand for the last time. His eyes were sodden from sadness or age or guilt, I didn't know. He knew that he had been beat and I felt a bit sorry for whatever advantages I took from him. He was a lost puppy without his master and he actually looked scared. "It was good doing business with you," I told him one last time before I steered my vessel west and headed towards Bahia de

Los Angeles, across the Sea of Cortez. The waters were still smooth and I opened up at full throttle for a few minutes to gauge my top speed. I never hit that speed before I slowed down in fear of ripping the boat apart.

If all went as planned, I would get to Bahia de Los Angeles before sunrise and come in as if I were just another fisherman coming off the water. I would stop and have breakfast somewhere and take my time, killing off a few hours before my next jaunt. I would then head north to a small fishing village called Puertocitos, 50 miles south of San Felipe, where I would meet up with my contact.

My boat had two 100 gallon fuel tanks on board, which would get me across the pond easily. The Sea of Cortez is still part of the ocean but at good times, could be reminiscent of a lake. It was ideal for small, faster vessels like mine.

Bahia de Los Angeles, or L.A. Bay as the gringos called it, was quaint and quiet with a local population of less than a thousand people. I arrived just as the sun was opening its eyes, shedding light on the small fishing village. I drifted my Ponga into the calm waters and followed my global positioning system's coordinates to a beach in front of a restaurant called Guierrmos for an early breakfast. I tied off the boat and secured it with a special locking mechanism that Old Man Robles had set me up with years ago. The restaurant was right on the beach and there was an outdoor patio with a handful of tables and chairs. The waiter met me at the patio entrance with a pot of coffee and a menu. The inside of the restaurant was inviting, but I wanted to keep close to the vessel. I had too much to risk by going inside just for some warmth.

I ordered *chorizo* and eggs, rice, beans, and flour tortillas. The salsa was hot but very unique and quite good. The waiter told me that it was more of a regional salsa, meaning it was from the Baja, and that you never knew what type of salsa you would get on any given morning. They had many and it changed daily. As we were talking, I had forgotten about the handgun that I was packing and decided to not talk so much and to concentrate on my mission. I quickly ate and a wave of sleepiness came upon me. I ordered some coffee to go when I realized that there would be no time for sleep.

I left the waiter 15 dollars and told him to keep the balance. He was pleasantly surprised and asked that I come back. "I sure hope to soon," I said with a smile. For some reason, as serious as the job I was undertaking, the whole concept of being in the Baja as my own boss was exciting, yet lacked the pressure that I sustained when I worked with the Robles Cartel. I knew the risk involved, but something told me that this desolate area lacked the scrutiny of the Gulf Coast.

Although I was making mental comparisons from my days with the Robles Cartel and what I was currently experiencing, I knew I couldn't get complacent. I untied the vessel and pushed it out into knee-deep water. I got my shoes wet, having little choice. It was back to business. I headed out of the bay, hoping that I wouldn't be taken by one of the famous gusts of wind that this area was known for. I had no troubles and headed north along the coastline. Soon, as much as I wanted to continue on, I was exhausted. I put up the canopy and anchored in the shallow waters that encompassed the shoreline. Twenty minutes of sleep was all I needed.

When I awoke, I realized it was a bit longer than a power nap but I obviously needed the rest. The excitement of my first deal in progress disinhibited my body's natural adrenaline, allowing me to continue on with fierce motivation.

I still had a good 75 miles up the coastline until I reached Puertocitos. There, I was to meet my contact, Lucy, at 10 o'clock in the evening. I had some time to kill, although I didn't want to be too conspicuous. I wanted some isolation but the comfort of knowing that I was close to friendly waters. I slowed the boat a bit and just took my steady time until I found an area that looked good for some fishing. I baited a hook and dropped my line. Within minutes, I was reeling in a good-sized corvina. They said the fishing was always good in the Baja.

I filleted the fish, throwing the guts and bones to the seagulls that perched on the bow. Then I poured some cooking oil into a large skillet and placed it over the small built-in stove that old man Gomez thoughtfully planned in the construction of the boat. It was propane and lit up after I bled the line of air. Within minutes, I was pan-frying *corvina* with a little salt and pepper. *If I could only get my hands on some of that famous Baja shrimp, I'd be in business,* I smiled to myself. Then again, fresh corvina wasn't a bad appetizer.

I slowly ate the meal, partly out of gluttony and partly out of hunger. I had eaten only three hours earlier but needed to kill a bit of time.

I cleaned up my mess and motored north. I found a small inlet off the peninsula and tied my boat up to a rock, with my anchor as a secondary. The Bimini top was like a roof cover and I slept peacefully until dusk. Tonight, the final leg of the trip would be made. My adventure had begun less than 24 hours ago and I felt I was practically done.

CHAPTER 37

The two small boys were enjoying their vacation at Mazatlan's Emerald Bay when they heard the scream. A little girl was running from the water with her hands masked over her face. All that the boys' could see was a blue tarp dangling in the ankle-deep water, close to the shore. The girl's mother looked puzzled as she met her halfway in the sand. She covered her mouth with her hand as she lost her balance and began to vomit. Attached to the tarp was a bloated body twice the size as normal. The smell caught the downwind and was competing with the nasty sight. Within minutes, local police surrounded the area and cordoned off the beach. This could not be good for tourism.

The coroner arrived and quickly recovered the body. Without an official autopsy, it was evident that the body was a result of a homicide. The throat had been lacerated and the head nearly decapitated. The authorities had difficulty placing the corpse inside the body bag. The coroner and his assistant were able to get the body placed in the back of an old station wagon and headed off to the morgue.

The local police concluded that the murder most likely involved drugs and contacted the federal drug task force. The body was quickly prepped and tagged for viewing upon the feds arrival. Attached to the body was a fanny pack that contained an address book, cell phone, gum, marijuana, and other miscellaneous items. These were placed into evidence for detectives to examine; an investigation into the identity of the victim began.

A federale in Mazatlan was called in to try and retrieve any data from the cell phone. Although the phone had taken on a bit of water, surprisingly enough the fanny pack was relatively waterproof and most of the evidence preserved.

The autopsy revealed that the victim suffered a deliberate laceration to the neck and ruled a homicide. Ironically enough, though, the laceration was not what killed him. The victim actually died from drowning. The autopsy also revealed that the murder occurred approximately two days prior to the discovery. Traces of cocaine, THC, and alcohol were found in the little blood samples that they were able to recover. The identity was quickly proved to be Raul Espendito of Mazatlan, Sinaloa, Mexico, a small-time drug trafficker who spent a jaunt in the local prison on the outskirts of the city for selling a large amount of marijuana to an undercover cop a few years back.

The technician examining the phone came across an interesting angle. Mr. Espendito had entered a text memo into his phone only three days before his estimated time of death mentioning a new acquaintance, Jose Cantino, from Tampico. Some of the text was missing but the last words of the memo read "San Felipe?" The DEA agent picked up his cell phone and dialed his counterpart in El Paso, Texas, to have him run the name "Jose Cantino," along with any aliases that existed in the drug trade. As the agent waited for the return call, he could feel the adrenaline running through his veins. It was always like this when he had to wait for any type of news that he could hand over to the detectives to help solve a case. And wait he did. Finally his phone rang. The Caller ID indicated that it was an international call.

"Fernandez?" the other voice on the line asked.

"Yes, Johnny, it's me," the agent answered, then waited in anticipation.

"Well, my friend," the American spoke solemnly into the phone, "you're not gonna believe this…"

CHAPTER 38

Puertocitos is a tiny fishing village roughly 50 miles south of San Felipe. The road was washed away by Hurricane Nora in the late nineties and had never been repaired. The 50-mile stretch by car sometimes took three hours, depending on how durable your vehicle was. Because the road had been destroyed, much of the desolate town dried up even further. The trip tested its inhabitants' patience and many people more or less abandoned their homes. The gas station was shut down and the local grocery was little more than a snack shack with essentials like beer and chips.

Puertocitos is well known in the region for its hot springs that line the coastal rocks. Generally the only time one can tolerate the springs is at high tide when the combination of cool water neutralizes the scalding sulfur baths. However, this didn't apply in the summertime when the waters were bath-like. Because Puertocitos was more or less a ghost town, it made perfect sense that drug runners used it as a hub in their drug operations.

Lucia, also known as Lucy, was one of those runners. She ran an orphanage and, ironically enough, supported the desolate and downtrodden souls of the region on her drug profits. She was my contact.

I could see the lights of Puertocitos shining back at me from the moonlit coastline. I was to meet Lucy at Lefty's beach home. It would be a casual first encounter on a personal level and I wasn't expecting anything out of the ordinary.

I had met Lefty years ago in Tampico while he was on vacation.

After the first meeting, he came back twice a year religiously because he loved the Gulf of Mexico so much. He sometimes brought his father, Pedro, who lived in the tiny town. Lefty and I became good friends—as close as I allowed anyone in my life, and we maintained contact frequently. We quickly learned that we both participated in the same trade of drug trafficking.

Lefty's real name was Pancho Serrano. However, Lefty stood out and knew that his name didn't. Lefty was unique and wanted every aspect of his being to reflect it. So he opted to change his name to Lefty after an old American country tune that he had heard in Juarez, Mexico, by a Texan named Willie Nelson. Lefty always maintained that his marijuana loads wound up in Willie's bongs. Over the years, Lefty had told and changed the story so often that I think he began to believe his own bullshit. The last time I heard him tell it he was now friends with Willie and that Lefty was the inspiration of that song made famous by the renegade country singer and his contemporary, Merle Haggard. I personally liked the song and didn't care if the tale was true or not. It made interesting conversation.

Lefty's old man had never known that Lefty was a drug dealer until after his death. It never sat well regardless of the personal fortune that Lefty had amassed for himself and his family. For the longest time, the old man never knew how he and his son went from being poor fishermen to owning a modest house on the bay in Puertocitos. At the time, some things were best left unexplained. But eventually, Lefty's life and times made a full circle and the old man was disappointed—a disappointment always countered with the good deeds that his son had performed for the poor and the community in general.

It was just about two years ago that Lefty's dad called me in Tampico to inform me that he had been killed in an accident. I wondered because he hadn't been to Tampico in quite some time and I hadn't heard from him. As traffickers, we didn't communicate on a consistent basis because of the authorities and their sophisticated surveillance. However, Lefty and I had kept in touch consistently through his dad and other contacts we had. When word had come from Lefty's old man, I was sad.

After the loss of Miguel, Lefty was really the only other person that

I considered a friend. Friends simply did not exist in my book. Perhaps if I had worked with Lefty day to day, I would have felt differently. Look at Miguel and what the drug trade did to him and the repercussions it had on me. Maybe in this business there were no such things as friends. Either way, I felt bad about his death and not being able to pay my final respects. It wouldn't have been smart to be seen at a known drug dealer's funeral. But one thing that Lefty always told me was that if anything ever happened to him and I decided to venture west, to look up Lucy who ran an orphanage outside of Puertocitos.

Lefty's dad, Pedro, continued to be in touch with me on a regular basis after I sent flowers to the funeral. I assumed Lucy was Lefty's sister, who looked after the old man. After I began calling the house to talk with the old man and his daughter, I had promised to come out some time and visit. Pedro knew that I didn't have many friends and grew up without a family. I sensed that he wanted me to fill the void of Lefty, I don't know. And after several conversations with Lucy, she and I were able to set up a deal that would complement my trip to the Baja. Neither of them knew that I was leaving Tampico for good.

After the events of my life, trust was not something that I placed in my fellow man. However, Lucy was different. I sensed that I could trust her not only because she was Pedro's daughter and Lefty's sister, but because she had an aura about her that I couldn't explain. What was bothering me was that she didn't fit the mold of what Lefty used to do and I wanted to continue doing. She seemed much too nice. So as we were making plans over the months, the whole trust thing drove me crazy. Conflicting thoughts and downright paranoia would come and go like a vacillating room fan on various speeds. It was crazy.

Lefty had told me years ago that Lucy could keep a secret like gold at Fort Knox. She knew of my profession and according to Lefty, Lucy did the same thing. I knew of their humanitarian efforts throughout the Baja. Regardless of the motives, however, we all dealt drugs.

When Lefty's dad broke the news to me about his death, he never expanded on any details and I didn't have the balls to ask. I knew how painful it was for him to make the call. Eventually, Lefty's right-hand man Francisco wound up in Tampico on some business and looked me up. He knew that Lefty and I had mutual respect for one another and that Lefty would have wanted him to stop by and see how I was doing.

He was the one who told me the intricate details that lead to his death. Lefty was ratted out by a snitch in jail who was cutting deals to get released. Lefty had another, more luxurious house in a development called Los Conchas in Puerto Penasco, also known as Rocky Point. Rocky Point was located in the Sonoran Desert about 70 miles south of the central Arizona border. It was made famous by weekend travelers from Phoenix and Tucson and had grown into a popular tourist destination.

His neighbors were shocked to find out how this wealthy young man, who loved to fish, was actually a drug dealer. They were let down no doubt as well. You would often see local and state dignitaries, along with many higher-ups in the church, visiting him at home. He was involved in many local charities and was well known throughout the Baja and the State of Sonora. People on the street would approach him with compliments and handshakes, even if they had never met him. People wanted to be like him and they knew that he had money.

Lefty was a master. He had three boats of his own in Rocky Point and they were all identical in make, paint, and registration. He would launch his boat in broad daylight and head out over the horizon where he would fish. Once out of view, he would swap boats with his connections. Because the boats were identical, no one thought he was doing anything but fishing. He would bring the Ponga back in and pull it out of the water on his private ramp next to his house. He would then put the boat back into his garage. At night, he would load one cargo vehicle each day over a period of a week and run the loads to most of the major border towns including Tijuana, Mexicali, and Nogales. It was a simple but brilliant operation. It would have gone undetected if it weren't for the mole. But like most drug runners, Lefty's luck eventually ran out.

He had graduated from doing a lot of work himself and had downsized his operation considerably after he had amassed his wealth. But he was still willing to get into the trenches once in a while to show his guys that he wasn't above any of it. So Lefty decided to run a load on his own. Yeah, he was far too important in some eyes to get caught but his ego wasn't something that he frequently massaged.

Outside of Mexicali on Highway 2, just as you begin your ascent through the mountains outside of Tecate, Lefty came across an Army checkpoint. There were sniffing dogs, but the packaging was virtually undetectable. But the Army knew. The authorities had been waiting from the tip they received from the mole. Along with the Army were federal officers. Lefty must have known something once he got there because he gunned the van in a hasty attempt to escape. It never panned out. The Army was prepared because about an eighth of a mile past the checkpoint was a machine gun nest and a spike strap sprawled across the road. It was over before it began.

When the news spread that Lefty had been shot up by the Mexican Army, many public officials called for an investigation into the matter. How could the Mexican government gun down one of its own, a man who had dedicated his life to helping the underprivileged and impoverished? And if he was truly a drug dealer, where were the drugs? Those in the trade knew the truth. The Army and the feds stole the dope and a group of guys made enough money to retire. The justification for the shooting was that Lefty had fled the checkpoint. Regardless of what they didn't find, the young sergeant on the scene was probably justified if Lefty actually tried to escape. But what transpired afterwards was what had the region in an uproar with rampant conspiracy theories and government abuse. In the end, all of the soldiers stuck to the same story and each one of them got a piece of the corruption pie.

The worst part of the scenario was that the authorities had Pedro identify the body in a Mexicali morgue. Apparently, Lefty's head had been literally severed by machine gun fire. The old man could only positively identify his son by the tattoo of Christ on his left forearm. His body was mangled and riddled with bullets. It was a terrible last sight of his son for a father.

The funeral was speckled with priests, nuns, dignitaries, volunteers, and hundreds of people who didn't know him personally but had heard of his reputation. Even the governor of Sonora came to honor his memory. Lefty was a modern-day Robin Hood. Yes, he enjoyed the money— what he truly enjoyed the most, however, was using his money to help others. Unlike me, he was a kind and benevolent man. I didn't think those characteristics existed among any of us in the drug trade, except

Lefty. And Lucy.

Years ago, while visiting Tampico, Lefty explained to me that there weren't practical means of helping people in poor, third-world countries. The governments were corrupt and stole from the people. So why couldn't he be corrupt and give back to the people? It was a rather unique way of viewing things. But as I always said, traffickers may have different motives for what they do, but it doesn't take away from the fact that we are drug dealers. And in many ways, Lefty was not so much different than me, except he was dead.

CHAPTER 39

Luckily I caught no one's attention despite the full moon shining over the Puertocitos Bay. As I drifted towards the houses that lined the shore, I called Pedro on his phone from my cellular. Within seconds, I saw a blinking flashlight from a distance and followed the incandescent beams. I gunned the boat and shut off the engines, gaining enough momentum to drift to shore.

I was met by a woman who surprised me with her youth and appearance—she was covered from head to toe in black, like a Muslim woman in a burka. I immediately noticed her slender figure and soft feminine hands as we touched in greeting. *This delicate thing is actually Lucy?* I thought to myself. We nervously tried to make small talk. A young man backed up a large trailer to the shore while a second companion jumped into my boat and fired up the engine.

"It's OK, Jose, they work for me," she ever so delicately spoke. I was still nervous but forced my trust into her corner. Within a minute, my Ponga was being pulled out of the water. My protective instinct had still not let up, but I bit my tongue as my Ponga disappeared with two strangers.

I trusted her only because of Lefty's regard for her. She grabbed my hand and led me through the sand towards a home with a large illuminated window. I could see the silhouette of a male figure pacing back and forth. *That had to be Pedro,* I thought.

We reached the back patio of the home where I greeted Pedro with a handshake and a hug. We exchanged pleasantries before they invited me inside. I followed Lucy and Pedro through the back door where I placed my backpack on the *saltillo* floor and took up Pedro's offer of a cold glass of water.

"Please, Jose, have a shower, while I prepare a light meal for you," she spoke to me softly, avoiding eye contact.

"Thank you, Lucy. A shower would be great," I replied.

She lead me down a narrow hallway to the bathroom. "Please, take your time, Jose. I know you've had a long day." She smiled and blushed simultaneously.

"Thank you, Lucy," I said and locked the door behind me.

The water was refreshing and helped to calm my nerves. I could feel the freshness wash away the salty feel of having been on the ocean for the last day. It felt even better to dry the water off my body. I wrapped the towel around my waist and realized that I was missing my backpack. I wasn't sure what to do until I heard a knock on the door. I cracked the door open. It was Lucy.

"Are you looking for this?" she asked with a smile. Our eyes briefly made contact and I took the backpack from her hands.

I quickly got dressed and combed my hair. Suddenly I heard several voices outside of the doorway and became confused. I grabbed my backpack and exited the bathroom.

"Surprise!" Lucy said as I met her in the hallway. "We invited a few friends and neighbors to welcome our friend from Tampico," she said with a laugh.

I was taken back and felt embarrassed. I didn't know how to react. No one had ever really celebrated anything for me except when I was leaving Tampico and that didn't feel like a party. It felt more like a termination.

As I scanned the room, I stopped in my tracks as I stared at Lucy without the veil over her face. She looked at me and nodded to come with her as she took the bag from my hand. I followed her signal as she quickly introduced me to her family.

"Let me show Jose to his room and we'll come back and join the party," she announced to the small gathering.

She took me by the hand and looked up at my face, eye to eye. There was a slight grin to her facial features and I was suddenly overcome with emotion. It was an emotion that I had never felt in my life—a feeling that I never knew could exist. And I had just met this woman.

She showed me my room and I dropped my bag at the foot of the bed. Lucy was standing in the hallway and I was hoping she was feeling the same about me as I was about her.

"Lucy, can I talk to you?"

She immediately recognized something was wrong. "Sure, Jose. Is everything OK?"

"I...I just don't understand."

"About what, Jose?"

"Why the big welcome? I don't even really know you."

Lucy looked at me and smiled with her perfect white teeth. "You're like family, Jose," she said as she grabbed my face and kissed my cheek. "Welcome to the Baja." She turned and ducked her head into the room. "Make yourself at home and then come out and get to know everyone." She closed the door and let me have a few moments alone. *Like family,* I mumbled to myself. *Wow.*

There was a small bathroom attached to the bedroom. I tried to rid myself of everything that I had eaten over the last two days. But the nerves wouldn't have it. I quickly shaved and brushed my teeth—all in all, I felt like a new man. But emotionally, I began to feel bad and my stomach was wheezing. Thoughts of my childhood began to come back and I didn't feel relaxed. My mind began to fill with paranoia. *This can't be right. This can't be genuine. I don't have a family,* I kept thinking to myself. I turned on the bathroom fan and took a quick hit to calm my nerves. I would have to face the music in a few minutes and my strength began to build.

My nervousness began to subside and I made the grand exit from the bedroom to be met by Lucy and Pedro and friends. We ate barbecued chicken with chipolte salsa and listened to mariachi music the rest of the night. I began to feel like part of the clan even though I my inner thoughts resisted. It was, however, the closest thing to family that I ever felt. I just didn't know why.

In the middle of the table burned a small candle and I was curious. I asked Lucy and her eyes became moist. "It's for Lefty," she simply said. "Ever since he died, Father always burns that candle night and day. It sort of represents his spirit, so in a way, Lefty and Father are still together.

"I see," I said, not knowing what else to say.

The party continued well into the morning and I couldn't get over how Lucy looked at me the whole night. I was beginning to sense that the feeling was mutual. But my thoughts and feelings were awry. When it came to love, I was a virgin.

CHAPTER 40

The federale waited anxiously as his DEA counterpart placed him on hold from a crackling phone line from El Paso, Texas. The goods were coming in on Jose Cantino and they were ready to find this guy and take him down.

"Are you ready?" asked the agent from the States.

"Yes, sir. I can't wait."

The details about Mr. Cantino were exciting. They had a live one. He was an orphan who grew up on the docks in Tampico. He went from fishing to the drug trade and was a warrior with the Robles organization since prepubescence. He went from deckhand to drug dealer. His accomplice, Miguel Rodriguez, was a member of the organization but was lured over to the DEA's side after several confrontations and detentions. Miguel provided most of the specific details in the Cantino file before he was tortured and murdered by the Robles' organization for treason.

The report was lengthy and specific. His close relationship with Old Man Robles himself was known, along with his many nightly jaunts in Key West and the Caribbean. But the file had been inactive over the past year. They thought that maybe he had been killed because he had dropped off the radar screen. This made sense because they knew that he had lost a handful of large shipments over the past two years because Mr. Rodriguez was double-crossing him.

"This guy is very calculating. I'm sure he is taking his talent to a new area. Perhaps, that's why he's showed up in Mazatlan?"

"What do you think we should do?" the Mexican fed asked.

"We'll immediately put out a warrant for his arrest for murder and spread it along the Pacific Coast and the Baja area. We can throw a cash reward in the mix too."

"Good idea," said the fed.

"We need to be proactive and get this guy now before he causes any more mayhem. He's been slipping through the cracks for a long time. And with guys like this, it's best to make sure that he never sees a courtroom or a lawyer, if you know what I mean."

The federale knew exactly what the American meant. Mexico was so corrupt and Cantino had so much money that you never knew how a conviction would go. He could buy anyone off. The best thing to do would be to kill him first and ask questions later. But then again, Cantino was only a catalyst for something bigger—the Robles Cartel? There were pros and cons and the situation would have to be weighed further as the investigation got deeper.

They made further plans to initiate the search for Cantino. "We need to put an agent from the States on this one and I have the perfect one in mind. Cantino just may be our key to dismantling the Robles organization if he is still alive."

"I agree, sir. That's a great point," the federale replied, agreeing with everything from his counterpart.

They concluded their plans over the phone. The DEA would have an agent in Mazatlan by 8:00 the following morning, when they would set up shop for the sole purpose of capturing Cantino. It would be the key to shutting down the largest drug Cartel on the east coast of Mexico.

The warrants were issued along with a handsome reward of $100,000 to sweeten the pie. Cantino had to be captured. The two governments were losing the war, but they were bound and determined to win this battle. Future job promotions would be imminent.

CHAPTER 41

The exchange was made in Pedro's garage; I peeled off 10,000 dollars to Lucy for her help in obtaining the contacts and logistic support. It was the easiest money that I had ever made in my life. All I did was transport some pot across the pond and the rest was done. Pedro was asleep during the entire transaction and Lucy promised me that I could wire money to my accounts in the Caymans from the Banomex Bank in San Felipe. However, she said I would have to do it in smaller increments that I was accustomed to because the bankers had to get to know me. She also recommended that I "expedite" the relationship with my banker by throwing him a few extra bucks. *Of course,* I thought. *Business as usual in Mexico.*

In Tampico, I could wire as much as I wanted because my banker was in my back pocket. A few 100-dollar bills always cured his curiosity, or any other employee of the bank. That was business—those relationships, however, were built over the years, not in a day.

It was three o'clock in the morning when we finished up the deal and I was wired. I needed a joint and went outside the garage door to light one up.

"No Jose! Not here. If you must, go out away from the house, down to the beach, where you can be more discreet."

"No problema," I said as I began to walk away in anticipation of getting high.

"Wait Jose!" she said, grabbing my arm. "Must you smoke that here?"

"No. That's why I'm going to the beach."

"No, by 'here,' I mean 'around me'?" she said as her eyes caught mine in a moment of weakness. I was taken back. This woman participated in the drug trade, yet she didn't want me to smoke my own stuff? It didn't make much sense to me.

"Why do you care, Lucy?" I asked with genuine concern.

"Because I do. You shouldn't use your own stuff. It's not good for you," Lucy replied, her words dying off as she glanced down at her bare feet. "I'm sorry, Jose. I really don't have any business telling you of all people what to do or not to do. I'm not your mother." She continued to stare at the floor. "In fact, I don't even know you that well..."

Another odd feeling came across me as I looked down at the top of her head. I had just met this woman in person for the first time and for some reason, she really cared about me.

"Can I ask you something, Lucy?" I said as my right hand caressed her shoulder.

"Anything you want, Jose." She looked up at me through her watery eyes.

"What's wrong? Surely my smoking pot is not the only thing bothering you."

"No, Jose...nothing," she said as she grasped for her words. "I just....I just....don't want you to be a victim of our sins. What we do is bad enough, supplying drugs and ruining lives...to save others...I just don't know." She wrapped her hands around my waist and buried her face into my chest.

I still couldn't describe the new feelings. The only feelings that I had ever had towards a woman came from my groin and lasted about ten minutes. It was short-lived and I trained myself that way. I had always thought that love was for fools. And I was right. Until now.

"Maybe you should get some sleep, Jose? I'll walk you to your room." She reached for my hand and lead me down the narrow brick hallway.

The room was immaculate and she had obviously been in to tidy things up and make the bed. But I noticed something that I hadn't noticed the night before. Everything in the room had a feminine nature. It was a girl's room. It was Lucy's room.

"Lucy, this is your room. I never noticed."

"Yes, Jose, it is my room when I'm here."

"I can't sleep in your room," I said with guilt.

"Of course you can, Jose. You're our guest."

"I can't do that. I just didn't realize it when I arrived."

"Don't be foolish, Jose. The couch is more comfortable than that bed anyway. You're doing me a favor."

I would have no part of it. Her white lie about the couch was just to make me feel better. We bantered a bit back and forth until I insisted on sleeping out in the garage in the boat. I had it designed so I could rest comfortably overnight whether I was on the water or not. She gave in after the short battle. We said goodnight as I rolled a blanket out over the seats. I gave her a hug and had to hold myself back from any further affection. She exited the garage and turned out the light. I stared up into the darkness, knowing that I should be sleeping but getting nowhere. A few moments later, a door opened up and the light snuck in, illuminating the garage. It was Lucy and she was wearing a nightgown.

"I just thought that you might want some milk or water before you went to bed," she said as she approached with two glasses.

"Thank you, Lucy. You really didn't have to do that," I said with a smile as I rose up from the bench seat of the boat. As I leaned over to take the glasses from her hand, she gently touched the back of my neck and pulled my face towards her.

"Thank you for coming, Jose. Father is not well and he sobs every night over Lefty. With you being here, I know he feels better."

My intuition was correct after all. Lucy was Lefty's blood sister. She wasn't just a drug dealer, she was family. Pedro's daughter. *I wonder why he never actually told me that he had a sister,* I thought. I'm sure it was just a protective instinct that most of us have in this trade.

"I didn't know. You know, about Pedro. His health."

"You do now," she responded, pulling my face to hers and kissing me on the lips. I opened my eyes and hers were still closed. She gently released her hand and walked back to the lit doorway.

"I'll see you in the morning, Jose," she smiled, and closed the door. *So that's what love is,* I thought to myself. I lay back down and didn't sleep a wink all night.

CHAPTER 42

I could hear the roosters and knew the sun was rising. The garage had no windows and was pitch black. I turned the helm light on so I could find my clothes. I placed a towel around my waist and went out the side door of the garage, around the back to the outdoor shower. I washed my face and brushed my teeth while the warm water took the chill out of my body. As I turned off the water, I heard the sliding glass door open up. It was Pedro and he was waiving me in. I quickly got dressed and dried my hair a second time with my towel. It was short and didn't need combing.

As I entered the home, the aroma of fresh coffee and baked bread permeated the air. The coffee was black and hot, giving my body the necessary wake-up after a long night of thought and restlessness. We ate freshly baked bread with papaya and watermelon. Even though it was light breakfast, it made me sleepy right away. I had to get back on a schedule and I had to get some sleep. My body couldn't take much more of this.

"So, what are your plans today?" Pedro asked.

"Well, I…" Lucy cut me off.

"We're going to San Felipe, Father," she said as she looked at me and smiled.

"I'm going to take Jose to the Mission afterwards." Her eyes were beaming with pride.

"Ah, the Mission," Pedro said as he closed his eyes and made the sign of the cross.

And that was that. It was the first that I had heard of these plans, but I was along for the ride. We had talked about wiring money from the small town of San Felipe but we never discussed when.

The Mission was started by Lucy and some Roman Catholic nuns ten years earlier, and relied on donations of food and money to help the needy. Most of the Baja Missions were founded in the 1700s by the Jesuits. Lucy's Mission was the newest on the peninsula and had many additional services that most missions did not have. Her Mission helped anyone. No one was ever turned away. The destitute made the Mission home on many occasions throughout the year, even if it were just for a day. It was the Mission where you could forget about life for a while and fill your belly and clean your body and mind. You could trade in your dirty clothes for clean ones and use the facilities. The only thing that they asked in return was for your love and commitment to God. Mass was held twice a day, every day. If you were at the Mission, you were expected to be at Mass, repenting your sins, and allowing the Lord, Jesus Christ, to guide you every step of the way.

Some fell off track with God. Many went back to the streets, pimping their bodies for a cheap high or buzz. Others resorted to theft to supply their habits. In the end, they were always welcomed back, because that was one of the canons that the Mission was built upon, and what their religion taught: forgiveness.

For the first time in my life, as we drove north on the bumpiest road I had ever traveled, I was actually interested in what Lucy had to say about God. Although I was not a believer, I respected this woman who spoke so passionately and with conviction.

It was a long 50 miles but our conversation made the trip go by quickly. We talked about our life experiences and what we were going to do when we got to San Felipe. Although the primary reason was to wire money, we could only send 50,000 bucks a day, so I naturally wanted to do other things to pass the time.

The town had about 20,000 locals and half as many gringos who lived there full time. It was a unique bunch of people who all seemed happy and content with their lives. Lucy dropped me off at the board-walk, better known as the *mulicán,* where I explored the curios shops and snacked on fish tacos and lime soda. She had to go to the bank to make contact with her friend before I went to deposit the money. Even though I had over 150,000 dollars on me, I fit right in with the rest of the crowd.

Lucy made contact with Benito, her personal banker, and set up a meeting for that afternoon. She then called me on a cell phone to ask where I was. She picked me up in front of the Bar Miramar and drove me around the block. I could have walked it was such a short distance but Lucy was afraid that I might get lost.

Lucy had met Benito through Lefty. He was fairly honest but could be persuaded to manipulate large amounts of money as long as he was being taken care of. He was able to do magic when it came to banking and would go out on the limb for clients if there were ever an audit or investigation. He was a powerful man in this small fishing village.

I liked him the minute I met him. Lucy saved me from the long, drawn-out, formal introductions that usually accompany situations such as these. She had laid down the rules and the scenario before I even got there. He was very upfront about the fact that he was on the take and expected to be paid up front.

I wrapped up my first day of business at the bank and breathed a sigh of relief. I was still nervous because I still had over a 100,000 bucks on me. But the load was lighter and I was ready to enjoy a few days with Lucy. I actually tried to convince Benito to do the whole thing at once, but both he and Lucy told me it would raise too many red flags. San Felipe wasn't used to seeing that kind of money and they didn't need the scrutiny.

"So what do you want to do now?" Lucy asked me with that curious smile.

"Honestly, let's check into a hotel where I can catch a nap," I said in all seriousness.

"Are you really that tired?" she responded as she placed her hand on the back of my neck and began to rub softly.

"I really am. I haven't been able to sleep and, worst yet, I haven't been able to go to the bathroom for two days." My frankness embarrassed Lucy.

"I understand Jose," she said, blushing.

We checked into the La Hacienda de la Langosta Roja Hotel located in the heart of downtown. We got two rooms, side by side, and then settled down for a light lunch in the restaurant. I think I was asleep as I was walking to my room because I don't remember ever lying down. I hadn't had a joint in over a day and I think my body was telling my mind to go screw myself. But adaptation was the key. And for the first time in my life, I found myself complying with the requests of someone else instead of making up my own rules. I was in love and maybe even knew it.

CHAPTER 43

The time went by fast. By the third day Benito had all of my cash wired to my account in Grand Cayman. Unfortunately, I spent most of my three days in San Felipe sleeping and filling my belly with goodies from the sea. I needed the rest and Lucy wasn't shy about encouraging me to sleep and rejuvenate myself; I wasn't shy in following her advice. So by the third day, I was back to my normal energy level and Lucy was ready to head south to the Mission.

We checked out of the hotel and I felt like a load had been lifted from my shoulders. The money was squared away and the idea of being caught with a boatload of drugs was a past memory. The risk had been taken; I was free and a few dollars richer. And speaking of memories, I had the best three days of my life. The little time that we spent away from the hotel, Lucy and I walked the beach, drank margaritas, danced on top of the Beach Comber Bar on the *mulicán,* and kissed under a full moon at high tide. It was magical and I didn't want it to stop. But the fun had to come to an end.

I reveled in my ability to grasp geography and history, but felt rather dumb as Lucy described the history of San Felipe and the Baja in general. What really sparked my interest was her overall knowledge of all of the Baja Missions. And as we trekked across the wash-panned road towards Puertocitos, I learned some fascinating history from my new-found friend.

According to Lucy, history had recorded a total of 31 Missions in the Baja peninsula. The first Mission built was in Loreto in 1697 by the

Jesuits. The Jesuits were commissioned to countries all over the world to propagate the Catholic faith. In the Baja specifically, the Missions were the glue that prompted Spain to colonize the area. It wasn't until Mexico claimed its independence from Spain that the Missions were cut off from their lifeline—the mainland of Mexico. Throughout the last two centuries and beyond, many of the Missions had been reduced to stone ruins. In one case, there is little evidence that a Mission even existed, except for writings and stories passed down over the years.

Unlike the vast resources that the mainland of Mexico offered, the Missions in the Baja were carefully planned because of the remoteness of the area and because it was hotter than hell a third of the year. Lucy explained that she had traveled to all of the Missions, some in excellent condition, others barely noticeable. Either way, many were in desolate areas and no longer practical in terms of their original intent.

It was ironic to learn that many of the supplies to build the Missions were primarily shipped from the Port of Guaymus, the same place where I would be shipping my own products.

She went on to explain that the Jesuits were not the only ones attempting to build Missions. The Dominicans and Franciscans followed suit, all trying to fulfill the Christian Piety.

Remoteness and desolation weren't the only factors affecting some of these sacred structures. To the south of the Baja, local Indians resisted the Christian movement disseminated by the missionaries. Many were polygamists, not buying into monogamous relationships between one man and one woman. And though little violence ensued, much of the Indian population was wiped out from foreign diseases to which the natives' immune systems were not accustomed.

"What is the name of the Mission that you work with, Lucy?" I asked with great curiosity.

"You'll see," she said as she winked at me, carefully maneuvering the car over the rough road.

As we made small talk during the ride, I paid close attention to my surroundings. We had gone about 40 kilometers before Lucy hung a right on a really rough road. The turn off was about halfway from San Felipe to Puertocitos and I was afraid that we might get stuck. Lucy's little car should have been a four-wheel drive Jeep.

Off to the right of the road was a large hillside where you could see the remnants of someone's desire to get rich. Lucy explained to me that it was an abandoned silver mine and proceeded to tell me a story about the old man whose heart and passion was to find the precious metal. He was so stubborn in his ways that he used every resource that he had to strike it rich, but the silver never came. Not being able to face his family over the failure of his expedition, legend had it that he jumped from the shaft to his death several hundred feet below. In his memory, the Mission closed up the main entrance to the mine years ago, turning it into a makeshift tomb and providing the unfortunate soul a proper burial. Every six months, members of the Mission visited the tomb to pray for the victim and his family and properly maintain the surroundings. *What a waste of time,* I thought to myself.

As we approached the outskirts of what I presumed was our destination, my fate was being decided. Little did I know that the authorities had arrived in San Felipe looking for a washed-up drug dealer named Jose Cantino.

CHAPTER 44

The police department in San Felipe is actually an extension of the municipality of Mexicali. Mexicali borders the U.S. city of Calexico, about 120 miles north of San Felipe. All of the police officers in San Felipe originated out of Mexicali and worked on a rotation. There was no field office for any of the state or federal drug forces in San Felipe, only in Mexicali.

A private, unmarked plane landed at the airport on the outskirts of Mexicali early in the morning. DEA agent Jack Hardlow was the lead investigator and was here to meet with his counterparts from Mazatlan regarding the Jose Cantino search. Hardlow was a 30-year veteran of the agency and it showed on his face. At one point in his life, he was handsome and fit, but years of stress and booze did everything to change that. He was a salty old dog but could fight with the best of them.

The entourage was picked up in a black Suburban and driven to the local police station in downtown Mexicali. The pilot stayed back to guard the plane and take a nap. Between all of the agents, the plane had enough computer equipment and weaponry to start and maintain a war. They had come prepared for the worst.

Jack Hardlow had a network of contacts, both legal and not, throughout the world. He knew that Cantino had a substantial amount of cash buried offshore in the Caymans. Through his contacts at the IRS, who in turn had cooperative government officials in the British Territory, he was able to verify that Cantino did business with one of the many local banks. However, when pressed for the information by

Cayman officials, the bank refused to cooperate without judicial over-sight. In essence, they would need a search warrant. In the interim, Cantino's personal banker attempted to contact his client to no avail. The banker would continue to try and reach his client and have him move all of his money to a Swiss Bank account where it would be untouchable for any government. This would occur for a small fee of course.

Although the Caymans used to be a haven for all sorts of unruly types stashing their money, it was a British Colony, and the United States was Britain's closest ally. Over the years, the U.S. government was able to convince the Brits that it would be in the best interest of their country to cooperate with the IRS and the Department of Justice when it came to the apprehension of tax cheats, drug dealers, and other dubi-ous people. Because of this type of tight-knit cooperation, Jose's banker could only do so much with such little time. He knew that they would have a search warrant soon enough and then the money would be frozen. Also, if the proper pressure were being exerted by the right peo-ple, he would have no doubt that his superiors would immediately get involved and cooperate with the authorities. Aiding and abetting would not be tolerated in the Caymans.

At the station, Hardlow met with local police and the head of the Army. He handed out pictures of Cantino. He also passed out a "want-ed" flyer with Cantino's mug shot and a list of crimes that Cantino had allegedly committed. Drug trafficking and murder were boldly high-lighted. Hardlow normally had better intelligence; unfortunately, he was following the information from the Mazatlan investigation and the floater that they found off the coast. It would take some time, but Hardlow would eventually be able to separate the good intelligence from the bad. Because of the reward being posted on the flyer, he antic-ipated hundreds of calls even if Cantino wasn't in the area. He instruct-ed everyone to follow the leads regardless. He was determined to nail this guy so he could get his career trophy, the Robles organization.

He instructed the officers to post the flyers all over the San Felipe area. He even promised some "off the record" cash to any of the officers who obtained sound information leading to his capture. He gave the standard "this guy's armed and dangerous" speech and let's get out there and make the DEA proud. Hardlow had little confidence in his corrupt subordinates but felt the money offered on the side would entice their loyalty and cooperation.

He quickly concluded the meeting and shook hands with each of the officers. They headed back to the airport, where he caught the pilot napping.

"Wake up, asshole!" Hardlow shouted, climbing into the plane. The rest of the entourage followed. Within minutes, they were taking off south to the San Felipe International Airport where they would begin their journey to find Mr. Cantino.

CHAPTER 45

The flight lasted about 30 minutes, during which Hardlow had an opportunity to down a Chivas on the rocks and give his cronies a pep talk about service to their country and a once in a lifetime case. Hardlow was a legend within the DEA and everyone wanted to not only work with him, but be like him as well.

The local authorities had a white unmarked van waiting for them and they were quickly whisked off north to the San Felipe Marina. Hardlow briefed the local police chief and his driver on Mr. Cantino and the initial operations. The Chief tried to ask questions but Hardlow forcefully spoke over him, in essence telling him not to ask questions until he was finished.

They arrived at the marina, where he briefed the local Mexican Navy and some prominent owners of some commercial fishing boats. They were given various pictures of Cantino and a description of the type of boat he was most likely using in his operation. He emphasized the pivotal role that the seamen would play as Cantino would most likely be transporting his dope by boat, not air. He then did something even surprising to the local chief's standards. He began passing out 100-dollar bills to all of the Navy personnel, promising more if they caught the crook.

The chief naval officer, in a weak attempt, tried to give the money back to Hardlow but the old man just walked away mumbling "just find the fucker" under his breath. He found his way back to the van and waited for the rest of the crew. The local police chief got into the van and began saying that he couldn't accept the money—it was against Mexican law. Hardlow blew the first of many gaskets.

"Do you think I look stupid, sir?" Hardlow stared the Chief down. "I've been working in this country when you were sucking on your mom's left tit. Don't give me this shit about not taking money. You're a cop for Christ's sake! In Mexico! Don't insult my intelligence!" Hardlow turned his head away disrespecting the Chief.

They headed back to the airport in silence. Upon their arrival, there were two young kids dressed in green khakis guarding the King Air turbo prop. Hardlow again noticed his pilot crashed out in the cockpit, taking advantage of the downtime. The van pulled onto the tarmac and dropped the crew in front of the plane. They were airborne within five minutes.

"Tucker, get me a scotch," yelled Hardlow as he leaned back in the executive chair.

"Yes sir," the young agent responded, making his way to the small galley in the rear of the plane. Hardlow piped up at the pilot, "How long until Mazatlan?"

"Little over two hours across the pond, sir."

The young agent handed him his drink. "Thank you, son, "he said as he slammed down the burning liquid, letting the last drop drip into his mouth.

"Wake me when we're landing," he ordered while he pulled the window shade down and reclined in his seat.

"No problem, sir."

As the plane ascended towards its altitude, the young agent stared down at the small white car making a dust trail in the middle of the desert. Beyond the dirt road was what appeared to be a small church.

CHAPTER 46

Mission De Lucia was written above the entrance like it was the name of a cattle ranch. I looked over at Lucy with a big grin.

"So that's why you wouldn't tell me the name," I said as I placed my hand on her delicate shoulder, rubbing it gently.

"I'm sorry, Jose. I get embarrassed. I don't want people to think the Mission is about me. It's all about the less fortunate, especially the children."

"So that history lesson that you gave me about all of the Missions in the Baja…"

"Yeah?"

"You just happened to leave this one out—the one that has your name on it?"

"Yeah." Lucy blushed.

"Well, are you going to tell me the story?"

"Of course," she said, parking the car. "Let's get out and I'll give you the story and the tour."

We both exited the car and walked around to the back of the vehicle. I met her at the rear as she opened the trunk and began to unload boxes of food and clothes. "Jose, if you could get the other two boxes and follow me, I'll take you to the kitchen area where we feed everyone." I picked up the remaining boxes and slammed the trunk shut. I followed her into the modest building that looked more like Army barracks than a Mission.

"Unlike most Missions in the Baja, this building is not made out of adobe or stone, just wood." As Lucy spoke, my eyes wandered around the large interior of the room.

"This is where we greet all of our visitors and guests." It was a giant reception area with chairs and couches strewn about. "We also hold all of our staff meetings here," she said proudly.

We continued to walk and I followed her lead. She brought me through a narrow hallway off to the side of the room that led to a rather large kitchen. I could tell by the number of burners on the stove that it was accustomed to feeding a large amount of people. On two of the burners, large pots were simmering away, giving off a spicy redolence throughout the air.

"This is obviously the kitchen," she said as she walked to the center and slowly panned the perimeter with pride.

"What's cooking?" I asked.

"Rice and beans, Jose—at every meal. It's cheap and every Mexican loves rice and beans," she smiled.

"But is that all they eat?" I asked inquisitively.

"No, but it's always the base meal. We get a lot of donated food. Pork, beef, chicken—all from local farms. Even though it's still a poor area, there are many big hearts around here."

"So this is your Mission, huh Lucy?" asking a question that I already knew the answer to.

"Well, Jose, God called me to do his work here on earth. Ever since I was a kid, I would do whatever I could to help others. After school, I would gather clams, trap crabs, even go fishing so I could provide food to the elderly and poor. We have this beautiful ocean that we call the Sea of Cortez, loaded with goodies. Yet we still have people who don't have the means to eat. It's terrible and makes no sense." Her voice was cracking as her eyes watered up.

"I'm sorry, Jose," as her smile made a comeback. "I just get very emotional and I always have been when it comes to my work."

"I understand."

"But back to the Mission. Lefty paid to have the Mission built. These were the types of projects that Lefty loved to get involved with." She paused and made the sign of the cross.

Even though Lefty was a drug dealer, I was reminded of the massive humanitarian efforts he facilitated up and down the Baja. It was all coming together for me. Lefty may have been a philanthropist, but Lucy was a Saint. *Mission de Lucia.*

"We don't have a full-time priest, only a deacon, but Father Francisco comes on Sunday afternoons from San Felipe to perform Mass."

"Oh?"

"And believe me, he literally is their father," she said, smirking.

"Whose father?" I asked.

"Let me show you," she responded, leading me through another entryway. "Now you must be quiet when entering this room because it's nap time and most of the children are young and restless."

Children? I didn't know! No, it can't be—an orphanage?

We walked into the room and I couldn't believe what I saw. There were at least 60 boys and girls, from infants to some in their early teens, crashed out on cots and blankets. Each child had his or her own makeshift territory with plastic boxes for dressers, and stuffed dolls and animals for friends. I say "friends" because the children all looked like brothers and sisters. There was a nun in the corner, watching over the children like a bear with her cubs. I couldn't believe what I was seeing.

It hit me all at once and it hit me hard. My eyes began to water as my childhood was being revisited right before me. I began drawing comparisons with the children that I grew up with. *That one looks just like Lupe—and it seems like Sister Maria is in the corner!* It was difficult; I had to step back before something really embarrassing happened to me.

I raced around the corner and broke out into a sob. My childhood was right before my eyes. Sister Maria, God bless her, who loved me like only a paternal mother could. My life—what a disgrace! A drug dealer, never sharing my wealth. A murderer! Where was my soul? Where have I been all of these years? I locked myself in the bathroom and continued to sob. I didn't have the answers. I just knew I felt dirty.

I spent several minutes in the dingy restroom and just couldn't get it together. I heard the knob on the door rattle and before I could decipher what was going on, Lucy had the door open and backed me up against the sink. As I kissed her beautiful face, my tears drenched her face. She knew it and so did I. I finally found my home. I was still an orphan after all of these years. And at that very moment, I had found my family once and for all.

CHAPTER 47

The plane touched down at the Mazatlan International Airport and Hardlow was stretching his body as he opened his eyes. The two-hour nap did him good and he was ready to get back to work.

"Does anyone know we're here?" he asked his young aide, Tucker.

"Yes, sir. They have a car waiting and we're all going to meet at our hotel suite."

"Good. Did you get the whores lined up for after dinner?" he asked with a grin.

"Everything's in order, sir. You won't be disappointed," he replied as he handed Hardlow his sports coat.

They exited the plane while the pilot stayed back to refuel. Hardlow was happy to be in Mazatlan, combining a lot of work with a little bit of pleasure. They would set the stage and plan the aggressive hunt for Jose Cantino. Before that, however, a night of partying was in order before they laid out the logistics for their mission.

They made it to the five-star resort, where he checked in. Hardlow had a lot on his mind. He knew Mexico and her incongruity well. It didn't have a death penalty, but Hardlow had his own rules and expected his Mexican counterparts to follow them. He wanted Cantino and he wanted information. He would do anything to squeeze every last bit of knowledge from Cantino before he finished him off for good.

But he hadn't met his team yet. He didn't trust the Mexicans. They were bent. They took corruption to the lowest form. He knew that whoever was assigned to his team could be on a Cartel's payroll. The Mexicans played cheap and he always started off with a threat when working for them. He normally received cooperation in return.

He made it up to his suite on the fifth floor of the Las Sabalos Hotel. He was greeted to a full meal laid out on the coffee table. He wasn't in the mood for a lot of food, but immediately opened the bottle of Red Label and poured up a drink. After a round of salutations to his colleagues, he made it clear that he wanted some time alone. They knew what he expected and could read the fatigue on his face.

As they all left the room, a young maid entered and began cleaning up the food and glasses. Hardlow let her be and went to the back room where he stretched his tired body onto the bed. The maid quickly followed him through the doorway with nothing but her bra and panties.

"Room service, sir?"

CHAPTER 48

My transformation from atheism to Christianity happened that quickly. There was a God and Jesus Christ was my Savior. Deacon Cruz and Lucy led me to the chapel, where I prayed for the first time in my life. I could feel the Lord's presence. He was with me as his spirit radiated from both of my hands into Lucy and the Deacon. I could see him but couldn't actually picture him. He was there and my soul was aching to confess my sins. I knew that Father Francisco would not be there until Sunday, so I asked Lucy what I should do.

"Deacon Cruz can handle your confession, Jose," she said as she gripped my hand.

It was in that dark room with the screen that I confessed my sins. I went all the way back to the murder of Reverend Tomas Ramirez, and up until recently, fellow drug dealer, Raul Espendito. It took more than 30 minutes for my first confessional and I silenced the good Deacon for what seemed like eternity. Unlike any confession that I had read about, there were no Hail Marys, no Our Fathers, just a man who removed the screen in front of me and held my hands. We both bowed towards one another as the tears poured from each of our eyes in deep prayer and sorrow. I was the sinner amongst sinners and could feel the pain drip away one tear at a time.

I had never felt guilty about anything that I did; today, however, the guilt piled on like an avalanche. Soon the avalanche subsided and there was sunshine to melt it away. As I stood to leave the confessional, I could feel the heavy load of guilt begin to lift. Like a drug addict, my recovery had just begun. I was now emotionally exhausted, but refused to lie down in the shelter. I needed to absorb everything that I could about the Mission de Lucia and her founder. My life was just beginning.

Lucy held me as I began the cleansing process. I didn't want her to know, but I had to tell her. I sobbed like a baby as I told her about the upbringing and the things that I did. Ironically enough, she didn't appear to be terribly surprised. Perhaps she knew of similar exploits from Lefty's days. She knew firsthand that most drug runners were indifferent to murder. It was part of the business. I knew, however, that Lucy epitomized all that was good in this world. Any differentiation had to affect her in a negative way.

Then again, she was wise to the world. It was obvious that she would not have the stage called Mission de Lucia if she hadn't acted among the corrupt. It was odd company, but obviously accepted. The benefit was one of sharing, among the poorest of the poor.

She brought me to her quarters that had a fold-out bed in the living area. It was very modest. "I don't want to live differently than my children. It wouldn't be right" she told me. However, it did offer privacy. As much as I wanted to take her and make love to her right then and there, I knew it would not be right given the circumstances. Plus, I doubted if Lucy would ever give in, because of our sacred location and her strong conviction in the Catholic faith.

We said our good nights and I lay my restless body and soul on the couch in the hallway under a light blanket. I was exhausted.

CHAPTER 49

The sleep wouldn't come and it was obvious why. My conscience would not allow me to forget any of my past; it was now on the forefront. I was afraid to start reading the Bible because I didn't need any additional reinforcement of what a bad person that I was.

Lucy heard me rustle out of bed and met me at the entryway of her bedroom.

"Come in here," she commanded me with a seductive look. My response was mixed as I followed her into the room. We continued towards the back, where we were met by an open screen door overlooking the southwestern desert. The cacti and rocks were illuminated by the Baja moon. We sat down on the patio and just stared up into the sky in silence.

"I couldn't sleep a wink, Lucy."

"I know what you mean."

"What time is it?" I asked.

"It's just after one in the morning."

I looked over at her and I could sense that she could see me in her peripheral because of her slight grin. "Jose, do you ever think about where Heaven is?"

I paused in discomfort. "Lucy, I didn't even believe in Heaven until yesterday."

"Would you mind if I poured us a glass of wine?" she said, quickly changing the subject.

"That sounds…that sounds nice," I replied.

As the fermented grapes touched my lips, the alcohol tasted wonderful for the first time in my life. *I wonder if the pleasant taste had anything to do with Jesus drinking wine?* I asked myself. I didn't plan on drinking more than one glass but I did plan on enjoying it with the one person that I loved.

"So, do you like it?"

"Like what?" I responded.

"The wine, silly," she gave me an odd smirk.

"Oh, yes I really like it. I'm not a big drinker, but this is very nice."

"It's from Santo Tomas."

"Santo Tomas?" I asked ignorantly.

"Yeah. Santo Tomas is outside of Ensenada. It's where all of the great Mexican wines are made."

"Oh," I paused, not knowing what to say.

The next minute felt like days. I was out of my element: in a good place with a wonderful person, caring for wonderful children. I knew I wanted to change my life. I had so much to make up for. I decided to break the ice.

"Lucy, I don't want to scare you off, but what happened today has changed my life." Lucy smiled as I made another confession.

"I want to move here Lucy and help your kids…help *our* kids. I've got all the money we need. We can…"

"Slow down, Jose," she said as her white teeth flashed inside the perimeter of her lips. "You just got here. Let's not rush into things too quickly."

I didn't know what to say. She was right. But I was once told that when you know, you just know. I never believed it until now. I knew what I wanted to do with my life and it wasn't selling drugs. Another half hour lapsed with very little said. We drained the bottle of wine and my head was feeling well. She led me back into the room where our bodies did the talking.

The two of us formed as one that evening and made passionate love into the early morning. As guilt-ridden as Lucy should have been—being the epitome of a good Catholic—I felt nothing from her but love and affection. I sensed that she felt the same. I knew that she was the one I wanted to spend the rest of my life with.

It was another night of little to no sleep. I got up, showered, and prepared for the day. Lucy was still in bed while I was dressing, hoping not to disturb her, but she was awake. She was just being courteous and polite as I finished up with the facilities. She had made a pot of coffee and I sipped it on the patio as she got ready for a long day of work. The desert looked the same except now it was sunlight illuminating the scenery.

It was an exciting day. The children were amazed when they saw me. There were no male figures around on a consistent basis, except Deacon Cruz, who spent much of his time on administrative duties and of course, praying.

I taught the children baseball with a rock and ocotillo branch and promised to bring the Mission all of the necessary equipment to have a proper baseball game, a promise that I intended to keep, and one of many things that the children desperately needed. It would be my first opportunity to give something back. I saw myself in every one of them. An orphan. *I'll adopt them all,* I told myself. *Every single one of them.* And I was serious.

Two weeks went by and I had never worked harder in my life. I was up before dawn and was designated the new cook. I had never cooked for so many people and bought out the store in Puertocitos twice. I felt guilty serving them rice and beans for every meal, so I cooked bacon and *chorizo* and *machaca*—anything I could get my hands on. I worked a deal with a local farmer who brought 50 chickens and committed to 50 every month. The children needed some meat on their bones and I was having fun every minute of the day.

After the kids lay down for their naps, I would start the laundry, another chore that I volunteered for. Before me, all of the laundry was done by hand. But on my first trip to Puertocitos, an American was having a garage sale. He had retired to Puertocitos 15 years ago. Since the road had washed out, he just couldn't take the 2½ drive into San

Felipe every month for supplies. He was getting out and selling things cheaply. I bought a washer and dryer, Onan Generator, three propane freezers, and numerous other items that would benefit the orphanage. He also gave me two closets full of clothes. They would be a bit big for the children but they would always go to good use.

The orphanage didn't have gas but it did have solar power for lights. I would fire up the generator that I bought and run the washing machine. Water needed to be added by hand, but I felt good about the unorthodox way I was helping out.

The children learned other sports from me too. And suddenly I was teaching them the value of reading and education. I would read the nap-time and bedtime stories every day and encouraged them to learn English so they could communicate with our neighbors up north and around the world. I taught them how to filet fish that I bought from the local fisherman in Puertocitos. All in all, I taught them the value of hard work, getting ahead, and loving the Lord. "With faith my children, no man is poor," I found myself quoting regularly. I used my own life constantly without revealing specifics as what to do and not to do. I was beginning to feel that I was born to preach the gospel and the teachings of Jesus Christ. It felt natural and my love for God was growing stronger and stronger every day.

I vowed to dedicate all of my fortune to these children. I would support them and help them get to where they needed to go in life. They were my sons and daughters. If they were going to be my sons and daughters, then I needed a wife—and because she was already their mother, I took drastic steps.

"Lucy, will you marry me?" I asked as I knelt on my left knee and displayed the modest band that I scraped up at the old man's garage sale.

"Yes, Jose! Yes!" She jumped into my arms and kissed my lips.

All the kids screamed in excitement as they watched the dramatic events pass before their eyes. That night, Lucy and I traveled to Puertocitos to tell Pedro the news. We were excited and were hoping Pedro would be excited as well. As we arrived at Pedro's home, we noticed that all of the lights were off and the door was wide open. A look of fear crossed Lucy's face as we slowly walked through the door.

"Father, are you home?" she spoke as we stepped through the foyer.

"Pedro," I spoke in a louder tone.

There was no response. Lucy turned on the lights. In front of us was Pedro, keeled over on the couch.

"OH MY GOD!" Lucy screamed as we ran across the room.

I placed two fingers under his jaw and felt his pulse. He was alive. I placed my ear under his nose—he was breathing.

"Lucy, he's alive, he's alive." I tried to comfort her. As relief set in, we both could smell the strong stench of tequila in the air. Our beliefs were confirmed with the empty bottle of Cuervo stuffed between the couch and the middle cushion. Pedro was drunk and had passed out.

"This is not good, Jose," she said with tears running down her face.

"Ah, hell Lucy. A good drunk once in a while never hurt a man," I said, trying to comfort her. She had no response, only concern.

Lucy walked into the kitchen while I laid Pedro on his stomach and went to find a blanket. As I returned, Lucy was staring at a bright orange piece of paper with an intent glaze over her face.

"What is it my dear?" I asked her nervously as I approached her.

She slowly looked up at me and I realized that something terribly wrong was happening.

"What!" I lashed out, trying to get her to speak.

She didn't say a word as the blood vanished from her face. She held out the paper. I knew, but I didn't want to face the music. Before I could take it from her hand, the paper dropped from her fingertips and floated side to side until it reached the floor. It landed perfectly on the tile like a helicopter on its landing pad. I looked down and it was as if I was standing in a mirror. My face was staring back at me. Above my picture, written in Spanish, was the caption "WANTED FOR MURDER."

"My God!" I exclaimed in disbelief. "How do they know?" I let the words run off my tongue.

"I don't know, Jose, but Pedro hasn't had a drink in 30 years."

CHAPTER 50

Lucy tried to rouse Pedro but it was no use. He was done. She was worried because he was 70 years old and knew his body couldn't take this kind of abuse at one sitting. She gave up and turned to me.

"My God! You haven't been here that long. How could they know?" Lucy said, placing her palm over her mouth.

"I don't know, but I need to leave, my dear. We need to let things cool off."

"Cool off, Jose! You just promised 60 children that you would be coming back with everything but Santa Clause himself!" she burst into tears and started for the front door. "How could I do this to myself? How did I let this happen to me?" she cried as she ran out the front door.

The noise temporarily woke Pedro, who stared right at me before shutting his eyelids. *Don't wake up now, old man. Your daughter is gonna be hard enough to deal with as it is,* I said to myself. I followed her out the door and walked briskly to the street. She was nowhere to be found. I walked briskly down the side of the house where I could see her silhouette along the shore. Quickly catching up to her, I embraced her fragile body.

"Lucy, my dear. I was honest with you. Please, we'll get through this," I said as I tried to comfort her.

"You don't understand, Jose. I can't lose another one I love. I can't take it, nor can the children," she replied, her sobs getting louder and louder.

Lucy buried her head in my arms as my shirt soaked up her tears. I wanted to cry myself, but knew that I had to act fast. I was in the crosshairs and didn't have many options. The authorities were probably in the vicinity. I pulled her face from my body and grabbed her arms firmly.

"Lucy, listen to me. We need to find out where Pedro got that flyer. We need to find out now!"

"Jose, I must make a confession," she paused with her words.

"OK?" I said in a drawn out breath, thinking that this was the last thing I needed at this moment.

"Pedro is not my real father."

"I don't understand? I thought…"

"Lefty was not my brother!" she blurted out.

"I'm lost, Lucy," I said, shaking my head. "I don't know what the connection is."

She paused as she contemplated her words carefully.

"Lucy, please spit it out. We don't have much time."

"We were engaged to be married," she said as she slowly raised her head and met me eye to eye.

"When Lefty was killed, Pedro was the only father I had. You see, Jose, I too was an orphan." Her words hit me like an eighteen-wheeler.

I'm sure my facial expressions said it all, but I said nothing. Why? There was nothing to say. The web of life was only getting more entangled and I didn't know how to react to what she was telling me. In fact, now was not the time to have this discussion. I changed gears and dismissed the hard-hitting news.

I kissed her forehead and wrapped my hands around her frail body. I comforted her with my physical presence, as my mind was a step ahead of my actions. I had to mentally map out an escape route before the authorities caught up with me. My boat was in Pedro's garage.

When I arrived two weeks ago, I had just over a quarter of a tank of gas in each tank. I would need more gas no matter where I decided to go. And of course I would need food and water. In fact, the idea of comforting Lucy had to come to an end. My freedom was more important.

"Lucy, listen. As much as we need each other right now, time is running out. I need to get out of here—and I mean now! They'll be hot on my trail in no time!"

"Perhaps you should come back to the orphanage?" she suggested in a tearful plea.

"No, Lucy, no. That would put you and the children in danger. I need to go now. Maybe north. They'll expect me to go south, so maybe I can ward them off for a while. While I regroup, we will need to formulate a plan. Right now, I need to get the hell out of here."

I stood silent for a moment because I really didn't have a contingency plan. I was a man with an overall plan, but I always had the advice and guidance from Old Man Robles and the Cartel. Now things were different. I was a one-man band and operating in foreign territory. I guess there were downsides to being self-employed.

"Lucy, please. We must be calm. Right now I need your help. We can discuss everything else later."

"Yes, Jose. Anything. Just tell me what you need from me."

"I need you to pack me some food while I siphon some gas from Pedro's truck. I will leave you and Pedro money—I have to make this quick."

"I understand. I understand...." Her eyes submerged with tears and desperation.

We quickly walked back to the house and I laid a 100-dollar bill on Pedro's kitchen counter. Lucy prepared sandwiches while I went to the garage and got a gas can.

I searched for a piece of hose in the garage to no avail, so I went to the side of the house where I cut a section of the garden hose and ran one end into the gas can. Returning to the garage, I unscrewed the gas cap of Pedro's truck. I was able to get about 15 gallons into the boat before the well went dry. I felt guilty about leaving Pedro empty, but I had no choice.

Lucy had the boat packed with food and water by the time I was finished filling it up. I backed her car into the garage and hooked up the boat to the rusty hitch. Within minutes, I was negotiating the trailer down the ramp and into the water. If it hadn't been so bright, I may not have noticed the spotlight shining on me from up above the hilltop. I jumped out of the car where Lucy met me at the waterline. We loosened the crank and the boat took to the ocean like a long-lost friend. I climbed into the boat and noticed the light getting closer.

"Lucy, I must go now. Someone is coming for us," I said as the initial stages of panic set in. "I will call you on your cell phone when I get out of here."

I turned the ignition. Nothing. I tried again—not even a crank. *Holy Shit!* I thought. I had a dead battery. I could now here the vehicle and noticed it was a police car. They were moving in on me quickly.

I ran to the back of the boat where I stowed the portable battery jumper. *I can't believe I left the fucking light on,* I told myself. I connected the clamps to the posts and prayed to God. I turned the ignition again and it cranked but didn't fire.

"Come on!" I yelled out loud while Lucy stared at me with her hands folded in prayer.

I tried it again and it fired immediately. I cranked the boat into reverse and drove it off the trailer.

"Lucy, I'm heading northeast. I will need help. Call one of Lefty's friends and find out where I can go."

"I will, Jose. I know many friends who can meet you. I will make arrangements." Her hands were now pointing out at me.

I turned the boat south and hit the throttle. "I love you, Lucy," I said as my voice drifted above the revs of the motor.

As I sped out of Puertocitos Bay, I looked into my rearview mirror and noticed the red and blue flashes illuminating Lucy's small frame.

CHAPTER 51

"Surely you're mistaken, officer. I don't know what you're talking about. This is crazy," Lucy said nervously as she paced along the side of Pedro's home.

"Ma'am, we have information to believe that Jose Cantino was here and left on that boat that was on the trailer hooked up to your car," the local officer explained.

"Well, I suggest you take me to jail then!" she said defiantly.

"Ma'am, no one is threatening jail yet," the officer grimaced.

"I run the Mission de Lucia. I would like to see you take me to jail. I'll have you're job by the time we get to San Felipe!"

The officer was a transplant from Mexicali and didn't know anything about local politics or a Mission that she claimed to run. It didn't add up, though He just couldn't picture such a beautiful young lady in charge of a Mission or an orphanage. Normally, fat old nuns did the charity work—not hot, young bombshells.

"Please excuse me," the officer said as he walked to his cruiser. He radioed his supervisor in San Felipe, who confirmed that Lucy ran the Mission outside of Puertocitos. It was quickly determined that it would be wise not to harass the young lady and he was ordered to back off. He got back out of the car and walked back to Lucy, who was standing in the doorway of Pedro's home.

"Well, everything checks out according to the brass," he said.

"Well, I would think so, rookie!" she replied, her words cutting off as she slammed the door in his face. The officer was stopped in his tracks. He was hoping to get some type of kudos in return for letting her go. Instead, he got shut down. He walked back to the patrol car and sped north. *Oh well,* he thought as he decided to get back to the sub-station and enjoy a nap. Maybe he would dream of the beautiful missionary? It didn't matter. He hated his duty because there was nothing to do. There was very little crime in the mostly American community. Ex-patriots came to Mexico to retire and get away from whatever they were running from up north. Why would they want to get in trouble at their ages? *So much for false leads,* he thought, placing his feet on the desk and closing his eyes.

He had fallen asleep thinking of the situation when the phone rang. It was a sergeant from the drug task force out of Mexicali ranting and raving about this and that. He couldn't understand his words because he was screaming so loud into the phone.

"Why didn't you take that woman into custody!" the sergeant yelled.

"But sir, I was told by my sergeant that everything checked out."

"She was harboring a fugitive, you idiot!"

"Sir, she's practically a nun. She runs a Mission…"

"I know what the hell she does and trust me, it's not missionary work. She was engaged to a drug dealer before he got gunned down. How do you think she built that place? It's a fucking laundromat for dirty money! Now go get her and bring her in before I come down there myself and arrest you for stupidity!"

The officer was dumbfounded. He was only here for a short amount of time before he would be rotated back up to Mexicali. All he did was confirm the woman's identity and stature and his superior had nothing but praise for the woman. Yeah, she looked suspicious but everything checked out!

He patrolled back into the tiny fishing village to look for the woman. As he drove up to the home, he noticed that her vehicle was no longer in the area. However, the boat trailer was parked on the side of the house. He exited his patrol car and walked the perimeter. There was no sign of her. He opened the side entrance to the garage where he detected a slight odor of marijuana. He turned on his flashlight and quietly walked inside. The garage was void of any vehicles, but he decided to look for the illicit drugs. He hadn't been stoned for over a month and some weed sounded good.

What was he thinking? He was ordered to find the girl. The only serious order that he had since his rotation began a few weeks ago. He quickly exited the garage and went around to the front door. He rang the doorbell, but no answer. He knocked but could hear nothing. *I know I missed her,* he thought. Her car was gone.

He turned and walked back to his car. Just as he started up the old jalopy they called a police car, the porch light came on and an old man opened the front door. He turned off the engine and got back out of the car. He shined his light on the old man, who looked to be in a daze.

"Buenos noches," he greeted the old man, but Pedro did not respond.

"I am looking for a young woman who was here earlier, sir? Would you know where she is?" he asked politely. Pedro just grunted as he stared through the officer in his drunken state.

"She was just out back about an hour ago saying goodbye to a man leaving in a Ponga. Would you know who that man was?"

"I think so," Pedro mumbled.

"We had an anonymous call that a man that we're looking for may have been in the area the last 72 hours."

"And?" Pedro said as he continued to stare at the young officer with his blood-shot eyes.

"Sir, are you OK?" he asked with genuine concern.

"I'm fine, and you?" Pedro said, slurring his words.

"I'm fine. Would you mind if I asked you some questions?"

"Go ahead, son."

"When I spoke to the young lady, I asked her about the man in the boat. I could see her talking to him while I was driving up. When I finally got close enough, he was gone like a bat out of hell and the young lady was defensive and very vague and told me all kinds of things like she ran a Mission and an orphanage and that she was going to have my job and that if I arrested her for any reason, she would have me jailed and she was just very angry as if I had done something wrong. All I was doing was my job. You know, it's an officer's job to investigate these things and this was rather suspicious..." he kept rambling. Pedro was patient as the inexperienced cop stated a confession as opposed to an inquiry. When he finally finished, Pedro piped up.

"Was that really a question?" he said with a smile.

"I'm sorry, I'm just anxious. I could be in a lot of trouble because I dropped the ball."

"I'm sorry for that son. Now, did you want to ask me a question?"

"Oh, yes sir. I was wondering...um...did you happen to see a man with that woman and if you did, would you know who that man was?"

"You mean him?" Pedro asked, handing the officer the flyer of Jose Cantino.

"My God!" he exclaimed. "This was the guy? He's plastered all over the Baja!"

"Yeah, that was him all right. Now I've got to go back to sleep," Pedro said as he turned around and headed for his front door.

The officer didn't know how to react. He could smell the tequila on his breath and knew the old man shined with indifference because he was drunk. He could always come back with a follow-up. He hopped back into his car and raced back to the substation. As he pulled into the dirt parking lot, he was greeted by two Army hummers and a black suburban. The feds had arrived and the young officer didn't know who was in more trouble, Jose Cantino or himself.

CHAPTER 52

The waters were calm as I headed the boat southeast. It was imperative that I went far enough south to get out of view from anyone in Puertocitos. My destination would eventually take me north to Puerto Penasco but I wanted to lead them astray in case there were any witnesses who saw me depart. I knew the Baja had limited resources when tracking drug dealers, so some of my worries subsided. I had been careless. I wasn't prepared and the reasoning was irrelevant. My freedom was almost taken and that's all that mattered.

The lights from Puertocitos were no longer visible. I followed my coordinates on my GPS and steered the boat 90 degrees east. My fuel tanks were low, but I had enough to get to the mainland. More prevalent on my mind was who ratted me out. I was panicked because, for the most part, I had covered my tracks. But now here I was, in the middle of the sea, trying to escape my past.

As I headed east, I had some semblance of how I was going to evade the authorities. I knew that they would immediately try and trace me back to Guaymus or down in Mazatlan because that's where I had left my tracks. So I dialed in some coordinates on my GPS tracking system and set the boat on autopilot. I was headed towards a small Indian village called El Desemboque. The only reason it had any name identification at all was because of Americans wanting to come down from the States and get in touch with their natural side—guilty white liberals attempting to reach out to poor brown peasants in the sake of understanding. Whatever the circumstances of El Desemboque, I just needed to get across the pond. It would be the last place that they would be looking for me.

My boat had the latest technology in marine navigation. As difficult as it could be, I trusted the instruments. The ocean could play tricks on you just as any pilot flying in the clouds or at night on autopilot could attest to. But you always trusted your instruments, because you had to.

I was able to get some rest at the orphanage so the added adrenaline was a bonus. I just prayed that I would be able to maintain my sleep schedule once I got to the mainland. This toying with my bodily clock had to come to an end. It couldn't be healthy.

I had been a good boy for days, but under the circumstances I gave myself justification to smoke pot to relieve some pressure. I had stowed a few ounces in my safe in the floor of the boat, normally used to store the cash. In this case, the small amount of crop was more valuable to me.

As I lit up the joint, the alarms on my radar screen went off and I immediately set into a panic. The alarms were set at high volume in case I was sleeping. I checked the screen, which indicated a relatively fast boat coming my way from the south. I immediately took the boat off autopilot and full throttled the vessel northeast. As I stared over my shoulder, I could see a large gray vessel. It was the Mexican Navy and they were aimed right at me. I tossed the joint in the ocean and placed the bag of weed back into the floor safe. I slowed the boat down, trying to be calm. But it was no use. How could I be calm when, with one wrong move, they could blow me out of the water? If they didn't know about the search yet, I could get out of this. If I were smart, I would toss the dope. But I was going to take my chances. The dope was the only comfort I had in this dilemma.

As the ship approached my vessel, I pulled out some old fishing nets with buoys and flags, camouflaging my true occupation. A loud bull-horn sounded and the amplified words stung my eardrums.

"Attention! Shut off your engine. We will be boarding your vessel!"

I was screwed. I thought the pot would calm me but now wild thoughts of paranoia were penetrating my brain. I didn't know how they could have caught me so quickly. I had nowhere to run. I left my pistol inside of my jacket in case of a last ditch effort. That would be as fruitless as a BB gun against a bazooka. But if I was meant to leave this world, I accepted it. No way would I spend the rest of my life in a Mexican prison. No way.

I killed the engine and could feel the pot taking effect. The darkness began to take a back seat to the rising sun. Two young boys, both toting AK-47s, approached the boat in a small dingy. As they came up aside me, I threw them a small rope and offered them a snack and soda. In total amazement, they smiled and accepted my small token. I smiled back, hiding my bloodshot eyes behind my shades.

While the kids praised Lucy's cold shredded beef burritos, I launched into a long diatribe of how I was a fisherman from Guaymus, but my dad was ill. He lived south of San Felipe and I had just crossed the ocean in hopes to see him one last time. But it had been too late. By the time I got there, he had passed.

My voice began to crack as I acted out the scenario. I told them that I had been able to make the funeral and pay my respects. But I didn't know if I could forgive myself for not being there earlier, and that I decided I would do some fishing to take my mind off of the guilt that I was feeling.

By the time I finished my story of immense bullshit, one boy was in tears and the other close in tow. It had paid off either through their naiveté or my conviction of the circumstances or both.

They went on to explain to me that they were only doing routine narcotic checks and thought that my boat was suspicious because of its size and distance from land. I told them that they were free to search the vessel and that I felt bad that I didn't have any fish or shrimp to give them. They declined my offer and both shook my hand. I was good to go and quickly realized how lucky I was. Obviously they had been out at sea too long. I'm sure as they made land, the two boys would kick themselves if they were to see the wanted posters.

God, I had to get off this ocean, and soon.

CHAPTER 53

Jack Hardlow sat in his comfortable hotel room in Mazatlan as he listened to the agent brief him on the latest information regarding Cantino. As he drew on his Cubano cigar, he couldn't help think of last night's girl as her scent faintly permeated the air.

"He was last seen in San Felipe, sir. We have it on good word that he's been there and was seen at the local bank on at least three days in a row."

"And what was he doing at the bank?" Hardlow asked calmly.

"We don't know, sir. We just have surveillance and confirmation from one of the employees that we bribed."

"Who was the employee?"

"Some assistant manager. Spilled his guts for a 100 bucks. We dangled a money stick at him telling him there could be a giant reward to him if we found Cantino. Took the bait like a blind fish."

"Get that banker on board. I want answers now. I want to know why and what he was doing at the bank. And I want someone to confirm that it was actually Cantino on the surveillance. Some of these dipshits will convince themselves they saw Jesus Christ if there's money involved."

"Sir, we have already tried to talk to the assistant manager and the branch manager has been very uncooperative. He said that all legal inquiries have to go through him if it involves the bank or one of their clients. And of course, he mentioned the standard legal jargon of warrants, etc. You know."

Jack Hardlow's face was beginning to turn red and he sat in silence. The young agent had seen this reaction before. He could go either way—patronizing or ballistic.

"Then get one of the boys down there and make him talk," he said, slowly enunciating his words while cigar smoke exhaled from his nostrils. "I don't have time to fuck around in this third-world shithole with peon bankers in the Baja." He placed his cigar in the ashtray.

"Ah, yes sir," the agent said nervously. "I'll get it handled."

"Good. And I want an update daily. We need to catch this prick so I can get on to some real business!"

"I agree, sir. Consider it done."

The young agent left the hotel room. He hated Hardlow because he was an immoral, unethical pig. *Make him talk,* he mumbled to himself. *I don't have time for peon bankers...*he thought about Hardlow's arrogant words. He reminded him of Jack Nicholson in *A Few Good Men,* always dressing down people in his own, special, condescending way. He was a jerk and was now asking him to do something that was not only unethical, but most likely illegal.

He caught a cab down to police headquarters where he met with his Mexican counterparts.

"Hardlow wants the information from the Mexican banker."

"But it's against Mexican law to release information about a customer of a bank without a warrant my friend."

The agent knew this information and didn't know what to say. He was nervous about giving the request in the first place because he was in a foreign country and his request consisted of breaking the law.

"Hardlow said do whatever it takes to get the information from the banker...and I think he means it," the agent replied as he turned his back and walked out of the room.

CHAPTER 54

I had run along the coast from El Desemboque for several hours and made it up to Puerto Penasco, also known as Rocky Point. I called Lucy on my cell phone and she put me in touch with a friend of Lefty's. He had been his neighbor and though he was quite a bit younger than Lefty, they were like brothers. The minutes seemed like hours and my paranoid thoughts couldn't help eliminate Lucy from being the culprit in terms of my outing. Unfortunately, in the drug trade, you had no friends. You trusted certain people more than the others. But when it came to getting caught, it was every man for himself. Or in this case, herself. But Lucy? *Lucy?* No.

The boat practically piloted herself and I continued to dwell on man and his modern technology. No more using the stars for navigation, just turn on the trusty old GPS.

As I approached my destination, it didn't surprise me to see a gringo waiving at me from the beach of a rather plush home on a bluff. He immediately knew it was me and had an F-250 truck running with an empty boat trailer backed down a launch ramp just west of his home. He walked over towards the truck and backed it into the high tide. I maneuvered the boat in front of the trailer. Little was said as I killed the engines and let the Ponga boat drift onto the trailer. Without an official greeting, we secured the boat to the trailer with a thick rope attached to the crank. The fit wasn't perfect but it didn't matter. I just needed to get off the water and out of sight.

Once the boat was secured, I began to eye my new friend. He was a tall guy packing some pretty big guns. He obviously worked out on occasion. With the exception of his beer belly, he looked like he was in pretty good shape. His tan was dark like a Mexican's but he stood out with his bleached blonde hair. Something told me that it wasn't his original hair color or that he spent a whole lot of time in the sun.

He introduced himself as Gilberto. I guess it was some American Mexican thing. You know, the gringo who wants to blend in with the locals. He obviously didn't have an ounce of Mexican in him. I shook his hand and told him my name.

I climbed into the boat as we traveled up the steep ramp that lead to the road in front of his house. His home was built on two lots and looked more like a compound, with an electric gate for security. My new friend had obviously pulled a boat or two in his day because he nailed it on the first try, maneuvering it up the drive and backing it into the garage.

We disconnected the trailer and quickly shut the garage door. I was told to stay inside while he parked the truck in front of the small casita at the rear of the property. The garage was a bit warm and very dark. My nervousness should have subsided at this point but my destiny was still in a stranger's hands. In an attempt to calm my nerves, I reiterated Lucy's words in my mind about Gilberto and Lefty being best friends. And if that was the case, then I guess we were friends indirectly. As I pondered these thoughts, I was taken by surprise. The garage door began to open, which sent panic up my spine as I saw two sets of tanned legs get slowly exposed by the rising garage door.

"What's up?" as the door came to a stop. In Gilberto's hand was an extra Pacifico beer and behind him was another gringo who introduced himself as "Hatch." He looked like a friendly enough guy, but now there were twice as many people who knew of my whereabouts in Rocky Point. But I had no choices at this point. I had lost control of the situation and again, my future lay before me.

"*Mucho gusto,* Hatch," I said in Spanish. "It's nice to meet you," I followed up, with my best English accent.

"Come on in, Jose, and let me show you around," said Gilberto as he handed me the beer. "*Mi casa es su casa.*"

I accepted the beer and just smiled.

As modest as Gilberto appeared to be, his casa was anything but humble. And the story behind it was nothing short of amazing. Knowing this man's energy and dedication to my situation in such a short time, I knew he wasn't exaggerating. He had credibility and I didn't need his resume to draw that conclusion.

He had been coming to Rocky Point from the Arizona desert for years as a kid. It was a simple family of four: husband, wife, son, and daughter. Years' before, his parents had built the home when Rocky Point had yet to be discovered by the waves of yuppies and baby boomers from the metropolitan cities of Phoenix and Tucson. They had gone several miles out in the middle of nowhere and built the home in a place called Los Conchas. Today, Los Conchas was a gated community with million dollar homes speckling the beach. It was a story of a dream that transcended into wealth—a massive return on the dollar. What we in the drug trade refer to as R.O.I. or return on investment.

His three-car garage was carved out just enough to fit my Ponga boat into. It was sizeable but paled in comparison to the 4000 square foot home and casita. The patio ran the length of the home and sat on the bluff, overlooking the ocean. The hot tub stuck out over the rest of the steepest part of the cliff, giving you the desperate sense of comforting exhilaration.

His dad was an early entrepreneur in a small town in Arizona located on the banks of the Colorado River. He had made a few bucks in California as a young man and decided to move the family to Arizona and take a stab at the virgin town. Lake Havasu City had a population of less than 10,000 people and had only been founded for a little over a decade.

Aside from the opportunity and growth that he saw in its potential, he knew it would be a great place to raise his family. He was a visionary. He then moved on to build his vacation home in a foreign country 350 miles away. And what did the cynics say? *You're crazy! In Mexico?* But he wasn't crazy. Not at all. He was just a step ahead of his time. And even if someone felt otherwise, craziness rarely equates to stupidity. In the investment world, we call it "progressive." And a progress it was, first with the old man, and now with his son Gilberto.

When Gilberto was in his twenties, his old man took ill and had a quick passing. Family and friends were devastated, and the community that he helped build, mourned. A pioneer was gone. Since then, Gilberto had formed new bonds with his dad's associates in both Mexico and the United States. He was no longer the little kid running around taking advantage of his good fortune. No, he had quickly matured and was forced to carry on what outsiders never saw—responsibility. He pledged to himself that he would honor his father's memory in everything that he did. So as he inherited the primary role of running the family business, he naturally inherited his father's business sense, which he conducted with the utmost integrity.

I sensed Hatch had come from the same stock or he wouldn't be in the presence of Gilberto. But I could sense that Hatch had another side to him that I just couldn't pinpoint. Maybe a practical joker? All in all, I felt good about the two of them and was quickly assured that what went on in terms of my harboring, would be kept within the walls of the Gilberto home.

I wanted to learn more about Lefty and their relationship. Gilberto told me that Lefty was more like an older brother to him. After he had lost his dad, it was Lefty with whom he found solace and comfort. He never wanted to look at Lefty as a father figure because he couldn't imagine anyone in that role except his father.

Neither Gilberto nor his family ever knew of Lefty's involvement in drugs until he was killed. But I suspect Gilberto knew deep down what Lefty did. There were too many unanswered questions. But his was a progressive mind and he only judged Lefty on how Lefty treated him and his family, not from rumors. What was out in the open was that Lefty donated his time and money to the poor. What was hidden was where he got the money.

I quizzed Gilberto further because a lot of this story sounded too simplistic. Then again, I knew Lefty well enough to know that he fit the mold that all of his family and friends attested to. It wasn't much of a quiz, it was just meant to satisfy my curiosity.

He was an interesting guy and he kept telling me to relax. But I was nervous and couldn't help it. He told me to never go out of the house until I spoke with him directly. It was ironic that he was buddies with the police chief yet undermining the efforts of law enforcement by harboring me in his home. I was jonesing for a joint but didn't want to offend my host.

We decided to eat a lunch of turkey sandwiches on white bread with lots of mayonnaise—an American favorite. I drank a soda and politely excused myself to the garage. A few minutes later, Gilberto came into the garage from the house and told me to make myself at home while he drove Hatch to the airport. I was surprised to discover that Hatch flew. I said goodbye to Hatch and decided that it would be a perfect time to calm my nerves.

As I heard the diesel truck leave the premises, I fired up a couple of roaches that I had within arm's reach of the helm. I practically swallowed one as I felt the heat burn my lips. I knew Lucy would be disappointed and I actually felt guilty. I missed her deeply and admitted openly to myself that I was scared. *How life has changed?* I said to myself. I placed the roach in an old Coke can and drowned the flame in the last sip that I never took. I then rolled a few more joints from the stash that I had in the floor safe for later in the day. I had done better, but most addicts weren't expected to quit overnight, or at least I told myself that. It was an excuse but under the circumstances, justified. You can't always do a 1-80 on a moment's notice.

Lucy had told me that Gilberto liked to have an occasional drink, but I couldn't tell in the short time that I met him if he was into God's herb or not. I didn't want to presume on our newly formed friendship, so I left the issue alone. At this point, just as Lucy said, I just needed to bide my time. She had nothing but praise for Gilberto and told me that he would think of a way to get me out of this mess. As comforting as her words were, I was still skeptical. I was a man who was used to doing things himself and under his own terms. And quite frankly, I was so far out of my realm and control right now, I was really thinking outside of the box.

I kept having these recurring dreams about trust and who could have possibly turned me in. I didn't know if I could trust anyone. I went to the refrigerator and grabbed another bottle of Pacifo beer. I just happened to study the label and didn't realize that the beer was brewed in Mazatlan. *Mazatlan?* And it triggered my mind. *Raul, Mazatlan* I then began to wonder what was really brewing in Mazatlan since my sudden divorce from Raul.

CHAPTER 55

"I simply am not in a position to discuss any bank matters with you whatsoever regardless of who you are," Benito said with a flare of arrogance.

"Well, sir, I guess I will need to speak to the man in charge" the Mexican agent said in his best manner of professionalism.

"Please, call me Benito," he said with sarcasm. "And, by the way, I am the manager of this bank and, like I said, without a legal warrant, I simply cannot satisfy your request. Not only is it against the law, it's against our policy and I will not compromise my own ethical standards because you haven't followed the proper procedures."

The agent picked up his cell phone and called his superior, who was sitting across the street at a curio shop, fending off desperate shop owners for the day's wage.

"Sir, I may need your assistance with this matter."

"I will be right in," the agent's supervisor said as he rang off and walked across the street to the bank.

"Mr. Benito, sir. My supervisor is on his way," the agent said as he stared at the banker.

"Well, young man, I must get back to my business. I see no need to meet with your supervisor. I will tell him the same thing that I told you," he said politely. "So, if you'll excuse me" as he got up from his desk and began to head for the door.

"Sit down, Benito!" the officer's demeanor shifting on a dime.

"Excuse me?"

The agent placed his right hand under his lapel of his sports coat. "You heard me. Now sit down until my supervisor gets here!"

"What are you gonna do, shoot me?" he said as he gritted his teeth in indignation.

The agent stood up and blocked his path. They met eye to eye for a second and then the banker looked down at his feet. The agent was prepared to use force if necessary and would crush him like an ant on the concrete.

"Again, sir, sit down and cooperate and there will be no trouble."

Just then, a receptionist from the bank opened the door and ushered the supervisor in. "What is going on here detective?" the superior said in stern words.

"This gentleman here, who goes by Benito, said that he was not going to wait for you. That unless we have a legal warrant, he will not disclose any information about Mr. Cantino."

"Who ever mentioned Cantino!" Benito yelled. "I would never disclose a client due to the professional privilege I uphold."

"Close the door detective."

"Yes sir," he said as he grabbed the handle and slammed the door into its frame.

There was a brief pause by all as the supervisor moved his lower lip above its opposite and pondered the situation. He slowly walked around the small office, staring blankly ahead, allowing the tension of the moment to climb. He then turned to the banker and bolted directly at him with a sadistic grin.

"Now listen here, you Ivy League wanna-be," he snarled, pulling his 9-mm from inside his jacket and placing it at the banker's head.

"My God! Who in the hell do you think you are?" he began to scream before the pistol was shoved into his mouth.

"I don't have to tell you jack!" the agent said as he pushed the gun deeper into his mouth. "The only person who will be telling anybody anything is you. Got that?" He removed the gun from his mouth.

"Fuck you," said the banker in defiance.

"Benito, my friend. Something tells me that every opportunity that I give you to tell me something and you don't, will result in further damage to your family," he smiled again.

"What have you done to my family?" he cried, bolting from his chair and hysterically trying to cross the barrier of the two agents. The young detective had him incapacitated within seconds and stuffed a handkerchief in his mouth.

"Something told me that you weren't going to play real well, Mr. Banker. So, unfortunately, we had to have a contingency plan in place." The banker just stared at the supervisor in complete disbelief.

"Detective, get the video," the man said as his face projected pure malice.

The detective pulled a small video camera from his pocket and proceeded to press play on the video monitor. Benito became enraged as a firm penis was shown in the corner of the frame with his wife's hair being pulled and a pistol at her head. The audio could clearly pick up the panicked voice along with laughter in the background. Screams of *Why are you doing this?* and *My husband is an honest man* permeated the scene. The last words of *He does not deserve...*were muffled by the perpetrator's membrane.

Benito was going crazy, trying to flail his arms and scream, but his actions were futile. He could do nothing. He was dealing with the devil's children. They had done something to his wife before he was even approached about Jose Cantino by these thugs.

Tears flooded his eyes and he began to nod his head in agreement to talk. The supervisor had the pleasure of removing the handkerchief and whispering, "If you scream you and your family will die," he said while screwing the silencer to the end of his weapon.

"I'll tell you anything, anything, just tell me you didn't harm my wife. I'm begging you."

"When was Cantino here and what was he doing?" the supervisor quickly asked.

"He was here for over a period of three days, depositing and wiring money."

"How much and where?"

The banker spilled his guts. He gave them the amounts, routing number, account number—everything. Hardlow would be proud.

"Now one last thing. Where is the surveillance system for this bank?"

"Uh, right here in my office. It's backed up permanently on my computer at midnight each night."

The detective walked over and emptied the trash from the trashcan in the corner. He then ripped the hard drive from the wall and placed it inside the receptacle. He tied the trash bag over it and picked it up with his left hand.

"Is there any other backup video of the surveillance here?"

"No."

"Are you sure?"

"Yes. There is no other camera or backup."

"Fine. But if you or any employee of this bank says a word about this incident, I'm sure I don't have to tell you what will happen. And in case you don't believe me, you may want to see this."

The small camera was turned back on while the handkerchief was placed back in his mouth. It showed one man holding her down as the other was raping her. It was an awful sight.

"Next time, it won't be this enjoyable." The sick words flowed through the audio speaker. With Benito's wife screaming in the background, the camera slowly panned up to the man's face, revealing the detective's smile. The banker went into another rage before the butt of the supervisor's gun struck his skull, knocking him out.

It was after four and the detective made sure that all of the employees left the bank before they made their final exit. They had left a sloppy trail, but the two agents were scheduled to be back in Mazatlan by the following morning. Hardlow knew that this little border town wouldn't give a crap about some banker's wife getting raped. If it became an issue, he'd trump up some charges on the banker for wire fraud, extortion, conspiracy, aiding and abetting, and whatever else came to mind.

Life was good for Hardlow.

CHAPTER 56

Lucy hadn't slept in two nights. She occupied her time with chores at the orphanage. Her life was embedded with worry and anxiety. She was in love and her lover was on the run. She had spoken to him but was afraid that someway or somehow, the authorities would trace her calls. She knew the Mexicans weren't that sophisticated when it came to tracking criminals. The Americans, however, were a different story.

She organized a meeting at the dining area to let everyone know that she would be taking a short sabbatical. Aside from being surprised, the kids and volunteers looked sad. They asked questions and Lucy avoided them by making general statements and empty innuendos. It was obvious that something was wrong but Lucy wouldn't budge. She quickly thanked everyone for their hard work and cooperation and exited the dining hall to meet privately with Deacon Cruz. It was the same story that she told the children just moments before. She needed some time away and everything was going to be all right.

She officially handed the baton over to the Deacon and prepared a memo to the volunteers and staff. She handed him a stack of cash and reassured him that there would be enough money to sustain the operation and continue the Lord's work. Although she wouldn't lie, she continued to be vague in her reasoning behind her departure. The Deacon knew and opted not to press the issue.

As they said their departing words to each other, Lucy found herself staring at the wet sand—tears dripping off her face. She squinted through her confusing emotions as she turned and paced towards her car. She stopped and suddenly turned with her eyes still focused on the dirt. "Deacon," she spoke softly without eye contact.

"Yes Lucy?"

She slowly stared up at him. "If I don't return..." she paused briefly, "...take care of the children."

"Lucy, my dear," he smiled gently, "we'll see you sooner than you think."

Lucy got into her car and drove out of the orphanage towards the sea. The short journey would seem like forever.

CHAPTER 57

"We got the information from the banker, sir," the young agent said in his broken English.

"Good deal, my friend," Hardlow said in a calm voice. "Give the info to your boss and I want to be briefed at my hotel room at eight o'clock tomorrow morning."

"Consider it done, sir," the agent's voice echoed through the phone.

"Anything else?" Hardlow said indifferently.

There was a brief pause before the subordinate answered.

"Actually, sir," the agent said gently.

"What is it, son?"

"The job of getting the information—" he slowed his speech, "we had to use unconventional means."

"OK?" Hardlow emphasizing his response.

"It was sloppy, sir."

"Sloppy?" Hardlow asked.

"Yes sir. Sloppy."

"So what are you saying, young man?"

"Well, sir, nothing really. It's just that we had some difficulty extracting the information from the banker and I just hope there isn't any fallout."

"Fallout?"

"Yes sir. Fallout."

"Well, I'm sorry to inform you that's really not my problem. Whatever fallout there is, is with you and your agency. I just needed the information."

"Yes sir."

"I would suggest that you speak to your superior and have him call me tomorrow and maybe I can give you some direction as to how to avoid any 'fallout.'"

"I think that sounds good. sir."

"Great, now I've got some work to do and I look forward to hearing from someone at my room by eight o'clock tomorrow morning."

"Yes, sir. Goodnight."

Hardlow placed the phone down without a proper exit. He knew that his next trip would be over to the Caymans where he assumed the banker would be more cooperative. The Caymans were British owned and he wouldn't have to resort to using gangster-type tactics to obtain the information that he was looking for. He would take care of it in the most moral and ethical manner.

If it was his last accomplishment of his career, he was going to nail Cantino to the cross personally and bring down the Robles Cartel. He stood up and walked over to the wet bar. He huddled over a bottle of Johnnie Walker Black and poured a stiff drink into a tall glass. He absorbed the fine scotch into the taste buds on his tongue before swallowing the blended aged liquid.

There's something better yet? He thought. He walked over to the closet and reached inside his sports coat and pulled out a small tin from the breast pocket. He opened the lid where he pulled out a small Ziplock baggie with some hydroponic weed that was confiscated in Culiacan last week. *Two hits of this shit will send me to the moon,* he smiled. He stuffed the end of his one-hit bat and grabbed a book of matches in the ashtray next to the bed. He went into the bathroom and turned on the fan. *This drug war,* he thought to himself as he lit up the weed and inhaled the substance deeply into his lungs. *What a fuckin' joke, he continued to himself,* coughing up the excess smoke filling his lungs. Within seconds, his mind slowly altered into new dimensions.

CHAPTER 58

Lucy told me that my new friend Gilberto would have the answers, but it seemed like days before we talked about anything substantive. My mind was racing in all directions and I was beginning to have withdrawals from my new love. I hadn't heard from her and I was just as worried about her as I assumed she was for me.

Gilberto and I had long talks. I eventually broke the news about my habitual pot use. I think he found it more comical than shocking. *A drug dealer smoking pot? How surprising!*

I spent most of my days hitting my pipe in the garage, thanking myself that I had saved a kilo for future means. I also began to relax my attitude towards alcohol and to enjoy fine vodkas with my new host. He would continually remind me that "this isn't vodka...this is Grey Goose...or Belvadere...." It was generally mixed with cranberry juice, which was also new to me. The combination alone satisfied my palette in a most unusual manner because I couldn't taste the vodka. Needless to say, the days went by quicker. This wasn't cheap Oso Negro, though I probably couldn't tell the difference. But according to Gilberto, it was the morning after that validated the 40 bucks a bottle.

It was the evening that I overindulged in both vodka and weed that seemed to do me in, regardless of the claims that good vodka leaves little damage the next day. I was passed out, but my guard was still up because when the garage lights came on, I bolted upright from my bed and immediately reached for my gun. I wasn't being invaded by the authorities, however, just my friendly host with an epiphany.

"I've got it!" yelled Gilberto.

"What, what?" I quickly put the gun down and tried to collect my senses.

"It came to me in a dream," he said, his smile beaming across the room.

"A dream?" I said with great distress. "A dream..." my words tapered off.

I squinted my eyes as they tried to adjust to the light. I didn't know if I was dreaming still or not. I thought for once I was in the middle of a decent sleep, void of nervousness or worry.

"Jose, it's simple!" he yelled.

"What's simple?" I asked in total disbelief as my mind prepared me for federal agents busting into the garage at any moment.

"Remember how Lefty used to do it?" he asked in excitement.

"Do what, Gilberto?" I began to get irritated at his irrational behavior.

"Jose, Lefty used to use more than one boat. He had three boats with the same registration, all replicating his fishing boat."

This was supposed to be news? I thought to myself. It was three o'clock in the morning and my host was informing me that a major drug trafficker had more than one boat? And this was supposed to be enlightening?

"Gilberto, I don't understand. Maybe we can continue this later this morning when we're both rested. What do you think?" I asked as politely as possible.

"I'm sorry for waking you, Jose. I'm just really excited. Please, just hear me out," he said anxiously.

"Fine, fine, but I'm really...." He interrupted me again.

"Just listen, Jose. When Lefty went out to fish, he would swap boats out on the open sea with his drug contacts. When he came back in, neighbors, authorities, whoever, would think that he was just coming in from another day's fishing!" he said excitedly, his smile radiating as if this was the invention of the Internet.

"He would then put the boat on the trailer and drive it up the ramp into his garage. No one suspected anything!" he reinforced his words with a karate chop through the air.

"Gilberto, I'm still confused. I just need to rest right now."

"I'll let you sleep. We can talk more about it in the morning."

It is morning, I said to myself. *Very early in the morning.*

"Before you go back to bed, though, I want you to think about something."

"OK."

"We can fake your death so that no one knows anything. We can make sure you launch your boat where people are aware of it and fake your death."

I didn't know what the excitement was about, but I played along. Perhaps I was just tired and had other things on my mind. I didn't know.

"Maybe we could go over this a little later this morning, Gilberto. I would love to hear more details—I just can't concentrate right now."

"I understand, Jose," he said as the excitement in his voice subsided.

Gilberto closed the door. I tried to go back to sleep—it was no use. I had Lucy's cell phone, but I couldn't call her. I didn't trust the situation. Who knows who was tracking her every move? In fact, I really didn't trust anyone at this point. I got up and turned on the helm light, then rolled a fresh joint. I smoked the whole thing while I tried to grasp what my host was telling me. Self-medication was my only choice at the moment. I quickly fell back to sleep and it only seemed like minutes before I was startled out of my sleep again with a tap on my chest.

"HOLY SHIT!" I screamed, trying to figure out who was screwing with me again.

"It's me again, buddy," Gilberto said quietly. "There's someone here to see you."

I slowly rose up from my mattress as Gilberto opened up the side door to bring some of the early morning light into the garage. As my eyes adjusted to the sunlight, Lucy was staring at me with tears in her eyes.

CHAPTER 59

It was eight o'clock sharp when the knock came to the door. Hardlow had been up bright and early nursing the effects of a routine hangover. "Oh, it's you again," Hardlow rudely greeted the young field agent. "I was expecting your boss."

"My boss told me to come back and see you, sir."

"Yeah, that's because your boss has tiny **juevos,** as you would say in your native tongue." He quickly shut the door behind the agent.

"So, where is the little whore?" Hardlow asked sharply.

"She left the orphanage yesterday, sir."

"And?"

"We tracked her all the way up the Baja to Mexicali."

"How did she get over to Rocky Point?"

"She changed buses and took the interstate."

"So, is she in a hotel or a private residence?"

"We can only assume a private residence because she was driven from the bus depot over to the Los Conchas subdivision."

"What do you mean 'assume'?"

"Well, sir, I know you don't want to hear this but we lost her at the entrance by the security gate."

Hardlow was visibly fumed. "You lost her at the entrance?"

"Well, sir, you need credentials to get in and our guy wasn't..."

Hardlow cut him off.

"What do you mean you 'lost her at the entrance'? How in the fuck did your flunky lose contact with a volunteer from a frickin' orphanage?" he said, his face turning bright red.

"Sir, the tire on his car blew out," he explained, looking down, too embarrassed to face Hardlow eye to eye. "It would have been too obvious to try and get through without credentials and the blown tire."

"You've got to be kidding me?" he said sarcastically.

"No sir. I wouldn't kid about something like that."

"Let me ask you a question, son. How long have we been tracking Cantino?"

"A long time, sir."

"And we lost him over a goddamned tire!" Hardlow screamed. "Get me that beaner's superior!" he continued his rant, pounding his fist on the table. "I'm gonna have his incompetent balls for breakfast!"

"Yes sir," the agent said, prepared to leave.

"Get the hell out of here and don't come back until you have some answers for me!"

"Yes sir," the agent replied as he quickly left the room.

Jack Hardlow had 30 years in government service and he was not going into retirement with his last project a failure. It wasn't about the drug war. Those ambitions would be left to the rookies. He knew they could never win the drug war by the way he was taught to fight it three decades earlier. It was only a game—but a serious one. A game that paid him handsomely on and off the books. He would work his job until he was 80 if they let him. But they wouldn't. He was obsessed and it showed.

He bypassed room service and went straight to the scotch. He was in a holding pattern with no way to land the plane. Within minutes, there was another knock on the door.

"Sir, I spoke to my superior and I've got a number that you can call. Do you want me to get a secure phone so you can…"

"Get the fuck out of here, son," he blasted, as he ripped the paper from his hands. "You're all worthless! Just a bunch of order takers! All looks and no brains!" He continued to toss the insults at the young agent even after he slammed the door shut.

As the agent trembled down the ritzy hallway of the Mexican resort, he could hear the old man screaming about the hundreds of thousands of dollars sunk into an investigation and something about flat tires. He was looking forward to his flight back home tomorrow where he was being transferred. This was an assignment that he did not need.

CHAPTER 60

The minutes seemed like hours as we squeezed each other tight. Despite the moderate temperature outside, we were both trembling out of nervousness and excitement.

"I'm really scared, Jose. Something just doesn't feel right."

"I know, my dear, I know. I've been hunkered down in this house for days now. No sunlight or ocean. Just darkness. Even during the day, I only see darkness."

"I've wanted to call you, but who knows whose listening?" she said as I could feel the hair on my chest being dampened by her continuous tears.

"We're together now, Lucy. That's all that matters at this moment."

I let up on my embrace of Lucy and sat up, resting my elbows on my knees. I rubbed my eyes and stared at her.

"Gilberto has come up with a plan that I think might work. We haven't discussed the details but it's rather simple," I said.

A smile came to Lucy's face. "What is it?" she asked anxiously.

"Well, basically, we're gonna take my boat out and fake my death somehow on the ocean."

"How do we do that?"

"We're gonna take it out and abandon the boat in the middle of the ocean and try and make it look like a drug deal gone bad. Again, I don't know the details but our host appears to be rather smart."

"That's a great idea, Jose!" she said with excitement.

"I hope so," I said, staring beyond her, unsure of our future plan.

Lucy leaned up and we both got out of the boat. She followed me inside of the house, where we found Gilberto cooking breakfast.

"Good morning, you two."

"Good morning, Gilberto."

"Today, we're going to have an American breakfast."

"It smells wonderful. What are you cooking?" Lucy asked with genuine curiosity.

"Well, we're going to have two eggs over easy, center-cut bacon, hash browns, and wheat toast. And we'll soak it all down with some fresh-squeezed orange juice," he said with a smile.

"I didn't quite realize how hungry I was until I smelled the bacon," said Lucy. "Now that I think of it, I haven't eaten anything since I left the orphanage yesterday."

"Well, I've made plenty, so I expect you two to eat it all."

Within minutes, the three of us were wolfing down our breakfast at the kitchen bar.

"The last time I had an American breakfast like this was in Key West a few years ago, but this is even better." I rudely spoke while I chewed some bacon. *The good ole days,* I thought.

"Well, now is as good as ever to start planning your demise, Jose."

Gilberto laid out the plan very simply. We would stage a crime scene out on the sea with my new Ponga. It would be purposely riddled with evidence of a drug deal gone bad: bullets, blood, dope—you name it. Gilberto would also notify his friend, the Police Chief of Puerto Penasco, that he might have seen Cantino, or someone who resembles the guy, in the wanted posters all over town. We would launch the boat late at night, followed by Gilberto's fishing boat, and stage the scene. Everything for the perfect crime scene would be provided, except a body of course.

Upon finding the floating boat, the feds would chalk it up as another drug deal gone south. I would go into hiding for a few weeks—even months—until everything settled down and efforts to locate my body were abandoned. Lucy and I could then live the rest of our lives together in happiness.

"So, what do you guys think?" he smiled, with his self-thought brilliance. Silence permeated the air. "If you don't think it's a good idea, just tell me," he said defensively.

"Actually, Gilberto, it's a great plan," I said with a smile.

"I knew it!" Gilberto yelled at the top of his lungs. "I hate to trash your boat, Jose, but it's a small price to pay for freedom."

Lucy and I nodded in agreement.

That evening, the three of us staged the crime scene on the boat inside of the garage. Gilberto drew blood from my arm, being a certified emergency medical technician, and began to bloody up the scene. As agreed, my wallet, marijuana, and several thousand dollars in cash were left in the safe of the boat to add credibility to the crime scene. It seemed too easy.

We decided that we'd take the boat out the next night after midnight. I would die in the middle of the Sea of Cortez in approximately 30 hours. It would be flawless and Lucy and I would be on our way to freedom. Or so we thought.

CHAPTER 61

It went down without a hitch. All we had to do from here was wait it out. Gilberto had made contact with the police chief, who confirmed that the authorities had stepped up patrols in and around the Rocky Point area. No one had thought to patrol the waters. The cops simply had gone to every hotel, bar, and restaurant in town looking for me. No luck.

Initially, Gilberto was going to shoot some holes in the boat to make it look like I got gunned down, but we were afraid that they might sink the evidence. So we stuck to the plan and left a few miles off the coast, south of Los Conchas. Surely it would be found.

The three of us were back within an hour, with Lucy and I hiding beneath a tarp while Gilberto pulled the boat out of the water with his utility quad. We made it up the ramp into his garage where the beginning of a long celebration began. Lucy volunteered to cook some fresh shrimp that Gilberto had fetched from the dock along with some Angus beef from the States. She wanted to grill everything, but Gilberto reminded her of the rule that no one leaves the inside of the home, except Gilberto of course. This included the back patio. It wasn't worth getting caught over complacency.

We called it an early evening after a few dinner cocktails. Lucy and I made love all night, cherishing the time that we had together. Although we were both tired, we couldn't seem to sleep. Our fate was hanging in the balance but there was nothing to play except the waiting game. So we occupied our time in the guest bedroom.

The following day, after a light lunch of grilled snapper and cottage cheese, the phone rang. It was a call to Gilberto from the police chief.

"You were right, my friend."

"About what?" Gilberto asked.

"The wanted man, Cantino. They found his boat this morning washed up on the beach north of Los Canchos."

"What about him? Was he in the boat as well?" Gilberto asked deceptively.

"No. The boat was covered in blood. It looks like someone caught up with him."

"But no body, huh Chief?"

"No. I think the only people who found the body were the sharks." The police chief laughed at his own humor.

"One less drug dealer, one better world I guess?" Gilberto said awkwardly.

"Well, I just thought you would like to know. He was definitely here."

"I appreciate the call, Chief."

"Oh, and one more thing, Gilberto," the Chief said in a serious tone.

"Yeah, Chief?"

"The feds want to talk to you. In fact, they're on their way."

Gilberto froze in a panic. He was just an American with little rights. As he stood frozen with the phone in his hand, he was staring at us sitting at the table.

"On their way?"

"Yeah, just routine stuff. Just tell them what you told me and everything will be fine."

"Ah, yes Chief. Sounds good."

Just as he hung up the phone, the doorbell rang. It was them.

CHAPTER 62

Gilberto was in a panic. Harboring a fugitive and an accomplice was not a bright idea especially as the federal police were ringing his door-bell.

"Quick, you guys need to hide! It's the police!" he yelled as quietly as he could.

The wanted couple jumped from the table and ran to the garage door.

"Just a minute while I get my clothes on," he said as he stalled the cops. He began praying that Jose and Lucy were smart enough to find a good place to hide. As he opened up the door, the plain-clothes fed-erales were holding their badges.

"Hello, sir. We are with the Agencia Federal de Investigacion," the man in charge said in broken English.

"How can I help you?" he answered with a nervous smile.

"We've been in contact with the local police and the Chief had mentioned that you called in a tip regarding a possible sighting of this man," he said, unrolling a wanted poster of Jose Cantino.

"Ah, yes, I did, sir. I called the Chief because he's been a family friend for close to 20 years," Gilberto said in confidence.

"Sir, could I get your full name?" the agent asked as pulled a pen out with his notepad.

"The last name is Gilbert—or Gilberto, depending on what coun-try you're in."

"Mr. Gilbert, may we come in?"

"Why, sure," he said, giving them his best poker face.

The two agents followed him into the large house. Immediately, both agents began to walk in separate directions, obviously approving of the living conditions of the rich gringo.

"Sir, may I ask why all of your windows are covered when the weather is so beautiful out?"

Gilberto blushed. "Well, sir, sometimes I get these really bad headaches. And they're like migraines. And they make be sweat real bad. So I have to strip down and of course, avoid the light. I don't have one yet but I can feel one coming on. So, sometimes, what I do, is take this medicine as a preventive…"

"OK, Mr. Gilbert," the agent interrupted suspiciously. "I get what you're saying but let me ask you another question."

"Of course."

"If that were the case, why are all of the lights on in the living area?"

Gilberto had to think fast before he dug the hole any deeper. He walked over to the couch where he sat down.

"Let me be straight with you guys, " he said, trying his best to relax.

"Do you remember that it took me a long to answer the door?"

"Yes, it was just a couple of minutes ago and it did seem like it took forever."

"Well, I like to walk around the house naked. That's it. I was naked. So I had all of the blinds closed. That's all!"

The detectives started laughing.

"OK, my friend, that makes sense. No more personal questions. We understand," as their faces turned red. "Back to the reason that we are here. The Chief, you're friend, said that you called in a possible sighting of Mr. Cantino."

"That I did."

"Can you give us any more details? Times, places, things of this nature."

"Well, I noticed all of the wanted posters around town and I thought I saw a man who looked just like him walking up the beach out front where I was swimming. To be honest, I wasn't a hundred percent sure. But I didn't want to take a chance. You know, I heard he was a very dangerous man." Gilberto did his part to look authentic.

"Well, he used to be dangerous," the agent smirked.

"Did you find him?" Gilberto asked, his voice rising in anxiousness.

"Only his boat, but we presume he's dead because we recovered blood from the vessel."

"So that man that I saw really was him?"

"I'd bet money on it that it was. His boat was found within the vicinity of your house washed up on the beach."

Gilberto was beginning to relax a bit as he played the part. He didn't think these guys suspected anything. But the fact that they were still inside his house made him uneasy.

"Gilberto."

"Yes, sir?"

"How is a man your age able to afford such a beautiful mansion on the beach?"

"It certainly isn't drug money," he joked, his laugh quickly muffled by their lack of response. "I'm sorry, gentlemen, that wasn't funny," he said, kicking himself mentally. "My dad built this home years ago when it was affordable and, unfortunately, he's passed on."

"I see. I'm very sorry to hear about that," the agent said with concern.

"Would you mind showing us your home before we move on?"

"Why, ah, sure," Gilberto said in disbelief. *Anything but the garage.*

He took them room to room, purposely avoiding the garage door. As they admired the interior, he was hoping to God that Lucy and Jose could hear him as he was deliberately raising his voice.

"Well, there she is," Gilberto said, leading them towards the front door. "Would you like to see the casita?" he asked with excitement.

"That would be great," they responded as they followed his lead.

They exited the front and walked towards the guesthouse. The one agent made a comment in Spanish about how he would like to use the casita to take his mistress to. Apparently, they didn't realize that Gilberto understood Spanish. As they came out of the casita, he noticed that they were both staring intently on the garage. But they left it at that.

He thanked the agents as they got back into their car. The further they pulled away, the harder his heart beat. Gilberto ran into the house and opened the entrance to the garage. They were nowhere to be found.

CHAPTER 63

Jack Hardlow was on a plane to Rocky Point not knowing what the hell was going on. The case began to twist into dimensions he could only speculate about. Obviously, Cantino had gone into hiding since he was outed by all of the wanted posters in the area. But a blood-soaked boat with no body?

His contacts in Puertocitos had informed him that Lucy from the orphanage had not returned. She had yet to be spotted in Rocky Point, where they lost her trail. Hardlow's mind was flooded with ulterior thoughts on what really may have happened. He never accepted conventional logic, which made him unique in what he did. There was more to the story and he was going to lift every rock to find the answers.

The Mexicans wanted to immediately close out the case without even matching DNA records with the blood on the boat. But Hardlow wasn't convinced that this was foul play. Further investigation would be in tow upon his arrival.

The flight from Mazatlan took about two hours. Hardlow was met by the local police chief and two agents from the AFI. The greetings were short as he wanted to get on to conducting business. They piled into a black Suburban and hauled away to the local police station. He needed to see the boat himself and collect samples for forensic testing.

Upon their arrival, Hardlow exited the vehicle, where he immediately identified the Ponga boat in a secured, fenced yard.

"What kind of forensic experts do you have here in Rocky Point?"

he asked in his typical cold demeanor.

"Well, our guy says that he'll be able to match the blood."

"That's not what I asked, Chief. Do we have a forensic team here?"

"No sir, we don't," the Chief said weakly.

"We need a forensic team and a ballistic expert down here yester-day!" Hardlow fumed.

"Where would you suggest we find…"

"I'll take care of it, Chief," Hardlow said curtly, as he turned and whispered an insult under his breath.

Hardlow strolled inside where he got on the phone and called the El Paso field office. He quickly arranged for a team of experts to fly down the following morning to review the evidence. When he hung up, he went back outside, where he did a visual inspection again of the boat. Doubting thoughts continued to fill his mind. The scene looked too good, too neat. As if it was staged. It wasn't adding up.

"Has anyone seen the girl?" he asked.

"The girl?" asked the Chief.

"Yeah, that whore from the orphanage who was followed up here from the Baja."

"No, sir. She has not been sighted since we lost her."

"Has anyone checked back with the orphanage today to see if she has returned?"

There was silence from the Chief and his cronies.

"Do you fucking people know what police work is!" Hardlow shouted and kicked the dirt below as he walked away. *Maybe it's time to retire,* he thought.

CHAPTER 64

"Sir, don't hold me to it, but this crime scene appears to be a setup. That's not a conclusive statement, but this, this is too good…," he said, his words tapering off as he shook his head in the negative.

Hardlow's decades of experience were beginning to pay off in this case. It wasn't definite but probable that Cantino's crime scene was manipulated. The amount of blood was consistent with a possible stabbing or gunshot wound, but there was no evidence that either action occurred. There were no particles of skin or clothing or remnants from any one else. That would include the girl or a would-be attacker. There was no gunpowder whatsoever or even any fingerprints. If it was manipulated, it was evident that they never expected an expert homicide team from the United States to review the evidence.

"Chief, you need to find that girl and I mean soon!" Hardlow said as he stared at the boat. "If it's the last thing you do in this world, find that girl."

The Chief nodded his head.

Police work was not about just reviewing evidence. It was intuition. It was making educated guesses based on patterns of criminal behavior. Of course, Cantino wanted the authorities to think he was dead. But with no body, it would never be proven conclusively.

Hardlow had had enough for the day. The experts confirmed his intuitions; it was just a matter of time until Cantino's past caught up with him. He picked up his tri-band phone and called his wife in Texas.

Hardlow's voice turned sweet and loving. He ended the call with "…I love you too, honey" and cleared the call on his phone. He turned towards the Chief.

"Do you guys have a whore house here in Rocky Point?"

The Chief was taken by surprise. "Well, ah, of course, Mr. Hardlow."

"Great. I would like to pay a visit."

"We can arrange something, sir."

"Excellent, Chief. Excellent. Maybe you can arrange a broad to come to my room."

"Yes, sir."

"Great. I'm leaving now and I'll expect some company soon."

"It'll be taken care of," said the Chief. Hardlow walked to his car.

As he picked up the phone, the Chief thought, *What a pig.*

CHAPTER 65

Gilberto couldn't believe they had left. The side door to the garage was unlocked. He opened up the door and walked down the easement between the house and his neighbors'. They were not on the beach—nowhere in sight. *Where did they go?* Gilberto thought.

He paced around the house and found nothing. Gilberto then got gutsy and aggressively yelled, "Are you guys here?" Nothing. His breathing became erratic and he started to get pissed. He was starting back towards the garage door when he suddenly heard some rustling from above. Looking up, he saw Jose pointing his finger at him as if he had a gun.

"You're dead, baby, " he said with a grin resembling a crescent moon.

"What the hell are you doing up there?" Gilberto said in a harsh whisper. "Are you crazy? Get down before we get caught!"

"Relax, Gilberto. I didn't know if they were coming into the garage or not. I heard you talking awfully loud as you were showing them around inside the house. We didn't want to risk it, so we snuck out the side door and climbed up on the roof."

As the two began to descend from the roof, Gilberto's instincts of paranoia kicked in. What if the cops had the house under surveillance? It was doubtful because he didn't think they suspected anything foul. But he was also cognizant of the ramifications of harboring a fugitive in a foreign country.

The two quickly slid into the side entrance of the garage. Lucy was visibly shaking. Gilberto's mind was racing. *What was I doing this for? Just out of loyalty? For Lefty, a dead man? I wasn't looking for the humanitarian of the year award. I must be certifiably crazy for risking my entire future, and life for that matter, out of what—naiveté?*

He made up his mind. Lucy and Jose had to leave—the sooner, the better. He didn't know what the feds knew. However, whatever it was, if anything, could bite him in the ass like a shark on a feeding frenzy. The heart to heart with his two friends had to be done immediately. Loyalty by proxy was quickly evaporating in Gilberto's book.

Lucy and Jose filed into the kitchen from the garage where silence filled the air. A minute or so passed before Gilberto said anything. He began to prepare one last meal for the two while he began to openly discuss the chain of recent events. They both agreed that he was taking on a monumental risk at this point. Lucy acknowledged that she also was completely exposed as an accomplice. The difference was that Gilberto wasn't in love with Jose. His plans demonstrated those feelings.

"You guys need to agree on an exit plan and I mean now. I'm sorry," he said as he stared at the both of them, reinforcing his strong words. "I simply can't risk this. I'm sure you understand."

The two looked at one another and slowly shook their heads up and down in agreement. Several seconds passed until Jose spoke.

"Gilberto, we do understand," he responded, staring at him, puckering his lips with gallant poise. "If it weren't for you, I might be dead or sitting in a Mexican jail." Gilberto remained silent but his eyes continued to fix on Jose's. "I mean that with all sincerity," he said as his eyes began to water.

As emotional as the moment had become, this was a life and death situation. Gilberto wanted to embrace him and give into the emotion, but he couldn't. He had to separate his friendship at this point with the pending business at hand and continue to take the lead.

"Then let's eat and get a move on."

They shared an early dinner of *carnitas* tacos from the pork that had been in the crockpot all day. Garnished with traditional beans and rice, their stomachs were full in no time. Jose finished first and excused himself from the table; he went to the garage to gather his things. Lucy just sat at the table and cried. This ever so powerful woman was wounded in helplessness, as she truly didn't have a plan. Within minutes, Jose was back in the house with a large backpack containing their items.

"I think it's best if you leave after dark in my boat. I've stripped the registration and filed the serial numbers off the boat and engine." Both agreed that it would be the safest escape route from Gilberto's home.

Gilberto found a small six-pack cooler in the garage and stuffed it with ham and provolone sandwiches along with a couple of sodas. He also prepared a bag of snacks that Jose packed inside his bag. The deal had been sealed and Gilberto was done. Lucy would stay back and take a taxi into town, then ride the bus out of town.

They launched the boat in some horrific winds. Gilberto hung on a line to the boat while Jose got the small outboard started. He would head towards Kino Bay, south of Rocky Point. He had three extra tanks of fuel and a case of bottled water. He would meet a contact of Lucy's who would harbor him for a month while things settled down.

Jose was not recognizable from a distance. Lucy had bleached his hair and shaved his mustache. He looked more like a Spaniard than a Mexican. Lucy said her goodbye in waste-deep water while Gilberto just waved. His heart was pounding from anxiety and relief. Loyalty for Lefty had placed him in a very risky situation that he was ready to wash his hands of.

Gilberto walked up the side of the house to the top. Turning, he found Jose and his old fishing boat slowly fading from his eyes. It was the last time that Gilberto ever saw him.

CHAPTER 66

As tired as Gilberto was, he couldn't sleep a wink. Lucy was still an accomplice and his mind was being attacked by worst case scenarios. The first bus to San Felipe didn't leave until seven in the morning, making it a long, restless night. He tried to read a favorite book, *The Old Man and the Sea,* but couldn't focus on it. He finally pulled out of the rack at five and put on some coffee. Lucy was already up and showering. Gilberto was sure she didn't sleep well either.

Gilberto made breakfast. They both picked at their eggs but ate very little. They talked about Lefty and what he would have done. Gilberto reinforced Lucy's commitment that if she were interrogated, she would not to drag his name into it. She agreed.

Lucy called a cab and told them to be at the Los Conchas gate by 6:30 a.m. This would ensure that she wasn't hanging out at the bus station for very long. Gilberto had made arrangements to leave for Arizona for an indefinite period until he felt comfortable enough to return to Mexico. The border was an hour away and he didn't plan on obeying the speed limit. He said his last goodbye to Lucy and made his last minute arrangements of closing down the house and packing up my truck.

Gilberto quickly got out of town; he was as nervous as a defendant in a murder trial. Mexico's judicial system was just the opposite as that of the States. If you were accused, it was up to you to prove your innocence. As a weekend warrior, he had a temporary visa that gave him certain rights. And he wasn't short on cash—money could buy you out of a lot of things in Mexico. But Gilberto's purpose in Mexico was to get away from all of the bullshit, not get in the middle of it. As much as he loved the country, the legal system was stacked against you. *Oh what the hell,* he thought. *Perhaps I'm just being paranoid.*

As Gilberto approached the border entry, the young officer from Customs asked the standard questions—and for whatever reason, decided to fill out a little card that he attached to Gilberto's wiper blade and directed him to the secondary lane. *Great,* he thought. With no explanation at all, he was in secondary with border agents grilling him while they ripped his vehicle apart looking for anything illicit. *Geez, I hope they don't find that orange that I forgot to declare?* It was a bit ridiculous. The only thing he ever smuggled across the border was an occasional extra bottle of booze.

"Well, sir, everything appears to be fine. You're free to go."

"Thank you, officer," he said with great relief.

He started up his truck when his cell phone rang. It was his neighbor in Rocky Point.

"Gilberto!" he said in a panic.

"Antonio, is that you?" he asked, surprised.

"Yeah, it's me."

His heart was temporarily relieved. "What's up?"

"I don't know but there are two black Suburbans and four police cars in front of your house. Are you still inside?" he asked.

"No, I just crossed the border. In fact, I am just leaving customs."

"I don't know, but besides the cops, the entire neighborhood is gathering around rubber necking."

"Did the cops go in?"

"No, it looks like they're ringing the doorbell. There's a couple of them around back on the patio."

"Oh shit" Gilberto said. And it wasn't because of the cops at his house in Rocky Point. There were police lights in his rearview mirror. Customs again. Within a minute or two, he was in the back of a green and white SUV with bracelets around his wrists.

CHAPTER 67

Jack Hardlow was actually enjoying his time with the hair-brained Mexican cops. These guys were so far behind when it came to police work that it was like trying to teach a retard calculus. He couldn't even get upset any longer. If it weren't so serious, it would be comical.

Hardlow and the DEA had all of the latest intelligence at hand, including satellite technology. He was reviewing a satellite video on his laptop from the night before, observing the Los Conchas neighborhood in Rocky Point. He was able to focus in on three people pulling a fishing boat out of a garage with an ATV and launching it on the beach. Only one man was in the boat and the boat never returned. The other two, a man and a woman, were seen driving the ATV back up the side of the home and parking in the garage. There was no activity until after 6:00 the following morning. A female left the home shortly before a man and was headed into town. Shortly thereafter, a man, now identified as Mr. Gilbert, was traced via satellite leaving his home and heading for the border. It was technology at its finest because there was no way to lose him.

It didn't take long for Hardlow to put two and two together. It appeared as if Mr. Gilbert had harbored Mr. Cantino and his girlfriend. If he could only go back a few days, but he couldn't. He hadn't ordered the satellite imagery in time for anything that precise. But the clincher was that the house from where the boat was launched was the same house that Mexican federal agents had visited the day before. It was the same house where the original call to the police chief was made about a potential sighting of Mr. Cantino. And it just so happened to be the house that neighbored the deceased notorious drug dealer, Pancho Serrano…Also known as Lefty.

CHAPTER 68

Hardlow knew that this whole saga with Cantino was a cover-up. He was licking his chops as he waited at the border, ready to move in on Mr. Gilbert. They had just placed him in the back of a border patrol vehicle and he was waiting for the green light.

Hardlow replayed the events in his mind. The trail on the woman had been lost when she entered the Los Conchas subdivision outside of Rocky Point. And the phone call from Gilbert to the Chief was suspicious at best. Hardlow had been smart enough to dial in satellite technology and have an agent from El Paso stake out Mr. Gilbert's house, where he verified a woman leaving the home shortly after 6:00 a.m. and Mr. Gilbert quickly after that. She was followed to the bus station by a federale working with Hardlow's gang. Upon her arrival at the station, surveillance was turned over to the local police department. "Don't lose her this time" said the federale, reinforcing his words. In the interim, Hardlow made a call to customs in Lukeville, Arizona, briefing them on Mr. Gilbert.

Gilbert was in the middle and would be able to provide the necessary answers to Hardlow's questions. He was going to put the squeeze on Gilbert and move in. The investigation was going well since he had arrived. Hardlow was doing his job. He was winning.

As soon as he got a hold of Gilbert, he would break the kid like an egg on the sidewalk. He was obsessed and anxious. Finally, the call came in from customs.

"Sir, Mr. Gilbert is in custody."

"Did you run a NCIC?"

"Affirmative, sir. He's clean."

"We'll be right over."

Hardlow had his DEA driver from the States but was smart enough to bring along one of the Mexican feds as well. He was going to pull a fast one. It may have not been constitutional from an American standpoint, but Hardlow often negotiated the laws to his favor. If you really thought about it, a border is simply a line drawn in the sand.

They flashed their badges to the entry guards and sped up to the green and white SUV detaining Mr. Gilbert. Hardlow flashed his credentials once again and overtook the situation.

"Place him in the back of my vehicle," he said with his famous arrogant flare, shining behind his dark shades.

"Well, sir, I'm not sure who has jurisdictional authority in this particular manner," the custom agent said.

"Shut up, rookie!" Hardlow burst out. "Thirty fucking years in this business and some college-educated punk is going to question my authority?" He placed his hand on the sidearm under his Docker's sport jacket. The young man immediately stepped back with caution as he felt the indirect threat.

Gilbert was placed in the back of Hardlow's SUV with his handcuffs intact. The Mexican agent driving turned the vehicle around and crossed back over the border into Sonoita, Mexico. He fired off an explanation in Spanish and they were on their way back to Rocky Point. The first few minutes were silent. Hardlow purposely said nothing to allow the young man to absorb some more fear. The atmosphere was awkward at best.

Hardlow then turned his head back from the front seat of the SUV and stared Mr. Gilbert down through his dark Ray Ban aviation shades.

"You've got some explaining to do young man."

"Sir, I don't know what is going on here. And I don't know why you are taking me back to Mexico. Are you guys real cops? Who are you?"

"Let's just cut to the chase, Mr. Gilbert" he said with a slight grin on his face. "We have evidence via the latest satellite technology that this man," he pulled a photo from his tweed jacket, "Jose Cantino, was harbored in your home at Los Conchas along with this woman," he pulled out the second photo of Lucy.

Dead silence ensued for several seconds before Gilbert spoke up. "I would like to see my attorney," Gilberto said with his fakest indifference.

"What attorney, asshole? What, do you think we're in the good 'ole USA right now? Didn't your daddy ever teach you the difference between the two countries and their respective laws?"

"You still didn't tell me who you are."

"My name is Jack P. Hardlow and I'm a special agent with the United States Drug Enforcement Administration. And you my friend are under arrest!"

"For what?" Gilberto screamed.

"For harboring an international fugitive. Aiding and abetting; the importation and distribution of drugs; and whatever else I feel like charging you with when I get around to it!"

Gilberto said nothing, knowing that he was in hot water. Hardlow turned back around and stared out the front window. The Mexican agent who was driving the car was oblivious to the situation because he either didn't understand much English or he was used to this kind of "justice." But the special agent in the back, sitting next to Mr. Gilbert, was obviously nervous about the situation.

"Agent Hardlow. You must afford me an attorney. At least a phone call."

"You're on foreign soil, son. I'll decide if and when you can get an attorney or a phone call. Right now, you'll be lucky to get a meal when I stuff you in that Mexican shit hole they call a jail," Hardlow grinned.

"You are violating your oath as a sworn peace officer. You work for the United States government, not North Korea's!" he yelled into deaf ears.

Hardlow was on the verge of retirement. He would nail Cantino and those involved if it was the last thing he did on this earth. He was obsessed over the case. These people were sloppy. They weren't smart.

As they made their way to the outskirts of town, silence again reared its head. Mr. Frederick Farrell Gilbert's heart was pounding as tears began to roll down his face. What had he gotten himself into?

CHAPTER 69

Little did Lucy know that she was being followed. The authorities picked up her trail that morning as soon as she left Gilberto's home, heading over to the bus station in a taxi. A local detective from the Puerto Penasco Police Department was on the old, dilapidated bus from Rocky Point, traveling to San Felipe. He would be relieved by an undercover when they arrived in Mexicali for the bus transfer.

It was apparent that Lucy was anxious as she tried to read a local newspaper, the *Rocky Point Times*. She had put the paper down more than once in an attempt to sleep, but to no avail. The slightest bump would rattle her awake. When she tried to eat, she would merely nibble while others around her stared at her snack in hand, wishing they could be nibbling on her granola bars or string cheese. The detective didn't know if this was because Cantino was missing and possibly dead, or if she was involved in his disappearance. It was a fifty-fifty scenario, but he didn't care. He just wanted to get back to Rocky Point where he could make some extra cash busting college kids smoking dope. He had a living to make and this boring assignment was interfering with that ability.

San Felipe is less than 100 miles across the Sea of Cortez from Rocky Point. But to travel by bus, it's a trip from hell. You have to go north to the border, then across to Mexicali, then back south again. It was an all-day affair, stopping in every little town dropping off or picking up, and generally boring the crap out of every passenger aboard. With this in hand, the detective decided that it wouldn't hurt to catch a few winks of sleep. And that's where his mistake began.

Lucy was nervously applying makeup when she noticed the middle-aged man staring at her constantly. Her intuition right there and then was that the man did not really belong on the bus for any other reason than to follow her. On their arrival in San Luis, a good-sized town bordering the southwest corner of Arizona, the detective was snoring loudly and never heard the bus come to a stop. It was there that Lucy jumped ship and disappeared into a busy shopping district, eventually finding a small table in the corner of a Chinese restaurant.

Aside from being a border town, San Luis was only 30 miles from Yuma, Arizona. Yuma catered to tens of thousands of snowbirds every season, who in turn looked to San Luis for cheap pharmaceuticals, shopping, and various forms of entertainment. She decided to check into a hotel and leave the trail cold for a while. If she was being followed, she couldn't go back to the orphanage just yet. She had to play it safe and decided San Luis was as good of a place as any. Also, she couldn't go back to the bus station because that would be the first place staked out.

The room was clean and adequate. She was thankful that the shower provided hot water. She showered in the water for over 20 minutes, cleansing her body and clearing her mind. The water became cold before she shut it off. She thought to find a day spa somewhere and have a day to herself. *Maybe a pedicure and a massage? Maybe a cocktail and a bite to eat?* She called for a cab and would make the appointment on the spot. For all she knew, she had lost whoever was following her.

CHAPTER 70

By the time the agent woke up, the bus and passengers had crossed over the Rio Colorado and were well on their way to Mexicali. The agent panicked because he couldn't see Lucy. *Maybe she's in the restroom,* he thought. He jumped up and climbed over the fat lady who was blocking him in from his window seat. She was asleep and snoring like a lumberjack, and never woke up despite his exit from the row.

He ran to the back of the bus and checked the bathroom door. It was vacant and unflushed. He almost heaved when his senses came into contact with the odor. He began to panic. He briskly approached the driver, checking each seat on the way. She was gone.

"Stop the bus," the undercover cop ordered, pulling out his badge. "Turn this bus around," he shouted to the driver in Spanish. Many of the passengers began to rubberneck above their seats to find out what all of the commotion was about.

"Sir, I just can't stop a bus! For what reason?" the driver pleaded.

The officer pulled his gun. "Did you hear me? Turn this bus around and take me back to San Luis!"

There was a loud hush from the observers behind. The driver turned the bus around and headed back to San Luis. What took minutes felt like hours. San Luis wasn't exactly a small place and the detective was not familiar with the town.

"Take me to the last stop that you made," he said.

"That would be the bus station, sir. Just don't hurt us, please!" the driver said calmly.

"I'm a cop. Why would I hurt you?"

"Well, sir, because you have your revolver pointed at me."

The cop was so agitated that he didn't realize that he was pointing his gun at the driver. He eased the pistol back into his holster and stood next to the exit way, refusing to face the passengers. He was nervous and not accustomed to real police work. He should have been a criminal. All he knew how to do was swindle money from foreigners. He really had no clue as to his sworn responsibilities. He had lost the woman that he was supposed to be following. He would pay, and pay heavily. His next phone call would be to his boss, who answered to the American bigwig, Hardlow. This would not be fun.

CHAPTER 71

The trip from Rocky Point was smooth sailing. My contact was there on time to pick me up at an unknown place. I had a portable GPS system and all I knew was that it was south of Rocky Point and north of Guaymus. His name was unknown and I liked it that way. The less I knew at this point, the better I was off.

I knew him to be a fisherman but I'm sure he was another player in the infamous drug trade that Lucy knew so well. Initially, he was quiet and reserved. The time passed slowly and my body was sore with anxiety.

I was waiting for Lucy to call so I had something to look forward to. I wanted to hear more news about my "accident." But the call hadn't come yet. I didn't know if she was OK or if they arrested her. For the first time since my early childhood, I felt completely lost. I was not in control and I knew I was a weak man.

I had vowed not to get back into the dope, but I asked my companion, who gladly scored me a solid ounce. I spent the next few days stoned and reading anything that I could get my hands on. I wanted to get out of this shack and go hit the town—to explore my surroundings—but it was too risky. I would have to bide my time in the few luxuries that I had at my disposal.

It took some time to get to know my companion. He was an apparent aficionado of tequila because he spent most of his days consuming it. However, the worm at the bottom of the bottle told me that perhaps he was a man of simple descent. Not exactly a high roller. In fact, closer to a scrote.

My curiosity got the best of me and I decided to partake in a session one evening. It was not good, nor healthy, but it was something to do. The taste replicated the smell of turpentine—something that my body could not handle. I carried on like a good friend anyway. After several shots and many blurred memories, I puked on the living room floor. Instead of being appalled, my companion filled with laughter as he called me a virgin and rambled on about by immaturity. It was OK with me because I felt much better after my body rejected the deadly liquid. In fact, I wasn't even hung over the next day. My body didn't even give it time to absorb before it exited back out of my esophagus.

I was always an early riser and the next day was no exception. My companion had passed out where my mind last remembered him—in a wicker chair on the clay patio. I was awoken by the red light blinking on my guest's Tel Cel phone next to me and its obnoxious ring.

"*Bueno,*" I said.

"Jose, speak English. How are you?" Lucy asked with desperation.

"My God, Lucy, are you OK?" I asked.

"Yes, I'm fine. I'm not at the orphanage because I think that I was being followed."

"What do you mean? Why wouldn't they have just arrested you?"

"I'm not sure yet. I'll have to explain later, but listen."

"I'm here."

"We need to lay low for a couple of weeks until the heat cools off."

"I understand, but what are you going to do?"

"I don't know, Jose."

"Do you want to come here?"

"No. It's too risky. I'll probably just stay in San Luis until I can come up with another plan. Just be careful and don't take any risks. I've got to go because my minutes are about to run low. I...." The phone went dead.

Lucy opted to stay in San Luis for another week relaxing at the day spa and spending her nights worrying about her future and her children at the orphanage. She pondered her life and the events of her life that led her to where she was today. She was a criminal, yes. But she justified it by neutralizing her actions with goodness, helping the poor and indigent. It was her true love in life. Everything else came in a distant second.

She thought a lot about Lefty and wondered if he ever made it up to meet his maker or if he was roasting in Hell. He too was a bad person who did many great things. The irony tore at her every night as she closed her eyes and prayed to God. She was devout in her faith and realistic when it came to feeding a young child.

She knew that life was unfair and that the system was corrupt. But for now, she was the surgeon who performed the quadruple bypass on the system for many years now and had gotten away with it. The local cops didn't go near her because of her humanitarian deeds. Yet they all knew the money was dirty. Some things were best unquestioned, at least for the local authorities.

Jack Hardlow felt differently.

CHAPTER 72

After two days of being unconscious, Benito Calderon finally arrived at a Mexicali hospital. He didn't know where he was, but he could feel the excruciating pain in his head. He had suffered a massive concussion and the physicians had initially rendered him comatose.

As he opened his eyes, a young nurse was wiping his forehead with a cool, damp cloth. "Mr. Calderon," she said quietly. "Can you hear me?" Her tone was barely audible tone.

"Yes, yes. Where am I?" he asked in a daze.

"You are in the hospital here in Mexicali. You have suffered a head injury," she said with gentle bed manners.

"How did I get here?"

"By ambulance from San Felipe."

It was slowly coming back to him. The two thugs who had pressured him for private information had posed as police officers. They were threatening him about his new client, one of Lucy's friends. And then it hit him like a rock. Benito Calderon sprung from his bed.

"My wife!" he screamed. "Where is she?"

"Calm down, Mr. Calderon," the nurse said as she used her large frame to push him back onto his hospital bed.

"You don't understand!" he yelled as he ripped his IV from his hand and tried to resist her restraint.

"Those men—those men raped my wife! I saw it on videotape!" he raged on with tears sprinkling from his eyes. The head nurse came running in and immediately added a sedative to the patient's IV.

"That won't work—he's ripped it from his hand!" the nurse yelled as she tried to restrain Mr. Calderon.

"I will kill those bastards!" he screamed on.

The head nurse ran from the room and came fumbling back with a large syringe and vial. She drew the sedative quickly and stabbed it into Mr. Calderon's arm. His energy quickly faded while they held the patient down.

"Yes, he remembers about his wife," the head nurse said as she slowly shook her head.

As Mr. Calderon recovered in the hospital, his wife sat at home traumatized. Not only was her husband almost beaten to death, she had been raped by two goons claiming to be detectives. They forced her to do things that God simply wouldn't forgive. She could have resisted more, but she eventually lost strength and gave in. She was to blame as well or at least that's how she felt.

Mrs. Calderon had been a strict Catholic her entire life and did not know how to handle the rape in her conversation with God. Technically, she felt that she had cheated on him. She had never been with another man and now two men had consummated a major sin with her. How would Benito feel—or the church for that matter?

She had spent the first two days under physical and psychiatric evaluation, but that didn't help at all. She even felt that her efforts at prayer were going unanswered. Her children were in care of her sister and they had no idea that their mother had been beaten and raped and their father could possibly die. What had she done to deserve this? It just didn't make any sense.

CHAPTER 73

The San Felipe Police Chief drove to Mexicali. He would be meeting with the Director of Internal Affairs. Unlike many of his trips to Mexicali, he was not being summoned from San Felipe, but rather proactive—to get some answers.

"Sir, I drove here this morning to find out about the brutal beating of our local banker, Benito Calderon. He is a pillar of our community in San Felipe and I need to get answers to some questions. We must ensure that justice will be served!" the San Felipe Chief pleaded.

"What exactly happened, now?"

"Well, our local banker was beaten almost to death at his office shortly after the bank closed and his wife was raped earlier that day by two men." He paused, trying to grasp his thoughts coherently. "They did this to get information about the fugitive, Jose Cantino." The Chief wiped his head nervously.

"I'm not sure what you would like me to do about it."

"Well, sir, we're trying to decipher if the information being requested was sought by the police or perhaps a competing drug gang."

"Well, what's your intuition?"

"I don't know, sir. I simply can't put a finger on it. I know this Cantino was wanted by both the U.S. and us, but who would rape a banker's wife just to squeeze some information out of him?"

"Well, Chief. I think you just answered your own question. Perhaps it was a fellow drug gang?"

"Sir?" the Chief asked smugly as he stared at the desk in front of the officer.

"Yes, Chief?"

"Could it have been one of us?"

"I don't see how. But why don't you give it a rest for a few days and we'll see how things come together."

"OK."

They shook hands and the Chief walked out of the Mexicali Police Department feeling about as relieved as a single pane window during a hurricane. What did it matter anyway? It was Mexico, wasn't it? It was just that corrupt system that Mexico was known for, wasn't it? It was just a person's life, wasn't it? The Chief was pissed and knew he couldn't do anything about it. If he wasn't careful, his life could be in danger as well. He smelled the rat, but decided to leave the trap behind. When he got back to San Felipe, he would send out a press release stating that a rival gang was responsible for the beatings and rape. It was business as usual.

CHAPTER 74

The Cayman Islands are located in the western Caribbean and is one of the world's largest financial centers. It's a haven for corporations and individuals alike, looking to avoid Uncle Sam and his evil, taxing ways. It's also a financial hub for terrorists, drug dealers, organized crime, and the like.

When Jose Cantino first became affiliated with the banking system on Grand Cayman, there were virtually no rules. His private banker asked no questions as to how he acquired his money, just how he could be of service to him in regards to his money. It was simple and plain cut. There were no questions asked—just the feeling of privacy and security.

Unfortunately, that changed when the U.S. Treasury enacted a bureau called FinCen, or Financial Crimes Enforcement Network. Financial intelligence took on a whole new meaning in the twenty-first century, especially after the 9/11 attacks on the World Trade Center and Pentagon. Because the Caymans' largest trading partner is the United States, it reasoned that there would be cooperation between the over 600 private banks nestled offshore, specifically, the Treasury Department and their ever-trusted kin, the Internal Revenue Service.

Since 9/11, it was paramount under President Bush that the various government agencies no longer compete, but cooperate in the interest of national security. A whole new feeling of brotherhood came about as agencies began to share information with one another, for the greater good of the country. It was no longer about power and ego trips, it was a part of the nation uniting against terrorism and holding the terrorists accountable.

Privacy laws took a back seat to "Homeland Security." Unauthorized wiretaps and the newly enacted "Patriot Act" were prime examples of "safety over freedom."

In the Caymans, much of the attitude was absorbed by the banking industry as well. Their so-called privacy policies that were guaranteed to their clients was often compromised for the betterment of humankind. The prevailing thought was that if they had to throw a criminal under the bus once in a while it was the exception, not the rule. It really didn't affect the Average Joe.

So it was a great day for Jack Hardlow when he landed in a government-owned jet in Grand Cayman for the sole purpose of meeting with a private banker who held over one million dollars of Jose Cantino's money. The banker, with leverage from his superiors, was to cooperate with the DEA on this one. Although Cantino was not a citizen of the United States, he had valid murder warrants from that country and they were expected to cooperate. And cooperate they did. Within minutes of meeting with Hardlow, Jose Cantino's funds were frozen and no longer accessible.

Hardlow thanked his counterparts and decided on a quick vacation on Seven Mile Beach. Why waste a flight to the Caymans if you weren't going to live it up for a few days, right? All paid for, of course, by the U.S. taxpayers. Jack Hardlow was really going to miss work when he retired.

CHAPTER 75

I can't keep living like this. I have done nothing wrong in my mind. I am not a criminal. At least they cannot prove that I am a criminal. Or can they? I don't think so. My life is so void without my children. What have I done to the children? They need their mother. Their lives are in jeopardy, all because of my selfish ways.

It is really love, or am I just desperately looking for an excuse? I really do love him, don't I? Is it possible to fall in love with a man who has done so many bad things in his past? I am devout, but can people turn on a dime? I wonder what he is doing now? I wonder if he's still with my contact? Does he miss me? I miss him, but I don't know if I can ever see him again. Can I? At least just one more time? Only fate will tell, I guess.

The ironic life that I have chosen. A twisted version of Robin Hood.

Lucy finally fell asleep trying to answer all of the questions in her head. She had to get back to the orphanage and face the music. She simply had no choice. The authorities had nothing on her except guilt by association. The children needed her and the orphanage was probably low on funds. She was no longer going to lay low, holed up in a hotel room in San Luis. She would catch a bus at the crack of dawn and pray that she got there safely to see her children. She wasn't looking forward to the bus trip. It would be treacherous both physically and mentally. She would make it though. She had no choice.

CHAPTER 76

"What do you mean you can't authorize the transaction?" I yelled into the cell phone.

"I am sorry, Mr. Cantino, your personal banker no longer works here and there is a problem with the account. I am your new banker, Jonathan Cannon, and you must come here in person to straighten this out." The English accent resonated through the phone.

"I'm in Mexico. I can't just get on a plane and fly over there. Please, Mr. Cannon. I need access to my money."

"Sir, I would be happy to get my superior if you could hold on for a minute or so..."

"No, I know what's up. You and your boss can go fuck each other!" I hung up the phone. *How do I even know that guy was a real banker and not some dick posing as a banker?* I thought to myself. *Betcha he and who knows who else was trying to get a trace.*

I didn't even know where in Mexico I was. What I did know was that I was in trouble. Somewhere, somehow, I had been exposed—how or why—who knew? I had done many things wrong in my life, but now that I had taken a leap to the other side, my luck had not only run out, but danger had set in. It was as if God didn't want me or something. Everything that I had worked for my entire life was being compromised. I was no different than a prisoner on death row. *Dead man walking.*

Two grand in American cash and a half an ounce of weed were my only possessions. I had given Lucy the rest of my money for the orphanage. I had some money in a Banomex account in Mazatlan, but didn't have the balls to try and access it. If his money was tied up in the Caymans, surely the authorities had the information on the alias I used to open the account in Mexico. It looked as if my banker had thrown me under the bus. It was a no-win situation. Something had to break. I needed to think. Plan carefully. Plot a course.

I lit up a joint to calm my nerves. *But I mustn't lose faith. I'm a believer. Perhaps God is punishing me for my past and testing me to see if I remain true.*

I vowed not to sway any further with the exception of the weed. I had to do it for Lucy and God. I had to take the initiative and get myself out the same way I hadn't gotten myself in—with my own two feet and no one else.

I smoked three joints before I was able to sleep for a while. I had been so absorbed with the transformation of my life that I had forgotten where I came from. My roots were in Tampico. The man who gave me a lift up early in life was the only other man who could help me. It was time to return to Tampico—visit my mentor and surrogate father, Mr. Robles. He was the one man I could trust. Why? Because he didn't kill me when he had enough justification to do so. I had to make the call and get back so I could lie low until things cooled off.

CHAPTER 77

To her own surprise, the ride home for Lucy was uneventful. Deacon Cruz was waiting as the bus pulled into the circle with the famous Arches of San Felipe, Los Arcos. It was a simple structure but was San Felipe's official landmark. The Deacon appeared to be much happier than Lucy. It was evident that she had a lot on her mind.

"It's so good to see you, Lucy," he said as his smile brightened up the mood. Lucy said nothing but managed a slight grin on her face as she placed her bag in the back seat and got into the vehicle.

"So, how was the trip?" the Deacon asked.

"It was OK, I guess."

Those were the last words spoken until the entrance of the orphanage. The ride, as usual, was long and bumpy, which did nothing to improve Lucy's mood. The Deacon could sense that she was not in one of her typical, cheerful moods. As they pulled into the Mission, Lucy pointed in the direction that she wanted to go. The Deacon drove the car around the back of the orphanage where the housing quarters for the staff were easily accessible and parked near Lucy's sliding back door.

"Lucy, I know you have a lot on your mind, but we should talk," he said in a dryer tone than normal.

"About what?" she said defiantly as she stared straight ahead through her dark sunglasses.

"Well, there's been some foreign activity on the premises. I mean, we've had detectives from the United States and Mexico City snooping around the property and asking a lot of questions."

"Questions like what?" she asked.

"Like, who runs the orphanage? Does she live on site? Where is she now? Obvious questions that everyone in this region knows," he said.

Lucy braced herself as her anxiety sharpened. Somebody knew something and her mind raced for suspects. Conspiratorial thoughts raced through her mind as she began to mentally question the loyalty of her staff and friends.

"So, did you talk to these men, Deacon?" she asked suspiciously.

"Not really. I just pretended that everything was status quo and that you would be back eventually. I didn't have any information to give them. I just told them that you were out of town and that I didn't know where you went."

Silence permeated the air for what felt like minutes. Neither was quick to speak or react. Lucy slowly opened the car door and departed from the car. She began to shut the door and suddenly stopped. She bent down and placed her head in the car doorway.

"Is that all that I need to know or is there more?"

"That's it, Lucy. If there was more, I would have told you."

"OK." She slammed the car door shut, put her bag over her shoulder, and entered the back door to her quarters. Closing the slider behind her, Lucy isolated herself for the rest of the evening. The Deacon was confused because she would have normally rushed through the front entrance to greet her children and her staff. But he reserved judgment on the matter. He was a man of the cloth and the Lord would look after him regardless of the circumstances. He got out of the car and went to his own quarters where he prayed for the world. Especially Lucy.

CHAPTER 78

Gilberto was stuck in the local jail in Rocky Point and Hardlow decided early on that he was going to have fun with the little prick. Immediately, he was served stale bread and tap water. A gringo's worst nightmare. He was not afforded an attorney or a phone call, all at Hardlow's doing.

The Chief wanted to step in and talk with his friend but was discouraged by the two younger agents guarding his cell. It was a real dilemma because the Chief had known Gilberto since he was coming to Rocky Point as a boy with his family. *How could this kid be involved?* the Chief kept asking himself.

Hardlow had gone back to his hotel for a couple of hours where he had a quick nap. He wanted to be rested for the interrogation. Hardlow took his time, knowing that every minute that went by created more terror and panic in the kid's mind. Psychology was always more deadly than physical force if the perpetrator knew his business. Hardlow knew his business.

He entered the jail at 4:30 p.m., where he made his presence known to those around him. He called the young agents over who were guarding the cell to get an update. "Speak up, young man, I can't hear what the hell you're saying!" as Hardlow's voice echoed through the chamber.

"Sir, there's been no change in the status of Mr. Gilbert."

"I guess we'll have to fix that. Have him placed in general population."

"General population, sir?" said the young agent, repeating Hardlow's request, dumfounded.

"Yeah. I want him in the same cell as all the drunks and drug addicts. In fact, if you got any queers in there, tell them Gilberto's nickname is 'banana man.' Let him know what life is going to be in a Mexican jail!" Hardlow laughed as he chomped on an unlit cigar.

Just as Gilberto's anxiety began to subside, the two young suits rushed into his cell and yanked him from his bunk. "Get your personals and let's go!"

"What's happening now?" Gilberto yelled defensively.

"We're just following orders. Now get your personals."

"I don't have any personals!"

The two agents grabbed him forcefully by each arm and dragged him from his cell.

"What the hell's wrong with you people? You're treating me like an animal!" he said belligerently.

"I would suggest that you just cooperate so you can be spared a life sentence in a Mexican prison."

"But I haven't done anything!" he yelled.

As they were dragging Gilberto down the corridor towards the main cell that held the daily vermin, he came face to face with Jack Hardlow. He could smell the alcohol on Hardlow's breath and a faint smell of marijuana. The two stared at one another for what seemed like eternity.

"You could have spared yourself the agony of this, but maybe you'll be ready to talk once you've lived with some of the animals down the hall," Hardlow smiled.

How bad could it be? Gilberto thought. *It's not a prison, just a small-time jail with petty thieves and drunks, right?*

His assumption was off base. The first thing the guards did was throw him in a cell where he tripped and fell on an old Mexican man covered in his own urine and vomit. Immediately, Gilberto was puking in the corner of the cell himself from the repulsive incident. It was disgusting. Those inmates who weren't passed out themselves began laughing at the gringo who couldn't handle a little puke and piss. Hardlow watched between the bars with an expression of pleasure written all over his face.

"Don't worry about being lonely tonight Mr. Gilbert," Hardlow spoke calmly through the bars. "I'll make sure you have a couple of friends to share an intimate evening with you."

Gilberto looked up at Hardlow through tear-soaked eyes and thought that he was staring at the devil. He was, in fact.

"No decent American in law enforcement would treat another man like this. You are here to enforce the law, not break it Hardlow. Where is my due process? Every one has the right to innocence before guilt!"

"Yeah," Hardlow said as he winked, smiled, and walked away.

Gilberto shook it off and noticed some of the inmates staring at him. One guy was laughing at him as he tried to wipe the vomit from his clothes. "Excuse me, sir," Gilberto asked boldly. "Do you understand English?"

"Go fuck yourself, *Americon!*" the man said with disdain.

Gilberto smiled as he slowly turned, staring each of them down before he landed his eyes on the wise ass. "Well, perhaps you understand this," he said charging the man and ramming his fist in the man's face. He snapped the guy's tooth and busted his nose open. The man screamed as blood poured out. Gilberto turned towards the man behind him, who stood up in reaction to the violence, and Gilberto kicked him in the groin. His screams were added to the American's first victim. He continued his assault on everyone until the guards were able to get in and restrain him, removing him from the general population.

The Chief made the call to put him in isolation, which was Gilberto's plan in the first place. All of the Americans had left to get a bite to eat. A medic was brought in to tend to the victims along with the aggressor. At this point, the Chief quickly decided that no one was taking over his jail. Not even a senior DEA agent from the United States.

CHAPTER 79

It was three o'clock in the morning and the Sonoran desert got very cold at this time of year. I was freezing as I made my way heading south from Kino Bay into Guaymus. Senor Robles had arranged for a private plane to pick me up at a discreet hanger at the Guaymus International Airport. There were no questions asked from the airport security guards, armed with AK-47s. I had forgotten how powerful Robles was and the culture of corruption that entangled my struggling country.

The plane appeared to have the capacity of carrying six people, but all of the seats in the back had been removed. Obviously, the plane was used for more than just transporting passengers.

I was briefly greeted by the pilot who said very little as we took off into the darkness. The airport was dead and I noticed the pilot did not radio anyone at the tower. I was scared but appreciated the fact that Robles had stuck his head out once again to save his protégé.

As worried as I was, the flight was uneventful. We had stopped for fuel once about two thirds into the trip; but I didn't ask where we were. While we were refueling, the pilot left the plane to take a leak. I had to go but was too afraid to take the risk. I would hold it.

He brought back a rather bad breakfast burrito consisting of a stale tortilla and cold eggs. But with the hot coffee, it actually hit the spot. We made it into Tampico by daybreak. We were ushered away in a compact car with tinted windows. The royal treatment, I guess.

I was briefly informed that Robles had sold his home up on top of the hill and had moved to an area outside of town. I knew Robles to be a respected businessman in Tampico, but it was generally known that his businesses were fronts for his massive drug operation. Consequently, he never lived in one place very long.

His new hideaway was several miles south of Tampico in a modest home atop a hill. I was barely spoken to and didn't dare ask any questions. My driver was new—at least I had never met him. I had the feeling that many of my old colleagues had moved on. Again, it appeared that no one stayed in one place for very long.

The small car pulled into a gated area at the base of the hill. A security guard opened the gate with no questions asked. The drive up the hill was rather long as the small car negotiated its way up the narrow road. At the top of the hill stood several armed guards with automatic weapons that ran parallel to their frames. All had dark sunglasses, standing rigid and on edge. I felt out of my element, as if I were a stranger not knowing what to expect. In fact, I recognized no one. I was a stranger except to the Old Man himself.

The guards waved us through and we pulled into the large garage area. The door behind us immediately closed. A sense of claustrophobia ran through my body. The driver turned around and told me to sit still while he made a few adjustments. My heart began to beat faster. I then heard a loud jerk, as if someone was trying to put a car into drive without starting the engine. More thoughts of paranoia ran through my mind as if Robles was trying to get even for some misdeed of the past. I was clean, but maybe this was his way of getting back at me—maybe he was going to torture or murder me. I took a deep breath and tried to relax as best as I could under the circumstances.

The car began to descend into the ground. It was an eerie feeling, but one I understood all too well. My life was a mixture of eerie feelings. It was evident that Mr. Robles had taken many precautions when deciding to relocate. *Maybe he was on the run,* I thought.

By the time we stopped descending, I guessed we were probably three to four floors down. Another garage door then opened into a massive tunnel. The driver placed the car in drive and we drove for several hundred yards. I broke out into a serious sweat. I opened my window and tried to inhale the air, but it was damp and stale. I tried to think of sunny skies on the Gulf guiding rich gringos to their fishing paradise. It didn't work. I puked out the window and left a surprise for my driver friend on the side of the car. But I felt better. Much better.

We had finally reached our destination. The driver said nothing about my episode as if he had witnessed this behavior before. He exited the driver side and opened up the back door. My only belongings were my backpack, but he firmly grabbed it from my possession. He pointed out the direction to walk and followed me from a modest distance. He obviously didn't trust me and was trained in proper security measures.

We reached what looked like an opening to an elevator. My driver asked me to stand to the side as he punched in a code into the keypad. The doors opened and we proceeded down a tunnel. The doors themselves were something out of *Star Trek,* but I played along as if it was old school theatrics. The scenery changed quite drastically once we began to walk through the tunnel. It looked as if it were a mine, with wooden supports every few feet and all. I began to count my steps. But I lost count. It was too bizarre. We finally reached a steel door that was secured. Again, my driver punched in a code and it opened. Incandescence lights took me by surprise. My eyes quickly adjusted to the bright light while I was met by a blonde, European-looking woman in her mid-forties.

"Mr. Cantino," she said as she me an inviting smile, "please have a seat. Mr. Robles will be with you momentarily."

"Thank you," I replied, admiring her beauty.

After a couple of minutes, a false door opened to my surprise behind the receptionist's desk. "Mr. Cantino, please follow me," she said as she got up from her chair. I followed her into the room where she sat me down in a chair, facing the backside of a man staring at a computer scene.

"So, Jose, how has life been treating you?" he said without turning around to look at me. I was a bit relieved because I was beginning to think that Robles wasn't around because I recognized no one. And Robles never had light hair like the man in front of me. But it was Robles—you never forget a voice like that.

"Well, sir, not very good, as you probably know."

"Oh yes, Jose, I know all too well—all to well." He gave out an evil-sounding snicker. "I hear that life caught up with you quick in the Baja."

"Actually, I think it may have started in Mazatlan. I've had a lot of time to think and I may have gotten careless."

"That's what I always liked about you, Jose. You always admitted when you were wrong. Just a really straight up guy."

I didn't know what to say because I couldn't look him in the eye and read his body language. I was assuming that he was telling me the truth, but I felt like I was talking to the Joker from Batman. He hadn't looked at me or even tried to shake my hand. So I sat silent and waited for his next move.

"Well, kid, I'm glad you called. We needed to talk anyway." He slowly turned his chair to face me. My heart practically jumped from my chest when I realized the man I was looking at wasn't Robles. Or was it?

CHAPTER 80

Jack Hardlow was enjoying the teenage hooker hanging on the stripper's pole at the Guau Guau club when his satellite phone rang. "Hardlow," he answered as he took another sip of his whiskey.

"Sir, Special Agent Robinson here."

"What can I do for you, kid?"

"She's back at the orphanage. I just got confirmation from one of our field agents."

Hardlow slammed his whiskey down as he paused briefly to let the good news sink in. He had been waiting for this moment.

"Good. I'll be there tomorrow morning. Keep her in your sights and I'll brief you on the operation when we're in flight to San Felipe."

"Aye aye, sir. We already have a reconnaissance team set up around the perimeter of the area."

"If she attempts to leave, have one of your Mexican counterparts detain her and anyone who's with her. Do you understand me?"

"Aye aye, sir."

"Let me repeat myself, kid. Do not let her out of your sights."

"Aye aye, sir."

"Good. And one more thing, Robinson."

"Yes, sir."

"Were you in the Navy at any time in your life?"

"Aye aye, sir."

"Yeah, aye aye, my ass. I was a fucking Marine who fought on the front lines while you boys sat on your little ship and fired rockets from 20 miles away."

"Sir?"

"Yeah, just shut up for a second. While you were sleeping in your comfortable bunks playing hide the sausage with your roomies, I was holed up behind enemy lines trying to stay alive. So I would suggest you don't use that 'aye aye' shit in my agency. It's 'yes sir' or 'no sir,' got it, Navy boy?"

"Ah, yes sir."

"Good." Hardlow hung up the phone. A surge of adrenaline immediately shot through his body as he washed the whiskey down with a cold Tecate. He was closing in and knew that she would be the key to unlocking the truth and confirming what he already knew: Cantino was alive.

He immediately ordered another whiskey and inquired about the teenager on stage. The bartender knew Hardlow and told him that she was available for him at any time. He smiled as he swallowed the little blue pill that he kept in his wallet. He would celebrate the good news back at his hotel room with the little whore who was younger than his daughter.

CHAPTER 81

It had been a long night and Hardlow was busy in his head. He remembered leaving the club with the whore and getting pulled over by one of the local police for running a stop sign. But the rest of the night was hazy at best.

Hardlow had fought alcoholism most of his adult life, always telling himself in the mornings that he would eventually change his ways. But come evening, it was the same routine. Now in his late fifties, he had come to the conclusion that he had lied to himself enough over the years. He was a drunk, but a functioning one. He always got his job done and it really wasn't a problem. In fact, he was good at his job and the end result was all that really mattered.

The plane took off from Rocky Point at predawn. The flight across the Sea of Cortez would take less than 20 minutes. As the sun was rising, Hardlow and his people were landing at San Felipe International Airport, south of the small fishing village.

The only personnel at the airport was that of the Mexican Army, who was there to give them a lift to the orphanage located between San Felipe and Puertocitos. The pilot tied down the unmarked government plane while the Hardlow entourage transferred their items to the Humvee awaiting them.

The orphanage was only about 30 miles south, but the road conditions were bad from Hurricane Nora during the late nineties. It would take over an hour to get to the orphanage. There would be no sleeping the rest of the way to kill time. The road was simply too rough.

As the sun was in full view creeping up over the water, Hardlow began to see the majestic beauty surrounding him. He couldn't help but feel the serenity of the mountains and how the desert met the sea. It was unusual to see an ocean surrounding the desert in this part of the world. The Baja was truly unique. For the most part, it was uninhabited and desolate. Maybe he would come back one day after he retired to find out what the fuss really was all about. In the meantime, he had business.

He radioed his field agents and announced that he would be there shortly. There was no need to make an aggressive approach to the situation. It was an orphanage after all, with only one way in and one way out.

The plan was that upon arrival, the task force would secure the perimeter surrounding the orphanage and Hardlow would go in with two officers as backup and apprehend their suspect. As much as he loathed this woman, this Lucy, he still respected the fact that it was an orphanage and young children were benefiting from the services provided. There would be no need to ransack the place with a swat team, scaring the children and volunteers.

As they made the turnoff to the orphanage, the entourage was met by a handful of field agents for some hot coffee, breakfast, and last-minute briefings.

"What do we have here to eat, son?" Hardlow said as he got out of the Humvee and placed his hands in his pockets. It was cold out and Hardlow was shivering.

"Well, sir, I had our boy Jorge here bring up some warm breakfast burritos that his wife made at home in Puertocitos. He just arrived and they're still warm," the young agent said, beaming with pride.

"Excellent, son," Hardlow smiled.

"Homemade salsa, too."

The young Mexican opened up a cooler and passed out the foil-wrapped burritos. They were still warm. Jorge pulled out a used pickle jar containing the homemade salsa. Hardlow unfolded his burrito and watched the steam escape into the cold air. He poured the salsa directly over the mixture of goodies and smothered it back up with the tortilla. *Something about Mexican food,* Hardlow thought. *There's nothing better.*

The burrito was spicy and delicious and hit the spot. A thermos of coffee was opened and poured into Styrofoam cups and passed around to everyone, taking the chill out of their bodies.

Hardlow crumbled the tin foil into his right hand and immediately began to lay out the contingency operation as the other men ate. Hardlow learned how to eat quickly in the Army because he was always the point man who did the talking. Nothing had changed in 30 years.

As simple as the operation was, Hardlow learned long ago never to take anything for granted. Whether he was interrogating a director of an orphanage or not, he was never complacent. Hardlow finished the briefing and they all loaded up and headed down the dusty dirt road.

The five-minute trip was uneventful. As they approached the entrance, the only noise they could hear were the roosters. Each of the vehicles split from one another and they surrounded the perimeter of the orphanage. Hardlow, gun by his side, was surprised to find the front entrance opened and took it upon himself to walk right in. He could hear something frying, accompanied by the smell of bacon and coffee. He followed the light, where he found two nuns preparing what appeared to be a breakfast of a hundred or more. He greeted the nuns politely in Spanish and asked for "Ms. Lucy," as she was called. The nuns looked surprised. Not only was it very early in the morning, the request was coming from a gringo in perfect Spanish!

"Que?" asked the nun, not knowing why he would want to see Lucy but also knowing that things happening around the orphanage lately were odd.

Hardlow pulled his jacket to the side exposing his badge and gun and said firmly, "Because I said so!" staring into her eyes.

The nun became visually panicked as Hardlow placed his hand on her arm and told her to take him to Lucy. The nun reacted by turning quickly and telling Hardlow to take his hands off her. Hardlow let go of her arm and asked her to lead him to Lucy. She pointed at a door and walked out of the room. Hardlow approached the door and attempted to turn the knob. It was locked. He backed up and kicked the cheap knob with his foot, extracting the door from the jamb. He walked through a narrow hallway, where he could here a shower running. He drew his weapon and slowly approached the light and sound of the running water. As he inched his way forward towards the bathroom, it was evident that whoever was in the shower had not heard him break down the door. Just as he reached for the door to the bathroom, the shower was shut off.

"Ms. Lucy?" Hardlow said, as a way to announce his presence.

"Who is it?" Lucy asked as she closed the shower door.

"I'm with the government and I need to talk to you," Hardlow said as he stepped through the door with his gun pointing at the semi-naked lady.

"What are you doing?" she screamed.

"Just put your clothes on before someone gets hurt," he said in a calm voice. "We need some information and you are the one who is going to give it to me."

Lucy tightened the already wrapped towel around her body and immediately knew what it was about. "You're an American. Why are you really here?"

"Shut up and get your clothes on before I haul your ass out of here naked!" he said as he cocked his pistol and aimed it at her head. "The game's over, Lucy."

She said nothing as she got dressed with her back turned on her intruder. Hardlow kept his pistol aimed at her as he admired her backside and perfectly curved buttocks. As soon as she was dressed, Hardlow handcuffed her. "I'd be happy to take you out the back so no one can see you like this," he said, trying to be courteous and have respect for the nuns and children.

"Go to hell, you bastard!"

Hardlow smiled at the petite woman and slapped her on the mouth. "I guess we're going to start this relationship off the hard way, huh?"

"Fuck you, gringo." She spit in his face.

"Have it your way," Hardlow said as turned her around and walked her into the room. He bent over and grabbed a sock, shoving it in her mouth. He then proceeded to grope her crotch area with his hands as she tried to resist and scream.

"Are we going to cooperate or do I need to take my aggression out on you in a different way?" Hardlow's perverted side was coming to surface. "And don't think for one second I won't get away with it."

Lucy stopped resisting and began to tear up. Hardlow removed the sock from her mouth.

"Any more behavior like that and you'll never see this orphanage again."

Hardlow opened up the back sliding door and signaled for an agent to come assist him. He transferred custody of the suspect to one of the field agents and told him to take her to the Humvee that he was riding in. "I'll be there in five minutes."

"Yes sir."

Hardlow ransacked the joint looking for anything of value. He found about three thousand dollars in cash and stuffed it into his pockets. But more importantly, he found a picture on the nightstand; the development date was within the last month. It was a picture of Lucy and Jose Cantino, sitting at a bar somewhere with the ocean in the background. "Priceless," he whispered under his breath and left the room.

CHAPTER 82

"Mr. Robles, I just can't believe it's you!" I was dumbfounded by the man sitting in front of him.

"Isn't it amazing what plastic surgery can do for you, Jose?" Robles smiled me. It was like a bad dream. The only thing that resembled Robles was his voice. His eyes were now blue and his mustache was gone. He was a different man.

"I don't understand, sir."

"Well, you should, Jose. Don't you realize that you're in a massive underground fortress? It's where I hide these days. They're on to me. Ever since the new president was elected last year, he's made it a mission to capture every Cartel boss there is. This all started right around the time you left us to go west. I had to do what I had to do." He flashed me his sadistic smile. I was speechless because I couldn't quite fathom the Old Man's plight. He was good friends with the police chief and on up—one silly election was going to change things forever? It made no sense. Surely they would buy off the new president like they've done for years? Anyway, it was beyond my comprehension and I chose not to take the conversation in that direction.

"So, you've gone out on your own and your past has caught up with you. That's a given. I'm assuming you want a job, Jose?"

"No sir, not at all. That's not why I'm here. I just need…" my words stopped as I stared into my lap and let the tears drip down my face uncontrollably. "I'm sorry, sir. You know me. I never cry. I'm just, just in a really bad situation right now."

"Jose, you're not broke are you?" Robles said with genuine concern.

"No—well, maybe..."

"Jose, look at me. I can't help you unless you tell me everything."

I took a deep breath and let out a long one. "Sir, they're on to me. They've got me on the run."

"Well, that's obvious, son."

"Sir, I gave up the trade. I met this girl. I fell in love. I found the Lord..." My tears swelled up again.

"No wonder it caught up with you," the old man chuckled. "Love is blind."

"Sir, I tried to contact my banker at the bank you hooked me up years ago. They say he's no longer there. They want me to come in and discuss my account before they release any of my money." And that was it—for the next three minutes as I broke down sobbing, trying to control my breathing and maintain the little manhood that remained. He let me get it all out before he said anything.

"Jose, from what you just told me, your money's gone. Forget about it. I got the call a few months back and I pulled it all out and took it to Switzerland. There's no questions asked there."

"There's more, sir."

Robles said nothing as I went on for 15 minutes. I proceeded to fill him in on all the details including the murder in Mazatlan. The story I unraveled was sad, but it could have been worse. I could have been dead.

"Jose, let me sit on this for a day or two. I have a lot of issues that I need to tend to as well, but I'm sure I can help you in one way or the other. In the meantime, I'll have my assistant set you up at one of our villas away in the mountains where you can take a retreat for a few days and not be scared that someone's on your ass 24/7."

"Sir, I was hoping just for a safe place to stay."

"Jose? Have you ever known me not to do anything top shelf? Come on, man. I'll send you over there and you can smoke some weed, drink some booze, screw a whore or two, and just get your mind off this stuff for a while."

I sat silent as Robles dished out a hedonistic plate from my past. He reached for his phone and touched a button. Within seconds, his secretary walked into the room.

"Make arrangements for Mr. Cantino to stay at the mountain villa tonight indefinitely. Be sure that the route is clear of all authorities before his transfer. And for God's sake, make sure this man is taken care of in any respect that he desires."

"Yes sir."

The old man stood up and offered his hand out of friendship and support. I didn't know what to think. Picking up my habits from my past life was what I didn't want to do, but I guess I had no choice. Although, honestly, a joint sounded really good right now.

"Thank you, sir. Thank you. I just need some time to lay low and then I need to get back to Lucy."

"Lucy?"

"Yeah, she's the woman who I fell in love with."

"I see," he smiled.

"Somehow, someway, I need to get back to her without bringing the problems of my past into our relationship."

"Good luck," he said sarcastically. "In the meantime, have fun, Jose."

I left the office after a long handshake and eventual hug. The secretary escorted me out and closed the door. Robles picked up the phone and called his contact in Grand Cayman. It was confirmed. Cantino's money had been frozen by the U.S. Treasury and he had a lot of heat coming his way.

"Sir, he'll never see a dime."

"Thank you." Robles hung up the phone. Cantino was screwed.

CHAPTER 83

Lucy would not say a word as they took the bumpy road from the orphanage back to the airport. Hardlow kept taunting her with snide remarks about living the rest of her life in a Mexican prison. His comments went unappreciated. Hardlow also couldn't help noticing how beautiful she really was. His thoughts continued to sway from the true purpose of his mission.

It took a little over an hour to get back to the airport. The plane had been refueled and the pilot was ready and waiting with a copy of *Travel and Leisure* in his lap. Lucy was re-cuffed with her hands in front and securely fastened in the back of the plane. Hardlow buckled up next to her and gave the pilot orders to get back to Rocky Point. They were airborne within minutes and Hardlow began his often-winded sermon of what he knew and what he expected from her. He wanted to give her an opportunity to think before the official questioning began back in Rocky Point.

"And, by the way, your Gringo buddy, Gilbert or Gilberto, is in our custody." Lucy said nothing but her face said it all. She reacted badly, confirming what Hardlow already knew—that she was in cahoots with Gilbert and Cantino.

They were back in Rocky Point within the hour. They were greeted on the tarmac with the same black Suburban that delivered them there earlier that morning. Once they arrived back at the police station, Lucy was locked up in her own cell while Hardlow and his men had a quick snack of *carne asada burritos*. Hardlow took his time eating and then excused himself to go to the restroom. He spent ten minutes relieving himself and took a few swigs from his flask. *Let the party begin,* he thought as he smiled and exited the bathroom.

Hardlow was in the driver's seat and made it perfectly clear to anyone who wanted to challenge his leadership. He entered her cell with a plastic chair and tape recorder, knowing that his subordinates would wait outside the cell in case she tried anything out of the ordinary. He didn't feel threatened by any means, but knew the situation could get volatile, and wanted to utilize good precautionary measures as an example to his men.

"Are you hungry, Lucy?" he smiled.

"No," she said as she stared at the neutral painted concrete floor.

"I can call you Lucy, right?" he said.

"You can call me whatever you like."

"Good. Now let's get down to business."

She nodded.

"I assume that you are fully aware of why you are being detained by myself, an agent of the United States Drug Enforcement Administration, working in conjunction with the government here in Mexico?" he said, showing off some official formalities.

"Actually, I have no idea why I'm being detained. In fact, I find you personally, legally, and morally repulsive! In fact, I am not answering any of your questions without an attorney present."

Hardlow had been down this road a thousand times throughout his career and decided to handle it the same way that he always had. "Shut up, you cocky little whore. Your nonsense will get you about as far as this jail cell. You have no rights nor will you have any in the future if I have my way!" Hardlow spit at her feet to emphasize his point. "You fucking Mexicans think that you live in a democracy, but you don't!" he smiled through his anger. "You think this is America? Well it isn't. You people go up to my country illegally and place your fucking children in our school's at taxpayer's expense. You apply for food stamps all on my dime. You use our emergency rooms for your primary health care because you know that some pussy in Washington, D.C., says it's OK.

You steal our money through the welfare system because some bureaucrat allows you to. Well, I'm challenging you otherwise. We're not in El Paso or Phoenix or San Diego! You're in your own country now, not the United States. No one gives a shit about you here—so don't fuck with me!" Hardlow stood up and kicked his chair across the cell.

It was a great part that he played. He could have been an actor. But Lucy didn't care about his little political diatribe. She had been around the block as well. She wasn't intimidated by his rhetoric. As nervous as she was, she had nothing to lose at this point. At least not yet. So her response was natural to Hardlow's rant:

"Go fuck yourself, gringo!"

CHAPTER 84

"So this is how it's gonna be?" Hardlow asked as he paced around her cell. "Don't you care about your children?" he said.

"Oh spare me your fake sentimentality, Mr. Hardlow. Of course I care about my children. It's something I do out of love and respect for God. I'm not on some government payroll mowing over human rights like a soldier in Tiananmen Square. The orphanage has nothing to do with why you have arrested me and taken me away from my home," she said indignantly.

"Do you think I'm a complete moron, Ms. Lucy?" Hardlow asked sarcastically. "Do you think that the U.S. government has nothing better to do than hassle with some coke whore posing as a humanitarian?"

"Coke whore? Who the hell are you? I've never done cocaine or any illegal drug in my life, you bastard!"

"Yeah, and Bill Clinton is a virgin," he said as he continued his pace around her cell. "You're a typical hypocrite, hiding behind your orphanage and mask of philanthropy. An orphanage supported by illicit drug sales and God knows what else!"

Hardlow stopped pacing briefly. "In fact, you should own a laundromat. You've been cleaning dirty money for a long time now, haven't you, Lucy?"

"I want to talk to my lawyer," she said calmly. Hardlow wasn't getting anywhere with her. She was obviously very smart.

"Is it the same lawyer that Cantino uses?"

"I'm not saying a word to you until I see my lawyer. He lives in Mexicali, but I don't have his number with me."

Hardlow knew that he would eventually have to cave in and allow her to make arrangements to speak to her attorney. How badly he wanted to just take her back to his hotel room and teach her a few lessons while fulfilling his perverse, sexual gratification. He knew that would be going too far but he was tempted. But he wasn't giving in to her just yet.

"I'll tell you what, Lucy. I'll get you your lawyer. But you're going to have to give up some information. And if you don't want to do that, your request will be seriously delayed. And who knows what can happen during that down time?"

"Don't threaten me, gringo. I've got nothing to say to you. You're a pig," she said as she spat at his jeans.

"Well, my dear, that was the wrong thing to do!" he screamed as he bitch slapped her mouth with his right hand and tore her blouse off with the other.

"Help!" she screamed. "This man is trying to rape me." Two Mexican guards came running down the corridor, into the cell. They immediately saw her torn blouse and grabbed Hardlow by the arms from behind.

"What the hell are you doing?" he yelled at the guards, who were dragging him from her cell.

"Mr. Hardlow, you cannot be alone in this cell with a female," the young guard said. "It's against our policy here." He stood his ground as his hand securely held Hardlow's arm.

"Let go of me you son of a bitch or I'll have your ass!"

"I am sorry, sir, we have rules here."

"And for obvious reasons" the other guard piped in.

As soon as they were out of the cell, Hardlow maneuvered his arms from the two men. "I will have your jobs!" he snapped as he tried to straighten his clothes. He adjusted his tweed jacket as he turned around in the hall. The Chief was standing about a foot from Hardlow as he turned around. They met eye to eye. The Chief was obviously agitated with what he just witnessed.

"Agent Hardlow, sir," the Chief said calmly but firmly, "may I see you in my office?"

"Gladly."

The two walked in silence to the Chief's office. The door slammed behind them. An immediate screaming match pursued. It was obvious that the Chief did not approve of the American's tactics.

CHAPTER 85

Mr. Robles's villa was located about 60 miles south of the compound outside of Tampico in very mountainous terrain. I had my own room and quickly adapted to the plush environment. It was a candy store for adults. Cocaine, marijuana, and something that was new to me: methamphetamine. The methamphetamine epidemic that had exploded recently in the United States made it very profitable for the Cartels to add to their menus. I had heard the horror stories, but again, it was a matter of simple supply and demand. It was cheap to produce and Robles had a grip on the market, producing massive quantities and still not able to meet consumption.

As always, I opted to enjoy the weed only. I knew that meth was even worse than cocaine and swore to never touch it. But what I did touch that evening was far worse in my eyes than either cocaine or methamphetamine.

She was in her early twenties, from Cuba, and was there to look after my every want and need. She rolled and lit my joints; made me sweet cocktails to cover up the alcohol—the only way I liked them; cooked me dinner, allowing me to choose anything that I wanted; and of course, screwed my brains out. It wasn't supposed to happen, but I felt my life slipping away by the minute. She was beautiful and obviously paid to wait on her guests in every capacity. I treated it like a minor indiscretion and swore that it would never happen again after the first time—until the following morning when she woke me up with a blow job. She was actually attracted to me, as opposed to the perverted old men who usually occupied the villa, away from their wives and mistresses. I was still young and she was the aggressor, not knowing if it would be the last time she was with anyone remotely her age. Unfortunately, I obliged and quickly developed feelings for her as well. How could I not? She was everything that a man could ask for.

The third day came around and I was quickly enveloped in my old ways—those of a guiltless, unethical, immoral degenerate... a hedonist who was living for the moment, not knowing what tomorrow would bring...someone who, after such a revelation in the Baja, returned to his old ways like a tweeker getting out of rehab. The difference was that I now held a conscience. I knew what I was doing was wrong and I felt guilty, but it didn't stop for the three days that I was there. Yeah, I knew it was wrong—but I did it anyway. Some may argue that it wasn't progress. I felt otherwise.

I had hours to think while at the villa; for the first time in my life, I realized that over the past few weeks, even when I was in Sonora, I was accomplishing nothing. I was holed up. It really wasn't much different than being in a prison in the sense that I could not leave and do what I wanted to do at any given moment. I had all of the amenities on the inside, but my true joy in life was on the outside—the freedom to roam and do what I pleased. I worked my entire life, so that I could have financial freedom and now that was gone. I had the freedom to go and do as I pleased whether it be fishing or running drugs—now that was gone. I wanted to break out on my own because next to Robles, I could never work for anyone but myself—that was gone too. Most importantly, I recently made the decision to change my life and have the freedom to give my money and time to those who needed it the most: the children. And now that was gone.

The children, Lucy's children, and now my children. *What have I done to the children?*

CHAPTER 86

"Who in the hell do you think you are?" yelled Hardlow. "You are obstructing a federal investigation. I don't expect a fucking beat cop in a small shithole that some marketing genius has labeled a sleepy little fishing town understand the complexity and seriousness of this case. What I do expect is some subordination. The United States and Mexico have an intergovernmental agreement, signed by Presidents Bush and Fox, that gives me the authority to do my god-damned job!" Hardlow was screaming and his face was beet red. The Chief, very composed, showed no reaction whatsoever.

"Are you listening to what I am saying!" Hardlow pounded his fists on the desk in front of him.

"Can I speak now Mr. Hardlow?" the Chief asked politely.

"Shoot!"

"Agent Hardlow, there is no doubt that you are a very influential individual in your government. But I will not stand back and watch a foreigner of all people, regardless of your status, mistreat a Mexican citizen and a female at that," he said with dignity. "That woman out there is still guaranteed legal rights that no person, especially a foreigner, can alter. Our country, just as yours, is not a nation of men, but a nation of laws. And as long as I am the Chief of Police in charge of that jail, I will answer to our constitution before anyone."

"Well, isn't that mighty poetic, Madre Mouse? Your little speech on the constitution brings a tingling sensation to the tip of my prick. You should've been a fucking legal scholar. I need a tissue," Hardlow said as he began to pace back and forth, wondering if he should knock this guy out.

"If you have a problem with what I said, Agent Hardlow, I will get the judiciary on the phone to not only advise you of how we do things here in Mexico, but to guarantee that she gets legal representation before anyone questions her. She will get the same rights as you, if you were locked up in a jail in the United States," the Chief said with a smile.

Hardlow gave the Chief a look of death. But the Chief would not budge. And because it was the Chief's jail, Hardlow had no control over the situation. *Typical corrupt cop. Protecting some scumbag bitch because she has a nice set of legs and runs an orphanage.*

"Well, Chief Pantywaist, I will be contacting my Mexican counterpart who will see to this nonsense. You, my friend, are a goner. Kiss your happy days of being the police chief goodbye." With that, Hardlow turned around and opened up the door.

"Agent Hardlow," the Chief said.

"What's that, counselor?"

"I would suggest that you do not threaten me with your bullying tactics. And your suspect will be meeting with her attorney this afternoon as soon as he arrives from Mexicali. Just thought you should know," the Chief smirked.

Hardlow saluted the Chief with his middle finger and walked out of the station.

CHAPTER 87

Four days had passed before Mr. Robles, showed up at the mountainside villa. A young girl who appeared to be in her late teens escorted him. His purpose was to stay and relax for a few days with his little friend. *What his wife didn't know, wouldn't hurt her,* I thought.

It was rather early in the morning, and my luscious Cuban had prepared a traditional Mexican breakfast consisting of *huevos rancheros,* beans, and hot flour tortillas. I was never a big eater, especially now. My body was running on pure nerves. My confidence had faded and my life was in receivership.

Very little was said at breakfast aside from the typical formalities and small talk. Mr. Robles would never bring up my plight in front of two whores. We would talk later, alone in a private setting. I'm sure that one of the reasons that Mr. Robles showed up was that he could use the rest. However, I could only assume that his primary purpose for coming to the villa was to try and solve my problems. Unfortunately, I could only imagine what I would have to do in return.

As my mind jumped around thinking about my options, I simply had no clear direction in which I wanted to take my life. For the first time ever, I realized that I was not a leader. Despite my independence, I had never been self-employed until now. And now, I was back at my old boss's mercy because my little business venture failed.

What I knew of Mr. Robles was that he was a businessman who was always looking for new ways to improve his bottom line. I knew that he wanted a piece of the pie in the Baja when I discussed my move west when I first left the Cartel. He had mentioned at the time that he knew the desolate peninsula was a great route for delivering his goods into the States. Somone had offered him a buy-in of a tunnel that went from Tijuana to Chula Vista for five million dollars. The tunnel had been in operation for only a couple of weeks and communication about it was so secretive that he himself had told no one. Robles could recoup his investment with a couple of major loads from his new base in Culiacan.

Without ever hearing about it from the old man, I knew that 90 miles north of Mazatlan, the town of Culiacan was a notorious narcotic hub. It was no surprise that Robles would want his hand in the pie. With less Mexican corruption and a lot more enforcement, it was getting harder and harder to deliver drugs to the States in conventional ways and routes. Robles was an innovator—always a step ahead of the game.

After breakfast, Mr. Robles and I sat on the veranda out back and breathed in the fresh air. Mr. Robles rolled a joint that we shared, then he broke the news about his phone call to the Caymans. He told me that because of my wanted status, certain RICO laws, and new governmental cooperatives between the British Government and the United States, my money was frozen. Only an international judge would be able to get the money released, and that would only happen if I were willing to face the charges, take a risk on bail, and eventually try to clear my name and prove my innocence in a court of law. We both knew that was not going to happen. In essence, I had to kiss the money goodbye.

My instincts were right when Mr. Robles quickly moved on to what he had in mind for me. He wanted to test new waters and me in the Baja was ideal. He wanted me to deliver 500 kilos of methamphetamine from Culiacan to San Felipe, where I would meet a contact from Ensenada to pick up the goods from there. I would be paid $75,000 cash upon successful delivery. In essence, it was a gift from Mr. Robles with a kick—one that could place me in even more danger than I already was in.

Yes, there was risk involved, but guys like Mr. Robles didn't just throw stray puppies into the jungle alone. Both Mr. Robles and I were seasoned professionals. Mr. Robles assured me that he had much of the narcotic personnel paid off. Yeah, there was risk, but it was mitigated risk. Robles couldn't risk losing that type of load and Jose couldn't afford to get caught.

"And remember, Jose, seventy-five grand for a skip across the pond is mighty generous," he said with a smile.

"Yes, sir, it is. It really is," I replied, staring straight ahead, as I soaked in the proposition.

"Also, if you're successful, you can make the run any time. I'll keep the seventy-five grand in tact as the going rate. You will be more of a partner, not an employee."

Further discussion of the specifics continued over the next hour; we both agreed to think about it some more. Mr. Robles excused himself, feeling the effects of the Viagra he popped an hour earlier. He disappeared into his master suite with the young whore and was not seen until dinner that evening.

In the interim, I had made the decision to take the offer, promising myself that it would be the last. I would have to somehow get in touch with Lucy and coordinate the effort with her. Not only would it be money that we now desperately needed, it would be a way to see her again in the near future. Regardless of my wandering over the last few days, I still wanted to settle down and spend my life with Lucy.

I began to plan my future. We would move from the Baja and start an orphanage somewhere else, out of the country obviously. The police would think that I was dead and the manhunt would be called off, case closed. Me and Lucy could slowly assimilate into another population in another country and bury our past. It really was rather simple. It could be done.

Dinner came around and very little was said. As everyone finished up, I joined the Old Man on the balcony for some Kahlua and coffee and some fine Moroccan hashish.

"I'll do it, sir. Thank you for the opportunity."

"Great, Jose, no need to thank me. This will be a mutual effort."

"I just need a bit of time to make some plans and allow things to calm down."

"No problem, Jose. No problem at all," he smiled.

I knew the voice, but just couldn't quite get over his face.

CHAPTER 88

It was a sit and wait game. The man had parked his car down the street from the police chief's house. He knew that he would be home soon. He could hear a lady in the house scolding some children, presumably the Chief's wife and kids. He then heard a sound and ducked behind an oleander.

A late model Crown Vic pulled into the Chief's driveway. The driver opened the door slightly and the dome light came on. He was preoccupied with some paperwork in the passenger seat and wasn't ready to exit the vehicle. The driver looked just like the guy in the picture. He finally got out of the car and slammed the door shut. As he began to walk up the concrete drive, he was approached by a middle-aged Mexican man wearing a long leather coat.

"Chief Espino," the man asked.

"Yes sir?" The Chief quickly turned around with a startled look.

"I have a message from Agent Jack Hardlow," he said as he pulled out his Glock and emptied the clip into his head.

CHAPTER 89

The killer was paid 10 thousand dollars cash in Hardlow's hotel room. All he had to do was show Hardlow a picture of the corpse that he took on his camera phone. *One obstacle cleared.*

Earlier in the day, Hardlow's Mexican counterpart had phoned, informing him to pick the girl up from the police station and fly her to Mexicali where she would be jailed. He would then have full access to her. He did as he was told, despite the meeting she had with her attorney.

The station was practically empty, not including the prisoners, of course. All of the available personnel were at the crime scene of their beloved boss, Chief Espino. There were no hassles. The dispatcher had received the faxed orders to surrender custody to Agent Hardlow and his Mexican counterpart. Lucy took offense upon hearing the news of the transfer and asked to speak with her attorney: denied.

There was no resistance and they were back at the airport within minutes, Lucy's hands cuffed on her front side. Within the hour, they arrived in Mexicali. A local police detective picked them up, taking custody of Lucy and transporting her to the jail. Hardlow filled out the necessary paperwork and was off to do his own business for a day. He accomplished his goal of getting Lucy out of custody in Rocky Point and placed in familiar territory. He would take the afternoon off to pursue his own plans.

Hardlow and Mexicali were like old college roommates who met up once a year for a binge. Hardlow's favorite place was a dingy strip club named Bar San Diego. The drink prices were not justified, but who cared? It wasn't his money that he was playing with. Hardlow loved the whores and Bar San Diego was more than just a strip club. He could dance all night with the cheap senoritas and then go upstairs to the "massage" parlor. The menu: hand jobs 40 dollars; blow jobs 80 dollars; full service 100 dollars. An extra 50 dollars usually bought him unprotected sex, which Hardlow preferred over those stifling condoms that did nothing for his stamina. Most of them went for it and Hardlow generally knew if a girl was clean or not. At least that's what he told himself.

So tonight was the night. He would interview Lucy again in the morning. He caught a ride to the Crowne Royal Hotel in the downtown district, where he cleaned up for his night out. He would formulate a deal in his mind to present to Lucy while he got jacked up on tequila and beer. Who knew? Maybe he would let the little bitch off in exchange for Cantino. Retirement was coming up fast and he wasn't getting any younger. Cantino was the last head he wanted mounted on his proverbial wall and he would do anything to get it.

CHAPTER 90

Eleven o'clock came very early for Hardlow. The pickings had been rather slim the night before, a Wednesday night, at the strip club. It appeared that all the real talent was waiting for the weekend. He hadn't remembered much at Bar San Diego except the Scotch binge he went on. The young hooker lying next to him didn't look nearly as good as she did last night. These early morning surprises always reminded him of the old Willie Nelson song: "went home with a ten and woke up with a two."

As he stretched out on the side of the bed, he yelled at the whore to get up. She quickly complied. He threw her a twenty for cab fare and told her to get lost. He latched the interior lock on the door and undressed for a cold shower. He began to go over the plan in his head. He would have preferred a hot shower but all that would do is make him want to crawl back into bed. As his body stubbornly adjusted to the cold water, his brain cells seemed to perk up, clearing his head of the many single malts from the night before.

He quickly got dressed in anticipation of his day at the police station. Packing his overnight bag, he left the key to the room on the dresser. He took the elevator to the lobby floor and found a small table in the corner where he set his complimentary paper and overnight bag. Grabbing a stale Danish and cup of coffee at the breakfast bar, he decided it wasn't worth sitting down to eat. He gathered his things and waived down the taxi parked in front of the hotel.

He gave the driver instructions and began to go over his future conversation with Lucy in his head. It was all on the line now. He would be deceitful yet civil to the young woman. If she didn't deal on his terms, he would have to resort to plan B and unleash a wrath that she had never seen.

About 15 minutes later, he arrived at the station, where he was escorted to the Mexicali police chief's office. Hardlow was fluent and they exchanged greetings. The Chief looked distraught. He then noticed the picture on the front page of the paper lying on his desk with the bold caption: "**Puerto Penasco Chief of Police Murdered. Drug Cartels suspected.**"

The Mexicans weren't known for their great detective work, so they often made up the news as they went. Of course a drug Cartel would be assumed. The problem was, there was no evidence pointing to that.

Hardlow thanked the Chief for his accommodations and did not mention what he just read on his desk. He was led to the interrogation room and requested that nothing be videoed at this time. He was more interested in cutting a deal with the woman than scaring the shit out of her.

As he entered, he noticed that her hands were trembling. His plan was already working. She was terrified. He didn't know if it was all him or the meeting with her attorney. It didn't matter—he had won half the battle.

"Good morning, Lucy," Hardlow said politely.

She stood quiet.

"Lucy, I would like to start fresh with you. I know that you're knee deep in this Cantino investigation, but I am willing to negotiate a few things for you so you don't wind up in prison for the rest of your life." Hardlow was a straight shooter from the get go. "And trust me, my dear, if that's what I wanted, I would get it."

Tears began to swell up in her eyes, but she still maintained control. Hardlow sat down in the chair across from her. Even he felt awkward being so kind to her in his initial comments.

"Now, I know that Jose Cantino is not dead. I also know that you know where he is. So, I'm going to make the deal very simple. If you give me this information today, I will guarantee that you will be a free woman. It will be in writing and delivered to your attorney as well. It's really that simple."

"Mr. Hardlow, may I speak?"

"Please my dear, you have the floor."

"Mr. Hardlow, my attorney specifically told me that I should not talk to you unless he is present."

Hardlow's temper began to get the best of him as he slammed his hands down on the table. He took a deep breath and tried to restrain his anger.

"Unfortunately, Lucy, that would not be in your best interest at this moment. Are you willing to listen to me about the deal that I'm about to offer you? Because if you insist on your attorney being present, I'm going to give this file over to the prosecutors and you'll be going on trial for aiding and abetting a murderer who just so happens to be a drug dealer. It's up to you."

They both sat in silence.

Momentarily, Hardlow got out of his chair. He closed the folder containing his notes and placed it under his left arm. He started to walk towards the door.

"Wait," Lucy said. Hardlow stopped in his tracks and grinned to himself before he slowly turned around.

"Agent Hardlow, please don't go. I'm willing to listen to your offer without my attorney present."

Hardlow thought he deserved an Oscar so far. He returned to his chair and sat back down. "Here's the deal. Jose Cantino has approximately one and a half million dollars in a bank account in Grand Cayman. I have had the account frozen so no one can touch it except the U.S. government, which just so happens to be me." He added himself in the equation for effect and intimidation.

"I know that you're a modern day Robin Hood type—you know, committing crimes and using the profits for good causes like that orphanage you got down there. Odd bit of philanthropy, though, you getting some kids hooked on drugs by dealing, then using the money to help other kids stay away from drugs. But as it looks right now, you have no future nor does your orphanage. In fact, I've had your own bank accounts frozen as of today." He stared at her as more tears swelled up in her eyes.

"Please go on, I'm listening."

"What if I were to 'un-freeze' some of those funds and give you say, 500 thousand dollars in exchange for the capture of Cantino?"

Lucy began sobbing. She knew it would be a Catch-22.

"Whether you do this or not really doesn't matter to me. I'll catch the son-of-a-bitch with or without your help." He stood up and leaned over at her. "And if you don't help, you'll be sitting in a Mexican shit-hole eating stale tortillas, braving off nasty butch dykes every hour of every day, for the rest of your natural life!" Hardlow said with a sadistic smile. "I'll be back tomorrow at the same time. You think about it and have a decision for me in the morning."

The real Hardlow had come out. He just couldn't be completely civil for once. It wasn't in his personality. He gathered up his things and left the room. Lucy broke into a sob as two guards entered and took her back to her cell.

CHAPTER 91

Hardlow called his pilot on his cell phone and was praying he hadn't hit the bars yet. Hardlow didn't like to hang out with the guy because he liked to conceal his illicit habits from others. He didn't need anyone holding anything over his head.

"Are you sober?" he asked seriously.

"Jack, it's only noon!" the pilot responded defensively.

"Yeah, that's why I asked. How long will it take for you to get to the airport?"

"I can be there in a half hour."

"I'll meet you there, then," Hardlow said and hung up the phone.

Two hours later, they were back in Rocky Point where Hardlow was quickly whisked away to the police station. His timing and luck could not have been any better. The place was practically empty as all of the cops were attending the funeral of Chief Espino. Dispatch recognized him immediately and let him in. He rounded up the only guard on duty and asked to speak to Mr. Gilbert.

"Oh, Gilberto," the guard said with a smile. *"No problema."*

Hardlow followed him down the corridor.

"Sir, would you like to speak to him in the briefing room?" he asked in broken English.

"No, I can chat with him right in his cell."

He followed the guard until he stopped in front of his cell. "Please excuse us, son. This will be a private discussion."

"Yes sir," the guard answered and walked away.

Gilbert was on the can with an obvious episode of Montezuma's revenge. Hardlow was having an issue with the smell but decided to tough it out.

"Mr. Gilbert, what a pleasant surprise. Tell me, was it the water?" He laughed at the poor kid.

"You have no right to do this to me. I have done nothing!" Gilbert yelled defiantly.

"Well, son, that's why I'm here. I think maybe I know of a way to get you out of this shithole."

Gilbert's tone changed immediately. "Sir, whatever I need to do, I will. Please, I just want to go home. I just want to see my family and friends." His voice sounding desperate.

Hardlow's demeanor turned completely serious. "I'll tell you what. I will have some bottled water and fresh food delivered to your cell along with some Bacterum to take care of the shits. But I'm going to need a thing or two from you."

"Sir, I'm ready to talk."

"Good. If you would have cooperated with me in the first place, you could've been home by now banging your girlfriend."

"Sir, anything."

"First off, how long was Cantino at your house?"

"Several days sir. The only reason that I put him up was because of a friend of mine who had known him for years. I didn't quite know the degree of trouble that he was really in."

"Yeah, I know who your friend was—not is. We killed that fucker a few years back. Another scumbag drug dealer, buying off half the crooked cops and politicians in Sonora," Hardlow said, emphasizing his message.

"Sir, I never knew that about him at the time. He was a friend of my father's and I can guarantee you that my dad never knew. They did a lot of charity work together and would go fishing on occasion."

"Charity work," Hardlow smiled. "What a great cover—until he got gunned down."

"Second question, pretty boy. Did Cantino fake his death?"

"Yes sir. I helped him plan the whole thing. In fact, it was my idea."

"Wow, Mr. Gilbert, you really have some balls admitting to all of this stuff."

"Sir, like I said, I want to cooperate."

"And cooperate you have."

"But sir, I can attest to you that Cantino's a changed man. He's found the Lord," Gilberto said with enthusiasm. This statement made the old man laugh out loud.

"OK, young man, last question." Hardlow looked down at the dirty concrete floor of the jail cell. "And this is probably the most important question, so don't tell me any fucking lies!" he said as he slowly drew his head up from the floor and stared at Gilberto in the eyes. They remained in silence, until he finally dropped the last request.

"Where did he go?"

At this point, Gilbert had no choice but to answer Hardlow honestly and in complete detail. As much as he wanted to tell him to go to hell and protect his friend, his options had been narrowed to the truth. Unfortunately, under these circumstances, the only thing that mattered was his safety and freedom.

"Well, sir," he began, pausing briefly, "the last I heard was Kino Bay. To hang out with a friend of Lucy's." He stared the old man right in the eyes. Hardlow knew that he was telling the truth.

"Sir, I had no intention of being involved in this…"

"Spare me the bullshit, Gilbert."

"Yes sir. It's not bullshit, but I understand what you're saying because…"

"Shut the fuck up son before I change my mind!"

"Yes, sir."

"Now, I have a follow-up question for you, now that I believe that you are telling me the truth."

"At this point, I have nothing to hide, sir. Any question you have, I'll continue to answer."

"OK, then." Hardlow paused, carefully thinking how to phrase his next request.

"How much money do you have liquid that you could get your hands on while you're here in Mexico?"

"Excuse me, sir?"

"You heard me, you little rotten son of a bitch. How much money do you have in the bank?" he pressed, his evilness shining through his bloodshot eyes.

"Sir, I don't understand. What does that have to do with anything?" he asked with overly concern.

"Answer my question you little prick!"

Gilberto knew where this was going and Hardlow's face was hard as stone.

"I've got a couple hundred Gs. Why?"

"How much does your mother have?"

"Wait a minute, sir. Leave my mother out of this equation."

"You didn't answer my question, asshole. How much money does she have?"

"Lots, I presume."

"Lots, huh?" Hardlow smiled. "And what should a dumb old redneck like myself interpret 'lots' as?"

"Millions, sir. Millions."

"OK, son, now we're talking."

Gilbert immediately felt a surge of diarrhea come on and raced back to the toilet at the end of the cell. It was a combination of the dysentery and the conversation that Hardlow was pushing him into. Hardlow patiently waited while Gilbert finished up, washing his hands without any soap at all.

"Are you through, poopy pants?" Hardlow chuckled.

"For now I am. I'm sure another episode is right around the corner of this conversation."

"I want you to come over here by these bars and give me your mom's number. And don't worry, the number will come up unknown on her Caller I.D." He waived the phone through the bars. "If I'm going to save your life, surely Mommy thinks her son is worth a couple million dollars?"

Gilberto's eyes widened in disbelief. He was being blackmailed.

"If not, I'm going to put you in a Mexican prison and let all of the inmates know that you're in there for raping little Mexican boys and girls. Now get over here and give me the number."

Gilberto slowly walked towards the bars and began to slowly rattle off the number. Hardlow punched it into his phone.

"Thank you, son. Now I'm going to sit here and listen to you tell your mommy what a bad little boy you've been. Then you're going to tell her to wire two million dollars to this Swiss Bank account on the back of this card," Hardlow instructed as he handed it to him.

Gilberto knew that Hardlow was bad news but was set back when he knew he was on the take. There was no more thinking. This guy was a pro. He made the corrupt Mexicans look like little leaguers playing in Wrigley field against the Cubs.

"I'll do it, you piece of shit, but how am I going to ensure that I can get out of here?"

"Number one, you disrespectful little cock sucker, if you ever refer to me as anything other than sir or Agent Hardlow, I will personally take you out into the desert and have you dig your own grave before I place a .45 bullet in your skull. Second, you'll just have to trust me that I'm going to get you out of here. But my word is sacred. The minute the money hits, I will personally see to it that my right-hand man drives you to the border."

"Fine. Dial the number."

Hardlow hit the green dial button on his phone and handed it to Gilberto. He listened intently on how he got caught up with a wanted felon and that he was looking at life in a Mexican prison. He could tell by Gilberto's end of the dialogue that the mother was terrified.

Hardlow's mission with the young man was accomplished, however, when he heard him giving her the routing and account numbers for the wire transfer.

"Mom, I promise that I'll pay you back. I promise." There was a pause. "I love you too and will see you tomorrow." He hung up the phone.

Hardlow then pulled a couple of pictures out of his sports coat. The date of the pictures was from yesterday. "And one last thing Mr. Gilberto," he said sarcastically. "You see these pictures?" he continued, placing them in front of Gilberto.

Gilbert's face turned red.

"They're of your mother getting out of her car in Phoenix yesterday. If I hear one word about this from anyone, she'll be meeting her maker sooner than she expected, and of course, you'll be right behind her," he smiled as he opened his jacket to expose his pistol.

"Understood," Gilberto replied, swallowing the lump in his throat.

"It was nice doing business with you, Mr. Gilberto. I'll have those things to you within the hour. And remember what I told you about leaking this to anyone. I would suggest you tell your mother the same. When the money hits, you'll be driven to the border." He walked away from the cell, and gave the jailer 20 bucks, telling him to bring the kid some food, water, and medicine.

Hardlow's pilot was waiting in the car outside, ready to fly back to Mexicali. He patted him on the shoulder as he got into the passenger seat.

"Where to next, sir?"

"How about Switzerland?" he joked as they drove back to the airport.

CHAPTER 92

"I am willing to cooperate," she conceded with her head staring at the table and her beautiful body being hidden by the orange jump suit that she was wearing.

"I'm glad that you've come around, young lady. You'll have enough money to fund your orphanage for the rest of your life, I'm sure," Hardlow said seriously.

He couldn't help think about how this deal was going to net him six hundred grand off of Cantino alone. The fact was, Hardlow had millions stashed away in Switzerland from his wheeling and dealing with drug dealers from around the world. He loved drug dealers because they made him rich beyond any means that the U.S. government could ever do.

"This is what we are willing to do. I will fly you to San Felipe today. Of course, you'll be under surveillance 24/7," he smiled. "I will have my Mexican counterpart make an official announcement in Mazatlan today stating that Mr. Cantino was murdered at sea by a competing drug Cartel and that the case has been officially closed. We will have it broadcast on all of the national news stations, along with the radio and Internet. We have tapped all of your phones and will be monitoring all of your calls made to and from the orphanage, along with all cell phone activity. Are you understanding all of this so far?"

"Yes, Mr. Hardlow," she said with surprising cooperation and composure.

"Good. We then want you to either find out where he is or lure him back to you so we can nab him. Remember, no missteps or you'll wind up right back here in this shithole, awaiting trial and a life sentence. Is that understood?"

"Yes, Mr. Hardlow," she answered forcefully as she met him eye to eye.

"All right, then, let's go." Hardlow stood up. He followed her out the door and waited while she was processed. Hardlow had requested that her clothes be washed, anticipating her cooperation. When she came out of processing, she looked like a new woman—a woman that he wouldn't mind getting to know on a more personal level.

They landed at San Felipe International Airport. Hardlow had tried to get a bit friendly with her, but she would have no part of it. It was obvious that she hated the man—with good reason. She was about to sell her soul to the devil. That didn't mean that she had to sleep with him as well.

"One last thing before you go, Mr. Hardlow," she said pointedly.

"Yes, Lucy?"

"I will need half of the money up front, wired to a third party of my choice, to ensure that you will actually carry through with your end of the bargain."

"Not a chance, Lucy!" he said as his nostrils began to flare. "We have a deal, now stick to it!" as his pisstivity began to climb new heights.

"No deal, Hardlow. I don't trust you. Without me, you have no Cantino," she responded as she held up her left hand and flashed the number one sign with her middle finger.

"I see you're attitude has changed drastically since you've touched down in your own little neck of the woods. Perhaps we should fire this plane back up and run you back up north where I'm sure there's plenty of room in general population."

"It's not going to work, Hardlow. I'm calling your bluff. Putting me in jail is easy. Your friends in Washington would look at that as the cowardly thing to do. It's too easy. You need me Hardlow and you know it. It you want to take me back to Mexicali, then let's go. But I know that your career is on the line!"

Hardlow had to think about this. This woman wasn't stupid. He was getting too personally involved. His little head was doing the thinking and she figured that out.

"OK, Lucy, you're right. There's nothing wrong with a little deposit down before a job is done. Your being in jail really wouldn't accomplish anything in terms of completing my mission. I'll tell you what—I'll give you a hundred grand down in good-faith money," he said.

"Five hundred grand or no deal. Take my offer and get the money, or take me back to jail," she said, standing her ground.

What do I have to lose? Only Cantino, he thought. "You know, Lucy, I could lock you up and throw away the key today." He smiled as he mentally fumbled for his words. "But I'm going to be nice to you today. I'm actually going to honor your request because if you foul up on this one, not only will I kill you," he paused momentarily, "I'll burn your fuckin' orphanage down while all those bastard children are sleeping, along with the rest of the Baja!" His flared temper screamed with desperation.

"No problem, Hardlow," she said as she smiled timidly. "Here's the routing and account numbers. When the money is wired and confirmed, I will put this deal together for you. And this time, I would suggest 'getting on it' before I change my mind."

"No problem," Hardlow replied as he bitch slapped her mouth with his open hand. Lucy was visibly hurt but did not react.

"Just remember, you little whore, you work for me. I don't have to be nice to you in any way. I run this peninsula you call the Baja and you of all people will never control me!"

"That's great, Hardlow. Let me know when the money's wired and I will look forward of having the pleasure of seeing you again."

Hardlow made a hasty exit and headed north to town from the airport while Lucy was bussed down to the orphanage by federal agents. Hardlow requested that he be dropped off on the boardwalk on the downtown coastline in San Felipe for some downtime and relaxation. He spent a half hour walking up and down the boardwalk listening to desperate solicitations from beggars and vendors alike. One punk even offered him a chance to buy some gonja and coke. Hardlow laughed it off as he thought to himself, *If only the poor peasant knew who he was dealing with!*

He decided to walk a few streets to Al's bar where he started off with a cold Pacifico and an order of deep-fried shrimp from the patio kitchen. He immediately moved to some rum and cokes and tied on a buzz. After being shot down by a few wealthy widows, he stumbled next door to the strip club where he had his night's catch within an hour. He thought, *Life is great.*

CHAPTER 93

The Cuban was riding me hard when I suddenly put a stop to her sexual appetite. My picture was on the news, along with some footage of a destroyed Ponga boat. The talking head was rapidly explaining how a certain Cantino had been murdered at sea and the case was officially closed. The girl immediately began to panic when she realized that she had been screwing a wanted murderer/drug dealer who was reportedly dead. She quickly gathered her clothes and left the room. I, on the other hand, was thrilled to hear the news. I may be broke, but it looked as if I might now have my freedom back.

My guilt over the current drug use and the young Cuban flooded over me as I began to feel God work his magic in mysterious ways. My good luck had returned—I owed it all to the Lord and that beautiful young lady, Lucy. I'd let the news die down and then make the call. I couldn't wait to see the love of my life.

I jumped out of bed and got my clothes on. When I went out into the kitchen, the maid said the Cuban girl had fled and asked if everything was all right. I nodded yes. It was a good thing that she left—her absence removed temptation. I couldn't do those things anymore. Except with Lucy.

CHAPTER 94

It was eight in the morning when the call came in. Lucy had been anticipating it at any time because all the news channels had carried the story for two days straight. She was bothered by the in-depth reporting about Jose and all the things that he had allegedly done.

"Honey, it's Jose! We're home free!" he yelled into the phone. "Did you see the news?"

Lucy began sobbing on the other end of the phone, as she was about to place her first nail into his coffin.

"Yes, Jose. I'm so happy," she replied. Her words were accompanied by wet sniffles into the receiver.

"Lucy, I'm going to be there shortly. I just have one favor I have to do for Mr. Robles."

"Where are you?" she asked nervously, knowing that the call was being listened to and recorded.

"I can't tell you right now," he said as Lucy sighed in relief.

Damn! the surveillance technician thought as he listened in on the conversation. *Come on, Lucy. Give me something here,* he said to himself under his breath.

"Jose, when am I going to see you?" she asked desperately.

"I'll be coming to San Felipe in exactly five days. In a boat. I'll need you and the crew to help me with one last deal. I'll explain the details later. But it's for my old boss. I owe him. It's also for you and our children."

"Jose, you promised. We have enough money..." Lucy said, her words tapering off into sobs.

"Lucy, the money's gone. I can't get to it. And I'll never be able to access it. I'll have to explain later."

He didn't have time to explain, but he didn't need to. She already knew. She was just playing the part for that evil bastard, Hardlow. She truly loved him, but was receptive to Hardlow's sobering words that people don't change. That attitude, however, countered all of her Christian beliefs. Still, she knew that Hardlow was a realist who had been dealing with drug dealers for decades. She was confused. *Jose has so much baggage,* she thought as she tried to justify her treasonous actions.

"Lucy, I will need you to meet me at the lighthouse on Sunday with at least two others. It's a major load worth over a million. I'll give you more details later, but you must be there for me."

"OK, my dear," she said softly, beginning to cry again. The phone went dead. Lucy knew that Jose would not spend much time on the phone, to keep the call from being traced. It didn't matter, though. The authorities were on his case. *My poor love,* Lucy thought, *he doesn't know.*

CHAPTER 95

The Deacon made his way out of the orphanage at his usual time that afternoon. He drove straight to the church in San Felipe like he had done every day for the last six years that he held the sacred position. The feds followed him expecting very little excitement. He knew that he was being followed, and they knew that he knew. Hardlow's surveillance team parked their car, walked down the street, and sat at a local restaurant where they ordered beers and fish tacos. *The Deacon's harmless,* they thought.

Religion is as much about power and control as believing. The Deacon was part of the Church's power structure and when he needed a favor, he knew what direction to turn. Who would turn away from doing a favor for a man of the cloth? So it was no surprise when the Deacon excused himself from the daily mass to make a phone call in the vestibule of the church. It was a local number and it was urgent. In a matter of minutes, a tall dark Mexican man showed up and was handed a sealed envelope from the Deacon. It was from Lucy.

The man opened the envelope and read the note. He immediately reached for the cell phone hanging from his belt and made a call as he walked outside of the church. Within seconds, he was back inside.

"Deacon Cruz. Who followed you?" he spoke in his machismo Spanish lingo.

"The two gringos who are at Tacos Carlos down the street."

"Thank you." The man walked out of the church towards the makeshift restaurant.

Sitting at a couple of tables away, he observed the two young agents laughing while they guzzled Dos Equis and ate their food. Down the road, two well-dressed men were bugging the communication system and placing a GPS tracking device underneath their car. *We'll see who's gonna be laughing now,* thought the Mexican as he stared at the gringo cops.

CHAPTER 96

Hardlow kept his promise to himself: he would always find time to enjoy his surroundings regardless of his work at hand. The third world was his to conquer. He was rather drunk the night before and remembered almost getting into a fight with one of the hookers next to Al's bar on the back street. His mind was a bit fuzzy, but he remembered some of the hooker's "masculine" qualities. He noticed that the bouncers were laughing at him; it didn't take him long to realize that the hooker was a dude.

He had grabbed her hand and realized that she had hands like a farmer and an Adam's Apple to match. So he did what came natural to him and grabbed the hooker's crotch, crushing the poor dude's package. As the victim began to scream, in a rather low voice for that matter, Hardlow kept squeezing. One of the bouncers approached Hardlow, but he turned and stared the man down. The bouncer stopped in his tracks and suddenly the bar fell quiet.

The victim's face was turning bright red as people began to move away from the scene. Hardlow head butted the transvestite, sending him across the room. He grabbed the young lady who was sitting in the corner with his left hand while he produced his federal badge with his right. He didn't need to say anything. The bouncers cleared a path as he dragged the young hooker out of the club.

No price was negotiated. She was too scared. They walked to the hotel where Hardlow was staying. He was drunk but really pissed about the dude in the club. He undressed the young prostitute and made his way with her as best he could. He was disappointed in himself because he wasn't 20 years old anymore. It didn't matter. She was for his pleasure only. He finally gave up and sent her home with a 100 dollar bill. She appeared to be happy that she got paid and offered her phone number to him in broken English.

"Get lost, you little whore," he said, slamming the door on her. He then passed out.

That was all that he could remember as he climbed out of bed and saw the condom on the floor, perfectly intact in its wrappings. *I really am a dirty old man. What would my wife and children think of me? If they only knew—maybe they do know.*

He quickly showered and gathered up his belongings. The fun was over and it was time to get back to work.

He checked out of the hotel and strode across the street where he found a small bakery with fresh coffee. It was a bit warm out to be drinking coffee, although the sunshine did help to clear his head. He made a couple of phone calls; within minutes, a black Suburban was clogging up traffic in the middle of the narrow street. Despite all of the horns honking, Hardlow made no effort to improve his pace as he walked to the passenger seat. A cop pulled up along the side with his lights flashing. Hardlow ignored him and the cop quickly figured out that it was the feds. He immediately tried to calm the irritated drivers.

Hardlow and his aides sped out of town towards the orphanage, where they would begin to set the trap for the catch of the day—or in this case, a lifetime.

CHAPTER 97

It was a quick turnaround for Hardlow and the boys. When they arrived at the orphanage, Hardlow made a personal point to escort her to the Suburban. She was dressed in a conservative black skirt with an off-white blouse. She wore flats, mitigating her beautiful legs. Hardlow followed her from behind to the vehicle, fantasizing about her wearing high-heeled pumps and a skimpy, revealing skirt.

"Lucy, are you ready?" Hardlow said with a sarcastic grin. "Your lover should be in San Felipe in just a few hours."

"Yes, I'm ready," she replied as she got into the vehicle and placed the seat belt around her lap and torso.

"Great." He followed her into the vehicle and made himself comfortable by widening his legs. "OK, kid, let's get rolling. We've got headlines to make."

The Suburban and its fellow vehicle exited the orphanage and made their way to Highway 5. Hardlow said nothing but kept staring at the side of Lucy's face. Lucy felt the uncomfortable stares; she, however, remained business-like, and kept her straight ahead. Hardlow placed his left hand on her right leg and began to gently stroke her soft, shaven skin. *God you're hot!* he thought.

"Mr. Hardlow, get your surly hands off my legs," she said sternly as she slapped his hand with her fist.

"My, my, aren't we grumpy today?" he remarked, pulling his hand away yet toying with her emotions.

"Do not touch me! We have an agreement and I expect you to keep this all business."

"Haven't you ever mixed business with a little pleasure? Contrary to what they say, it's been a habit of mine for decades."

"Mr. Hardlow." She turned and stared at him directly. "It would be in your best interest, trust me, to keep this all business!" She turned her head back to look straight ahead.

"What do you mean by that?" he asked as his perverted eyes were temporarily diverted once again by her body.

"You'll see, gringo man."

"Gringo man, eh? That's awfully arrogant coming from a woman who's desperate with very little options."

Lucy ignored him and tried to close her eyes, but it was impossible. To her left, the sun was dropping over the San Felipe Sierras. She became lost in thought,

Hardlow decided to lay off Lucy. He was excited but had an anxious feeling about his lack of connection with some of the officers in the local entourage. *Typical, flaky Mexican cops, he thought. Half of them are crooked, the other half stupid.* They had been subordinate, but his mental antennae sensed that they cared more for the caretaker of the orphanage instead of the mission at hand. He realized that Lucy was well known in the area, but didn't they know how crooked she was? If not, they'd eventually find out.

It seemed like forever before their convoy reached the pavement of the road. Within minutes, they were coming up to an Army checkpoint. They were quickly waived through as the teenagers with AK-47s acknowledged their superiors. Hardlow calculated that they were within a half hour of their destination. It would be relatively soon that the trendy little fishing village of San Felipe would render Jack Hardlow, a record-setting catch of a lifetime.

CHAPTER 98

As the popular tourist destination that it had become, Puerto Penasco, or Rocky Point as it was known to by Americans, was still a small, close-knit community. The murder of Police Chief Espino had left the community in fear and anger. These types of needless, brutal murders only happened in places like Mexico City, Tijuana, and Nuevo Laredo, but not Rocky Point.

The Chief was a devout Catholic who had a reputation of being fair, known to keep most of his officers as honest as he could. But there were simply no known leads. No one had heard the shots, which indicated the killer most likely used a silencer on his pistol. It was obviously a professional hit. But who? Espino had no known enemies except the small percentage of petty criminals found in every town that had contempt for any authority. And why so many shots? An entire clip? It was dumbfounding and, unfortunately, the case was quickly becoming cold.

CHAPTER 99

It was 9:30 in the evening and Elian Castro was drunk. Ten thousand dollars cash went a long way with the Cuban dissident and he wasn't about to give up the party. He had decided to stay in Rocky Point a while and enjoy a new hooker every night. But the drunk Elian was a different person than the cold, skilled, professional killer that he was when he was sober. Like so many people who had some Indian in their blood, Castro and alcohol was a deadly combination.

So when the young stripper tried to explain to him that she didn't sleep with men, only danced at the strip club for money to pay for school, he took great offense. In fact, when he grabbed her by her bikini underwear, it was then that the two massive bouncers had taken action. They grabbed him from behind—they quickly received foul insults and physical resistance. Not only was he loaded but he was careless as well. The 9-mm weapon that he had on his person was the first sign of trouble.

As the first bouncer placed him in a headlock, the second one bound his hands behind his back. He then placed bracelets around his ankles. The suspect continued to resist with futile results.

A weapon in Mexico, unless you are permitted to carry, is a major crime. The police were called. Castro was immediately arrested and taken to jail. It was there that they were able to determine that the 9-mm pistol was the very same pistol used in the murder of Chief Espino.

Because of Chief Espino's popularity, and the tight bond between Rocky Point and the gringo community, several professionals from both the United States and Mexico had come together to investigate the murder. It was there, for the purposes of leniency, that Mr. Castro spilled his guts about Agent Jack Hardlow, and his contract hit.

He then became belligerent and was once again restrained. This time, he was injected with a sedative and quickly became unconscious. By the time he woke up, he had a splitting headache and had no idea where he was. He had forgotten everything—until they played him the confession video.

CHAPTER 100

There were two Suburbans in the caravan coming from the orphanage. Hardlow and Lucy with the two local cops up front, and the rest of the entourage in the Suburban behind them. Hardlow still had several agents stationed in and around the orphanage, making sure everything stayed calm while they were gone. Hardlow purposely left his men in the other vehicle so he could get away with groping Lucy and acting anything but becoming. It was a bit of a shock when he turned his head around and realized that the Suburban following them was no longer in sight.

"Hey, fellows," he said as he turned his head back around, staring at the backs of the two cops. "The boys behind us are gone."

Suddenly, the Suburban pulled over as the cop in the passenger seat drew his weapon and pointed it at Hardlow.

"Agent Hardlow, where is the money?" said the young cop as he cocked the old wheel gun and pointed it at his face.

"Excuse me, son!" as he said in defiance. "What money?"

"The money that you promised to wire our friend here," he replied as his eyes rolled towards Lucy for reassurance.

Hardlow moved his hand towards the inside of his jacket.

"Don't you dare reach for that gun, Mr. Hardlow, or I'll blow you're fucking head off!"

"Why, you son of a bitch!" he screamed. "Do you know who the fuck I am?"

"Lucy, slowly remove Agent Hardlow's gun from the inside of his jacket. One wrong move, Hardlow, and you'll be swimming in your bloody brains."

Lucy slowly reached inside of his cheap tweed sports coat and unholstered the weapon.

"Now hand it to me," the cop said, staring at Hardlow, who suddenly found himself facing two pistols at his head.

The front seat passenger holstered his own pistol and got out of the car. He walked to the back door while the driver kept his eyes on Hardlow. "Get out," he said, opening the door.

Hardlow begrudgingly stepped out of the vehicle, where he was told to place his hands up against the side of the vehicle. While the one cop drew out his gun again and kept it pointed at Hardlow, the driver came around the vehicle and frisked the agent.

"Now listen, sir. We're not here to hurt you. We only want to guarantee the rest of the money. Trust me when I say, if you don't cooperate, you won't see the sunrise."

Hardlow was taken back. He underestimated the influence Lucy had with the local cops. His abusive nature obviously didn't help either.

"I've already given her a down payment. I can't imagine why she wouldn't trust me," he said, smiling sarcastically.

"None of us trust you, unfortunately."

"Well, we have a deal and I plan on sticking to it. Upon Cantino's capture, she'll get the rest of the cash."

"That deal has now changed. We want it all up front, or the deal's off."

Hardlow swallowed hard and bit his tongue. He was in no position to negotiate. But he also knew that the other vehicle had to be on its way. He thought he would stall them a while.

"Well, what do you expect me to do, call the Caymans now? It's too early in the morning. The banks are closed."

"Yeah, you're right. But you can call your bank in Switzerland at this hour," the young cop smiled, calling his bluff.

"Switzerland—are you crazy?"

The young cop stepped closer to him. "Open your mouth," he said as he drew his weapon to his face.

Hardlow's eyes raged with fear.

"One more chance, sir. Open your mouth or I'll blow it open."

Hardlow slowly opened his shaking lips as the officer placed the tip of his pistol to the back of his throat. "Now listen carefully, you crooked son of a bitch. You are going to have that money wired now or I am going to take you up behind that rock and have you dig your own grave. I'm then going to blow your brains out through the back of your head and watch your body follow them into the pit. Is that descriptive enough for you?" He slowly backed the pistol out of his mouth and wiped it on his shirt.

"I will need my laptop out of my bag along with my satellite phone. I can advance the money to the lady, I suppose."

"Good. That's what I wanted to hear."

"You're a bastard, Hardlow," as Lucy kicked his shin.

Hardlow hit the ground hard, not being able to break his fall. "Son of a bitch!" he yelled. "You want me to get this money wired to you or what?"

"You're going to get the money wired, Hardlow. I just thought it would be nice for you to put yourself in my position for once." She then kicked him in the groin.

Hardlow screamed as he curled up into the fetal position.

"Hopefully, that little thing will be permanently disabled," she said, turning around to get back into the truck.

It took him minutes to recover and Lucy was enjoying every moment of Hardlow's pain. For the first time since basic training, Jack Hardlow's life was out of his control. He hadn't been this scared since Vietnam. And to his dismay, the other Suburban never showed up.

CHAPTER 101

The Suburban suddenly lost power. Little did the DEA agents in the back seat realize that the driver had placed the vehicle in neutral when they were on the highway and shut the engine off. He flipped the ignition forward, lighting up the dashboard with multiple red indicator lights, without fully turning over the engine.

"We've lost power, gentlemen," he said as he coasted to the side of the road.

"Great," said one of the agents in the back seat. "Hardlow's gonna be furious."

"I'll call ahead to Agent Hardlow and tell him what's going on when I look at the engine."

"Good, because Torrence and I don't know shit about mechanics," the DEA agent replied.

"Why do you think we joined the DEA?" Torrence said. They both laughed.

The Mexican driver got out of the vehicle and popped the hood, pretending that he was diagnosing the problem. He also pretended to call the other Suburban, making his voice loud enough for the DEA agents to hear. He left the hood open and walked back to the car and jumped in.

"I think it's the alternator. The battery seems to be really low."

"That's OK. I'll call Johnson back at the orphanage and have him come get us. What did Hardlow say?"

"He said the same thing, call the orphanage. They had to continue on so they could get ready for the ambush. He said just to hurry up. If he didn't see us in an hour, he would send a helicopter."

"Good enough," the agent said as he pulled out his satellite phone and made the call. A half hour later, a Humvee pulled up with Johnson and a kid from the Army. They all piled in except the driver.

"I'll stay here with the vehicle and have a tow truck come pick me up."

"Good enough. We've got to get going. We've got a criminal to kill."

Once they were out of sight, the Mexican fired up the Suburban and cranked on the air. He called his counterpart, who was transporting Hardlow.

"Mission accomplished. They're on their way."

"Gracias amigo."

CHAPTER 102

All of the local cops knew Lucy and were not opposed to helping her through this dilemma. Unfortunately, everything was in a quagmire because they were pretty much left in the dark. It was a multi-task effort and the local cops were at the bottom when it came to details and information on the mission.

Jack Hardlow was in charge and at the top of the chain of command. He had DEA agents, federal police from Mexicali, the Mexican Army, and the local cops for backup and support. With Hardlow as the point man of the operation, orders from him were to be followed.

The local cops had a difficult time doing this because Hardlow had no respect for anyone in the operation, including his own agents. He was abusive and had a tendency to go off on tangents and rants. He had a "I've got nothing to lose at this point in my career" attitude and was blatant with his reckless actions and obnoxious outlook. There was no loyalty to him.

On the other hand, they all shared an affection for Lucy. Many had known her for years, along with her boyfriend, Lefty. They had always taken care of the cops, whether it was legitimate or not. They also did a lot of charity work that benefited the community and the Baja in general. So it was a Catch-22 working for Hardlow, whose actions could only hurt Lucy. And if Jose Cantino was a friend and lover of Lucy's, he was a friend of the cops, regardless of what he was wanted for. And although the Chief of Police gave orders to his subordinates to back up Hardlow and his task force, he did so in a half-heartedly way and his boys knew it.

The call had come in just after sundown that evening while the operation was in motion and the Chief was falling in and out of sleep on his lounge at home. He wasn't happy about being jarred from his sleep, but his wife said that it was an important call from the Puerto Penasco Police Department.

"Yes?" the Chief said as he took the call.

"Sir, this is Detective Carlos Espinoza of the Puerto Penasco Police Department..."

The Chief listened and suddenly jumped out of his chair.

"You can't be serious, detective?" the Chief said as he stumbled around looking for his shoes.

"Yes sir, it's true. The weapon used in the crime was found on the Cuban. He said that Hardlow hired him to do the hit."

Anger quickly built within the Chief as the detective continued to brief him on the events of the murder of his comrade and friend, Chief Espino.

"Don't worry, detective, I'm on my way. I'll personally arrest the son of a bitch myself!"

CHAPTER 103

Jose Cantino was expected early that morning, when the fog would be dense and the town asleep. Because the bars closed at two, the authorities guessed he would be in shortly after the drunks went home and sometime before the sun rose. It was a rather short window of time, but easily managed from a tactical operation.

Hardlow made a difficult, self-conscious effort not to discuss the wire transfer performed earlier to anyone. It was water under the bridge and it wasn't like he had to do something that he didn't agree to do. But it bothered him immensely. Hardlow was a control freak and he simply was not in control. *What if they had wanted more?* he kept thinking to himself. *Never again will I travel alone with local cops, unless I plan on killing them,* he smiled to himself. In fact, that option was certainly one within reach.

Hardlow knew that Lucy and the two cops had witnessed the transaction along with the confirmation number. He also assumed that the local cop driving behind them was in on the heist because the second car were not behind his when the assault and wire transfer took place. *I didn't think these bastards were that smart. But then again, they certainly knew how to play the game.*

Hardlow would find out for himself later why they had been left alone for so long. It would be interesting to see what the other agents stories were. He would, however, mark the two cops in the front seat of his Suburban permanently in his head. One day, perhaps even after retirement, he would track the two hoodlums down and personally torture the little criminals. If he held a grudge, it was for life.

Hardlow tried to switch mental gears. Incessant thoughts of failing himself could make him lose focus on the big prize. He would just have to move on and forget about this afternoon in the interim.

The Humvee that replaced the second Suburban arrived in San Felipe just after sundown where they all met in a small room at the Costa Azul Hotel. The two beds had been stood up on their sides and stacked in a corner to make room for chairs and an easel that detailed the operation. A plain-clothes cop walked across the street and ordered 30 fish tacos to go and various sodas from a taco stand and brought them back to the room. The tacos filled the void.

Hardlow began speaking and carefully went through the game plan, getting verbal confirmation that everyone knew their duties in the operation. As he began his closing, he opened up his briefcase, revealing tens of thousands of dollars.

"This, my friends, will be divided equally among you all when Mr. Cantino is successfully killed or apprehended!" he said as he pulled stacks of 100 dollar bills from the leathered box. "This is no joke. This is money that was confiscated recently in a drug bust in Culiacan. I have been authorized by both the U.S. and Mexican governments to give you this money if we nab the son of a bitch tonight. *Comprehende?"* he said, then slammed the case shut and expressed a fake smile.

There was no response from anyone, just their complete attention.

Hardlow picked up the case with his left hand and held out his right. "This is it, my friends."

One by one, they each stacked a hand one upon one the other.

"Let's move out."

They all filed out of the hotel room with Lucy by Hardlow's side. He would not let her out of his sight. He was obsessed with her and they both knew it. Within minutes, all of the vehicles involved in the operation caravanned out of the hotel parking lot and headed north. When they got to their destination, they were on top of a hill with a view of the ocean. Directly above them to their right was the famous lighthouse that overlooked the small fishing village.

Two high school kids were interrupted from their groping session and were quickly escorted from the property. The restaurant across the street was closed. Evening was winding down and San Felipe was getting ready for bed.

Hardlow again took the reigns and reinforced the original plan that he had just laid out at the hotel. As he spoke, he became more and more pissed off every time he eyed Lucy and her crooked cohorts. His style had become more timid as thoughts of weakness kept entering his mind.

"Agent Jackson will be giving the signal as Cantino comes in. He will flicker his flashlight at Cantino's incoming boat and direct him to shore. As the boat approaches land, we will beam in on Cantino using an infrared scope. And remember, this guy is armed and very dangerous. As much as I would like to detain and arrest him, do not hesitate for one moment to shoot and kill. He's too big of a risk unless he flat out surrenders."

Lucy held back her tears as best she could. Her friends on the force would look the other way but not the Federal Policia or the Mexican Army. This is what these guys lived for and Cantino's capture would mean lots of money and promotions.

Hardlow continued to lay out the logistics and made sure that every agency involved was dialed in on the same frequency. He could have easily summoned more personnel, including the Mexican Navy, but they would probably screw it up. It had become personal with Cantino now. An obsession. Hardlow would break the rules on this one and let his personal ambitions outride good conservative police work.

I'm going to personally kill the bastard. He smiled. He couldn't wait.

CHAPTER 104

Detectives Morales and Fox had both known Lefty for years before he was gunned down; they were still personal friends with Lucy. They had all grown up together and were as tight knit as most families. Years ago, Lefty had gone to the other side, but blood was thicker than water. If it weren't for Lefty and his generous donations to the town of San Felipe, Morales and Fox would have probably headed over to the mainland to find more lucrative work. It was Lefty who insured regular bribes to all of the local officers, including 20,000 dollars to the two detectives for turning the other way on a deal of a lifetime. Unfortunately, corruption was a core part of an officer's salary.

The San Felipe police force had few officers who were permanent and stable. The young officers transferred down from Mexicali were often bored. Although the blonde tourists caught their eyes, for the most part, the town was slow. They wanted action. San Felipe only had action with tourists and fishing.

With the exception of the Chief, Morales and Fox called most of the shots when it came to the field. Because of the circumstances regarding the covert operation of capturing Cantino, the two made the call to send all of the rookie personnel down south to patrol the minute fishing village of Puertocitos, protecting the desolate town from the few aging ex-patriots who occupied most of the township. It was an exercise in futility, knowing that the worst thing that could happen was a drunkard pissing in public. But then again, who was watching? They justified the trip to the officers by stating that they had to show an occasional presence 50 miles south to let everyone know that they still had a grip on things. It was a bit flimsy—the justification that is—but no questions were asked. Morales and Fox were well respected and if they said to go, their subordinates went.

Both detectives knew that if there were ever an investigation, their hides would be up for auction. They were now part of a conspiracy; the fewer witnesses, the better off the two men would be.

The detectives had been in contact with the entourage from the orphanage. Hardlow did not know that the cop in the passenger seat was sending text messages the entire time, communicating every word said and move made. Hardlow and his boys also didn't know about the bugs and the tracking systems that were secretly installed while Hardlow's agents were fucking off their surveillance responsibilities by drinking at a taco stand. The cop in the passenger seat had confirmed via text that Hardlow had transferred the money. Retirement was now secure for all of the officers because Lucy had agreed to split up the pie in return for their help and cooperation.

Morales led the meeting back in the conference room at the station. Fox and three officers were present. They had all worked together for over a decade; trust and loyalty was never questioned. Not only was their friend's life at stake, so was there own future, both physically and financially.

"We have tracked their car and monitored Hardlow's communications. They're guessing that Cantino will be in between three and four o'clock in the morning..." His voice cut off with a cough. "Excuse me." He cleared his throat. The nervousness was setting in.

"This makes sense as the town will be dead. If he waits until sunset, he'll be in direct conflict with the fisherman."

The detective stood up and walked over to an old chalkboard. He began to lay out his own plan. Without getting into specific details, he reinforced that there may be several options for executing their plans. Missions of this nature never went as planned, but he needed to know what each officer would do in case events didn't play out in their favor. Scenarios were gone over and Morales made it very clear that he was relying on 100% of each officer's trust, loyalty and discretion.

"Just for the record," he said, then paused and stared at the floor, "the money has been transferred." He waited for their reaction. There was none. As he looked up, however, he flashed a slight grin that immediately brought smiles from his comrades.

"Are there any questions, gentlemen?"

"No sir," said the officers one by one.

"Then let's get going and get this behind us."

Morales walked over and put a hand out. Simultaneously, each officer put a hand into the pile one upon one another.

"Be safe, my friends, and be sure to have one another's backs."

As they gathered their things and walked towards the door, there was a loud ruckus coming from the lobby outside. It was the Chief.

CHAPTER 105

"Chief, what's wrong?" Morales asked with concern.

"Hardlow is what's wrong. The DEA guy from the States."

"Yes, we're familiar with him," said Morales. "He's got quite the reputation."

"I just got a call from Rocky Point. They think they have the guy who killed Chief Espino," he said in anger.

"You mean in custody?"

"Yeah," the Chief acknowledged as he bit down on his lower lip.

"Chief, that's great news!" Detective Fox piped in.

"Yes and no," said the Chief in a slow, crescendoed tone. "The suspect claims that Hardlow hired him to do the hit."

The room fell silent as the officer's faces met the distress on the Chief's brow.

"You know, Espino was my cousin," the Chief said as his eyes swelled up with moisture.

Morales' insides began to surge with panic. *This could screw up the plan...really complicate things.* The Chief's demeanor switched from sentimental family member to pissed off cop.

"We're going to go down there and arrest that son of a bitch! And I mean tonight!" the Chief yelled as he smacked his fist into his palm.

"But sir," Morales piped in with a bit of hesitation. "We should think this through before we make any rash decisions."

"I agree Chief," Fox said, choosing his words carefully.

"You guys don't understand," the Chief responded, placing a handkerchief over his face. "He was like my brother." He quickly broke down and started to wail like a baby.

The roller coaster of emotions that the Chief was experiencing made it imperative that he not get involved at this point. He was too close to the victim and that never rendered good police work.

"Chief, Chief …I'm sorry," Morales said, searching for comforting words that didn't exist.

"Fox and I can handle this. We'll bring him in—but it may have to wait until the morning."

"Absolutely not!" the Chief screamed. "We must get him now. I mean tonight!" The Chief got up and started walking towards the lobby. Everyone was comatose as they watched him leave the room.

"What do we do now?" asked the local sergeant.

"I'm thinking," said Morales. "Maybe this is a blessing in disguise. Maybe, just maybe, if we tell the Chief where Hardlow is, it will disrupt Hardlow's plan. One less cop might just be the ticket."

As good as it sounded, little confidence was portrayed by the local constabulary. It sounded more like a dream than reality.

"Are you guys coming or what? We've got a murderer to catch!" yelled the Chief in the other room.

"Well, this should be a real showdown," said Morales under his breath.

"Should we contact our counterparts to give them a heads-up?" asked the sergeant.

"You know, my friend, that's why you're still a beat cop and not a detective," smiled Fox. "Don't you remember, they're all on the same radio frequency?"

The aging man looked down at his boots and shook his head in embarrassment.

"Let's go, guys, before the Chief fires us."

The five men walked out of the station wondering whether they would ever return to their normal jobs again.

CHAPTER 106

It was a five-minute drive from the police station to the lighthouse. It was all the time Morales had to tell the Chief what Hardlow was doing.

"You mean to tell me that Lucy is dating this guy that Hardlow's after?" the Chief said with confusion.

"Sir, it's very complicated, but yes. You know, Jose Cantino."

"No, no, no, detective," the Chief said as he shook his head. "Cantino was killed off the coast of Rocky Point a couple of weeks back. Where in the hell have you been? It's been all over the news."

"Chief?" he paused briefly, using the time to think of the best way to give him the news. "Unbeknownst to all of us, it was a setup. A public relations campaign to force him out of hiding."

Silence ensued as the Chief absorbed the news from his subordinate.

"We just found out about it this morning. Hardlow kept it secret until the last minute so no one would leak the information. You know what the DEA is capable of—all those secret agencies that the Yanks have."

"Detective, I am still confused. Why wasn't I notified of this immediately?" the Chief said in a stern voice.

"Sir, Agent Hardlow has the soul discretion in this matter. He has the authority to do as he pleases when it comes to this operation. His Mexican counterpart, whom I've spoken to personally, thinks Hardlow walks on water. He refers to him as a legend and backs him 100%. My hands were tied."

"You didn't answer my question, detective. Why didn't you notify me as soon as you found out it was a setup?" The Chief's words floated in the air as Morales thought of how he was going to answer the awkward question.

The truth was, both Morales and Fox didn't want the Chief to know anything. He was too honest. He would have thrown a monkey wrench into the wheel of events and further confused the matter. The two detectives would need to justify it by saying they had too little notice and time to get the Chief involved.

Before the detective could begin to answer, their vehicle came to a stop in front of the discotechque behind the famous landmark lighthouse.

"Detective, you have some explaining to do when this is over," the Chief said as he opened the door and jumped out of the truck. "Where's Hardlow? The son of a bitch!" the Chief yelled.

It was about to get ugly. The Chief approached the two young boys enlisted in the Mexican Army. "Where's the gringo?" he demanded.

The two boys were scared and said nothing, only raising their shoulders and shaking their heads.

"Damn it!" he yelled. "Then what the hell are you two doing here if you don't know anything?"

"Sir," one of them answered. "I don't know much. We were told by the narcotic officers from Mexicali to back everyone up." He had worry on his face.

"Do you know anything about the operation at hand?" said the Chief to the second soldier.

"Sir, all I've heard is that we're waiting for a boat to come and if there's trouble, we're to follow orders."

The Chief shook his head. "What kind of operation is this? Uninformed people?"

As he left the two boys, a tall Mexican dressed in dark blue fatigues, wearing a protective helmet and goggles, approached the Chief.

"Who are you?" he asked without mincing words.

"Who are you?" the Chief responded indignantly.

"I am with the Mexicali Narcotics Office and your ranting and raving is breaching the integrity of this operation."

"I need to speak to Agent Hardlow of the DEA."

"You still haven't answered my question," the narc said as he gripped his AK-47, demonstrating that he was serious about what he was doing.

"I am the Police Chief of San Felipe and Agent Hardlow is wanted for the murder of Chief Espino of Puerto Penasco!"

The agent laughed. "Impossible. Agent Hardlow works with us to stomp out drug trafficking. Let me see your credentials and a warrant." He pointed the tip of his rifle closer to the Chief.

"You are in my town and I would suggest that you put that rifle away," the Chief as the showdown began. Before the federal agent could respond, Detectives Morales and Fox simultaneously drew their weapons on the narcotic's agent.

"Drop the gun or your dead," said Fox. The Chief stepped back, hesitant as to what to do.

"Sir, we will explain later," said Fox.

"These men are planning to kill a fellow citizen who has not been afforded the opportunity to plead his case in a court of law. I have everything on tape," said Morales.

The Chief continued to withdrawal. "I'm beginning to see things a bit more clearly now."

The federal agent did not move and certainly didn't drop his weapon. So Morales and Fox did what they had to do and cocked their pistols that were aimed at his chest.

CHAPTER 107

As if the little town of San Felipe needed any more fireworks, the scene erupted into pure chaos. Many of the members of the operation were not aware of what was going on because they were spread throughout the scene.

"Where's a radio?" the Chief demanded. Fox grabbed the radio off of the narcotics agent, who did not move his weapon aimed at the Chief's head. He fumbled with the device, and quickly figured out how to operate it. He handed it over to the Chief.

"Now listen up, all personnel. We are calling off this operation immediately," the Chief spoke loudly into the receiver. An echo from down the embankment could be heard in English.

"Who in the hell is compromising my operation?" a bewildered Hardlow screamed as he came up over a hill.

Jack Hardlow and a Mexican sharp shooter had set up an ambush point on the beach directly below the lighthouse. Hardlow based his tactical decision on information that he had extracted from Lucy. This was the point where Lucy had originally planned to meet Jose for his final drop and their reunion. From there, they would escape the Baja and find a new home with a new life. Lucy felt the strains of guilt as she divulged the information to Hardlow, knowing that she would never speak to Jose again.

According to the original plan, when Jose's boat came in, a high-powered beam of light would be used by Lucy to signal her presence and lead him to shore. Hardlow's plan was similar but once Jose was in range, several other instruments of support would be used to kill the wanted drug dealer. Perimeter lights were set up along the beach together with two machine gun nests at different angles to ensure the kill.

It was right after they finished setting up and the plan was playing out with little to no flaws when the Chief showed up and everything flipped for the worse.

CHAPTER 108

"This better be a joke," Hardlow huffed into his radio as he tried to assess the situation. His voice was stiletto from his heavy breathing, being out of shape. "And even if this is a joke, whoever you are, you're gonna pay!" The radio went silent as you could hear Hardlow walking at the edge of the hill, ascending onto the plateau.

Detective Fox began the mutiny by yelling to those within the vicinity that they must abandon the operation. As he held his pistol firmly at the narcotic agent, another federal officer out of the blue yelled "Bullshit!" Fox was startled and moved his head towards the direction of the voice.

"Put that pistol down, Fox. It's not worth it," he said.

"I'm not moving my pistol until your sidekick takes the Chief out of his sights with that AK-47."

"You don't know what you're doing, Fox. I've worked with Hardlow for years and for whatever reason you're doing this, you're career is over."

"Hardlow's wanted for murder!"

"Since when?" said the fed.

"Since right now," the Chief jumped in.

"Murder for who?"

"Espino. The Chief from Rocky Point."

"Where's the warrant?"

"I don't need a warrant."

"The hell you don't. You're obstructing an international police operation—you best come to the table with more than that," he said with cockiness.

The federal officer was obviously getting nowhere with the Chief and his two detectives, so he decided to join the standoff by grabbing one of the local sergeants and putting him in a headlock. He then stuffed the tip of his automatic weapon into his mouth.

"The game's over you bastards. Anyone who tries to obstruct this operation any further, is going to see Sergeant Dickwad here get his god-damned brains splattered over the dirt!" he screamed and emphasized it with a wad of spit into the man's head. "And if that doesn't work, I will single-handedly kill every one of you so you can rot in hell for eternity!"

It was then that Hardlow appeared in full view and noticed all of the guns drawn on one another. He didn't have to say much because it was written all over his face.

"What the hell is going on here?" he demanded. "And who the hell are you?" He approached the Chief with his M-16 in hand.

The Chief didn't say a word but just stared.

"OK, then, if you don't want to answer, let me rephrase my question," he said as he continued walking. "Who the fuck are you and what are you doing here?" he screamed as he pointed his gun towards the Chief.

"Are you Agent Jack Hardlow?" the Chief asked calmly.

"You didn't answer my question!"

"I am the Chief of Police here in San Felipe and you, Mr. Hardlow, are under arrest," he snarled like a trapped bear.

Hardlow's face turned to a sarcastic smile as he marched even closer to the Chief. "I am going to have your balls for breakfast in the morning. Do you know what you are saying and who you are talking to? This is a federal operation that you are interrupting."

As Hardlow approached closer, the Chief began to back up. Detective Morales cocked his weapon, which caught the Chief's attention.

"Not so fast, sir," said Morales.

The situation now had gone from really bad to even worse. It seemed as if every agency involved in the operation, from the locals to the feds, had guns drawn on each other. Even worse, the faint sound of an outboard motor was quickly approaching the scene.

CHAPTER 109

Jack Hardlow was never one to lack leadership. But he now knew that despite his efforts to run a tight ship, some of the Mexicans involved in the operation could not be trusted. He had already been forced to wire a substantial amount of money earlier that day, along with getting his ass kicked around by two flunkies and their female cohort. Perhaps it was time to change his tactics and approach. His mind went into overdrive trying to think. If he moved, the plain-clothes detective would most likely blow his head off. But what few people knew was that Jack Hardlow had an earphone hidden in his ear and was wired to a microphone.

"Gentlemen, let's take a deep breath here. I think we've all gotten lost in the shuffle. We're here to apprehend a major player in the war on drugs," he said as he held his bead on the Chief. It made his statement a bit insincere but Hardlow was a realist. "In fact, we should all lower our weapons and talk this out. There is obviously a misunderstanding here."

No one moved. Everyone was afraid of what the other one would do.

"Agent Hardlow?" the Chief asked.

"Yes, Chief?" Hardlow's words came out reluctantly.

"I was just contacted by the Puerto Penasco Police Department. They have a suspect in the murder of Chief Espino."

"Well, Chief, that's very good news. However, what does that have to do with this situation at hand?" he said with frustration.

"Well, Agent Hardlow, the suspect says that you hired him," the Chief said without backing down.

"Is that right?" Hardlow said in his most serious tone yet. "And I bet the moon is made out of cheese, Chief." He cocked his M-16.

Events immediately changed as Hardlow's attention was taken by the voice in his earpiece.

"Sir, I can see the boat," said the young agent on the beach. "Please advise."

"Keep him in your sights," said Hardlow. "We'll take him out when I get this little problem solved I'm having up here on the hill."

"Is everything OK, sir?"

"It will be shortly."

A few of the men were confused as to whom Hardlow was talking.

"Hardlow," said the Chief.

"It's Agent Hardlow to you or sir," he yelled. "In fact, you have ten seconds to think this through or I will personally have the pleasure of blowing your brains out across these rocks—*comprehende?*" His words pierced all of the ears listening on the frequency.

"Ten...nine...eight...seven...six...five...four...three..." He gripped his weapon firmer and maneuvered his finger on to the trigger.

"Sir, I've got the boat within sight and I can make out a silhouette behind the helm."

"Flash the light and draw him in," Hardlow responded.

"What's your decision, Chief?...two..." he said with a smile, "...one..."

Everything went silent. The Chief had called Hardlow's bluff, at least for now. Hardlow stepped closer to the Chief and grabbed him by the jacket with one hand and placed the tip of his weapon at his left temple.

"Is this how you want to die?" asked Hardlow. He knew that if he shot the Chief, other lives would be taken, and possibly his own. Guns were pointed in all directions and at one another.

"Agent Hardlow," said Morales as he reached the bottom of his countdown.

"I'm sorry, detective, I didn't get your name as you rudely interrupted me."

"My name is Morales, sir."

"Oh, you must be one of the assholes involved in this conspiracy?"

"No, sir. The Chief is my boss and friend. I will not allow you to kill him if I have any control over the situation!" he said.

"Good enough, son. I hope you had a nice dinner with your wife and kids this evening because when I'm done with you, you'll be sitting in a Mexican prison for the rest of your life. Or better yet, meeting your maker."

"Not if I kill you, sir," said the detective whose hand was beginning to tremble with fear.

"You don't have the balls," said Hardlow.

"You're a bastard, Hardlow." Morales's eyes began to water.

"Yes I am, my friend. Yes I am."

"Sir." Hardlow's earpiece went off again. "The boat is beginning to slow down. Is everything OK up there?" the agent down below asked with concern in his voice.

"Everything will be fine. Just don't let him out of your sight. We'll be up and ready shortly."

"Listen up, gentlemen," Hardlow said, withdrawing his focus on the Chief and slowly turning in all directions to get the situation under control. "Our man is within our sights and someone is gonna have to make a move—or we're gonna have to work together on this."

As he was sizing up the situation, he quickly noticed that something had gone terribly wrong. In the midst of all the confusion, Lucy was missing.

CHAPTER 110

Lucy was able to grab a large police flashlight and hide it under her jacket. She knew Hardlow and his goons had every intention of killing Jose. She was suffering immense guilt for having given up so much information to Hardlow and could not stand the thought of not helping Jose. Her entire life had been about helping others. Whether Cantino was a drug dealer or not, she was in love. He had made the first step toward change and was risking his life for her and the orphanage. She would do whatever it took.

She quietly slid down the sandy embankment where the young agent was flashing a powerful light at what appeared to be the boat being piloted by Jose. The fog was thick and she could barely make out the young man in the black uniform. It looked as if the agent was a gringo. He was using a pair of infrared binoculars to monitor the boat's position.

She reached the bottom of the embankment and was met by the shoreline. Her goal was to neutralize the agent before he was able to shoot and kill Jose. Although the fog was thick, she would still be visible on the open beach. She had to make some quick decisions because she was not armed.

About three feet above the shoreline, there was a small pathway that ran above the sand, probably a walkway for when the tide was high. Dense brush separated the pathway from the beach. It would be the perfect cover.

Lucy crawled along the pathway, hiding behind the brush, trying not to make any noise. She was moving quickly towards the agent. She made it to where she was almost directly behind the man in black when the embankment gave out. Lucy lost her footing and rolled onto the beach. The agent turned around with the lamp in hand as Lucy lunged at him with the long, metal flashlight. She knocked him solid on his forehead as the agent's large halogen lamp dropped into the sand. He was rattled but by no means was he out. He reached for the rifle nestled upon a makeshift tripod that he had made out of a large rock and some firewood left over from campers. He butted Lucy across the face, sending her to the sand. Thinking she was out, the agent turned and opened up fire in the direction of the boat's engine.

Suddenly, a frightening noise came upon them like the rumbling of an earthquake. From over the embankment came a helicopter, creating a massive sandstorm. The agent dropped his weapon as he placed his hands over his eyes for protection. The helicopter drowned out the boat's engine, furthering the chaos.

As the helicopter hovered over the coastline, Lucy stumbled over to the crouched agent and rendered the second blow to his head. The agent dropped like a rock, face first into the shallow tide. The blow didn't kill him but Mother Ocean did. He drowned within minutes.

The helicopter now had its massive spotlight on the small vessel. The light was so powerful that it penetrated the fog. The boat was moving quickly towards the beach. Lucy had only one option. She picked up the long rifle and aimed it at the cockpit window. She squeezed the trigger and rattled off several accurate bursts. Within seconds, without any mechanical failure, the copter crashed into the ocean.

The noise from the boat's engine could be heard once again, still approaching the shoreline fast. *Slow down,* Lucy thought to herself as she couldn't believe the quick turn of events. But it was no use. She backed up to being in direct line of the speeding boat, and heard screams and noises from up above. As she turned around to see what all of the confusion up top was about, she found herself staring at the barrel of a 9-mm pistol in the hands of a federale.

CHAPTER 111

The Chief didn't have to make a decision because it had been made for him. Stiletto bullets down on the beach, along with the roar of the helicopter, made everyone take their eye off the ball. The helicopter was a clandestine idea that Hardlow had coordinated on his own without anyone else's knowledge.

Just as the Chief turned his head, his body took a round of Hardlow's bullets. He hit the ground hard from the impact, landing on top of Detective Morales.

"Well, Chief, I guess you blinked," "Hardlow emptied a few more rounds into the Chief's forehead, ensuring the kill." Morales tried to push the dead Chief off of him before the narc filled them both with a few bursts of gunfire. Morales never had a chance. When Hardlow turned around, Detective Fox was pointing his shaking pistol at his head.

"You murderer, you!" Fox's lips fidgeted in anger. "You killed my friend!"

Hardlow said nothing, but only stared at the young cop. "My friend, put your gun down. You've got nothing to gain but everything to lose," he smirked.

"I have nothing!" Fox yelled. "Especially now that you killed my mentor, my boss…my friend!" He broke down crying.

"Look behind you and you will see who actually killed your friend," Hardlow said, catching the ignorant cop by surprise.

"Who's behind me?" Fox asked nervously.

"Just take a look," said Hardlow.

"I will not," said Fox.

Hardlow grinned and shook his head. The noise was deafening as the Mexicali narc blew a hollow point through the back of Fox's skull. Hardlow wasn't happy with the remnants of brains and blood in his face, but it was better than being dead like the two detectives on the ground in front of him.

The other cops were smart enough not to take on the professionals. Hardlow had been at this game too long and seemed to always have a contingency plan. They laid down their arms and quickly surrendered. Then the unthinkable happened. Just as he prepared to head down the hill, he heard gunfire and then the crash.

Holy shit! he thought. *The copter's down.*

"OK, gentlemen. Make sure none of these clowns have any backup on them and get them cuffed. We've got a drug dealer to catch."

Hardlow turned and began running towards the embankment. Before he could get ten feet away, bullets sprayed just below his legs. Hardlow's natural instincts from Vietnam kicked in as he dove to the ground. Set up from behind their black Suburban were two civilians, both heavily armed.

"Everyone, drop your weapons," the first civilian said as two armed men pointed their weapons towards Hardlow and his men. "You have three seconds or you'll be rotting in hell!"

Hardlow hadn't had a chance to give up his rifle when a single bullet ripped through his calf. He began screaming and everyone immediately dropped their weapons. A command was given to the newly freed hostages to stand up. The second civilian removed their handcuffs, setting them free to guard Jack Hardlow and company.

The two civilians now had custody of the situation. They had been brought in by Morales and Fox—both friends of Lefty, as a last-ditch effort in case all went south. As they began to take a human inventory, they quickly realized that two federal officers working with Hardlow were missing. And so was Lucy.

CHAPTER 112

The boat hit the beach, causing a massive jolt that violently jerked my body forward. If I hadn't been lying on the floor of the boat, protected by its shell, I would have been catapulted onto the beach like a rock from a slingshot. There was blood smeared everywhere and I temporarily lost consciousness. Coming to again, I rolled over to my side. I had forgotten where I was or what I was doing—then it came to me. Someone got tipped off. I had been shot and was slowly dying. The feds had me. *I will never live my life in a Mexican jail,* I told myself. *I'd much rather die.* And so I did—an ocean away from Tampico. Or at least I thought I had.

CHAPTER 113

The officer turned around and pointed the gun at Lucy. Lucy became hysterical as she witnessed Jose crash into the shoreline. She fell to the ground, screaming at the world for what just happened. The officer kept the tip of his rifle pointed at her until she finally looked up through her drenched eyes.

"He's dead," the officer said with a grin. "Gone. History. Now get up off the ground, you bitch!" Lucy didn't move. Nothing else could happen that would be any worse than what she just witnessed and it was all because of her.

The federale walked over to her and kicked her in the ribs with his heavy black combat boots. "Get up before I shoot you!" he screamed. Lucy just fell to her side, holding the broken ribs that had just been delivered.

A single shot ripped through the air. The next thing she knew, the officer toppled over her. She could feel the warm blood pooling onto her skin before she could finally maneuver out from underneath him. On top of the embankment, was a civilian with a rifle in his hand.

CHAPTER 114

I regained consciousness again. They were dragging me up a steep embankment in an Army blanket. When we reached the top, it looked like a killing field. Bodies were strewn across the empty lot that overlooked the ocean. I blacked out again. I was losing too much blood.

I had no recollection of the time between the time I blacked out and when I woke up at the local clinic in downtown San Felipe. A local surgeon had performed emergency surgery and had pieced me back together, pumping donated blood into my system. The surroundings were grim, but much better than a field hospital in a war zone. I really didn't know what was going on, nor did I care. All I knew was that I avoided the ultimate blow. For some reason, I was going to make it. I could feel it. I later found out that I was mumbling in and out of consciousness for Deacon Cruz. Being unsure, he had administered by last rights. Prematurely, thank God.

I was drugged with more anesthetics but could sense the urgency beneath the tears in Lucy's eyes. I was in despair, just as she, but I knew somehow, someway, that this woman had saved my life. The same intuitions I had my entire life that guided me from childhood took hold about my fate. I was a survivor, despite the rapid decline in my life's fortune.

We had little time and had to get out of San Felipe fast. I sensed the danger. Federal and local officers had been killed and it would be only a matter of time until the Baja was turned upside down, looking for the culprits. Or in this case, infamous drug dealer, Jose Cantino.

I was taken from the clinic on a gurney and placed into an old conversion van with California plates. I was unconscious again in no time. When I came to next, I was being loaded onto an airplane, overhearing the pilot voicing his concern about the weight of the plane. I recalled that we were carrying the dope that I had brought over from Culiacan. The plane was made to hold eight people and I had the luxury of being laid in the cramped aisle. I had no choice. I could feel the surgeon dressing my wounds and the sharp piercing of a needle in my arm. I knew I was tore up, but couldn't feel the pain. Even the uncontrollable vomiting session didn't seem to bother me. It was all a big blur.

I could overhear everyone speaking in English, including the gringo pilot who appeared to be in his early forties. He looked and sounded familiar, but I couldn't pinpoint him. I was too drugged up to care.

Wait! I thought to myself. I did remember. He was the American who hailed from Arizona who I had met at Gilberto's house! Lucy's network was beginning to kick in. I remember his name being Hatch or something odd like that, but Lucy kept calling him Phil. I had met him only briefly. He appeared to be calm and collected, rattling off his pilot's jargon over the radio as if this was a routine flight.

Phil was speaking on two frequencies: one to the airport authorities, the other to Lucy and our entourage. I'm sure he didn't want to know what had been loaded into his plane and I'm glad he didn't know because he may have opted not to do us the lifesaving favor. For reasons that I would probably never know, he was a loyal patriot in Lucy's army. As I drifted in and out, I heard something about the Pacific side, Tijuana and Ensenada. It jolted me out of unconsciousness as I suddenly tried to get Lucy's attention. I tried to talk, but I just couldn't get the words out. I tugged on her ankle; she quickly unbuckled her seat belt and came to my aid.

"Jose, what is it?" she said with deep concern.

"In my shirt pocket," I barely sputtered the words.

"What about it?" she said confusingly.

I tried to look down but it was too painful. Lucy then reached into my pocket and found the folded-up sheet of paper that included a detailed map and contact information regarding the dope I was to deliver. It had times and places to meet the smugglers. Lucy patted my forehead and said that she had what she needed and for me to get some rest. She climbed back into her seat and fastened herself in. Phil dialed in the coordinates on his GPS. I knew that we were still climbing because I could feel my body at an angle. I briefly saw through a window the mountains west of San Felipe and knew that there was a large range separating the Pacific side. Whatever questions were being asked, I could no longer hear them.

What does Phil know? I asked myself. I guess it really didn't matter at this point. It was life or death, doom or freedom. I preferred the freedom along with everyone else in the plane. I hated how my life had panned out, always on the run and not knowing what was around the corner.

As I continued to dose off, my body and spirit felt a sense of ease that it had not sensed in many years. Odd, considering I was lying shot up in the aisle of a small airplane, wondering what life would deal me next.

My life was always riddled with conflict and emotions. From the time that I was an orphan, always anticipating a family, to when I was adopted, having to kill that pastor, to my drug-dealing days and the murder of my best friend, and even to the time I actually had time to relax in Mazatlan, I've never felt peace. The pain and stress of my life seemed never ending, up until now.

I continually thought of the orphanage, which filled me with inspiration. That inspiration, however, was coupled with the fact that I would always be looking over my shoulder, regardless of what my life looked like. But up here, in this little airplane, hanging on to my life, I felt at peace with who I was and forgiven for what I had done.

CHAPTER 115

It was a short flight across the peninsula. Before I could ask for another painkiller, I felt a sharp sting in my ass. Within seconds, I was feeling as high as our altitude once again. Something told me I shouldn't miss my first touch down in a plane and I programmed my mind to be aware and semi-cognizant.

The sun had peaked over the mountains as Phil began his descent. "There's no stopping now," he said in a determined yet cautious tone.

I began drifting off until I heard the retractable gear lower and lock into place. It was below me, so I could only assume we were preparing to land. But the drugs had tricked me because although I thought I was awake, the landing of the plane jolted me from my sleep. The sense of time had escaped me and I told myself that I must have only been asleep for a minute or so.

There was no conversation between Phil and any air traffic controller, which told me that this flight had not been logged with any aviation agency. In fact, the landing was rough and I quickly determined that we were on a dirt runway. I remember what I saw on the small piece of paper and the instructions that we had and who to meet to consummate the exchange. The meeting place was outside of Tijuana in a vast, desolate place.

My mind was alive but I felt as if I was living in a dead body. My physical features simply would not cooperate with what my mind was telling me.

"Oh shit, are we in trouble," Phil said.

Lucy began to scramble for things; she was visibly panicked. I tried to get a question out about what was wrong but the words wouldn't come. Phil and Lucy began to argue back and forth. For a moment, Phil talked about taking off again. All I heard after that was, "Don't Phil, they'll kill us!"

Then the heated conversation subsided. It was evident that cooler heads had prevailed. I heard Phil draw a deep breath before he spoke.

"OK, let's keep calm. If we panic, we have no hope of getting out of this situation."

I was thoroughly confused. My recollection was that we were to meet some guy named Chuy, who had been Robles's point man in the northern region of the Baja. They knew each other indirectly through other Cartel members but had never had the opportunity to do business one-on-one. Chuy's reputation, however, was legendary as a no-nonsense guy who fired the bullet before he said "freeze."

I later found out that the scenario was much different. The reason for the panic was that when they landed, there was a contingent of Mexican policemen all over the airstrip. This was not expected and never disclosed to me or anyone by Robles. But then again, you never knew how a drug deal would go down. The drug trade constantly changed and operations had to adapt.

Phil shut down the plane propellers and opened up his side window.

"Buenos dias, Officer. How are you?" he said with intense sincerity.

"Buenos dias. Could I see some identification please?" the officer asked sternly.

"Would you like my passport, license, what do you need?" he said calmly.

"How about your wallet?" the officer said.

"What?"

"Show me the money, gringo!" the officer said as began to laugh hysterically. Phil was caught off guard. "Pardon me?"

"You heard me, gringo. Show me the money!"

Phil turned to Lucy and then to me as if that was going to help any-thing. As he searched for answers from our expressionless faces, he slow-ly turned back towards the cockpit window.

"Sir, I don't understand? We're just…"

The cop interrupted him again with a burst of laughter. "How are you, *American?*" he said with a bright smile.

"Good, sir, good I think," he said tamely.

"My name is Chuy." The entire plane let out a "Thank the Lord" sigh when we realized that our contact was sporting an officer's uni-form.

"I know it's not Halloween, but I wanted to dress up anyway," he said with that hysterical laugh.

It was then that Lucy started rattling off in Spanish as a contingent of Mexicans piled out of the back of an old Chevy three-quarter-ton van. Within seconds, Phil and Lucy had their headgear off and were climbing over me to open the door of the plane. Before I knew it, Chuy was inside the plane with his briefcase while Phil conducted the unload-ing of the cargo. I was privy to the details but wasn't in the mental state to comprehend the details of the transaction. What I did remember was that hundreds of thousands of dollars were given to Lucy in return for the delivery. The words *rapido* and *andele* were emphasized in the midst of cluttered sounds from the workers unloading the illicit packages.

The cops had been on the dole because Chuy was a sworn peace officer in Mexico. It was corrupt, but he was our friend at the time and he kept us safe. As the deal wrapped up, Chuy exited the plane. Phil climbed aboard and was mumbling something derogatory about drug dealers and why he was there in the first place.

Within minutes, we were airborne again and circling south. I could hear Lucy and Phil arguing about money and how Phil would not accept anything from her if the source involved drugs. He was adamant in his position.

"I did this as a favor to you Lucy and the man that you loved. Your intentions are good but the money in your hands is dirty. It's no differ-ent than blood."

"I understand Phil and thank you," she said as she began to cry. "It will never happen again. If you only knew…." she paused, "then you'll believe me that it will never happen again."

Phil was pissed because he may have had a suspicion about what was loaded onto his plane but his sacrifice was for Lucy—Lucy the humanitarian, not the dope peddler. He had sacrificed his life and livelihood only to participate in something that he was very against. The irony hit him like a hammer. Lucy, the petite beautiful soul who cared for hundreds of orphans throughout her life, who Phil only knew through their mutual friend Gilberto, showed a side that should never be exposed. Loyal despite his own convictions, Phil was disappointed and let her, and myself indirectly, know it. Lucy knew that he was right and had enough dignity not to say another word. For myself, it was rather obvious that I was the cause of all this, so was a good time to leave the argument and let my medications work their magic. I drifted off into a deep sleep while my body tried to fight off the invasion of Phil's diatribe.

I was awakened when we touched down on a small airstrip south of Ensenada. Reality began to set in. I was feeling rather dirty for bringing these two wonderful people into my life of rancid deprecation.

CHAPTER 116

We had touched down south of Ensenada somewhere near a vine-
yard in the Santo Tomas Valley. Although I would have been opposed
to this plan if I had a say, the owner of the farm was a friend of Phil's.
Phil's rationale was that it was close to where we had to go and that his
plane was a frequent sight at the airstrip in the middle of the vineyards.
It made sense, but I think I was against it because I was no longer in
control. However, the wine apparently was a bonus to the trip.

The shades in the plane had been drawn prior to our landing and I
was left alone to bask in the monotony of the day. The door was left
open for ventilation and I was tended to by the doctor on and off for
the next ten hours. Although it may have been over cautious, I was not
to be moved from the plane until sundown. So I slept as much as I
could, only feeling comfortable when a new injection of drugs was
rushed into my system.

In the interim, Phil visited with his friend the winemaker, while
Lucy arranged for medication, rations, and supplies, to be delivered to
the winemaker's home. One more short flight, then we would go into
hiding for several weeks. We hoped that with time, our case would go
cold and the authorities would give up. Lucy and I only wanted our
lives back. If we succeeded, it would be a new life for the both of us.

CHAPTER 117

Dr. Ferdinand temporarily left the plane, probably to get something to eat or take a leak. As I drifted back into a deep sleep, I was awakened by our pilot Phil. I was still not in a position to say much but I owed this man much more than just my life. I owed him my loyalty, because he not only helped save me, but Lucy as well. I did my best to concentrate as he quietly delivered his opinion on the matter.

"Jose, my friend," he said with genuine compassion.

"Yes, Phil?" I replied, barely whispering his name.

"Do me a favor," he said as he placed his forefinger over his mouth, "and just let me talk." I nodded as I stared into his blue eyes.

"I know what you do and I don't like it." His upbeat face momentarily turned somber.

I didn't know what to say, but apparently my facial expressions said it for me. "Don't say anything, Jose," he said firmly. "It's my turn."

I again nodded in agreement.

"I came here to help Lucy and we had a good conversation during the flight. She's told me the history between you two and, quite frankly, I'm pissed off. In fact, I'm beyond pissed to know that you've sacrificed my safety, freedom, reputation, and principles over the drugs that we transported over the peninsula." His words reinforced his stare.

"But I'm forgiving her, knowing what Lucy does for others," he continued, with his lips tightening around his face. "But don't underestimate how I feel about those fucking drugs in my plane and the fact that you have probably ruined thousands of lives with your greedy, selfish ways and means!"

I tried to say something, an apology, but he placed his hand over my mouth.

"I'm not done," he said as he gave me a disingenuous smirk. "I'm here to make a point."

My eyes gave him an approval to continue on with his sermon.

"If you ever make it out of this mess, which I have my doubts," he said as his hand fisted into rage, "promise me you will never deal drugs or profit from them in any way, ever!"

The cabin of the plane permeated with silence. Although it was brief, Phil's diatribe was truthful, emotional, and to the point. This man had no tolerance for drugs and allowed the weight of the situation to lie on my shoulders. Without hesitation, I responded accordingly. "You have my word, brother."

"Thank you," he said as he slapped me on the shoulder. "This conversation is done!" On the last word, he held his hands up like a referee calling a touchdown.

CHAPTER 118

I was carried out of the plane at dawn and we stayed at the ranch in Santo Tomas for two weeks while I recovered from my gunshot wounds. My bedroom looked like a makeshift hospital; I had round-the-clock care from a local nurse. When I was healed up enough to travel, we headed north to a small town called Las Salinas, where we made arrangements to have a surgeon from Tijuana perform plastic surgery. It was too risky to travel to Tijuana, so we scheduled it in a clinic in Ensenada.

Lucy had the surgery first because the doctor said that I was not well enough. Her face was badly bruised for several weeks. When it healed, she looked much different, but was still beautiful. It was eventually my turn and I was very happy with the results. I actually thought I looked much more handsome. I shaved my mustache and colored my hair a light brown. Every week, I would mix the die into my hair, maintaining a consistent look. I was beginning to feel a lot better about life.

How I survived this fiasco, I would never know. It was an impossibility, according to most. But once again, I persevered and prevailed. I was not out of the game, though. In fact, the game went into overtime.

It was evident that Lucy and I needed to flee the country and live in another part of the world. I knew no one outside of Mexico; however, Lucy had friends throughout South America. I knew why, but opted not to ask too many questions. Because I had given Phil a promise to abandon anything to do with drugs, the thought of being around Lucy's network of friends made me nervous.

We both healed and the doctor gave us the green light to begin our journey out of the country.

CHAPTER 119

It was in late October when we boarded the private boat and headed south from the Las Salinas Marina, towards our new beginning. The
trip would turn out to be rather lengthy, even in a luxurious yacht. The
captain had ties to Lefty, which in turn made Lucy and I like family.
There were eight crew members including the captain, a full-time chef,
two maids, and four deckhands. Lucy and I had our own cabin and
spent most days making love to the rhythm of the sea and munching on
longosta and shrimp.

I was looking forward to my life with this woman. The trip south
gave me plenty of time to contemplate my beginnings and all of the
things, both good and bad, that I had done in my life. This time, however, I didn't feel any pressure and was actually able to relax and enjoy
myself. Lucy was teaching me how to savor every breath of life without
the stress from my past.

Speaking of my past, I spent days confessing my sins to the Lord
without the luxury of a priest. I never did have the gall to tell Lucy
about the Cuban. It would only complicate matters—I would take that
one to my grave. I did feel, though, that I had a new lease on life and it
appeared to have a very good warranty.

When we decided to leave, we knew that regardless of how much
we would miss Pedro and friends, our only way to freedom would be to
go as far south as we could endure while still being able to perform the
Lord's work in a legitimate manner. Because I was literally along for the
ride, I didn't probe too much as to our final destination. Lucy didn't dis-

close much either, afraid that someone may overhear our conversations. Unfortunately, in the drug trade, everyone is suspect; most conversations and actions revolve around distrust and paranoia. The likelihood that the authorities would find us was small, but no one really had to know who we were or where we were going. It was that simple. The further south we traveled, life got easier, one nautical mile at a time.

CHAPTER 120

Colombia was famous for smuggling the world's best cocaine out of its borders, so it was ironic that we were smuggled in. We had fake documents and wound up at a compound outside of Bogota that once housed the infamous Medallin Cartel leader, Pablo Escobar.

From there, we traveled to Ecuador for a few days and wound up on the outskirts of Lima in Peru. We never stayed long in any one place—we didn't want to develop any patterns. We were back on a boat in Peru where we sailed further south to Santiago, Chile. It was there that I found my love of Chilean wine. Alcohol never played a role in my life until Chile, where I learned to view wine not just as an intoxicant, but as a wonderful finish to a lengthy, non-glorified process. It was very similar to my life—the making of a fine wine. Although aging has its drawbacks, in the end, I knew that I would be fine as well.

After several weeks in Chile, we headed east to our final destination, Buenos Aires, Argentina. I later found out that Argentina was well known for its expatriated foreigners, beginning with many Germans prior to the Second World War. Ironically, many Nazis and Jewish Germans escaped the mayhem of Adolf Hitler, and settled among one another in South American countries such as Paraguay, Chile, and Argentina. The stereotype of non-Jewish Germans hating the Jews was thrown out the window in this country, along with any other discriminated race in the world. Argentina was simply a melting pot of people who wanted to enjoy the finer things in life without the politics and hate. It was rather refreshing.

In hindsight, the network of people who helped us along the way was beyond amazing. Although I'm sure most of it was related to the drug trade, we were treated like family and well protected. This was true of authoritative personnel as well. Police officers and customs agents didn't bat an eye and I could only assume that the system never changed whether they killed guys like Pablo Escobar or not. There was always someone to take their place when it came to Cartels or anyone associated with them.

Lucy and I settled in a modest villa on the outskirts of town, where we quickly began volunteering at one of the local orphanages. With almost 15 million people living in Buenos Aires, orphans were not exactly scarce.

Within a year, Lucy and I, living under aliases, were married in the Catholic Church with only a priest as a witness. We were able to purchase a small farm on time, leaving the modest amount of cash that we had virtually untouched. Because of Argentina's robust business climate and Lucy's amazing ability to sell her ideas of protecting the young and the innocent, she was able to raise thousands of dollars to construct the orphanage and keep it maintained on someone else's dime. So without donating our funds, we donated our time and had full capacity within six months. Upon completion of the orphanage, we had a formal ribbon-cutting ceremony and over 200 children who were full-time residents. Although we missed our children desperately back in Mexico, our new family surrounded us.

We recruited a local priest, several nuns, and volunteers to help us complete the mission in life that Jesus Christ taught us. We also were able to hire two paid staff members to help us with administration. Life could not be better, unless we were to live on the ocean, of course. The ocean was near, however, and we never missed an opportunity spend time with her. She, as well, was part of our family.

CHAPTER 121

His body looked aged but his eyes were still focused and sharp. It had been over a year, but he still had not found what he was looking for. He was getting close, picking up a scent here or there. He landed at the Jorge Newbury airport outside of Buenos Aires on a military transport plane and rented a cheap economy car. He planned to stay a while as it was his first time in Argentina. He knew where he would eventually wind up, but he wanted to explore the city and get a taste of the country.

He checked into a hotel without a reservation and pulled a flask of scotch from his bag, which he nipped on while he cleaned up for the evening. He was within walking distance to many bars and tried his luck at a Latin nightclub. Unfortunately, he found that he could no longer pull the ladies like he could in the old days. No woman wanted to bed an old man unless he had some money. In this case, the streets of Buenos Aires were no place to flash the cash. Like so many endings in his life, he was once again, let down.

He called it a night and woke up bright and early; he packed up his belongings and hit the road. It was a heavily populated city and he wondered when the urban surroundings would end. After close to an hour, rural Argentina came into play as he neared his destination.

The rolling hills of Argentina appealed to the old man. Although the river de la Plata and the ocean could no longer be seen, the environment was simple and attracted many of his senses. He imagined himself living somewhere in South America, perhaps Argentina.

He pulled over his car from a distance and watched a large group of children play among the fields, wandering happily in directions that only they knew. There were only a handful of adults supervising, mostly nuns, looking after the innocent. It was peaceful and hopeful and generally nice as he observed the harmonious activity of the children, all getting along. His thoughts were mesmerized as he dwelled upon his entire life and began to think what would have happened if he had made a few different decisions in his life. It was oddly comforting. Then again, not really odd at all because all old men eventually think about their time on earth and the fact that they are mortal.

He pulled the car closer, and decided to park in the dirt parking lot that was freshly cut from the surrounding pasture. The building was newly constructed and epitomized a house of love and caring and most importantly, support—a building that embraced a sense of safety and security for the innocent and unguided.

His life represented a history of violent actions to achieve what his government thought was the best way to accomplish peace. It was a tough world out there, and for the first time in his adult life, he realized that all in all, his life lacked merit and contentedness. But it was his life and he could not change the past. It was the direction that he chose.

He inched the car closer to the entrance, where he eventually shut off the engine. He smiled in the rearview mirror and placed the gun that was in his attaché case into his shoulder holster. He touched his temples with both of his hands and physically reassured himself why he was here. He exited the vehicle and walked towards the entryway. There were no security guards or electronic gates, just a door of welcome in his path. He opened the door and scanned the small lobby of the building. Nothing but bare walls, saltillo floors, and a smiling receptionist.

"Buenos dias," she greeted him with a smile as he walked through the front door.

"Good afternoon," the old man said in English.

"Good afternoon, sir," she responded as she smiled at the gringo from so far away. "How may we help you?" she said in perfect English.

"Well, ma'am, I was admiring your operation here and I thought that while I was in the area, maybe I could drop by and meet the directors of your orphanage."

"Oh, yes, I would be pleased to make that happen," she said candidly. "Could I inquire as to the nature of your visit?"

"Well, sure," he said with smirk on his face. "I've come a long way and thought maybe I could make a donation to mankind, or in this case, your orphanage."

"Well, of course," she said ecstatically. "And who may I tell them is here to see them?"

"Jack."

"Jack?" she said with a grin.

"Yeah, Jack Hardlow."

ACKNOWLEDGEMENTS

If you've never been to Hawaii, Front Street in Lahaina (Maui) is an absolute must. I'll never forget walking into The Bubba Gump Shrimp Company and seeing a sign that said, "Never let a few facts get in the way of a good story." On the flip side, for whatever reason, when a piece of fiction is written, there are generally many "real" stories involved in creating the tale. More importantly, it's the people you have surrounded yourself with over the years, that help you solidify these events mentally, enabling you to document them in a "fictional" faction. Whether it is out of experience, witnessed events, things that I've read, or just my plain imagination, I owe the following people a debt of gratitude for their motivation, friendship, and experiences relating to this book.

The Late Don Aldridge. My Dad passed on in 1999. My Dad was my mentor. I was always told that I was a carbon copy of the old man, minus my faults. Dad was the Speaker of the Arizona House of Representatives, served on the Arizona-Mexico Commission, and is the primary reason that I've had a place in Mexico since I was 25 years old. My Dad was a world traveler. I hope to visit as many places as he did in his lifetime. Dad, your memory lives on, along with the inspiration that you have given me to tell a few more stories in my life.

Mary (Aldridge) Rock. Mom, thank you for being the "Mother Theresa" of my life. I don't know of a more amazing woman. A woman who bore and raised 8 kids, and was still the best in her profession. Thank you for everything and always being there for me. Always know how much Evan loves his Grandma.

Evan Michael James Aldridge. As I said in the dedication, "The backbone of my life." Every thing I do in life is for you. As most parents would agree, I only want you to have a better life than your Dad. Who you got it from, I don't know? But you're the greatest guy on earth! Always take care of the ones you love, especially your Mother, and that little brother of yours, Garrett. When you get older, I hope that you understand that all of those times that you came into my office asking why I couldn't watch the entire episode of Sponge Bob with you, I was dedicating a small portion of my time typing away with my imagination.

Tamera Holman. Tam is my oldest sister and we have a very special bond. I happen to be the youngest of the Aldridge clan and for some reason, Tam has always believed in me. She's an awesome business partner as well.

Beth Sawyer (and family). Beth is number two out of the eight of us who has always been there for her little brother. Beth, your help during my younger years enabled me to drink beer when I should have been paying the rent as a student at Arizona State University. Go Sun Devils!

Sophia (Soph) Aldridge. Soph is the angel of the family who cared for my Dad 24/7 while he was ill. We all love you, sis. Hurry up and get to Havasu so you can cook for us!

Ray Aldridge (and family). My brother Ray is the guy that I want sitting across from me in my fishing boat while on the Sea of Cortez. He is by far, the most appreciative guy I know when I deliver him fresh, jumbo, Baja, shrimp (muy grande camarones). Not only an expert outdoorsman, but truly the guy I see the least, but would like to spend my time with the most. I'm flattered to know that his wife Mary still considers me her favorite brother-in-law. My little niece, Allyse and nephew Taylor, are no longer little.

Dan Aldridge. My brother Dan is a US Naval Academy Graduate. A former Naval Pilot who bought me my first car. Dan, your knowledge of life is amazing!

Nannette Wilberding (and family). Nan, we don't hang out much any more since you've moved across the country but thanks for being a great sister. Next time you and Al and the kids decide to go to Hawaii with Andy and family, add me to the invite list, would ya?

Dr. Andrew Aldridge (and family). My best friend. My humble brother who does more in a day for mankind than I'll ever do in a lifetime. Thanks Brother: for your guidance, advice and love. I also want to thank his awesome wife, Jacque, along with their kids, Will, Loren and Ellie, for putting Evan and I up on those wonderful summer nights in Flagstaff, Arizona to cool off from the heat and catch up on old times. Andy is one of the top surgeons in Arizona, having been recognized by his peers.

Dave Rock. Uncle Dave, you're the man! Thanks for always looking after Mom. You're still one of the best cooks I know. God Bless Aunt Roe and all of my great cousins: Colleen, Marci and Ed, and their families.

Donald "Brady" Sawyer. Technically you're my nephew – but in reality, you're more like a brother. Your talent has gone "un-tapped" for 26 years as of the printing of this book. Walk with me "neph" to bigger and better things!

Patrick Wilson. Pat's my old roommate who has seen the inner workings of this author, first hand. I want to thank his Mom, his Dad Lenny, the late great "Pops," his wife Tina, and their daughters (my nieces), Karlie, Courtney and Whitney. Thank you all for putting up with Uncle Mike!

Dan Johnson. My best friend from high school whom I seldom see, but think about often. His wife Merritt, their two little guys (Spencer and Perry), Brother Rick, and Dan's parents (Don and Marcia Moore), are as solid as a Buffett concert in the middle of the Caribbean. "You know Mike, I would put this song in my all-time favorites…" Dan was referring to Buffett's *The Captain and the Kid* during a conversation in the early 1990's. 20 years later, all I've got to say is "Amen, Brother."

Ron "Ronnie" Crawley. Ronnie is one of my neighbors down in Mexico. He also happens to have a house in Lake Havasu City, Arizona, where I reside. We're good buds and we've spent many days down south together, including a 2 week trip down the Baja peninsula in 2006. Ronnie is a few years older than me (sorry for the disclosure) and has taught me a lot about life and what to expect. He and his family (JoAnne, Jesse, and Jr) are great friends. I have a financial advisor but he doesn't come close to Ronnie's advice: "Go See Your Brother (Andy does vasectomies) and get a Pre-Nup!" Classic advice from a first- class guy.

Dennis "Big D" Martin. Your presence always brings a smile. Your kids, Rick and Jim are always welcome on the golf course. Just remember my friend that good guys like yourself always outlast tough times. Thanks Pop!

Malcolm Graham. A great friend and business partner. An entrepreneur who has shared many of the same business experiences that I've had in my own life. I've traveled extensively with my friend from England, including his hometown of Barnsley in the United Kingdom. Thanks "Buddy" for being the guy you are. Vista at the Heights will be the greatest RV Park in Arizona when we're done!

Matt Rhoades. Matt is one of my friends who gives me good advice on things in life. However, sometimes I don't listen.

Jeff Gilbert. Jeff is a friend who I rarely see these days due to our schedules. A guy who does what it takes to look after the people he befriends and encounters. Jeff, although we don't see each other that much thank you for your friendship and your support on my endeavors. Furthermore, thank you for the many evenings at your place in Rocky Point, Mexico, which I "exported" to make this novel better. God Bless your Mom (Jackie), your Dad (the late Brian S. Gilbert), and your two great kids, Alena and Jarrod. And to your wife Tanya, for keeping you in line! Jeff is the inspiration for one of the characters in the book.

Jeff and Dean Cannon. Jeff and my Dad went way back. My Dad was a politician and all Jeff wanted was a green light to pursue his dream of becoming an entrepreneur in the United States (Jeff is from England). With a little help from my Dad, and a lot of perseverance from a stubborn Englishman, Jeff not only made it but made it big! His son Dean is another great guy. "Deano" has been to my pad in Mexico and is a world traveler and brilliant musician. His rendition of "I love this bar" by Toby Keith in my own bar off the back of my house in San Felipe, will be a living memory for years to come. Jeff, thanks for always being there if I needed anything. Deano, conquer the world brother!

Phil Hatch. Phil is the official "Baja Bush Pilot" and the inspiration for another character in the book. If I ever broke down in the middle of the Baja, I could call Phil (and his co-pilot Gilbert) on a tri-band phone and he would be off in minutes to my rescue.

Evelyn Perricone. Evelyn is my editor who has taught me so much about writing by her reviews of my work and her constructive recommendations. Evelyn, I look forward to working with you on the final version of *The Golden Zone.*

Ed Spinella. Ed is my publishing agent from **1st World Publishing** who tells me what I can or cannot do in the writing world. Thank you Ed, for your knowledge and experience.

Walt Lietz and family. When my Dad died in 1999, Walt was my surrogate "Dad" on many occasions when I was married to his daughter, Kristen. Knowing Walt has reinforced my desire to continue to travel the world as he has done, and give a little bit back to mankind once in a while, as he has his entire life, especially after 911. And to his wife Donna, who has been the "sturdy hull" guiding everyone within her path over the years. To the both of you, always know that Little E loves his "Nana and Papa."

The Westwood Family. Kristen, thank you for being such a great Mom to our little boy (who's not so little anymore); Zach, thank you for being such a good influence in Evan's life; Cheryl, your kindness takes up an entire room; Rusty, thanks for bringing ice cream over on a hot summer day for Evan, Peyton and Spencer – I'll always remember that. You're a stellar guy who actually appreciates the fact that I wear cowboy boots on occasion (and your own kids don't!). Rusty reminds me of a song line from the late, great, country singer, Chris LeDoux "…he's the last to quit, the first to buy the beer…"

Aaron Goldstein. Thanks brother for the "cover" of *An Ocean Away.* Aaron's website is on the jacket of the book. Aaron has spent a few weekends down south at the pad living the old adage of "What goes on in Mexico stays in Mexico!" The photo on the front cover was taken in Mexico (by Aaron) and he's an intricate part of my team. I'm looking forward to many future projects.

Greg Fichter. Greg is an old friend who is a genius when it comes to software development. So I'm gracious that he "stepped down" to put together my website. Thank you for creating and administering **www.MikeAldridge.com** and **www.AnOceanAway.com.**

Dr. William Gibbs. By far, my most influential professor in my academic life. I once dropped his logic class and 20 years later, I will never live it down! Thank you Dr. Gibbs for being the best professor and academic Dean NMMI ever had.

Jerry Shea. Jerry is a graduate of Georgetown Law School who once worked with John F. "Jack" Kennedy as a young man on my old stomping grounds, "The Hill." Jerry eventually made it out West to California where he became a successful corporate attorney for a major corporation. At the age of 81, Jerry and his wife recently left his home outside of La Bufadora, Baja, Mexico for Lake Havasu City. Sporting a pair of Van's slip-on shoes, and a ponytail, Jerry has taught me so much in such a little amount of time not only about Mexico, but life in general. Jerry, it's guys like you that inspire me to write.

Senator John McCain. I had the honor of working for John in the U.S. Senate along with many of his Senatorial campaigns as a paid staffer. I almost got paid on his first presidential run in 2000 but we didn't quite make it that far. Though I never saw him in flip-flops, he has been a gracious friend and big influence in my life. I was saddened to see him lose to Bush in 2000, although he was clearly more qualified. In fact, our nation would be much better off today if we would have elected him in 2000. But that's just political hindsight by a Monday morning quarterback (me). The last time I saw John was on a flight to London in 2005. Although I'm sure he was jet-lagged, I saw fatigue in his eyes, and wrinkles in his skin that represented a lifetime of service, honor and dedication to both his country and mankind. And today, at the age of 72, he still has not slowed down, even after losing the presidency to President Obama. John, life isn't always fair, but you were never one for excuses. They don't get any better than you. Screw the political pundits. You are one of America's great heroes in my lifetime. Your service to your country will always trump any political office you desire. And America deep down knows that.

Jimmy Buffett. In May of 2009, I witnessed my 44th Jimmy Buffett concert in Las Vegas. Jimmy is a man who has brought utopia to the common folk through his songs and books, along with a general inspiration for all of us to make enough money to drink a cold concoction on some deserted island, sharing experiences with the ones we love. Jimmy has been a part of my daily routine since 1989 when during a tough time at military school my roommate (Tom Jenney) dropped a cd on my desk called *Songs you know by heart*. Since that day, I have realized that with all of today's problems in the world, the cure is not to hire some sociologist to try and figure all this crap out. No, no. The solution is to make Jimmy Buffett albums more accessible throughout the country and the world. Problems solved! I have introduced countless people to his music I might add. "Drink it up Jimmy, this one's for you...."

Melrose Larry Green. I first met Larry at a "Republican" fundraiser in Los Angeles for a minority politician running for city counsel. We hit it off right away and he threw me a stunner! He invited my date and I to the Cat Club (next to the Whiskey Go Go in Hollywood) where he does stand up. I had the privilege of meeting Slim Jim Fantom (Drummer for the Stray Cats and the owner of the club) and quite a few other "different" types. Melrose used to be a regular on the Howard Stern show and is also a published author who told me that night that he never gives his books away? However, by the end of the night, I walked away with a signed copy of *Why the Clinton's belong in Prison*. Thanks Larry. A signed copy of *An Ocean Away* is on its way.

I have so many other people that I would like to thank. For those of you that I missed, I apologize. Since I don't want to make the acknowledgments longer than the book itself, I would like to make a general thank you to the following people: **First World Publishing; Discover Baja Club;The Rocky Point Times; The Sonoran Sky Resort; Patrick Butler and the El Dorado Ranch (San Felipe, Baja, Mexico); The staff at Ads Pay USA; The Yeller Seller; Brian and Heather Wedemeyer; The Freedom Bridge Foundation; Edward J. Lynton; Masonry and More; Phil Hatch's "Bodyline;" Scottsdale Resort and Conference Center; Sunburst Studio (sunburstdesignstudio.com); Aldridge Insurance Services, LLC; Vista at the Heights RV Development; and Lake Havasu City, Arizona.**

LaVergne, TN USA
08 August 2010
192521LV00004B/23/P